# THE IGUANA'S SCROLL

## NOVA 01

THE IGUANA'S SCROLL

NOVA 01

C. T. EMERSON

IGUANA PUBLISHING, LLC

Copyright © 2022 by Iguana Publishing, L.L.C.

All rights reserved. No part of this book may be reproduced in any form or by any electronic or mechanical means, including information storage and retrieval systems, without written permission from the author, except for the use of brief quotations in a book review permitted by copyright law.

Paperback ISBN-13: 979-8-9867134-0-3

ebook ISBN-13: 979-8-9867134-1-0

*Cover and illustrations by Andie Eikenberg.*

This book is a work of fiction. Any names, characters, companies, organizations, places, events, locales, and incidents are either used in a fictitious manner or are fictional. Any resemblance to actual persons, living or dead, actual companies or organizations, or actual events is purely coincidental.

CTEmerson.com

*To my family, Ecclesiastes, and Tampico.*

Contents

| | |
|---|---|
| Prologue: Nova Rising | 1 |
| Chapter 1: Daydreamer's Delight | 13 |
| Chapter 2: Of Magic and Dogs | 31 |
| Chapter 3: This Side of the Key | 45 |
| Chapter 4: The Other Side of the Key | 67 |
| Chapter 5: At the Sign of the Anvil | 83 |
| Chapter 6: The Shadow | 105 |
| Chapter 7: Above the Skydraft | 125 |
| Chapter 8: A Headmaster's Welcome | 137 |
| Chapter 9: The Dean's Threat | 157 |
| Chapter 10: An Introduction to Coatlball | 177 |
| Chapter 11: Shadows of the Past | 203 |
| Chapter 12: The History Professor | 217 |
| Chapter 13: Beneath the Swirling Fog | 235 |
| Chapter 14: The Ceremony of the Gifts | 257 |
| Chapter 15: The Prophet's Advent | 285 |
| Chapter 16: A Word to the Wise | 313 |
| Chapter 17: Light Refraction | 335 |
| Chapter 18: Under the Willow Tree | 365 |
| Chapter 19: The Teacher's Lounge | 389 |
| Chapter 20: A Yeti's Decor | 409 |
| Chapter 21: Family, Honor, and Reputation | 429 |
| Chapter 22: The Forgotten Wood | 443 |
| Chapter 23: Boy, Shadow, and Ghost | 471 |

## Prologue: Nova Rising

It was a muggy August morning when Jeff Hamilton first heard the news.

"They're calling it the discovery of the millennium," his daughter told him as he dropped her off at school. "Bigger than Y2K, whatever that is!"

"Yeah, yeah," he replied through the car window, "don't you think it's just Pluto back in the swing of things?"

"Don't be stupid, Dad. Pluto's not a planet."

"It was when I was your age," he mumbled as she walked off to join her friends.

Even though Jeff found it difficult to understand why the news mattered, he couldn't help but marvel at the way everyone else was reacting to it.

Even now, as his daughter joined her friends, he could see them pointing up at the sky, sharing their excitement with animated fingers and astonished faces at the only news that mattered.

Overnight, a Japanese astronomer discovered a ninth planet in the solar system.

According to the articles his daughter had read to him over breakfast, the planet only neared Earth every two hundred years out of a thousand. Now, anyone could see it by stepping outside at night and looking just past Neptune.

# * Prologue: Nova Rising *

What the articles failed to mention, Jeff had told his daughter with bacon in his mouth, was why any of this mattered. The only real takeaway in his mind was the eerie thought of a new planet joining their solar system after being enveloped by darkness for close to eight hundred years.

"Thank goodness for our planet," he thought as he drove the car forward with a worn boot on the gas pedal. "No creepy things going on here ... everything is proper and normal as *per* usual!"

And that's how Jeff's morning continued – properly and normally.

"Good morning!" he said to friendly colleagues entering their offices or sipping their coffees.

"Excellent," he muttered to himself as fat squirrels darted to and from the ash and oak trees littered across campus.

"Brilliant!" he thought when he walked past upper-school students dressed in ironed shirts and slacks or skirts.

All proper and normal.

But as he strode past the final crosswalk before his office, Jeff noticed something that brought him out of his entirely proper and normal reverie.

Underneath the marble-blue sky and fluffy, white clouds, a brightly colored bird stood on the branch of his favorite oak tree. It looked a lot like a toucan, he thought. But toucans didn't live in the United States, let alone North Carolina, did they?

Naturally, he tried stepping closer for a better look, but by the time he managed to adjust his glasses and squint his eyes, the bird had already flown away.

*Caw-caw!*

"Must have been a cardinal," he surmised, twitching his mustache and turning back to his office door.

Shrugging, he placed his coffee and briefcase on the doorstep before taking out his keys and unlocking the door. A light kick later and the door opened.

But when he stooped to pick up his belongings, something else improper and abnormal disturbed his morning.

Seated at his desk was a man he hadn't seen in ten years.

Gallantly dressed in a button-down shirt and pants ensemble that matched the outside sky, the man stood and flashed a brilliant smile.

"Cardinals don't *caw*, Mr. Hamilton. They sing."

All Jeff could do was sputter in response.

Still smiling, the man crossed the gap between them and offered up a handshake. Ordinarily, Jeff would shake hands with anyone, stranger or not. But there was something *different* about this man. Even though his shirt and pants looked normal enough, he also wore a form-fitting frockcoat and a frayed, sash belt. On top of it all, his hair ran past his shoulders in a tight ponytail, marring, he thought, what was otherwise a very handsome face.

Unperturbed by Jeff's lack of an immediate reply, the man continued smiling at him pleasantly. "You never submitted an application, Mr. Hamilton. Why not?"

There was a long pause while Jeff gathered himself. He had spent the past ten years convincing himself this well-dressed man was a figment of his imagination. How could he exist?

# * Prologue: Nova Rising *

Finally, he shook the offered hand in front of him, perhaps more gingerly than he would have liked. "I thought I hallucinated the last time we met." He took another look at the mysterious stranger, hoping he might fly away like the toucan had.

He didn't.

Groaning, Jeff slumped into the visitor's chair in front of his desk.

"Well, that explains a great deal," said the man, stooping down next to him. Behind a tall nose, green eyes stared at Jeff. "Do you at least remember my name, Mr. Hamilton?"

"Cato Watkin, of course," said Jeff, unable to stop his eyes from shifting to Cato's. A warmth lived there that didn't belong to someone so young and fit.

Incredulity seeped into the corners of Cato's smile. "After all this time, you remembered my name, and yet you never submitted an application?" He chuckled and stood up. "Well then, what *have* you been up to, Mr. Hamilton?"

Jeff thought that was rather unfair. He was the best college counselor in the area, placing more students in elite institutions than any colleague before him. He did have to admit, however, he hadn't been placing students in Mr. Watkin's particular school.

Indignation bristled across Jeff's mustache. "I've been getting students into college, Mr. Watkin!"

"Please, call me Cato."

At this point, Jeff stared at Cato, refusing to believe he existed. But Cato did exist, perhaps even more so than Jeff.

# NOVA 01

After a moment, Jeff's visitor dropped his smile and picked up a walking stick from the side of the table before looking back and tapping it against the ground.

*Clunk!*

Without any prompting whatsoever, the door behind them slammed shut. An instant later, Jeff's forgotten briefcase and mug zoomed around the room and came to an eventual halt on his desk.

The coffee sloshed around in his mug as Jeff thought of what to say. By the time it came to a stop, he made a mental note not to drink it.

"So," Jeff finally managed, "last time … you weren't a hallucination?"

Cato shook his head, still looking pleased.

"Are you a magician or something, then?" As Jeff said the truth out loud, he felt a knot ease in his chest.

Though Cato shook his head again, this time he adopted a pitying expression. "A wizard, actually. Not that it matters, I suppose, but a magician practices parlor tricks and sleight of hand. I, on the other hand, channel magic." Cato's eyes twinkled as he spoke. "I told you all of this last time, too, you know. Don't you remember?"

Jeff growled. "How could I? I've spent all this time trying to forget."

Cato nodded his head at that. Before continuing, he walked back to the other side of the desk and resumed his position in the swivel chair, placing his walking stick across his lap. A large, green jewel on its pommel grabbed Jeff's attention.

# * Prologue: Nova Rising *

"Last time," Cato continued, "I told you that I come from a place called Tenochprima Academy. It's an educational institution that includes a few courses you won't find at even your most eccentric liberal arts school."

Jeff pursed his lips as he switched from staring at the jewel to Watkin. "Courses on magic, right? That's great and all, but I clearly didn't get enough sleep last night. There's just no way this is real! Why would you wait ten years before returning if you weren't getting any calls or emails from me?"

Cato hesitated. "It was in my own best-interest not to prod ... and if we're being honest, it's not likely one of your candidates would have been accepted anyway."

Rattled, Jeff looked back up at Cato, his eyebrows furrowed. "Not likely one of my candidates would have been accepted? I've gotten my students into the Ivy Leagues!"

"Well now's your chance to get them into something greater," said Cato. "Do I really have to prove to you I'm real? That my school's real?"

Jeff waved his hand dismissively. "D'you know what would happen to me if a student disappeared and I tried telling the board that I sent them to a magical institution?! They'd think I was a maniac! Or worse!"

"Oh that," said Cato, stifling a chuckle. "You won't have to worry about anything other than producing a candidate or two every year. We will bewitch everyone at your school to think you've sent these children off to – what did you call them? Ivy Leagues?"

"*Bewitch*?" repeated Jeff, a concerned expression his face.

"We just cast a spell, Mr. Hamilton – it's really not that complicated. Your fellow counselors across the country all produce candidates! Why can't you?"

"You can't possibly think that I'd fall for a trick like –,"

But he stopped speaking. Cato had stood up and the green jewel in his staff began to glow.

Jeff felt his heart beating quickly in his chest as the light grew brighter and brighter. Expecting to be transformed into a toad at any moment, he stood and scrambled to the door, hoping to escape.

Before he could even take one step, green smoke puffed into existence above his desk, followed by a half-dozen envelopes.

"There you are, Mr. Hamilton," growled Cato, motioning to the envelopes as they fell onto his desk, "these are some of the applicants your colleagues have submitted. Go on, open one! See for yourself!"

Torn between fear and curiosity, Jeff reached out and grabbed the topmost envelope with a shaking hand. Maybe the stranger could have faked the slamming door and flying cup of coffee – but these forms, they'd appeared from thin air!

Fingers fumbling, he managed to open the envelope, revealing a dossier featuring a boy named Beto Warren. The word "Accepted" was stamped onto the form – he was fourteen years old at time of submission.

It was very well written, Jeff had to admit. Whoever had taken the time to fill out this form had done so with the same level of effort and care he exhibited when writing one of his many university contacts. *Proper and normal,* he thought.

# * Prologue: Nova Rising *

Steeling himself, he looked across the desk at Cato and tossed the dossier back down on the desk. "Very well," he said, feeling his throat catch, "this is a proper application – I think I *might* just begin to believe you."

Cato beamed. "Excellent! Are you ready to move onto candidate selection?"

Jeff narrowed his eyes at the enthusiasm but raised a hand to his chin all the same, thinking hard.

"What do y'all look for in your students?" he asked, surprised to find himself regaining his confidence. It was with a straighter back that he now surveyed Cato. "I'm assuming you want top athletes, near-perfect SATs, stellar GPAs? I'm not going to lie, Cato, I hope you don't take any of these kids. I've got a reputation to keep – these top candidates need to make the *real* Ivy Leagues. Even if I begin to feel a personal pride in sending kids away to, uh, … learn … magic, the board is going to want to see my quota maintained."

Cato was smiling at Jeff again.

"Submit whomever you'd like, but there's one particular trait that's a dead giveaway for a future witch or wizard."

"And what's that?" asked Jeff, sounding suspicious.

"I believe your side calls it attention deficiency. Yes, it's a common issue in your world. What the condition really is, is a child bundled with magical energy without any means to express it."

Jeff gaped. "You're telling me our ADD kids are magicians?"

"Wizards, Mr. Hamilton. And yes, most of them are. But the thing about the magical realm, Jeff – may I call you Jeff?"

"Yes of course – not sure why you didn't ask sooner."

"Common courtesy, Jeff. We are in the South after all. Proper and normal, wouldn't you say?"

Jeff raised his eyebrows in alarm, but before he could interrupt, Cato continued.

"Well, *Jeff*, the magical realm isn't firing on all cylinders yet."

Jeff furrowed his eyebrows at that. Thinking hard, he took his chair before Cato could sit back in it, ushering him towards the guest chair instead. "What do you mean isn't firing on all cylinders? You made those forms appear easily enough, didn't you?"

"Did you read the morning papers today?" asked Cato, looking pensive. He sat down in the offered chair, rubbing the green jewel on his staff. Jeff no longer thought he'd be turning into a toad.

"Well," said Jeff, "the S&P 500's down, Spieth just sealed the cup, and a Japanese gentleman discovered a new planet. But what does any of this have to do with your, uh, magical realm?"

"That new planet has everything to do with the magical realm," said Cato, his eyes lighting up. "You see, magic, as a force, ebbs and flows on our planet. Think of how the Moon pushes and pulls the tide." Cato gestured the movement with his hands. "We have reason to believe this 'new' planet brings magic out of matter whenever it is near. This is why we've seen such an increase in children 'suffering' in concentration over the last couple of decades."

## \* Prologue: Nova Rising \*

"You mean to tell me that, like some kind of gravity, magic is making us all ADD?" Jeff had to resist the temptation to laugh out loud because, even though what he was hearing sounded insane, it almost made sense.

Cato nodded his head. "That's our best guess, and it's important to emphasize that this *is* guesswork, because the last time this ninth planet drew near us was around one thousand to eight hundred years ago, which is consistent with the calculations being performed by even your astronomers." He pointed at Jeff as if he represented a society of human astronomers.

"This time period overlaps with the High Middle Ages in Europe, the height of the Byzantine Empire, the early life of Genghis Khan ... But, as you can imagine, records from that long ago are difficult to come by, hence the guesswork. Either way, the ebb and flow of magic means that our world's infrastructure is weak when the ninth planet is first visible to us every millennium. For the most part, we haven't been able to *use* magic for several centuries. This is why I say we are not firing on all cylinders yet. Though our school is the greatest there is in the Americas, we don't have the ability to admit more than sixty students every year. Our realm can't handle more than that at the present."

There was a pause as Jeff digested what Cato had told him. He gazed at the wizard and his staff, reevaluating his own understanding of the world. Why didn't the history books ever mention magic? Why on Earth was Cato trusting him, of all people, to select applicants?

"Very well," said Jeff, "I'll submit one to two applicants to you every year. What's your, umm, phone number? Do y'all use phones?" he asked, trying to be polite. Now that he thought about it, how would a witch or wizard communicate? Surely by phone.

"Unfortunately, our mirrors cannot interface with your *phones*. That said, I did use a burner once when I lived for an extended period on, as they say, your Side of the Key." Cato looked at his watch and raised his eyebrows. "Do you have a pet, Jeff?"

Jeff paused. "Come again?"

"A pet? Dog? Cat? Goldfish? Any of those squirrels outside yours?"

"I have a dog at home," said Jeff, finding it difficult to keep the confusion out of his voice.

"Perfect. We'll be in touch through either your dog or a squirrel if you're at work. I noticed several on my way in. Fluffy tails and whatnot – very well fed." He nodded his head repeatedly as if the matter were finalized.

"Through my dog?" Jeff tried asking.

But at that moment, a tapping noise interrupted them.

It came from the window to the right of the office door.

"Oh," said Cato, flourishing his fingers, "that'll be Jaiba."

The window opened, and to Jeff's astonishment, the same toucan he'd ignored earlier stuck its enormous beak through the opening.

*Caw-caw!*

Did Jeff imagine the bird saying, *'get going, you're late!'*?

"That I am," mumbled Cato. He stood up, offering Jeff a handshake. "My good man, I really have to dash – whole day planned out – you understand. Whenever you've completed an application, just ask one of

## * Prologue: Nova Rising *

your squirrels to let me know, and I'll send Jaiba to pick up the paperwork from them, sound good? Ok? Bye now."

Before Jeff could say another word, Cato had opened the door and walked outside.

Still filled with questions, Jeff bolted after the wizard into the sunlight. "Cato! Cato!" he yelled, crossing the door's threshold.

But Cato had gone. He wasn't on the sidewalk. He wasn't even crossing the street. Desperate, Jeff turned to see if Jaiba was still in the oak tree, but the toucan had gone, too.

But where Jaiba had been earlier, there now stood a fluffy, brown squirrel. It cocked its head at Jeff and adjusted its whiskers. It looked an awful lot like Jeff when he twitched his mustache.

## ❦ NOVA 01 ❦

# Chapter 1: Daydreamer's Delight

*I finally met someone from the 'Other Side' today. All those years watching and waiting by that door finally paid off! I knew I wasn't crazy.*

*28$^{th}$ of June, the first year of the 10$^{th}$ Age*

Oliver García never enjoyed history class. For all the heroes and cultural upheavals they studied, he just couldn't get past how dusty the subject felt.

It didn't matter. He'd be at soccer practice soon enough anyway. If he strained his neck just far back enough, he could see the fields through the classroom window. Maybe if Mrs. Caldwell would just let them out a bit early today.

Panic-stricken, he realized he'd been daydreaming again. Had Mrs. Caldwell noticed?

He glanced at her, placing a thoughtful but dishonest hand on his chin.

To his great relief, she was still mid-lecture, somehow managing to bore even the kids at the front of the class.

"Now remember," she said in her most southern drawl, "Cortés used a translator to convince the Aztecs and the Toltecs to fight each other, and then, after they had nearly destroyed themselves, he commanded his forces to attack the capital city of Tenochtitlan …"

Oliver pushed his bangs over his eyebrows and slumped back into his chair with a sigh of relief. The last thing he wanted was to be caught daydreaming again. And for good reason.

# * Chapter 1:  Daydreamer's Delight *

The last time Mrs. Caldwell caught him, she dragged him to the principal's office where he was yelled at for over thirty minutes.

"You're throwing away your education!" Mrs. Caldwell had screeched.

"You're ruining your chances of getting into college!!" Principal Foster had bellowed.

"You're going to get kicked off the team!" Coach Myers had spat.

But none of them could make him understand why it was so important that he couldn't pay attention to a set of very boring people. He was frustrated because his teachers, his coach, and even his uncle were telling him he was throwing away his future when he knew a larger issue was in the way – an issue he could not quite pinpoint.

Nonetheless, as a relatively responsible freshman in high school who always did his homework, Oliver knew they couldn't suspend him or hold him back a year. Not only were his grades decent over middle school, but he was also a tenor in the school choir and had just made the soccer team.

That said, a different kind of threat was tossed around the last time he'd been in Principal Foster's office. At one point during all the screeching, Mrs. Caldwell mentioned having him see the school counselor, Mr. Hamilton – and not for college counseling, but for *general* counseling.

Now that was a legitimate threat.

As far as Oliver was concerned, being sent to see Mr. Hamilton for any reason other than college counseling was the equivalent of getting pantsed in front of the whole school. Worse yet, if anyone found out, well, even his soccer teammates would stop speaking to him. *What'd they make you see Hamilton for, Oliver?*

# NOVA 01

He pushed his dark bangs up and over his forehead again. They always fell back down, giving his face the slightest of shadows. Scared of the possibility of seeing Mr. Hamilton, he looked up at Mrs. Caldwell, feigning all the attention he could muster.

"And it's really a shame they razed the city," continued Mrs. Caldwell, "because, and I'm not exaggerating here, Tenochtitlan was the Native American equivalent of Venice."

Most of the class looked around at each other, unable to appreciate the comparison. "Venice is in France, right?" a boy in the back of the room asked his friend.

Fortune favored the boy as the bell rang before Mrs. Caldwell could belittle him for his mental lapse in European geography. It was three o'clock, and her reign was over.

Elated, Oliver began stuffing his belongings into his backpack as fast as he could. The shuffling of students around him doing the same thing filled his ears, so he allowed himself to crack open a smile. Soon he'd be safe and heading to the soccer fields.

When he finished packing, he chanced a nervous glance at Mrs. Caldwell with his peripherals. She had her back turned to the room as she erased the whiteboard. Stunned at his luck, Oliver took his opportunity to escape. He could almost smell the soccer field at this point, but just as one of his skinny legs reached the door, Mrs. Caldwell spoke with her back still facing the room.

"Oliver, could you stay behind for a moment?"

# * Chapter 1: Daydreamer's Delight *

Oliver's heart skipped a beat as he stopped mid-stride. This was it. He was going to be sent to the counselor. He'd have to transfer to a new school. Maybe in Venice.

With a resentful roll of his eyes, he readjusted his backpack and turned towards his doom, shuffling towards it like a nervous penguin.

"Oliver," said Mrs. Caldwell, her drawl torturous. "I noticed you weren't paying attention in class *again*." She emphasized the repeat nature of his offense as much as humanly possible. Oliver glared at her back, determined to weasel his way out of visiting Mr. Hamilton.

"Was this another daydream?" she continued. Oliver wondered if it were possible to erase her neatly scribbled notes any slower. She had to know how annoying she was.

"No, ma'am," he replied determinedly. He attempted to bore a hole in her with his eyes.

As the final notes disappeared from the whiteboard, she turned to face him with a cruel grin on her face. Above her nose, cerulean eyes bulged with disturbed satisfaction. They contrasted against her thin features, making Oliver feel nauseated. Any more pressure or stimulation and an eyeball might pop out.

"Oliver," she breathed, "there's no use in lying to me. You and I both know that you *weren't* paying attention."

"I was!" Oliver lied. He tried remembering the few snippets of monotony that he had managed to register. "Cortés took over Venice after forcing the Aztecs to fight themselves!" he said, somewhat loudly. He was surprised he absorbed even that much.

# NOVA 01

"Tenochtitlan, Oliver! Not Venice!" shouted Mrs. Caldwell through gritted teeth, her smile forgotten. "I told Principal Foster you shouldn't have continued on to high school this year! If you don't pay attention in my classes, we'll just have to – we'll just have to …"

She seemed unable to find a verb strong enough for what they should do to him. Either that or she had become physically incapable of speaking due to the continued expansion of her bulging eyes. Her demeanor had changed from satisfied to angry and it didn't take a genius to see the vein on her forehead meant danger.

"Mrs. Caldwell," Oliver pleaded, "I'll do my reading and pass my tests as always!" He couldn't see any other way out. Was he doomed to receive *general* counseling?

Mrs. Caldwell opened her mouth, threatening a screech, but then a knock came on the classroom door.

As she gaped at the door, looking much more like a church gargoyle than a human, Oliver thanked the heavens. Maybe he'd be able to sneak off to soccer practice.

But then the door opened.

There, stood Mr. Hamilton, the school counselor.

Oliver felt the world narrow in around him. His stomach went hollow and his mouth dry. *How on earth could Hamilton have gotten here already? How did Mrs. Caldwell tell him to come? Did the other students notice him walk in?*

Mr. Hamilton smiled and said hello to Mrs. Caldwell in what sounded like another dimension. Petrified, Oliver only picked up on garbled noises as they continued exchanging pleasantries. Mrs. Caldwell stopped looking

* Chapter 1:  Daydreamer's Delight *

like a gargoyle, and Mr. Hamilton smiled as only a school counselor could. Throughout it all, Oliver stood motionless, unable to take in anything.

Unless he was handed a miracle, his life was over as he knew it.

Finally, Mr. Hamilton put a hand on Oliver's shoulder, snapping him back out of the ether.

"I was just wondering if I might have a word with Oliver here."

Mrs. Caldwell smiled disingenuously again. "Of course, Jeff," she said, her southern accent somehow becoming more pronounced. "I take it that Principal Foster's been in touch with you about him already?"

"Been in touch?" asked Mr. Hamilton. "Who was in touch with me?" He furrowed his eyebrows and cocked his head, looking between Mrs. Caldwell and Oliver.

Mrs. Caldwell's smile dropped. "Yeah, Jeff ... about his ... attention deficit disorder?" She widened her eyes, intimating that to not pay attention to her was a cardinal sin.

Mr. Hamilton snapped his fingers and pointed at her. "Oh right!" he exclaimed, grinning. "Yeah, sure thing. That's *exactly* why I'm here. In fact, I just finished speaking with Principal Foster about it."

Oliver could tell Mr. Hamilton was lying. His smile wasn't matching his eyes and hands. *But why would he be lying?*

Knowing Mr. Hamilton wasn't the only person in the room stretching the truth calmed Oliver slightly. Even if he wasn't good at paying attention to history lectures, he had always been very good at reading people.

## NOVA 01

Mr. Hamilton glanced from Mrs. Caldwell to Oliver some more. "I'll just, uh, take Oliver to my office, and we'll discuss his academic options, shall I?"

Both Oliver and Mrs. Caldwell looked confused, but Oliver was curious enough to not protest. He wanted to know why Mr. Hamilton was lying. *What's he hiding?*

Before Mrs. Caldwell could say another shrill word, they were both out the door headed to Mr. Hamilton's office, leaving her to resume her impersonation of a gargoyle.

"D'you have a good summer, Oliver?" Mr. Hamilton asked as he led Oliver towards the crosswalk to his office. Surprised, Oliver noticed Mr. Hamilton looked just as nervous as he did.

Oliver peered around as they walked to make sure nobody could see him talking to Mr. Hamilton. "It was okay," he breathed once confirming nobody was in sight. "Played some video games and a lot of soccer at the park. My uncle works a lot, so plenty of time by myself."

As they walked across the street, he noticed a fat squirrel twitching its tail on a tree branch in front of Mr. Hamilton's office. It rustled its whiskers at him before darting to hide on the opposite side of the stand-alone office, chattering mysteriously as it scampered away.

"How about you, Mr. Hamilton? Good summer?"

"I had a great summer, thank you. My wife and I went out west and hiked around a place called Crater Lake in Oregon. Beautiful spot. Never seen anything like it. Almost magical ..." Oliver thought he heard Mr. Hamilton's voice crack towards the end of his sentence.

*19*

## * Chapter 1: Daydreamer's Delight *

When they reached the office after a few more moments, Mr. Hamilton opened it and motioned Oliver inside towards a chair in front of his desk. Without saying a word, Mr. Hamilton slumped into his swivel chair and rubbed his eyes.

"Crater Lake?" asked Oliver, trying to prod the conversation along.

Mr. Hamilton wiggled his mustache and readjusted himself in his chair. "Oh, never mind Crater Lake. Please, call me, Jeff."

Oliver looked at him, confused. "Mr. Hamil - umm, Jeff, what the heck is going on?"

Jeff didn't look at him at first. He stood up, sat back down, then stood up again before facing the window behind his desk. After a long, quiet moment, he spoke.

"Oliver, I had a visitor earlier this week."

Oliver growled and crossed his arms. "Yeah, I know. You talked to Principal Foster, right?"

"No, not Principal Foster," said Jeff, turning to reface the room. He took a deep breath and looked directly at Oliver. "A man from another school visited me, Oliver. He's looking for candidates for his, um, academy."

"Huh?" said Oliver, scratching his head. "You mean you didn't bring me here to talk about my daydreaming? Isn't it a little too early for college counseling?"

"No, not exactly. I brought you here to talk about this other … well, I'm pretty sure you can call it a school. He kept using the word institution, though."

# NOVA 01

Oliver felt his mouth go dry as Jeff placed a thoughtful hand on his chin to remember what the "man from another school" had said.

"You're sending me to rehab?!" he shouted. "For my mental health?!" He began breathing heavily, looking left and right around the office to see if there was anyone nearby, ready to lead him away in chains.

"No, no, no," said Jeff. He waved his hands apologetically. "I'm sorry. Let me start over. We're not sending you anywhere you don't want to go … but this really is tough to explain. Are you calm?"

Oliver snorted. "Am I calm? You're about to send me to rehab! For daydreaming! The four of you should go! Not me! I'm just trying to survive the start of my freshman year, no thanks to y'all! I told Mrs. Caldwell! I do my homework! I pass my—,"

"Oliver!" interrupted Jeff. "The man from the other school, well, he teaches … well, let's just say he'll teach you about a different dimension!" He shook his head with a twisted smile as he spoke. "One, where there's … magic."

Whatever Oliver had expected Jeff to say, it wasn't that. He must have misheard. *A different dimension? Magic? Is that why I daydream?*

"Come again?" said Oliver, raising his eyebrows. "Did you say you're sending me to a school in a different dimension that teaches magic?"

"Only if you're interested," said Jeff with a grimace. He sat back down in his swivel chair, head in his hands.

Oliver didn't know what to say. He wanted to yell, to tell Jeff he was crazy, that this was an obvious trap to send him to a psychiatrist, or to hold him back a year. But he didn't. He thought about making an escape from

* Chapter 1: Daydreamer's Delight *

the small office so he could run away and move to another city. But he didn't. Deep down, something in Oliver stirred, assuring him that Jeff wasn't lying, that there was something out there that needed exploring. Was magic guiding him on?

"Oliver?" said Jeff, prodding him in the shoulder with a finger. Oliver shook his head and looked up. He hadn't noticed Jeff walk past the desk. How long had it been since he responded?

"Sorry! I – I don't fully understand."

Jeff chuckled. "Well, how could you? I, myself, just found out about this magic opportunity earlier this week."

"No, not that," said Oliver. He had no problem envisioning magic as a reality. After all, hadn't magic's presence been sprinkled throughout history? Only dismissed in the modern-day? His gut feeling guided him on.

"Why me?" Oliver continued. "That's what I don't understand. Am I the only one at our school?" To make sure Jeff could tell he was entirely calm, he straightened his back and folded his hands together in his lap.

"Oh?" said Jeff, raising his eyebrows. "It took me much longer to accept magic was real." He took a moment to return to his chair before speaking again. When he did, he rustled his mustache with a finger. "I'm impressed. The man who visited me earlier – Cato – he had to *prove* it to me." When he finished speaking, he pointed at the door and then back at the desk, tilting his head as if he were revealing something to Oliver.

Oliver dismissed the look, opting instead to focus on his momentary hastiness. When Jeff told him he could do magic, his gut feeling guided him on – he didn't need proof. But was that too trusting of him?

# NOVA 01

"I guess you have a point, Jeff. How do I know this isn't part of your nut-house pitchbook?"

Jeff twitched his mustache. Perhaps more excitedly than before. "Now, that's more like it, Oliver. If I'm sending anybody to a new school that teaches magic, they'd better not be gullible, eh?"

Before Oliver could respond, Jeff walked to a cabinet to the left of his desk and removed an envelope with green scorch marks on it. As he returned, he shook the envelope in his hands. "Do you know what this is, Oliver? Don't answer – rhetorical question, sonny. This is what Cato Watkin, the wizard – well, he might have been a professor … an administrator? Doesn't matter. He's from your new academy and brought this as proof. Go on, take a look."

Torn between excitement and fear, Oliver reached out with his hand and grabbed the envelope. As his fingertips met the parchment, a tingling sensation shot down his body. He ignored it, assigning the feeling to plain, old nerves.

At the top of the envelope, he noticed a copper restraint and string keeping the envelope shut. He motioned to untie the binding, but before he could, the envelope flapped open on its own accord. He paused to look at Jeff, his eyes narrowing suspiciously. Was that a trick? Or was that magic? Despite his excitement, he couldn't rule out the thought of a cameraman jumping out at any moment, revealing him to be the main event on an internet prank highlights reel.

But no cameraman appeared. Instead, Jeff simply urged him on with a patient, if sweaty, nod of his head.

*23*

# * Chapter 1: Daydreamer's Delight *

Deciding that his curiosity would never forgive him if he walked away, he placed a trembling hand inside the envelope and pulled out a surprisingly dense piece of parchment.

Jeff ushered him on with a wave of his hand. "Get going, kiddo. I can't keep you from Mrs. Caldwell all day."

Seeing Jeff look a bit calmer as he retook his seat behind his desk eased Oliver's own nerves. His hand no longer shook as he looked down to read what had been written in royal blue ink on the parchment.

"Tenochprima Academy Admissions Request" was stamped at the top. Below it, several sections asked for features ranging from Full Name to Behavioral Qualities. Even further below, Oliver saw free-form areas, one of which was titled "Gift Predisposition."

"What does it mean by 'Gift Predisposition'?" asked Oliver as he read over the questions. He frowned when he came across a section titled "Head Circumference."

"You know what?" said Jeff, "I never actually got around to speaking with Cato about that last area in the application. But I did take a look at a sample application, and it looks like a different counselor went into a great amount of detail over the applicant's power and, uh, strength." Jeff's voice trailed off as he looked at Oliver calculatingly.

Oliver shifted uncomfortably in his chair. As confident as he was, he had never thought of himself as powerful, let alone strong. Between his skinny legs and narrow chest, it'd be a flat-out lie to describe himself as some kind of powerful sorcerer. Is strong what the school wanted? If so, why did Jeff pick him?

# NOVA 01

Jeff coughed from across the desk. "But I'll have a word with Cato and tell him everything I know about you, eh?" He stepped forward and placed a hand on Oliver's shoulder. "I have no doubt you have a Gift of some sort in you. So far, this entire process has felt almost predetermined to me. I wouldn't be surprised if magic is guiding me on, too."

Feeling more cheerful, Oliver smiled. "Thanks."

"Don't mention it," said Jeff, rustling his mustache with a finger. He walked back to the other side of his desk and put on reading glasses. "Now, let's fill out this application and send it off to Cato ASAP!"

"But why me?" interrupted Oliver. "You never answered my question."

"Ah," said Jeff, furrowing his eyebrows. "Well, don't take this the wrong way, Oliver, because it's really nothing to be ashamed of, but I picked you because of your attention deficit disorder. I've been told that it's a clear-cut sign of a magical child – something about magic attempting to burst forth from you. If Mrs. Caldwell's repeated reports on you are even remotely accurate, you'll be the next – erm – Merlin."

Oliver couldn't help but smile. Mrs. Caldwell's annoyance wasn't even well-placed.

"The next Merlin," he repeated to himself more than Jeff. For a moment, he imagined wearing a pointy hat, growing out a long, flowing beard, and attacking goblins with a staff in his hands. But then he wondered if magic would really exist as described in European fairytales. "Jeff, how do wizards do magic?"

"You know what?" said Jeff, laughing, "I don't have a single magical bone in my body. All I know is that Watkin fella simply tapped his staff to

# * Chapter 1: Daydreamer's Delight *

get his magic going." Jeff stood up again and looked out the window. As far as Oliver could tell, jealousy didn't straddle his voice, only joy. He turned back and smiled down at Oliver in the chair, excitement brimming in his eyes. A foreign look on the man, as far as Oliver could tell.

"I'm not going to lie to you, sonny. I wish I could have gone off to learn magic when I was a kid. Though adults won't admit it, we spend our entire lives wishing things could be a bit more exciting. When you're a kid you hope it's a wizard knocking on your door or a dragon's egg in your yard,"—he paused to sigh— "but then one day, you grow up, and stop dreaming for opportunities to leave the dull world behind. You instead wish for a shinier car, or a better job. But Oliver, your wizard, your dragon, it's here! For everyone out there who didn't have their dream come true, do them a favor, and go to this school! Dare to be something different!"

The gut feeling of assurance returned to Oliver. It made him feel warm and confident, not scared or intimidated. He knew he wanted to go to Tenochprima Academy, and that Jeff was going to help him get into it. So, he stood up and offered his hand to Jeff saying, "Okay, Jeff, I believe you."

Jeff grinned some more, his mustache askew, and stepped up to Oliver to shake his hand. "Excellent! Let's get your application filled out!"

Most of the application details, as it turned out, were easy. Height, dominant hand, address, and date of birth were straight forward enough. The legal guardian section made him uncomfortable, but he was used to that feeling. Every form always asked about his parents. Truth was he didn't have any. Well, that wasn't exactly true.

"My uncle," he muttered when Jeff looked down at him over his reading glasses. "He's been my guardian my whole life." He breathed a sigh of relief when Jeff moved down the list.

"And what about your 40-yard dash?"

"Why do they need my 40-yard-dash time?" asked Oliver towards the end of the hour.

"I really don't know, but you're on the soccer team, right?" asked Jeff. For once he twitched his nose instead of his mustache. Then again, the motion looked similar.

"Yeah, I can run a 5.3," said Oliver, straightening up again, "but unless they're playing magical football or soccer, why would it matter?"

Jeff raised his eyebrows. "5.3! That's amazing at your age!" With a glance at his watch, his eyebrows dropped back down into a sterner expression. "But let's wrap this application up. I'd say we have fifteen more minutes before Mrs. Caldwell or Coach Myers start poking their noses around for you. Last on the list is your 'Gift Predisposition' … now, for this one, I think we can put down *fast*," —he looked at Oliver for a moment appreciatively— "and *wise for his age*. How does that sound, hmm?"

Oliver scratched the back of his head. "Well, I don't know about all that. There are faster players on the team. And wise? Isn't that for like old kings?" He had never felt the fastest and certainly not the wisest. *Better wise and fast than strong and powerful. That'd just be lying.*

"Yes," Jeff agreed while continuing to scribble on the form, "like King Solomon or somebody like that. Alright, we'll add 'modest and earnest,' too."

# * Chapter 1: Daydreamer's Delight *

Oliver crossed his arms and sunk further into the chair. "Alright, fine. Do you want to put that into an envelope, and then I'll put it in my mailbox tonight?" As soon as he'd asked the question, however, he felt a bit silly. He had no idea where to send the application. "What's the address for Tenochprima Academy, anyway?"

Jeff didn't respond immediately. Instead, he slowly crept to the window behind his desk. "I think we do – erm – have a way to communicate with them."

They both jumped as a squirrel landed on the windowsill. Just as Oliver began to ask what on Earth was going on, the *squirrel* tapped on the window.

Oliver's jaw dropped as he looked at Jeff, wanting to ask what was going on.

Jeff shook his head and approached the window with an uneasy gait. When he opened it, the squirrel darted past him and planted itself on the desk, looking directly at Oliver.

It twitched its nose.

"Wait a minute!" said Oliver. "This is the same squirrel we walked by earlier! Right before your office!"

"Yes, it is, isn't it?" Jeff replied. He looked unsure of himself again. "Cato said it'd either be a squirrel or maybe his toucan."

"His toucan?"

Before Jeff could answer, the squirrel interrupted them. It squeaked at Oliver and held out a paw. Without hesitation, Oliver fist-bumped the paw, but the squirrel didn't seem to like that. It twitched its whiskers at him, looking like Jeff when he twitched his mustache, and pointed at the envelope covered in green scorch marks. It chattered at him now, hinting at a sense of urgency. The squirrel, no doubt, had a busy day ahead.

"Oh, right," Oliver mumbled. If this was a magical squirrel, then maybe it wanted his magical application. He handed the squirrel his form and looked at Jeff for some approval. But Jeff looked back at him with wide eyes.

But he needn't have worried. A second later, the squirrel took the application and began rolling it into a cylinder between its paws. As it did so, Oliver was shocked to see the application shrink with every turn. By the time the squirrel was finished, the application was no larger than a walnut.

"Hey!" Oliver exclaimed. "How's anybody going to be able to read that?"

The squirrel chattered at him again, dropping the miniature application on the desk. Gingerly, it then picked up the parchment with its teeth and resumed squeaking at Oliver, the sound now muffled. With a final twitch of its tail, and what could only have been a nod of its head at Jeff, the squirrel darted back out the window.

Oliver quickly stood up and tried to chase after it, but by the time he got his head outside, the squirrel had vanished. He thought he might have seen a fluffy tail disappear behind a bush, but then again, maybe it was just a cloud of green smoke.

**\* Chapter 1: Daydreamer's Delight \***

## Chapter 2: Of Magic and Dogs

*The man I met. He sounds a bit crazy but there's just something compelling about the way he wants to change the world.*

*6*<sup>th</sup> *of July, the first year of the 10*<sup>th</sup> *Age*

Oliver had a hard time thinking of anything but Tenochprima Academy for the rest of his afternoon. After the squirrel disappeared with his application, he and Jeff agreed to meet again by the end of the week if they didn't hear back. Oliver then bid Jeff farewell and darted to soccer practice, over an hour late, with a note explaining his tardiness. When he showed up, Coach Myers accepted the note with a raised brow while his teammates avoided his eyes altogether.

But it hardly mattered.

Nothing could change the fact that *he* might become a magician – er – wizard!

Knowing his life might change at any moment filled Oliver's stomach with a flurry of excited butterflies. The idea that, in a few months' time, he might be able to cast a spell, shape an element, or even duel an enemy in heroic fashion, gave him plenty of daydreaming material. Would he wear a long, billowing cape like a witch in Salem?

Every now and then, however, the butterflies in his stomach churned in a more uncomfortable direction, bringing his attention to one *major* problem he was intentionally dodging.

# * Chapter 2: Of Magic and Dogs *

Though he'd never had too many problems at school, the monotony of living with his uncle screamed out at him, begging for a change. For as long as he could remember, he'd taken the bus home after soccer or track practice, prepped a microwave dinner, and settled down for the evening with homework and television shows. Then, after a little while, his uncle, Santiago, would come home after a long day's work, say goodnight, and disappear into his own room on the other side of their one-story house.

Oliver was fortunate to be introverted by nature, otherwise the relationship might have driven him crazy long ago. The dynamic worked during the school year when he had classes and practices to keep him occupied.

The summers, however, were a different story altogether.

With day after day of nothing planned, all Oliver could do was apply himself towards the few sources of entertainment available to him. One day he might have a go at playing a Nintendo game if his uncle was out of the house. Another day, however, he might only be able to go to a park and hope to play a pick-up game of soccer with strangers.

Though he might not have overtly thought of it yet, going away to learn magic excited him not simply because he would learn to become a wizard.

He'd also be offered an *escape*.

Eventually, the thought did formally pop into his head, showing up unannounced and past the restraints of compartmentalization as Coach Myers' whistle announced the end of practice. *What is Santiago going to think? Will he be okay with me applying for a school of magic? How much is it going to cost?*

## NOVA 01

As he showered and got onto the school bus, Oliver thought of the options available to him.

He could lie to Santiago and say he had applied for boarding school with the help of his school counselor. But this idea caused him to shake his head, much to the protest of his bangs, which fell unevenly above his eyebrows. Even if he wasn't close to Santiago, he couldn't lie to him for the rest of his life.

He looked out his window on the bus, oblivious to the paper planes, spit balls, and general bedlam playing out around him.

Alternatively, he could simply ask Jeff to see if Tenochprima could bewitch his uncle. If they were beguiling his old teachers and classmates so nobody would ask questions, why not include his uncle? Santiago wouldn't be able to understand the lie because he'd be under a spell. But that didn't feel right to Oliver, either. He was trying to rationalize the lie, and that sounded worse than just flat-out lying.

Finally, he realized he could do something that every fourteen-year-old struggled to do when making a difficult decision.

He could tell the truth.

Whenever he thought hard, he tended to rub his old, frayed sneakers against each other. He was doing so now.

If he told Santiago the truth, one of two things would happen. Either Santiago would be angry and refuse to send him to Tenochprima or he would become more interested in Oliver, opening the door to a closer relationship. There would be no in between with his uncle. Truth or lie, a conversation with Santiago was in the cards.

## * Chapter 2: Of Magic and Dogs *

He let out a sigh. He'd have to feel out Santiago's mood by the end of the week before he brought up anything. And besides, if Tenochprima didn't end up accepting him, there'd be nothing to talk about anyway.

Feeling confident, he straightened his back and took in his surroundings for the first time since he had stepped onto the bus and sat down.

To his right, a window winked sunlight at every bump of the road. To his left sat a girl he'd never met before. She wore black headphones over red hair, so he knew not to talk to her. Behind them, a half-dozen remaining students aimlessly perused their phones on their bus route home.

As they turned past a grove of dogwood trees, marking the entrance to his neighborhood, Oliver pressed his knees against the seat in front of him to brace himself for the turn. When the bus evened out, he thought he saw an unusual blur of green in between a few of the trees, but the sun had just reflected into his eyes so he couldn't be sure. Seeing as it wasn't entirely unusual to glimpse splotches of green between grass and trees, he shrugged and picked up his book bag from beneath his legs, readying himself to exit the bus.

When he did step out of the bus, he tensed.

Santiago's van was parked in the garage.

He hadn't expected his uncle to be home already and didn't relish the idea of talking to him about the application before dinner.

They had no gate, so he walked past the dried-up oak leaf hydrangeas in the front-yard and straight to the garage door. Unlocked as always, he creaked it open, hoping he'd be able to sneak inside and barricade himself in his room on the eastern side of the house until supper. He'd have to get past the kitchen and living room to do so. Inwardly, he hoped Santiago might be in the shower, but as soon as he crossed the garage door's threshold, he stopped in his tracks.

It wasn't Santiago who'd caused him to squeak to a halt on the tile kitchen floor. A medium-sized dog sat in the main room, staring directly at him.

*What on Earth?* he thought to himself. Was it a stray that wandered in through the unlocked garage door? Was Santiago pet-sitting for someone?

Slack-jawed, Oliver stood there, trying to understand what was happening. He didn't want to startle the dog, in case it barked and brought Santiago into the room. But then another thought, a much more exciting thought, trickled into his head. Could this be a communication from Tenochprima? Could this *dog* be here to tell him if Tenochprima Academy had accepted his application? He scrutinized the dog more closely now. It had all the markings of a boxer. Short, little ears. Little-to-no fur. Surprisingly thin legs.

The dog cocked its head and made a soft exhaling noise as Oliver surveyed him, almost returning the favor. But then …

*Bark!*

"Shush," Oliver hissed at the dog. But it ignored him, continuing to trumpet the sound of its kind. *Bark! Bark! Bark!*

"Oliver?" a deep voice asked from a room towards the rear left side of the kitchen. A man followed the voice, appearing from within a hallway.

Tall, strong, and stoic, Santiago exuded a no-nonsense attitude leftover from his military days. For as long as Oliver could remember, his uncle had

## * Chapter 2: Of Magic and Dogs *

been a quiet, unwelcoming man. And yet, for all the times he had thought he was going to be punished for not cleaning up after himself, or for straying into his uncle's room to play a video game, Santiago had instead given him a steely glare that accomplished the same purpose. The look affected Oliver so much, by the time he reached his rebellious middle-school years, he never dared cross him.

But today Santiago looked unsure of himself. He reached a lumbering arm behind his head and scratched his short, thick hair – a reminder of how different he looked from his nephew. Though Oliver's black hair was thicker than most of his classmates, it certainly fell short of Santiago's stiff copper wiring.

"Uhh, Oliver," he grumbled, scratching the back of his head. "I got out of work early today and thought, este," —he pointed at the dog now— "you always wanted a pet, no?"

Dumbfounded, Oliver forgot to respond. He didn't understand what Santiago was doing. He remembered asking for a dog once when he was seven, but he hadn't dared ever bring up the subject again after the glare he'd received then.

"What?" he finally said, looking from his uncle to the dog. It cocked its head to the other side.

"Well, you know," Santiago said, blustering, "you said you wanted a pet a few weeks ago."

Oliver raised an eyebrow. "A few years ago?"

"Was that really years ago?" said Santiago. He'd switched to scratching the stubble on his chin

"Yes, Santiago! I was seven, now I'm fourteen. That was half of my life ago!"

Santiago's eyes flashed. "Quick thinking. You paying attention in school now?"

Oliver's cheeks reddened. Opting not to reply, he narrowed his eyes at his uncle and stepped towards the dog. Pure bliss was etched across its face as Oliver began ruffling its ears.

"I'm sorry," said Santiago.

Oliver stopped ruffling and raised both his eyebrows at the apology. This was unusual territory for his uncle.

"That was a jerk thing to say," Santiago continued, "and you don't deserve that." He stared at Oliver for a few more seconds, the usual steel flashing across his eyes, then lumbered towards the kitchen counter. From below, he pulled out a black, countertop stool and offered it to Oliver. When Oliver shook his head, Santiago shrugged and settled down on it instead.

Oliver's mind raced as he thought of how to respond. Usually, an insult in his house resulted in slammed doors and scrounging for food in the pantry during the late hours of the night. This current situation, however, made Oliver feel even more uncomfortable – it was an actual confrontation requiring a solution.

All he could think to do was to follow suit. So, he stepped away from the dog, much to its dismay, and sat on one of the wooden chairs circling the dining table that stood across from where his uncle sat. The dog sat in the middle of the kitchen, between them both. It cocked its head back and

## ✳ Chapter 2: Of Magic and Dogs ✳

forth at the two of them, and, after much internal deliberation, scuttled over to Oliver for more attention.

"Hah!" said Santiago with a hint of a smile. "See? I had the right idea! Archie likes you already."

"Archie?"

"You think I'd call a dog *Archie?* When I adopted him at the shelter in Mooresville, he already had the name. Doesn't listen to anything else."

Oliver looked down at Archie. He was tempted to speak to him in a baby voice, but that felt too cliche to do in front of his stoic uncle. Instead, he simply smiled back.

"But seriously," continued Santiago. "I am sorry."

Oliver pressed his lips together and mumbled, "there's nothing to be sorry about – I know you didn't mean it."

An awkward silence filled the air. Unsure of what else to say, Oliver fixated on the blender sitting on the kitchen countertop behind Santiago. A full minute passed by before either said anything else. Just as Oliver was about to stand up to barricade himself in his room, a third voice reverberated through the air around them.

"*Well, this is awkward, isn't it,*" interjected the voice. It was deep, crunching, and foreign, like a Spaniard speaking in a posh English accent.

Oliver jumped out of his chair, his heart racing. He had thought he and his uncle were alone in the room.

Santiago stood as well, catapulting the stool behind him as he scrambled for safety. It ricocheted off the kitchen counter and fell to the floor, clattering to a halt.

## NOVA 01

"WHO'S THERE!" boomed Santiago.

"*I'm right here, good man,*" declared the voice. "*No need to yell.*"

Oliver glanced at Santi as he surveyed the room, looking for the voice's source. He was glad to see him look just as confused and scared as he did.

The voice chuckled like crunching hills of stone. "*My, my, isn't it obvious? I'm the dog!*"

Santiago let out a shriek that sounded a lot like "*demonio!*" and darted behind the counter.[1] Oliver, however, stepped toward the dog with quick and long strides.

"You can talk?!" he asked incredulously. "The squirrel couldn't!"

"*I think loud enough for your thick skulls to hear,*" the dog said without moving its mouth. It was unmistakably smiling at them now, looking from Oliver, who was grimacing, to Santiago, who was cowering.

"Think loud?!" yelled Santiago with his hands over his temples. "What the heck are you talking about, DEMON DOG?!"

"*Demon dog? Now really, Santiago. You already told Oliver I go by Archie.*"

"OLIVER, WHY IS THE DEMON DOG TALKING TO ME?"

Oliver started to laugh now too. The situation made a little more sense to him after the afternoon's events. But when he put himself in his uncle's shoes, the scenario seemed much weirder.

"Santi! It's fine! He's just a dog – not a demon dog!"

Archie's jowls folded into a grin. "*Well, that's not entirely true, now, is it?*"

---

[1] Santiago moved to the United States from México in his early twenties. He speaks in his native Spanish from time to time. "Demonio" translates to "demon" in English.

## * Chapter 2: Of Magic and Dogs *

"THAT'S IT, DEMON DOG! NO MORE JOKES!" With a shaking arm, Santiago pulled a kitchen knife from a drawer and brandished it at the dog from behind the counter.

"SANTI! Calm down! The dog's here for me!" Oliver looked down at Archie to confirm. "You are here for me, aren't you?"

*"I'm certainly not here for Santiago, if that's what you're asking,"* said Archie. He backed up behind the kitchen table, peering at Santiago through the gaps in the chairs. *"Now, really? Put that thing away before you hurt somebody. I'll stop with the jokes. I am here to deliver something to Oliver!"*

Oliver's heart began to race at the mention of his name – this had to be about Tenochprima Academy! He looked to where his uncle was hiding and saw him emerge, knife in hand. Though he no longer yelled, his eyes narrowed, flashing steel.

Oliver hissed at the look and gestured for Santiago to stand next to him. "Hurry up! You heard the dog! Get over here!"

With measured steps, Santiago lumbered towards them, muttering "hallucinations" and never taking his eyes off Archie.

*"Now, now, Santiago,"* Archie quipped, *"leave the knife on the counter, will you? You're starting to make me nervous."*

"How do I know you won't suck out my soul or something, huh, *demon dog*?"

Oliver rolled his eyes.

With a scuttling noise, Archie slinked from his hiding place to sit immediately in front of them on the kitchen tile. *"Perhaps I was having too much fun. In my defense, it's this dog-like form – leaves the brain addled."*

Oliver raised his eyebrows at that.

"*Santiago,*" Archie resumed, "*I am nothing more than a dog-messenger on This Side of the Key. For our purposes today, that should be enough. I mean you no harm.*"

Santiago continued flashing steel at Archie, but then, to Oliver's surprise, he rotated to place the knife on the kitchen counter next to a bowl of bananas. Inwardly, Oliver cheered as Santiago turned back towards them with his arms crossed.

Archie nodded appreciatively. "*Now, Oliver, I'm sure you've already had a moment to speak with your uncle about Tenochprima after you applied earlier today.*"

"Erm," Oliver muttered. He tried to gesture a stop-speaking-now gesture to Archie but the damage had been done.

"Tenochtitlan?!" Santiago asked. "What are you talking about demon dog? Are you an Aztec descendant?" He shook his head ruefully as he spoke.

"*No,*" Archie exhaled, "*not Tenochtitlan. 'Teh-knock-pree-muh.' It's a magical institution.*"

Santiago let out a baritone, false laugh at the mention of magic. "Magical institution for Aztecs? I think you woke up in the wrong dimension, demon dog." Then, with a more serious expression, he added, "come to think of it, I think *I* woke up in the wrong dimension." He began closing and opening his eyes and waving a hand in front of them. "Oliver, did you apply for a nuthouse or something?"

Before he could answer, Archie interrupted. "*Well, that's unfortunate. A scenario B? My apologies, Oliver. I thought all family members would be up to speed when I felt the magical readings outside the house.*"

# * Chapter 2: Of Magic and Dogs *

"I didn't get around to telling him," Oliver mumbled. He worried they only had seconds before Santiago might get nasty. "What do you mean about magical readings?"

"*I scanned the house when Santiago and I drove up and the readings spiked more than—,*"

"SCENARIO B?!" shouted Santiago. "MAGICAL READINGS?! SCANNING MY HOUSE?! YOU BETTER START MAKING SENSE OR I'M TAKING YOU BACK TO THE POUND." He rotated back towards the counter and picked up the knife again, wielding it at Archie and then Oliver. Though Archie returned to his safe space behind the kitchen table, Oliver stood his ground.

"The demon dog is telling the truth, Santi!" He thought if he used Santiago's descriptor of Archie it might help his uncle feel in charge. After a quiet moment, he knew his tactic had worked because Santiago didn't interrupt again. "A – well, a wizard is the only word for him – he came by school earlier this week and told the counselor, Mr. Hamilton, to submit applications to this magical school called Tenochprima. Mr. Hamilton submitted *me*, and I think this dog will let me know if I got in or not!"

"*That's precisely correct!*" added Archie from behind the table.

Santiago flared his nostrils in the dog's direction and then looked back at Oliver.

"Oliver! You see how crazy this is?! The only reason I'm listening is because I'm pretty sure I'm hallucinating!" He waved at Archie with the knife. "There's a *talking dog* in my house!"

"Santi, it's true," Oliver pleaded. "Can we just hear the rest of what the dog has to say?"

Santiago grimaced. "If this is a joke, Oliver," he said threateningly, "it's a really bad one." Flashbacks of La Chancla[2], Santiago's favorite tool of choice for scolding, crossed Oliver's mind. He was in for a whooping if things didn't go well.

"*Well, thankfully,*" said Archie, peering his head around the table, "*I'm real, and I can prove the existence of magic for you right here and now!*"

*Finally,* Oliver thought to himself. His mouth felt dry – surely, they'd have just mailed him a letter if he'd been rejected? Then again, he didn't know how these people operated. It could be a formal denial.

Santiago smiled sarcastically at them both. "Ok, demon dog." He spoke in a sing-song voice Oliver had never heard from him before. "Show me a neat card trick."

Archie looked at Santiago with an unamused expression before emerging fully into the space between the table and the counter again. Then, with a soundless twist of his body, he disappeared inside a puff of gold smoke.

*Plop! Clang!*

---

[2] A "chancla" is a sandal or flip-flop. In Mexican culture, it often doubles as a disciplinary tool used by distressed parents and/or teachers. In this context, Oliver is reminded of Santiago's use of La Chancla.

## * Chapter 2: Of Magic and Dogs *

Oliver and Santiago exchanged surprised stares as the smoke subsided. Next to Archie, a shiny key and rolled-up piece of parchment teetered to a halt.

There was a brief pause as Oliver and Santiago digested what they had just seen. Inside his chest, Oliver felt his heart pound. He thought he knew what lay in front of him. A letter from Tenochprima Academy.

He stooped down to pick up the letter and glimpsed cerulean ink.

*"Wait!"* Archie implored. He had resumed smiling like a mischievous cat. *"Before you read the Instruction Manual, let me be the first to say CONGRATULATIONS on being accepted into Tenochprima Academy!! Our Admissions Department believes you will make a fine addition to our one-of-a-kind institution!"*

## Chapter 3: This Side of the Key

*I was right! Magic does exist – but for reasons I can't yet understand, it's restricted to the 'Other Side.' Why would there be two sides and not just one?*

*29th of July, the first year of the 10th Age*

Oliver whooped and hollered as he ran around the kitchen, digesting the news. *He'd be going to Tenochprima Academy to learn magic!* The same thoughts of grandeur that had enveloped him in Mr. Hamilton's office returned, causing him to absentmindedly twirl his hands as he cast imaginary spells.

"*Oliver!*" Archie barked. "*Focus! Lots of logistics to get through.*"

"Sorry!" Oliver mouthed, not feeling sorry at all. He shot Santiago two very excited thumbs up, but his uncle didn't return the enthusiasm. Instead, he lumbered towards the stool he'd tipped over earlier and picked it up. He looked a bit green in the face as he dusted off the cushion and sat down.

"What's the key for, then?" he rasped. For a moment Oliver wondered if Santiago might vomit.

Archie beamed. *"Excellent question!"* His claws clicked on the tiles as he stooped down and picked up the shiny key. Then, he padded over to Oliver and dropped the key in his outstretched hand.

When the metal touched his skin, Oliver let out a faint gasp. It was surprisingly warm to the touch.

*"This key,"* said Archie, *"is your ticket to the Other Side!"*

"Other Side?" Santiago and Oliver asked at the same time.

# * Chapter 3: This Side of the Key *

Archie chortled in his chest, louder and deeper than seemed possible for his frame. *"Yes, you two are sharp."*

"*Ha-ha*," Oliver feigned. "But what do you mean by the Other Side? Of the street?"

Santiago nodded his head as Oliver spoke. His posture had regained *some* composure and a bit of color was returning to his face.

"Yeah, no more jokes, demon dog," he growled. "Do magicians and wizards have their own hidden kingdom or something?"

*"In a way,"* said Archie looking cryptic. *"Around nine hundred years ago, the greatest magical wielders in the world congregated and made a controversial decision to place everyone who could channel magic in a dimension running parallel but distinct from the existing one."* Oliver glanced at Santiago and saw the same look of awe on his uncle's face. *"You both live in the original, unmodified world, whereas I'm from the parallel dimension."*

*"And that brings us to your key question, Santiago,"* Archie mused. *"Currently, the only known way for humans to travel between both worlds is by key. That is why you'll hear folks in our dimension saying, 'the original' or 'other' Side of the Key."*

Oliver raised the key Archie had placed in his hand earlier, looking at it in a different light. Goosebumps spread across his arms and legs as he stared at the shining metal. Out of the corner of his eye, he caught a glimpse of reverence in Santiago's eyes. A chortle brought Oliver's attention back to Archie.

*"It's worth noting that these inter-dimensional keys are exceedingly rare. No man or sacred beast possesses the knowledge to forge another. We must use those that already exist. Your key, for example, was created at the time of the initial concealment."*

"Initial concealment?" Oliver asked.

Archie let out a doggish whine. *"At this rate the questions will never end! Leave some for school! Professor Watkin, no doubt, would prefer you learn about the dawn of magic and the ages of magical proximity from him first."* Pausing, Archie took a moment to scratch his left ear with his paw. *"Now! Let us turn our attention to the Instruction Manual that came with your key! It should answer enough of your questions to have you comfortably reach Tenochprima."* He motioned with his nose and eyebrows at the parchment that still lay on the floor.

Absentmindedly, Oliver handed the key he had been holding in his other hand to Santiago so that he could pick up the parchment.

In his hands, the instruction manual felt thicker than expected. Even so, he handled it with care between his fingers, not wanting to rip it by accident. Flipping it over, he traced folded-down corners that met under a wax seal bearing an emblem he'd never seen before. On it, he made out a snarling bear, a giant eagle flapping its wings, and a floating serpent. It had a beak, multi-colored feathers, and on-closer inspection, narrow wings. Beneath the creatures, the words 'Tenochprima Academy' were etched into the wax.

"Open it already!" said Santiago with raised fists. Oliver lifted an eyebrow at his uncle, surprised to see him displaying this much emotion about anything. At Oliver's look, Santiago coughed and lowered his hands. "I mean, be careful opening that, Oliver. It may be a trap or something."

Archie rolled his eyes. *"Yes, careful you don't get a paper cut."*

Oliver laughed, deciding it best not to comment, and removed the wax seal from the parchment. It made a satisfying sticky noise as it separated

# * Chapter 3: This Side of the Key *

from the paper. With the seal undone, he unfolded the corners of the Instruction Manual, revealing a list of directives written in cursive.

Dear Mr. Garcia,
Congratulations on your admission to Tenochprima Academy. Kindly refer to the instructions below to arrive on campus by Sunday, the thirtieth of August.
1. Take your key to your prescribed doorway to enter the Other Side (your Guide will show you the way)
2. Upon entry, make your way to your nearest Khufu Ship, Trundholm, Sky Disk or Quadriga
3. Board the Southern Line towards Tampico, México
4. Exit at Charleston, South Carolina (eighth stop on the Southern line)
5. Follow signs to Tenochprima Academy
6. Board the Tenochprima Shuttle and arrive on campus where ushers await
7. Orientate yourself with your fellow extramen

Note:
1. You will require (i) all textbooks for Tenochprima extramen, (ii) a magical channel of your choice, and (iii) clothing in compliance with the school dress code
2. You may pick up your textbooks, supplies, and uniform at your local village
    a. If necessary, all items can be purchased at the campus bookstore

Warm Regards,

Madeline des 'Moulins
Cuahtemoc Ohth Tamul
Augustus Thomas Henderson

Oliver's brain raced with questions when he finished reading the Instruction Manual. He had no clue what his prescribed doorway was, let alone what a Khufu Ship could even begin to be.

"*Don't worry if it doesn't all make sense,*" said Archie, exhaling doggishly. "*I am here to serve as your Guide throughout your time at Tenochprima.*"

Oliver nodded appreciatively and offered Santiago the list. He returned the key he'd been holding onto in exchange.

After he finished reading, Santiago shook his head. "What's a Quadrangle Ship, man? This list doesn't make any sense."

"Thank you!" said Oliver pointedly. He looked at Archie with sarcastic satisfaction, as if it were the dog's fault the list didn't have enough detail.

Archie narrowed his eyes and smacked his lips at them both disapprovingly. "*A Quadriga is just one of the possible vehicles of transportation available to novas. So are Trundholms, Sky Disks, and Khufu ships. They are all relics from bygone ages that served as public transportation – we just got them back up and running in the last ten or fifteen years.*"

"Magic ship, eh?" Oliver interjected, "Sounds cool. But what's a Nova?"

Archie huffed at the question. Looking around, his eyes lit up at the sight of the living room couch next to the dining table. A moment later, he'd stretched his legs and curled up into a comfy spot, his eyes closed. Oliver almost berated the dog for not answering his question but then he and Santiago jumped again as Archie's voice sounded in their heads. Though he appeared to be settling in for a nap, his voice continued just as before. "*A nova is our term for a witch or wizard. Not very clever, now, is it?*"

# * Chapter 3: This Side of the Key *

It was Santiago's turn to huff. A noise Oliver was all too familiar with. "How the heck are we supposed to know if it's clever or not, demon dog?"

*"My apologies, Santiago. Our source of magic – the solar system's forgotten planet – is called Nova. And humans ... well, when they discovered magic, for some reason they opted to call themselves the same thing."*

"Forget about it," Santiago blustered. "We don't have nine planets anymore – Pluto got demoted."

Archie exhaled in tired fashion. *"Not Pluto, Nova. It's the reason why magic exists. Like gravity from the moon pushes and pulls the tides, Nova pushes and pulls magic from the fabric of life."*

Oliver blanched. "You mean magic is caused by that new planet the Japanese spotted a few weeks ago?" His voice cracked as he spoke, betraying his excitement. Santiago meanwhile gasped and Oliver could practically see cogs shifting in his head.

*"Right again!"* said Archie. Oliver thought he heard a hint of pleasure in the dog's voice, but it was difficult to tell with his eyes being closed.

"Okay then," Santiago replied belabouredly. "Where do we take the key?"

Archie's ears perked up and his eyes opened. *"It's quite simple really."* He stretched for a moment, extending his front paws and arching his back. *"I had the faculty at school bewitch your key to work with your kitchen-to-bedroom door. Oliver, if you wouldn't mind, hand me the key and we can proceed!"*

Santiago and Oliver looked at each other, confused. "What kitchen door?"

*"The one to the bedroom ..."* Archie began. He scanned the kitchen for any door whatsoever.

Santiago boomed with laughter. "Archie? Is this the part where you tell us it's all a joke? We don't have a kitchen to bedroom door!"

*"Preposterous. I was told there'd be one!"* But Archie didn't look as confident as he sounded. Oliver thought he may have even detected a sliver of embarrassment in his tone.

"Well, there isn't," said Oliver, crossing his arms, "but can't we just reprogram the key for another door or something?"

Archie stopped. His ear had drooped down to folds on the sides of his head. *"Well, yes. But your first day exposed to magic is supposed to go smoothly!"* He took the key from Oliver's hand with his mouth and darted over to a pantry door, attempting to unlock it. But the door didn't have a keyhole, just a handle.

*"Gah! I thought that may have worked! Why couldn't I just have assigned it to a bathroom door?"* He was thinking aloud now, ignoring Oliver and Santiago as he spoke. *"I bet Cato did this on purpose. My first student since ... gah! What a cruel joke."*

Pity flooded Oliver's core as he watched Archie dart back and forth around the kitchen. Only last summer Santiago had renovated the main living space. Where there used to be a wall and door separating the kitchen from the living room, only open space now remained. "Okay ... Archie, how else can we get to the Other Side?"

Santiago chuckled dryly at Archie but then coughed as Oliver shot a reproving look at him.

## * Chapter 3: This Side of the Key *

Archie slowed to a halt at the question and cocked his head at Oliver. *"We can enter another way, but we'll have to head to the nearest Master of Keys in your area. Thankfully, there's one in the village of Davidstown."*

Santiago gave Oliver a look. "You mean Davidson? They only have a bookstore for the local college and places to eat. No key shop, no magic, no nothing.

*"Remember what the Instruction Manual said? You can pick up your textbooks and school supplies on campus or in your local village."*

Santiago blustered. "There's no—,"

*"Haven't you been listening to anything I've said?"* interrupted Archie. It was his turn to exchange a look with Oliver – he bore his doggish smile again. *"Once we're on the Other Side of the Key, you're never going to want to see Davidson ever again. In Davidstown, you'll be able to get your books for your extraman classes – although I'm pretty sure there's a convenience fee if you don't pick them up at school."*

That got Santiago's attention. Oliver wilted as he saw the steel in his uncle's eyes harden.

"Convenience fee?" Oliver asked, giving Santiago an uneasy look.

*"Well, you can't expect our Side of the Key to just hand out things for free, can you?"*

Santiago grumpily pulled out a billfold from his pocket. "Will a twenty work?"

Archie scoffed. *"Imagine using paper as currency – I cannot believe your people abandoned the gold standard."* He continued chuckling and padded across the tile to yank the twenty from Santiago's hand.

Santiago let out a yelp. "Hey," he tried adding in a deep voice, "don't slobber that thing up too much. The cafeteria at work only takes ca-AAAAARRGG!"

But Santiago abandoned his efforts at being manly and began to scream because Archie had suddenly disappeared. This time, no smoke hid the magic. Oliver saw him turn on the spot and wondered what he was up to with the bill, but he had vanished entirely before he could even think to ask.

No sooner had Santiago finished screaming when Archie came back into sight. For the briefest moment, Oliver thought Archie looked different as he reappeared – almost leathery – but he dismissed the thought just as quickly because Archie looked perfectly doggish after another second or two.

*"Aha!"* Archie exclaimed. *"Observe!"* He stepped forward to Santiago, whose eyes were bulging, and dropped four lavender coins from his mouth onto the floor.

"What are these?" Oliver asked. He stepped forward and quickly picked up one of the coins. It shone purple and light blue and sterling silver rimmed the circumference. "They look like pieces from a fancy board game or something." Santiago couldn't help himself, also stooping to pick up one of the remaining three pieces.

*"Those are amethyst pieces, gentlemen. And they are worth about five dollars each. We call them "Ameys" for short! They ought to cover any administrative fees we come across as we buy your supplies. We can go first thing tomorrow to beat the crowd. And then maybe a spot of lunch will do us good – there's a tasty spot with fresh bugs that are just the crunchiest. If you go at the right time ..."*

## * Chapter 3: This Side of the Key *

Oliver glanced at Santiago as Archie continued talking about bugs, but Santiago looked deep in thought. Probably about bugs, too, or maybe the money situation.

Ignoring them both, he glanced at the kitchen oven. It read 9:17 PM. In the rush of excitement, over three hours had passed them by.

*"The hour does grow late,"* said Archie, following Oliver's gaze. *"Shall we head out early tomorrow? I'll make myself at home on the couch."*

Santiago shrugged his shoulders and allowed them to fall. "If you say so, demon dog. I'll call in sick. No chance I'm missing seeing the *Other Side*." He used air quotes to demonstrate his begrudging use of the foreign lingo. "I'll heat up a frozen pizza for dinner – you guys good with that?" The invitation to agree or disagree was more of a formality as he was already on his way to the freezer.

*"Very well,"* said Archie, curling into a ball on the couch again.

Oliver felt mutinous at the sight of Santiago making pizza and Archie settling down for bed. As far as he was concerned, it was a crime to wait to explore Davidstown until morning; a world of magic and wonder was only a key's turn away! Inwardly, he wanted to knock Archie's and Santiago's heads together for denying him the immediate satisfaction of seeing the Other Side. Instead, however, he opted for a long sigh.

"I'll preheat the oven," he grumbled.

## NOVA 01

Unable to sleep, Oliver tossed and turned the whole night thinking about Archie, the Other Side, Santiago's decent reaction, and lastly, Tenochprima Academy itself. He wondered if he'd fit in or if he'd be ... well, more like he was at Hunterton High. Boring and friendless.

It was almost a relief when his alarm went off at 7:30.

In a flurry of motion, he shot out of bed, put on a fresh set of clothes, and tied his frayed pair of sneakers before bolting to the kitchen.

But Archie had beat him to it. As Oliver rounded the corner from his room, he was greeted by scrambled eggs, crispy bacon, and sizzling sausage on the kitchen table. Next to it, Archie waved at him with his right paw. Impressed, Oliver waved back and nodded his head to indicate his thanks. He grabbed a piece of bacon and began eating. "Santi up yet?"

Before Archie could answer, Santiago appeared from around his side of the house as well. He was drying his hair with a towel, but otherwise looked ready to go.

*"Oh-ho!"* sang Archie. *"Good to see Oliver isn't the only one excited to see more magic, now is he, Mr. García? Now that you've received a taste, you're dying for more, eh?"*

"You betcha, demon dog." The term now carried familiarity, not animosity. "Thanks for making the eggs, jefecito[3]," he added in Oliver's direction.

---

[3] In this context, "jefecito" can be best translated colloquially to "bossman." An affectionate way to describe somebody in charge. Literally translatable to "little boss."

## * Chapter 3: This Side of the Key *

"Not me," said Oliver through a full mouth of sausage, egg, and cheese. "Archie."

Santiago glanced at Archie appraisingly. "Really? How can a dog cook breakfast?"

*"A friend delivered it on my behalf."*

"Hmm," Santiago replied. He gave the eggs an uneasy leer before shrugging his shoulders and digging in.

Within twenty minutes, the spread of food had been eaten and the dishes loaded in the dishwasher. It helped that Oliver was a growing boy and could eat several eggs, four slices of toast, and six pieces of bacon without issue. Santiago, built differently, always marveled at how much Oliver could eat and still be so skinny.

Between the delicious food in his belly and the prospect of magic in his future, Oliver had reason to smile by the time they clambered into Santiago's van. And smile he did. Like a clam.

Within an additional fifteen minutes, Santiago had parked a short walk away from Davidson's Main Street, where the local Master of Keys was supposed to be. During the car ride Oliver had bombarded Archie with questions but Archie insisted he wait until they reached Davidstown on the "Other Side" before he answered any more.

*"Now,"* Archie began telling them as they walked underneath oak and ash trees towards Main Street, *"I've never interacted with the Master of Keys before, but from what I've heard, he's quite the curmudgeon."*

"So what?" Oliver asked. He skipped ahead of them. "Aren't we his customers?"

"Yo, slow down, Oliver!" grunted Santiago. "Master of Keys ain't going anywhere." Oliver slowed down an indiscernible amount.

*"Even then,"* said Archie, ignoring Santiago, *"something about the fumes makes every Master – erm – unpleasant."*

Oliver raised an eyebrow. Santiago, meanwhile, grimaced as they rounded the corner onto Main Street.

*"This way!"* Archie beckoned.

As always, Main Street was a pleasant affair. On each side of the wide thoroughfare, old-fashioned brick sidewalks gave way to early American style storefronts with sash windows and pre-civil war facades. Each window display offered something different to the surveyors outside. In one, preppy clothing enticed potential customers to dress, lounge, or golf in pastel colors. In another, a classic diner's jukebox rocked and rolled as waiters and waitresses served burgers and fries. They didn't stop until they reached the only eye sore on the street – a small, bizarre shop with a display of gnomes.

*"Here we are!"* said Archie, bringing them to a halt at the gnomes.

"For real?" Santiago asked, leaning as far away from the gnomes as he could. They all stared at them with bulging eyes from behind long, thin noses and wizened, gray hair.

*"What? The gnomes?"* Archie asked after seeing the incredulous looks on both their faces. *"They are the sign of a Keyshop. They're supposed to bring good luck to travelers."*

"Isn't that just superstition?" Santiago asked with a sneer.

Oliver laughed. "In a world of magic, talking dogs, and key dimensions, you really think a good luck charm is ridiculous?"

# * Chapter 3: This Side of the Key *

Archie chuckled and shook his head. *"You two are more like brothers than father and son."*

Awkward silence followed, threatening to poison the mood. Oliver half expected Santiago to walk away, or worse, to kick Archie, but instead his uncle leaned back and belted out a laugh.

"Hah! You may be right, demon dog," he said, offering a rare flash of his teeth. "But Oliver knows better than to provoke me too much."

Oliver felt his muscles relax. Santiago rarely talked about Oliver's mother, and never once his father. He looked at his uncle who was wagging a finger at him.

"Don't think you becoming a magician changes anything," he said in a hushed tone. "I'm still the boss around the house." He pulled Oliver into a headlock and ruffled his hair before releasing him and turning back to Archie. "Vámonos[4] – we've got some magic to see."

Archie chortled. *"Ever the man of action, Mr. García. After you two, then."* Oliver could have sworn Archie gave him the slightest of winks. Less subtly, he motioned with his head at the doorbell. *"Well, I can't press it. We'll get funny looks."*

Oliver didn't need a second invitation. Between the magic he imagined in the air and Santiago's good mood, he was feeling very excited indeed.

He jabbed his finger at the doorbell, unintentionally setting it off twice. *Ding dong! Ding dong!*

Santiago slapped him on the back of the head. "Just once."

---

[4] "Vámonos" means "let's go" in English.

###  NOVA 01

*"And remember,"* Archie added, *"we have reason to suspect the Master is unpleasant. Don't get testy with him."*

With the back of his head stinging, Oliver barely noticed a middle-aged man open the glass door to the left of the window display full of gnomes.

The man rang out through the screen door that still lay between them. "Watchu want?!" His voice carried the gravel of ten thousand cigarettes.

Archie spoke first, which was a good thing, because Oliver had no idea how to respond to a voice like that. *"We wish to modify the entry point of our Key."*

The man glared directly at Archie after he spoke. "Ye do, do ye? Are ye going to Tenoch, kiddo?" His eyes kept switching between them all.

"Uhh," Oliver began.

"Doesn' matter," he looked at Archie now. "Why's your key need reimaging? I ain't got much fuel left."

Oliver blustered. "Fuel? What are you—,"

*"Wouldn't it be more prudent,"* Archie interrupted with a raised paw, *"to discuss inside, away from wandering eyes?"* With a tilt of his head, he drew attention to the dozens of passersby running their errands.

The Master of Keys' jowls quivered. "I'll decide what's prudent, ye mangy mutt. That is, if you even are a dawg. Who knows what you might be on the Other Side, eh?"

*"Now, really!"* Archie huffed. *"I think we got off to the wrong start. My name is—,"*

"Don't care what yer name is. What I do care about is that yer the fifth group of cartoon misfits to come by with a key mapped to the wrong door."

## ∗ Chapter 3: This Side of the Key ∗

*"I can assure you,"* Archie blustered, *"this mistake will be thoroughly investigated!"*

Looking up, Oliver saw Santiago shake his head while Archie continued babbling. *"As the local Master of Keys, we require your services to—,"*

"I ain't got an obligation to do nuthin," the Master said, sneering. He took a moment to spit out chewing tobacco.

Just when Oliver began to wonder if they were wasting their time, Santiago exhaled loudly. With a large hand, he grabbed the screen door and yanked it open before lumbering inside with a lowered shoulder.

"Hey!" the Master protested, "ye ain't got the right to—,"

Santiago cut him off as he entered, pushing him aside with his shoulder.

Oliver darted in behind him, side-stepping the grouchy Master and squeaky screen door. Archie, meanwhile, scampered in between the three sets of legs.

"If I'd had me staff on me," the man grumbled, rubbing the shoulder Santiago had barged through.

"I'd have beaten you with it," Santiago growled.

Oliver flared his nostrils at Santiago. "I'm Oliver, the bulldozer is Santiago, and my Guide is Archie."

"I already told ye," grumbled the Master, "I don't care what yer names are." He walked towards the rear of the shop and situated himself behind a counter and ancient cash register. "Gimme yer key and let's be done with it."

It took Oliver a moment to register the request because the room itself had begun to distract him. In the same space of a small studio apartment, nearly a hundred wooden shelves had been installed. Everywhere he looked, shelf after shelf covered the walls, and on them, sat dozens of gnomes. Each wore a different expression – some sad, others glad, all certainly mad. In each set of little arms, keys of varying color and size reflected light at him from a gas lamp behind the counter where the Master now sat. The effect was, whether intentional or not, spectacular as each key winked at them in iridescent colors of green, red, purple, or blue. Oliver took out his key so it could soak in the presence of its brethren. As always, it felt warm to the touch.

"Gimme the key, boy!"

Oliver snapped out of his reverie at the marble-voiced request. "Sorry!" he said, jumping away from the shelves. He approached the Master, dodging another slap on the head from Santiago along the way.

But before he could hand over the key, the shop's screen door squeaked open again. A girl and a magnificent golden retriever waltzed in as the door shut behind them. The girl somehow looked familiar to Oliver. She was as tall as he was, with straight, red hair that hinted at shades of brown. Her frame was thin, but her posture and expression exuded a fierceness Oliver typically only saw in people as large as his uncle. Black headphones rested on her shoulders, and though it took him a moment, Oliver eventually realized she was the girl he had sat next to on the bus.

*"See I told you, Emma,"* said a new telepathic voice, *"this is the Keyshop. You'll find—,"*

## * Chapter 3: This Side of the Key *

"ABSOLUTELY NOTHING YE MUTT! WHAT MAKES ALL Y'ALL THINK YE CAN JUS' BARGE IN?!" The Master of Keys' face was a shade of red Oliver didn't know existed: almost maroon.

*"Now really, good man!"* the new voice continued. It was deep, like Archie's, but silkier, and with less of an accent. *"Oh, Archie! I didn't see you there. I've never been able to master these dog forms on this side. Terrible eyesight, and my tail won't seem to stop wagging!"*

"NOBODY IS GOING TO THE OTHER SIDE IF Y'ALL DON'T QUIT YER YAPPIN AND FORM A LINE! THIS IS GETTIN RIDICULOUS!"

*"Well, I never,"* the golden retriever huffed. He stepped back and forth uncertainly behind Archie. *"Come along, Emma. The Master of Keys demands we form a line."*

*"Don't you think introductions are in order, Rasmus?"* said Archie, smiling his boxer grin at the golden retriever.

*"You're quite right,"* said the golden retriever. His tail kept wagging into Oliver's leg, making his knees buckle. *"Good morning, all. My name is Rasmus, and I am Emma's Guide for her tenure at Tenochprima Academy!"*

"Good to meet you," said the girl, sticking out a hand towards Oliver. "We sat next to each other on the bus yesterday." Oliver took her hand and shook it. He almost winced at how firm she shook back.

"I thought you looked familiar! My name's Oliver García. You're from Hunterton, too?"

Emma crossed one arm over the other, stretching her shoulders. "Actually, I go to Davidson High and live just up the road. But I do theater after school at Hunterton, so I usually take the Hunterton bus home." She turned towards Santiago offering her hand up again. "And you?"

"Santiago but you can call me Santi. I'm Oliver's uncle-and-or-guardian."

Archie snorted. *"You didn't tell me that. I've been calling you Santiago or Mr. García for more than a day now."*

Santiago gave Archie an affectionate pat of the head. "Yeah, but I don't like you, Archie." He winked at Oliver and Emma as Rasmus snorted on Archie's behalf.

*"Ha-ha,"* Archie replied sardonically.

"I'm never gonna get rid of y'all, am I?" the Master of Keys sighed in the background. He picked up a staff studded with jade jewels and banged it on the counter, red in the face. "GIMME THE KEY, BOY! I AIN'T GONNA ASK YE AGAIN!"

"Sorry!" Oliver yelped. He hurried towards the counter and placed his key on it, before turning back to face Emma. "Your key mapped wrong, too?"

*"Yes!"* Rasmus barked. *"Completely outrageous. Somebody in the admissions department is having a very unprofessional laugh!"*

"It was mapped to a balcony door," Emma added with a shake of her head. "It's a sliding door with no keyhole – just a latch."

*"Preposterous!"* Rasmus finished.

"Quit yer chattering and focus here, boy!" the Master of Keys growled in the background. "Ye better give me yer key too, girl."

# * Chapter 3: This Side of the Key *

Emma placed her key next to Oliver's. Hers was a dark red that nearly matched the color of her hair. "No need to be rude, mister."

The Master ignored her. "Finally," he muttered. "Dang dogs never stop yappin'." Taking the keys, he turned to face a mysterious machine Oliver hadn't noticed yet. It looked like an old-fashioned typewriter but with added levers of varying lengths. Where paper might exit a real typewriter, a keyhole existed, and on the right-hand side, a thin, dirty hose connected it to a tank on the floor. Fuel sat idle in the tube, looking celadon through the muck that covered its surface.

"I'm gonna set y'all's keys to work with my door out back, ye hear? You'll have to use this entrance if you want to come back. If you want to change yer entrance, get yer school to provide more fluid – terribly expensive to make – yer usually only allowed one change, and we're doin' it now."

"Utterly preposterous," Rasmus sniffed, wagging his tail and shaking his head some more.

Ignoring him, the Master grabbed and pulled the longest lever on the machine. Oliver took a step back as it began to vibrate violently. In the tube, the idle fuel turned a shockingly bright green, visible even through the grimy surface.

"Don't look directly at the fluid!" the Master said with a cackle hinting at insanity. "Few ways to get you blind quicker than that!"

"Tell us that before you start!" Oliver yelled through the racket. He threw a hand partially over his eyes and saw Santiago do the same. Archie and Rasmus, meanwhile, continued watching unperturbed. Nuts and bolts flew in every direction as the machine continued to rattle, occasionally clipping Santiago, who took up the most space.

Unconcerned by the racket, the Master stuck Emma's key into the keyhole and began to coo at the contraption. Just when Oliver thought there was little chance of the machine doing anything other than destroying the entire shop, the Master picked up his staff and yelled an indiscernible set of words that sounded an awful lot like *Abra-Kadabra* to untrained ears.

With an unnatural clang, Emma's dark red key shot out from the opposite end of the machine towards a quench tank on the other side of the counter. Steam erupted as the key touched the surface of the tank's thick, dark liquid. What Oliver assumed was water spritzed and boiled even after the key settled at the bottom. A moment later, Oliver's green key followed Emma's, dousing them in steam for a second time.

"And there ye have it!" the Master said, turning around to smile at them for the first time. He tapped his staff on the ground twice, ridding the room of smoke and, Oliver realized, drying the clothes and fur of his guests.

Oliver touched his shirt, confirming it really was fully dry. He looked at Santiago who marveled back at him, also dumbfounded.

*"Now, now, gentlemen,"* Archie chuckled, *"you're going to need to stop guffawing like buffoons every time you see magic."*

Next to them, Emma dropped her hands from her dry hair. Not too bothered, however, she shrugged her shoulders and gave Oliver and Santiago a grin before darting over to the quench tank to grab her dark red key.

## * Chapter 3: This Side of the Key *

"Nah-ah-ah!" said the Master of Keys, wiggling a fat finger before Emma reached the tank. She stopped and furrowed her eyebrows at him.

"I'm more than capable –,"

"Don't even think about it! Ye'd lose yer arm if ye stick it in there. Trust me – I'll do it." He picked up a set of thin tongs that sparkled in the iridescent lights of the room. Oliver raised his eyebrows when he realized the sparkling came from rubies encrusted on the exterior of the tongs. The gems continued to glow as the Master pulled the keys out from the quench tank, placing them on the countertop for Oliver and Emma to grab.

Without any further hesitation, Oliver and Emma grabbed their keys. Then, with his free hand, Oliver offered Emma a high five.

"Woo!" she shouted, accepting the high five.

"Thank you, sir," Oliver added to the Master.

"Nah, boy," said the Master, scratching his right jowl, embarrassed and sweaty. "Now go on and git! I won't tell you again. The door to the Other Side, *the real side*, is out back, between the trees!"

"Don't we owe you a fee or something?" Santiago tried asking.

"GAH! GET OUT BEFORE I CHANGE ME MIND!"

Scrambling, the rag-tag gang ran out of the Keyshop. None of them, not even Archie or Rasmus, wanted to be left alone with the Master and his rage.

## Chapter 4: The Other Side of the Key

*On the 'Other Side' they call our side the 'Original Side.' It's all so unfair that only a select few get access even though all of us should – that's at least what he's told me so far. The 'great artificial barrier' he calls it.*

*1$^{st}$ of August, the first year of the 10$^{th}$ Age*

"Weird dude," Santiago grunted when they were safely on the other side of the squeaking front door.

*"Indeed!"* Rasmus exhaled.

But Oliver and Emma couldn't care less. They were already sprinting around the shop towards the rear, desperate to find the doorway that led to a world of magic.

"What are y'all waiting for?" Oliver shouted back at them.

"Wait up!" Santiago yelled, gearing up to join them. Archie and Rasmus darted ahead of him, quickly outstripping them all to reach the back of the shop first.

When Oliver and Emma caught up, they found the serpents levitating in front of a small, sky-blue door. Seconds later, Santiago arrived, slightly out of breath.

If he were being honest, Oliver thought the door looked rather plain. The only distinguishing feature it offered was a gnome sentinel seated to its right. As quickly as the thought entered his mind, however, he berated

# * Chapter 4: The Other Side of the Key *

himself for it. Did he expect his first entrance into the Other Side to be like entering a palace?

"I expected something more ... awesome," said Emma, echoing Oliver's previous thoughts.

*"Not enough red carpet for you?"* Archie quipped. Rasmus snickered in his throat.

Emma crossed her arms embarrassed. "That's not what I meant! How does this work anyway?"

*"Good question!"* began Rasmus. His tail could not be contained at this point. It kept hitting Santiago's leg as he wagged back and forth.

"Easy there, dog!" Santiago grumbled, batting away the tail.

*"Oh, excellent point, Santi!"* said Archie. *"One more bit of housekeeping!"* He padded towards the door, blocking it. *"While we certainly aren't 'demon dogs,' Rasmus and I will revert to our original forms when we cross back into the Other Side. Do not make a scene."*

Rasmus looked solemn as Archie stepped aside from the door. *"I will miss this coat of fur. Everyone is so very happy to see me as a dog."*

Emma raised an eyebrow. "What are you two on the Other Side?"

Oliver thought back to when Archie had reappeared in his house the previous evening, looking leathery.

Santiago grimaced at them all.

*"You'll see us both soon enough,"* said Rasmus mysteriously.

Oliver fought the urge to roll his eyes. Whatever Archie and Rasmus were, they seemed to enjoy secrecy and surprise far more than they should.

*"Emma,"* Rasmus continued, *"you first."*

Emma stamped a foot into the ground and placed her hands on her hips. "Why? Because *ladies* first?"

"No, child. You are simply closer to the door."

She let out a *harrumph* and walked up to the door. "There's no keyhole!"

*"Bring the key closer to the door-knob,"* said Archie with an exhale. *"If the key has been reimaged correctly, a keyhole ought to—,"*

"Got it!" Emma interrupted. "But it won't budge! Why – GAH!"

*WHOOSH!*

A great gust of air pillared into the doorway, disappearing within its cracks. Emma darted back to the rest of the group, her hair askew. Behind them, the alley had gone very quiet, and above them, the leaves in the trees no longer rustled.

"Well, that was creepy," Santiago whispered from behind Oliver.

Archie chuckled again for the umpteenth time. *"Oh, nothing to be concerned about. Look! The door is now open!"*

"What are you talking about?" said Emma with her arms in the air. "It's still closed!"

But Oliver noticed it first.

What had previously been a solid door was now a shimmering, *moving* surface. Slowly, he stepped up to the door and swiped with his fingers. He gasped as his hand and wrist disappeared within what felt like standing liquid. Around where his arm had broken through, the surface shimmered more aggressively, as if he had disturbed a still pool of water in a forest clearing. And there, through the surface, he saw it.

## * Chapter 4: The Other Side of the Key *

"The Other Side," Emma whispered into his ear. He jumped and tensed up as she gave him a light push on the back. "Are you going in or not? If you need a boost, I can push you in no problem."

Oliver swatted her hands away and shook his head. "Here goes nothing," he said, bracing himself. And then, he stepped through the liquid, entering the Other Side.

Breaking through the barrier felt so much like stepping through sticky gelatin that Oliver couldn't help but take a moment to pat down his clothes. Once he confirmed he was being stupid, he took stock of his surroundings.

Instead of jumping into a creepy wood, or a foreign country locked in a different era, he stood in a brick-laden alley, just as he had a moment ago, with oaks and dogwoods looming overhead.

And yet, there was something different about the alley – something he couldn't quite put his finger on. Eventually the answer hit him like a bucking horse.

It was as if the world's color-palette had been swapped, dialing everything up with superior vibrancy, saturation, and contrast. Where a light-green tree might have stood on the other side of the door, a bright, vibrant viridian took its place, and overhead, sunlight no longer twinkled yellow, but shone as golden saffron. He resisted the temptation to dive into his surroundings, but just barely. Around the corner, a loud hubbub bounced off brick-laden streets he could only glimpse. He had to physically hold his legs in place to stop them from taking him away.

He thanked the heavens as he heard a voice break the silence from behind him. He didn't know how much longer he could wait for the others.

But as the voice spoke, his curiosity shifted. It was Santiago speaking, yes, but he spoke in a slow tenor Oliver barely recognized.

"No … no puedo creerlo."[5]

Oliver turned away from the street of magic to get a better look at his uncle. It wasn't often he reverted to full Spanish. Growing up, Santiago had always insisted they speak English every day, leaving Spanish for Sundays and mass. It drove Oliver crazy since he was proud of their heritage, but he knew Santiago must have had his reasons.

Santiago lumbered forward, glancing left and right as his military training demanded of him. When Oliver looked into his eyes, he expected to see the usual steel, but they didn't look cold or stern at all. In the face of magic, they looked glassy and skittish as they moved from tree to tree. For a moment, he thought he saw tears forming where they weren't allowed to exist, but then Santiago saw him staring. A blink later and the steel returned. Oliver fired right back with a smug smile, ensuring his uncle knew he'd seen his machismo collapse in the face of magic.

As Santiago ruffled his hair in revenge, he squirmed away and saw Emma emerge through the doorway. As soon as she saw them, her face split into an enormous grin. He couldn't help but feel lucky for going first – he got to see everyone else's reactions. Emma quickly moved on from them to step towards a tree and flick a tree branch extending from a golden dogwood. She whistled appreciatively when the flowered leaves hissed at her in reply.

---

[5] Translates to "I can't believe it."

## * Chapter 4: The Other Side of the Key *

Finally, Rasmus and Archie emerged as well. With each additional ripple of the door's surface, Oliver's jaw dropped further and further at the sight of them. Instead of two dogs, two enormous, winged, and feathered serpents slowly emerged from the entryway, floating gracefully in the air. First, their heads appeared, looking angular and ferocious. Archie's was a golden, blue whereas Rasmus' shone a brighter silver. The plumage on their torsos rippled yellow, purple, blue, and green, creating a rainbow effect as the marigold sunlight danced off their bodies.

Santiago took one look at the two beasts and let out a long whistle. "You really were a demon dog, Archie."

*"I wouldn't dream of lying to you,"* said Archie, circling past Oliver's right shoulder in a sharp, quick motion. His deeper voice suited his real form far better than his boxer one. He stopped above Emma, continuously flapping short, narrow wings like a hummingbird. *"Are you surprised? I thought you may have caught onto my difference at the house yesterday."*

Oliver jumped in place as the answer came to him. "When you disappeared to get the coins! I did notice! But I thought I was imagining it."

*"You'll learn to trust your imagination in due time,"* said Archie with a tut-tut. *"Despite what your adults tell you, imagination is never ill-founded."*

Nearby, Rasmus circled downwards towards Emma. She didn't hesitate to reach out, and he obliged with a tilt of his head.

"The feathers," she said marveling at the plumage. "They're all flawless. Are you two dragons?"

Archie snorted. *"We know you meant no insult. We are feathered serpents. Our kind has existed within the Americas for millennia. But really, Rasmus – no need to have them serve your vanity. They won't look twice once they get used to our appearance."* Rasmus looked grumpy but didn't respond. *"And besides, I'd prefer we take the children to get their books before lunch, not after. Otherwise, we'll have to wait in a line."*

Emma huffed indignantly. "We don't worship you!"

Santiago, who had been rolling his eyes, coughed loudly. "I agree with Archie – I only took the morning off work."

*"Indeed. They'll have a list at the bookstore around the corner. I'd expect a host of introductory courses for your extramen year. Let us not wait any further."*

Before waiting for a response, he zoomed ahead in a flurry of circular movements, disappearing around the corner onto the bustling street Oliver had noted earlier. Rasmus grunted and followed, leaving them scrambling to catch up.

Bursting out onto the street, they saw the feathered serpents circling ahead to their left. Elsewhere, dozens of fascinating shops and restaurants caught their eyes where normal ones had stood on the Original Side. As they stopped to gape at the new scene, several passersby on the street pointed at them rudely, chuckling at their shocked faces. Long-tailed frock coats and frilly shirts appeared to be the norm among them.

Where asphalt had been before, brick now connected the shops and restaurants to one another. An armory lay directly in front of them, bearing an extravagant set of swords and hammers in its window display. To their right, Oliver quickly caught a glimpse of a restaurant where a waitress was serving a group of wizards what appeared to be a plate of enormous, wriggling insects. Even further away, he saw a little girl running away from

# * Chapter 4: The Other Side of the Key *

her mother to enter a shop with a sign embroidered by feathered serpents and the words *Tupper's Coatlball Emporium.*

Before he could focus too much, however, Emma tugged him by the arm saying, "C'mon! You heard Archie! We've gotta get the books before lunch!" Santiago pushed them both on their backs in the direction of the feathered serpents, seemingly agreeing, but even he couldn't resist sneaking looks at the weapons in the armory.

A moment later, they followed Archie and Rasmus into a bookstore. A bell sounded when they entered, and from behind a counter stood a wizened man with a pencil-thin mustache and a neatly pressed green suit. Well, Oliver wasn't entirely sure if it was a suit — the long-tailed coats on this side of the key looked foreign to him.

"Ah, mon children!" the man said with a French accent. "Monsieurs Archie and Rasmus 'ave jus' told me about your acceptance into Tenochprima Academy!" He gestured at Archie and Rasmus levitating near a tower of books before bowing. "My name is Monsieur Lafitte. Please allow me to point you in the direcshun of your extramen books in the rear of the shop."

When he finished speaking, he waved vaguely towards the rear of the shop, past several columns of cascading book towers. Archie and Rasmus didn't wait for a second invitation and shot past an older boy navigating a pile of unkempt books. The boy waved an annoyed hand at the gust of wind that followed the serpents, but otherwise treated the disturbance as if only a fly had bothered him.

"Thanks ... mister," Oliver and Emma said together, both unsure of how else to respond.

"Not a problem, mon children!" He gestured again towards the rear of the shop.

Santiago cleared his throat and nodded at Monsieur Lafitte. A moment later, Oliver felt a nudge in his back as Santiago ushered him and Emma towards Archie and Rasmus. "C'mon, mon children," he whispered into their ears. "That guy ain't helping us."

When they passed the boy at the book tower, he ignored them, completely focused on a book called *The Prince*. Only then did Oliver notice the tower was labeled "Hardmore-year books." A moment later, Santiago had shoved him all the way to a different tower that read "Extramen-year books."

"Umm, Archie?" Oliver began with furrowed eyebrows. He picked up a book titled *Lycene's Lance: The Lost Treasure of the Peloponnesian War*. "What years does Tenochprima teach? I've never heard of hardmores or extramen."

Archie circled towards him with embarrassed feathers where eyebrows might have been. *"My apologies, Oliver! It's been ... a few years since I've been a Guide! All magical institutions teach courses to students from ages fourteen through seventeen. Afterwards, students will become apprentices for specialized fields before eventually becoming a master."*

*"The students,"* Rasmus added, *"are referred to as Extramen, Hardmores, Juniors, and Seniors."*

# * Chapter 4: The Other Side of the Key *

Archie nodded approvingly. *"Yes, quite. Which means you and Emma are entering your extraman year."*

Oliver glanced at Emma and breathed out a sigh of relief when he saw her looking just as confused as he felt. At his stare, however, Emma impressed him by shrugging off the uncertainty and moving on to the list of books pinned to the wooden tower – it was the only section of the wood visible beneath the mountain of books.

As they looked through the books, Oliver's uncertainty continued growing until it filled his stomach. "How do we even begin to do magic?" he finally asked, relieving some of the pressure.

Archie chortled in his chest. *"Do magic? I wouldn't presume to know. Your species is strange to us – we do not require a channel or a source to perform magic as your kind does."*

"Channel? Source?" Oliver tried asking, but Emma interrupted him.

"Easy there, Einstein," she said. "We'll find all this out with our books!" She pointed at the tower in front of them emphatically. "Let's focus on getting these first, huh?" Santiago chuckled behind them both.

"What are you laughing at?" Oliver asked, jeering slightly at his uncle.

"Emma's got her head screwed on right and you're going to have a heck of a time keeping up with her."

Emma laughed. "I just want to get us to that armory. I saw you looking at it too, Santiago, don't pretend." She traced the book list with her finger. "It says we'll need that first one you picked up, Peloponnesian something or another, along with *An Introduction to Channeling Magic, World History Throughout the Ages; Dawn of Magic through the Seventh Age, Destruction 101,*

## NOVA 01

*Introduction to Magical Political Systems, Potions and Embalming 101, Biomes of the Magically Inclined,* and … *Magical Pre-Algebra?* No, that can't be right? Magical pre-algebra?"

Oliver stepped up next to her, frowning at the sight of *Magical Pre-Algebra*. He groaned as he began sifting through the pile. "Looks like we can't even escape math on this side of the key. But, hey, maybe it'll be better with magic."

Emma brushed her fine hair behind her ears. "No chance pre-algebra is good anywhere, but you've gotta admit some of these do sound good." She picked up a copy of *Biomes of the Magically Inclined* and shook it with one hand before waving *An Intro to Channeling Magic* inches away from his eyes.

*"Your first year should be manageable if you do the classwork and homework assigned to you,"* said Rasmus. *"Introductory courses across the board."*

*"Agreed,"* said Archie. Oliver noticed his eyes were directed at the front of the shop where he saw half a dozen families milling inside. Monsieur Lafitte greeted them all with raised hands and a smile Oliver hadn't received.

*"We really must get a move on, though,"* Archie continued. *"Grab your books and let's pay the convenience fee and proceed to the armory."* Without waiting for a reply, he fluttered his wings and shot towards the exit. Rasmus followed, as always, but took a moment to circle around Emma's head before disappearing with Archie behind the shop door.

Oliver smiled at Emma as her hair settled. "That's never going to get old." She flashed her teeth back at him as Santiago handed them some drawstring bags that had been hanging from a nail. They placed their books

# * Chapter 4: The Other Side of the Key *

in their bags and tossed them over their shoulders. Santiago offered to carry Emma's bag, but she returned a fierce expression indicating she needed no help whatsoever.

Moments later, they found Archie and Rasmus levitating just outside the armory. Santiago peered past them towards a scimitar in the window display.

As Oliver approached, Archie circled lower to the ground to hover directly in front of him. Caught off guard, Oliver stumbled back. When he righted himself, Archie couldn't have been more than a foot away from his face, staring directly into his eyes. The pupils were vertical, like a cat's, but layered with depth Oliver had never seen before. He had to tear his focus away from them when Archie spoke.

*"It is against my doctrine as a sacred beast to participate in your selection of a magical source and channel. Humanity's relationship with magic is ... different than mine."*

Oliver peered past Archie's plumage to exchange a nervous look with Emma.

Archie nodded at the exchange, which made Oliver snap his eyes back to his guide's, wondering if feathered serpents could read human minds. He tried nodding back, but a gulp in his throat stopped him halfway.

*"You need not worry. I have a feeling you are blessed with the Gift of Wisdom."*

Oliver repeated the words to himself more than anybody else. "Gift of Wisdom?" Hadn't that also been what Hamilton jokingly scribbled in his application? Before he could think on it too much longer, Archie fluttered his tongue between his beak-like mandibles. It was a testament to Archie's character that Oliver didn't scream and run away with fright as the tongue disappeared back into the beak. *"I've been at this business for a very long time, Oliver. Your Gift, whatever it is, bursts at the seams. Your schooling will teach you to hone it, but for now, trust your instincts."*

"Wait!" said Emma, poking Archie near his middle. "Why can't we trust my gut?" Oliver couldn't help but be impressed as he watched Emma's small frame angrily poking the flank of a flying snake the size of a horse.

Rasmus chuckled. *"Because you are so very obviously blessed with Bravery. It will be of no use inside a place of corrup—,"*

Archie snapped his head towards Rasmus, growling in a language Oliver couldn't understand. Steam leaked from his nostrils, from which Emma had enough sense to back away. She crossed her arms as she stumbled, ignoring the language the serpents spoke, and maintained a mutinous glare even as she tripped into Santiago's arms. When Santiago propped her back up, Oliver shot him a concerned look, pointing at the quarreling serpents with his eyes. He followed the gaze, returned to Oliver's eyes, and winked.

Oliver felt a mix of dread and delight as he watched his uncle approach the hissing and steaming serpents. "Archie?" Santiago asked, looking momentarily earnest. But then he flexed his biceps, one down, the other up. "What do I have the gift of? Machismo? Good looks?"

Rasmus gaped as Santiago changed his pose to that of a bodybuilder's. Eventually, the serpent managed to sniff and say, *"Positively preposterous."*

*"Absolutely mad,"* Archie agreed.

"Y'all are boring," said Santiago. "But don't worry, while we wait outside, I'll tell my favorite jokes."

"Won't you at least come with us?" Emma asked.

## * Chapter 4: The Other Side of the Key *

Santiago shrugged. "If these two bags of feathers can't enter, no chance I can."

Inwardly, Oliver agreed, but one look at the armory's dark entrance made him wish otherwise. Even if he did have *Wisdom*, he was sure he could use some parental guidance once inside. But he also recognized there'd be no use in delaying his choice, or Emma's. Feeling determined, he stuck out his right foot to enter.

But Santiago surprised him with a hand on his shoulder.

The usual steel glinted at him, which was to be expected, but a new, warmer layer now softened the gaze. Oliver briefly wondered if it had always been there and he'd just never taken the time to look for it.

"The demon-dog is right," Santiago grunted. "Trust yourself, yeah? You're a smart kid. You've got a whole lot of your mom in you."

It took everything Oliver had not to tear up – where had this been his whole life? They never talked about his mother.

Then Santiago winked and the moment drifted away as quickly as it had arrived.

"Aaand, if you see an extra magic gun in there, you already know I won't say no."

Emma snorted with laughter. "A gun? Maybe an axe. Come on, Oli. Five minutes inside and we'll officially be superheroes."

Before Oliver had time to register that she'd called him 'Oli,' she tugged his shirt, along with his body, inside the armory's entrance. Behind them, he heard Santiago clasp his hands and rub them together. "How 'bout some jokes?"

## NOVA 01

*"Oliver,"* Archie pleaded in Oliver's head, *"do carry about your business quickly."*

Oliver grinned, shooting a quick look behind his shoulder.

"Rasmus, what do you call a cow with *one* leg?"

*"Now, really, Mr. García?"* Rasmus' voice begged. *"Is this altogether necessary?"*

But Oliver never heard the rest of the joke. He followed Emma, dashing deeper and deeper into the armory. It was only when he couldn't see anything at all that he realized the voices outside had become muffled. It felt as if a blanket had covered them, shutting out all light and noise.

"Okay," muttered Emma, squeezing his hand in the dark. "It's driving me crazy. What's the punch line?"

Oliver smiled. "Really? We're in a creepy armory, unable to see a thing, and you want to hear the rest of *that* terrible joke?"

Silence followed, but only for a second.

"Yeah, otherwise I'll be thinking about it all day. What *do* you call a cow with one leg?"

Oliver cringed as he prepared to say the punchline. *What would she think?*

"A steak."

For one painful moment, Emma's grip loosened in his hand, and Oliver dreaded the worst. She thought they were idiots.

But then, she surprised him, chiming with laughter layered by glee, and maybe a bit of pity.

He squeezed her hand back.

# \* Chapter 4: The Other Side of the Key \*

## Chapter 5: At the Sign of the Anvil

*He's just like me. I finally found someone who understands. All the injustice — the disproportionate spread of wealth and inequality across the world — it exists on both "Sides of the Key." The kings and queens of old used to think their Power was preordained so that they could deliver a better future. I'm starting to think they were right — that he's right.*

*12th of August, the first year of the 10th Age*

Inside the armory, it was so quiet they could hear their hearts thumping in their chests.

After a few moments, flames flicked into life in a nearby lantern.

"*Oooo,*" Emma whispered as she skipped forward. "It's supposed to be spooky, isn't it?"

"Hmmm," agreed Oliver.

The entryway led them into a foyer of sorts. There were no thrills or towers of books. Instead, brick-laden walls stared imposingly at them from every direction. The only exception was a second doorless entryway leading further inside. From behind it, further darkness loomed, accompanied by a heat that ebbed and flowed against their faces.

"Feels like an oven," Emma murmured.

"Could be magic," Oliver countered.

"Well, there's only one way to find out," said Emma. She grabbed his arm and pulled him forward.

# \* Chapter 5: At the Sign of the Anvil \*

Bracing himself for a blast of heat, Oliver was surprised to find the air in the room felt cool against his face.

"Hah! It *was* magic," said Oliver triumphantly. Emma fake sneered at him as they took stock of their surroundings.

The only light source in the room was an overhead, old-fashioned light bulb. It illuminated an anvil in the center of the room and little else.

"Anybody here?" Oliver asked as they approached the anvil. Unidentifiable shapes loomed in the dark but there was no hint of a quiver in his voice. Emma gave him a thumbs up.

"Who's there?" came a deep voice from elsewhere in the room.

"Uhh," Oliver began.

"Two customers, if you're selling," Emma finished confidently.

Fingers snapped and blinding lights flamed into existence. Blinking, Oliver and Emma saw they were in a large room that looked more cavern than building. Tall cabinets and shelving units formed neat, circular rows, within the open space. The rows became shorter and shorter as they congregated around the illuminated anvil and each shelf hosted dozens of weapons, instruments, and devices, categorized according to an order only fully understood by the owner.

"Welcome," the unknown voice continued, "my dear customers, to my humble armory!" The contents of the shelves winked light at them as the voice spoke. Some shone bright white from diamonds while most others reflected subdued colors of jade, turquoise, ruby, and sapphire.

"One for the theater, this one," Emma whispered into Oliver's ear. He smiled and pressed her aside with his forearm.

## NOVA 01

"Thank you, sir," he said. "Where are you exactly. We've come to select a channel and a …" He trailed off, unable to remember the word.

"A source!" Emma finished for him.

"Tenochprima, no doubt?" the voice continued.

At last, a heavy-set man with hairy forearms stepped out from behind a tall cabinet. He wore a strange, yellowish green helmet over his head and what might have once been a white, ruffled shirt over his chest.

"Forgive me," the man growled. "I like to work in the dark except when I'm at the anvil." From his helmet, a viewing apparatus extended over his left eye while another lay angled off to the side, unused. If it weren't for the axe in his left hand and the polishing rag in his right, Oliver wouldn't have been able to stop himself from laughing.

"Oh, thank goodness for that," said Emma, dryly.

"Indeed," the man said with a flat expression.

"What do we call you?" said Oliver.

"Miyada."

"Miyada?" repeated Oliver. He'd stupidly been expecting a last name like Smith.

"Yep," said Miyada. He walked over to a nearby stool and resumed polishing the axe, ignoring them.

"Is that a weapon we can select?" Emma asked, crossing her arms.

"Depends," said the blacksmith mysteriously. He stood up and squinted at the axe before placing it against one of the shelving cabinets. "You're clear as day gifted with Bravery, so the axe might suit you. But your friend here is harder to read. Are you a silent Wiser, or a stoic Powerhead?"

# * Chapter 5: At the Sign of the Anvil *

Squatting down slightly to get a better look at Oliver, he placed both of his apparatuses over his eyes and peered at him, looking like a jeweler inspecting a stone.

"Umm," Oliver stammered, "our Guides seem to think she's Bravery and I'm Wisdom."

"Hah!" Miyada laughed. "You're clearly extramen so you wouldn't know any better."

"Know any better?" asked Emma incredulously. "What's that supposed to mean?"

"Bah!" said Miyada with a dismissive wave of his enormous hands. Ignoring Emma, he walked over to a cabinet filled with what appeared to be sheets of webbed cloth studded with hundreds of small jewels. Each sheet couldn't have been wider than ten inches or longer than thirty.

"What are those, Mr. Miyada?" Oliver asked. A green weave with white gems caught his attention.

"Sleeves," the blacksmith grunted. "And don't call me Mister."

"Sleeves?" Oliver and Emma echoed.

"Yeah, that's right. What do you think of 'em, girl?" Miyada asked, gesturing at the cabinet and speaking to Emma. "What are your names anyhow? These won't suit you, boy."

"Emma."

"And I'm Oliver."

"Doesn't matter. Try one on, girl."

With a glare, Emma began reaching for the green cloth with white jewels. Before she reached it, however, Miyada slapped her hand away.

## NOVA 01

"No! Not that one. It'll be out of your budget and wasted on an extraman."

Emma huffed, crossing her arms again. "What do you mean, *wasted*?"

Oliver glared now, too, and thought back to Archie's words outside. Was Miyada, this grumpy man, the blacksmith they needed?

"Y'all really don't know a thing, do you?"

Neither of them responded. Emma even refused to select another sleeve before they received an explanation.

Miyada slapped the side of the wooden cabinet and chuckled. "Well, you're brave alright. Still unsure about you, though. Oliver, was it? Forgive an old man for being crotchety. You interrupted me from making … well it hardly matters to the two of you. Just know I'll make sure we get you both properly fitted."

Nodding, Miyada reached towards the top of the cabinet and selected a red colored sleeve with dark purple jewels. "Try this, Emma. It's a weave of Red Adler branches serving as the channel and Amethysts as your sources. Weak channeler but decent sources with the amethysts. I'm pretty proud of how it turned out if I'm being honest …"

Emma held the sleeve in her hand for a moment, looking unsure of what to do. Then, she pulled it up on her right arm using her left. It slid over a majority of her forearm and half of her upper arm. Where her elbow bent, a gap had been left in the weave. At first, it looked eight sizes to large, but just as Oliver was about to comment, the sleeve tightened, fitting her snuggly. As Emma flexed and rotated her arm, Oliver gaped at the weave.

# * Chapter 5: At the Sign of the Anvil *

On closer inspection, even though it looked like tough tree bark, it flexed as easily as elastic.

Emma grinned as she continued moving her arm around. "What's the best way to use it?" She closed her fist and brought her elbow down elegantly.

"Woah!" cautioned Miyada. "Easy there! Don't go setting my shop on fire or anything."

Emma laughed as she continued to flex and relax her hand into a fist. "But I don't even know how to use this."

Miyada stopped her forearm with one, strong hand and glared at her. "Keep on with that, and I'm sure something *will* happen."

Emma nodded her head, but otherwise maintained a reproachful look as Miyada released her and continued speaking. "Sleeves make a great weapon for beginners. And between you and me, I always liked wearing one at school because during the winter you can hide it under your clothes and nobody will know the better until you've already got them tripping over a rock."

"I'll take it!" said Emma, smiling down at her sleeved arm. Her smile wavered, however, when she saw Oliver staring, too. *"What?"* she mouthed. Oliver shook his head and looked away, feeling some heat rising to his cheeks.

"That's the spirit!" said Miyada slapping the wood again. "I offer thirty day returns if you're even remotely unsatisfied. We can always upgrade you to a weapon or gauntlet when you're ready."

Starting to feel left out, Oliver coughed in his throat. "What about me? What do 'Wise' beginners use?"

Miyada didn't answer immediately. Instead, he stared into space while scratching the stubble on his chin with the backs of his fingers. "Well, that's the thing, isn't it? I'm not convinced you're a Wiser, but there's really no way to find out until you pass the Ceremony at school, is there?"

Oliver didn't have a clue as to what Miyada was talking about, and by the looks of it, neither did Emma, but he didn't want to interrupt or sound stupid. Miyada saved him from both options when he waved his hand dismissively a moment later. "Don't worry. We can always upgrade you down the road if we get you wrong." He spoke to himself more so than Oliver at this point, leaving the cabinet with the sleeves. As he stepped away, he grabbed his axe and then paced over to a cabinet with necklaces, rings, and bracelets.

Emma giggled behind him. "A necklace?" Oliver turned around to shush her, but now he felt heat in his ears. The array of jewels in front of him made him feel ridiculous. Surely a normal weapon would make him look more intimidating at school.

"Don't be silly, girl," said Miyada, frowning. "The most trained wizard in the world would only need a twig and dust of jade to obliterate a novice with a diamond-studded mace."

"*Hmph!*" Emma responded indignantly.

"At least not a necklace," said Oliver uneasily. Even if the greatest wizard could get by with a simple piece of jewelry, he didn't feel like a necklace with a big rock on it would make him many new friends at school.

## * Chapter 5: At the Sign of the Anvil *

"Are you sure, boy?" Miyada growled. "Necklaces can be hidden under the shirt."

Oliver tried laughing but it came out more as a cough. "What is it with you and hiding weapons? Do you have a knife hidden up your sleeve, too?"

"Bah!" Miyada half-yelled. He waved his arms again at them. "Not too long ago, everybody had a reason to hide a weapon on them! But you're too young and new to this world to understand."

"What are you talking about?" Oliver asked. He gave Emma a quick look of surprise.

"Oh, he's just being dramatic!" Emma interrupted. "It's all he does. Dark room, lit anvil, spooky entryway. Yes, very scary, Mr. Miyada." Oliver wasn't sure if he agreed with Emma or not. Miyada had worn a grim expression.

"Being dramatic, am I?" Miyada growled. "You wouldn't dare say that if you had any idea. But I'm not the one to tell you about *him* anyway ..." He sat on a stool next to the cabinet with the necklaces, rings, and bracelets. "So, what's it going to be, Wiser? If not a necklace, how about a ring?"

"Sure," said Oliver, shrugging his shoulders. He wanted to ask more about the person Miyada had alluded to but knew a lost cause when he saw one.

Miyada shot him a tired look. "Inspiring response. Here, try on a few from the third row from the bottom. I'm not in this business for the profit so much the passion. You're selecting high quality materials on that third row there, boy ... but this is so unusual."

Emma rolled her eyes and muttered, "how *dramatic*."

Oliver's curiosity, however, got the better of him. "Why unusual?" he asked. He'd already moved past the subject of the sinister man Miyada had mentioned.

"Because," said Miyada, twisting his hands on his axe, "I can always tell what Gift someone has. *Always!* But you," he pointed at Oliver with the axe, "you've stumped me! I haven't been stumped once – not once! But now, for the first time ever, I'm guiding an extraman towards a ring with rubies and diamonds rather than jade or amethyst." When he finished speaking, he stared at Oliver with both viewing apparatuses on his strange helmet clinking into place. Lens after lens appeared, making Oliver squirm.

Emma huffed and waved a hand in front of the gadgets. "Quit being so weird! It looks like you're X-raying him or something."

"Bah! I'm not being weird or dramatic! But you're right in that there's no use worrying about it. Oliver – here, try this one on first." He picked up a ring off a small purple cushion and offered it to him. It was a single sapphire ring made of a light-colored wood. An elaborate design that resembled Archie's plumage had been etched into the wood.

Before Oliver could even reach his hand out to take the ring, Miyada pulled it back. "No that's not right at all, is it?" He began tugging tufts of hair that stuck out of his helmet before selecting another ring. "Try this one instead."

He offered Oliver a simpler ring this time. Where most of the rings bore elaborate twists, turns, and prongs to incorporate their jewels, this one hosted a darker colored wood that had been sanded down to nothing but a smooth surface.

## \* Chapter 5: At the Sign of the Anvil \*

"Where's the jewel on this one?" Oliver asked, curious more than surprised. Didn't Archie say he needed a source and a channel?

Miyada tapped a finger pretentiously against his nose. "Ah, I used an advanced method for this one. The jewel, and it's a rare one, is Red Beryl. You can't see it because it's a solid ring welded into a wooden sleeve of American Chestnut. Now, normally, I'd have sold this ring for seven hundred and fifty ameys owing to the resources I used, but I'm giving you a significant discount because, frankly, I think you're special."

At Miyada's words, Oliver felt a humming sensation in the back of his head. It felt like when he'd first heard Jeff talk about Tenochprima. Was Miyada right? Was he a special case? He dismissed the thought immediately because it felt vain. Even then, however, Archie's advice came back into his head. *"You'll learn to trust your imagination in due time."*

"Well, that's entirely unfair," Emma huffed from behind them.

Miyada waved a dismissive hand at Emma without even looking at her. "Life isn't fair. I'd suggest you get used to it. Boy! Try on the ring!"

Oliver jumped a bit at Miyada's tone, but he took the ring without question.

Like his green key, the ring was surprisingly warm to the touch as it sat it in the pommel of his right hand. Time stood still as he admired its perfectly smooth surface for a moment. Then, he pulled it onto his right ring finger. Like Emma's sleeve, the ring shouldn't have fit at all, but as it crossed his knuckle, it shrank to a perfect fit.

As soon as the ring adjusted itself, a feeling unlike any other erupted across Oliver's body. From his right hand where the ring lay, to across his arms, head, torso, and legs, energizing waves of energy pounded throughout his veins, threatening to destroy him. He gasped at the new feeling, unable to do much more than close his fist and shut his eyes as he fell to his knees. Had Emma felt this way when she put on her sleeve?

After what felt like ages, the sensation began to subside, allowing him to return to his body. The first thing he felt, was the ring. It beat like a second heart over his finger, but what did it channel? Outside the ring, he felt a roaring tempest in the world, waiting to be pulled into his frame and refined. He didn't know if he could do it.

He opened his eyes and saw Emma's looking back at him, etched with concern. She had placed her hand on his shoulder and crouched down next to him. Miyada, however, bounced around gleefully from just behind her.

"You're the Prophet's Advent!" he said, pushing Emma's hand off him. "I've never seen anything like it! You're ... you're ..." He helped Oliver up, incapable of articulating his thoughts. "Go on, get out of here! Free of charge. But write down what you just felt when you get the chance! Augustus himself wouldn't have reacted like that!"

Goosebumps crawled across Oliver's arms and neck. Hadn't he read the name Augustus recently? What was a Prophet's Advent? He glanced at Emma, looking for a clue as to what happened. But she only bit her bottom lip in reply.

He turned, ready to ask Miyada the questions in his head, but the blacksmith had already stepped away towards a desk on the other side of the room. As he passed the anvil, he took off his helmet and placed it on

## * Chapter 5: At the Sign of the Anvil *

top. "Go on and get to school, y'all," he yelled back at them. "I'll be writing my contacts at Tenochprima about what Emma and I saw just now."

From the desk, they heard him snap his fingers, returning the room to its original state of semi-darkness. Their audience with Mr. Miyada was over.

When they stumbled outside, Oliver wasn't sure he'd tell Archie about Miyada's theatrics. Hadn't he warned him something dramatic might happen?

Emma, however, clearly felt otherwise. Within seconds of stepping outside she'd asked Archie and Rasmus about the Prophet's Advent.

*"Preposterous!"* Rasmus sneered as Archie seethed with his eyes shut. *"The Prophet's Advent is nothing but a myth!"*

"You don't understand!" Emma huffed with her hands on her hips. "I put my sleeve on and felt a little excited. But when Oliver put on his ring,"—she paused to make an expanding gesture with her hands— "he looked like he was about to explode!"

Archie's eyes clicked open as a trail of smoke, not steam, began circulating up and out of the nostril slits on his upper mandible. *"I don't doubt the blacksmith made you feel as if something special happened."*

"It wasn't like that!" shouted Emma. "You weren't there!"

## NOVA 01

*"No use,"* said Rasmus, turning to face her. *"Blacksmiths across the country have a tendency of convincing children they are more than meets the eye. It's a sales pitch to make you buy more expensive weapons."*

"But he gave Oliver his ring for free!" shouted Emma.

*"Enough!"* Archie growled. He circled closer to Oliver, changing to a warmer tone. *"Promise us you won't overthink it. We're only trying to help you. Nobody at school is going to want to hear about an extraman saying he is a mythological being. You'll be a laughingstock!"*

Oliver thought for a moment. Though he was certain he would never forget the feeling of magic coursing through his veins for the first time, he also understood Archie and Rasmus only wanted to help him succeed. It didn't matter if he still felt a raging hurricane outside of his finger, begging to be syphoned inside him. If Archie and Rasmus thought this was normal, who was he to question them?

"I won't overthink it," he finally said to them both.

Archie visibly relaxed his muscles and let out of sigh. *"Good. You would have been bullied relentlessly. Shall we get some lunch?"*

Based on the stern look on Emma's face, Oliver could tell she wanted to keep talking about prophets, magic, and Miyada. Thankfully, she proved street-smart enough to not protest. He tried shooting her a comforting glance, wanting her to understand they could talk about it later.

Moments later, they spent the better part of an hour enjoying an unusual lunch at *Jacque's Joint*. In addition to indoor seating, the restaurant extended outward, onto the edge of the cobblestone street, underneath a dark-purple veranda. Given the size of Archie and Rasmus, a waitress with a drawl like

# \* Chapter 5: At the Sign of the Anvil \*

Mrs. Caldwell's seated them outside where their tails had space to flick and swish. Archie and Rasmus wasted no time ordering platters of fajita bugs, which turned out to be an array of enormous insects served on large hot plates – Rasmus was delighted to see some were still wriggling. To Oliver's amazement, Archie and Rasmus doused the bugs with fire until they exchanged stuffy nods of the head. *"Al dente is as far as you want to go,"* Archie mused.

Santiago gagged several times at the sight and smell of the oversized bugs, but otherwise managed to not get sick. Oliver and Emma skipped the bugs and ordered cheeseburgers accompanied by macaron flavored milkshakes. The milkshakes left them feeling light-headed and liable to laugh at anything Rasmus or Archie said or did. Emma became so affected, they had to order her an antidote. Oliver made sure to convince her to eat a crunchy bug before the antidote could take effect. At this, Santiago excused himself from the table, heading straight to the restroom.

After they calmed down a bit and Santiago returned from the bathroom, Emma gave Oliver a pointed look before speaking in a matter-of-fact tone. "Archie, I know you say we're wrong about Oliver's reaction to the ring, but can you at least explain something else to us?"

Smoke returned to Archie's nostrils. *"I thought we told you that the idea of a Prophet's Advent is a lie spread by——,"*

"It's nothing to do with a Prophet!" Emma interrupted. "Miyada also mentioned that not so long ago, everybody had a reason to have a weapon on them. What was he talking about?"

## NOVA 01

Archie didn't react to Emma's words, but Rasmus did. He looked panicked for a moment, giving Archie a look of uncertainty. But Archie shook his head at him before responding in a diplomatic tone.

*"Well, Emma,"* he said. *"For one thing, you are incorrect, as this subject has everything to do with the myth of the Advent."*

"Wait, hold up," said Oliver, nonplussed. "A second ago you said there's no such thing as —,"

*"Of course, there's no such thing!"* interrupted Archie. He grimaced slightly and lowered his voice before continuing. *"I only tell you this as a brief issue of facts prior to going to school."* Oliver, Emma, and Santiago leaned in to listen, which was pointless as the communication was telepathic. *"Around thirty years ago, a young man, not unlike yourself, Oliver, checked all of the boxes to become the Prophet's Advent."*

Rasmus interrupted with a snort. *"Is this really in order, Archie? Let the headmistress tell the students if she must!"*

*"I'd rather they hear a recounting of facts from me instead of a sensationalized story from other children,"* Archie retorted with finality.

None of them dared interrupt as the serpent squirmed in place with flames licking across his face. *"This boy believed himself to be the Prophet's Advent based on an incredible distribution of the Gift of Power. He went as far as to publicly label himself as the Advent after graduating so that he could persuade others to follow him into bringing about a new world order. When he spread his manifesto, I'm sorry to say, countless lives were lost."* He paused to exhale, and Oliver was surprised to hear his tone change to a mournful one. *"And then, when humanity was on the brink of succumbing to his deceit, an experiment of his went horribly wrong. He had*

## * Chapter 5: At the Sign of the Anvil *

*become so blinded by his purpose, he unburdened himself from any sense of conscience, and attempted to do what nobody has ever done."*

"Which was?" Oliver asked quietly.

*"To bring back the dead,"* whispered Archie, shaking his body as he did.

"Ay-ay-ay," said Santiago, shuddering.

*"We can only be thankful it ended poorly for him,"* whispered Archie. *"The attempt failed, leaving him imprisoned in a spiritual purgatory. Without him around to lead his manifesto, the populace returned to reason, and his remaining followers disbanded."*

"What happened?" Emma murmured. Even she, with her Gift of Bravery, sounded timid.

Archie sighed. *"Nobody knows for certain. All we do know, is the temple where his experiment occurred was completely sealed by an unknown power. The greatest type of evil in the world slumbers within it now, imprisoning him and his most faithful supporters ... or worse."*

"So that's why everyone had a weapon on them?" Oliver asked. "To fight this man and his followers?"

Archie nodded grimly. *"Prior to this most humans stopped carrying weapons. There was no need since they thought they'd reached a state of society where no conflict could exist – the End of History some called it."*

"What was the man's name?" Emma interrupted.

*"His name?"* Archie coughed, slightly flustered. *"Well, it's been forgotten entirely."*

Oliver's skin crawled at that. "What? How can a name be forgotten?"

## NOVA 01

"*Nobody knows,*" said Archie, as if this was an ordinary thing to occur. "*He must have been close to succeeding in that temple because a greater power erased his name from memory. We can only refer to him now as … The Damned.*"

"*The Damned …*" Oliver and Emma repeated.

"*Yes, but don't go saying it too loudly,*" hissed Rasmus. He peered his head around the restaurant tables to make sure nobody was listening to them. "*People will think you're among those who are trying to resurrect his terrible manifesto – and yes, Emma, they still exist.*"

"*Did he die in his prison?*" Oliver asked. He didn't like the idea of a murderous enemy preaching for a new world order.

"*Most say that a sleepless malice sealed within that temple is his purgatory,*" said Archie with a grimace.

"Purgatory?" asked Emma, her face puzzled.

Rasmus flitted his tongue. "*Some believe he attempted to perform magic so dark it backfired on him, leaving him to be punished by the aftermath in that temple forever.*"

"Some?" said Oliver. "What do you two believe?"

Archie gazed at him appraisingly for a moment before responding. "*Well, Rasmus and I believe no evidence exists to indicate he has perished. Yes, the temple is sealed by corrupt—, erm, dark magic, but is possible he has survived and is imprisoned to this day, waiting for the opportune moment to reignite his movement.*"

Santiago shuddered. "Sheesh, y'all are giving me the heebie-jeebies! I feel like the internal man might come grab my leg and drag me down to the afterlife."

## * Chapter 5: At the Sign of the Anvil *

Rasmus and Archie stared at Santiago, completely shocked. Santiago tried shrugging it off with an unconvincing high-pitched laugh. "What? That can't happen, can it?"

*"You couldn't have known this,"* said Rasmus shaking his head grimly, *"but that was likely The Damned's fate when his ritual failed him."*

Oliver put a hand over his mouth and saw Emma doing the same, stifling a squeak.

Santiago, meanwhile, stood up from his chair and neatly folded up his napkin before placing it on the table. "Nope, nope, nope," he muttered. "I'm outta here. Oliver, give me your key. I'm finna go to a church and pray or something."

*"You're making a scene, Santiago!"* Archie warned. The occupants of a nearby table were looking at them, whispering into each other's ears. *"You four go on ahead back to the door,"* Archie continued, warily surveying the room. *"I'll pay the check and meet you there."*

"You don't need to tell me twice," said Santiago, issuing a mock salute. "Kids, let's go." With alarming speed, he navigated past the other tables and onto the cobblestone street. After exchanging a concerned look, Oliver and Emma followed, but were unable to catch him until they stood outside the Master of Key's door.

Once there, Oliver let out a long whistle. "This infernal man sounds like a nightmare!"

"That's what I'm saying!" Santiago half-yelled with a shudder. "Dragging people to hell? Everything sounded great until we heard about him."

"But he's imprisoned," said Oliver, emphasizing his words. "There's nothing to worry about." With a look, he tried getting Emma to back him up. But that made him more worried about her than Santiago. She wrestled more than a couple emotions on her face, chief of which appeared to be frustration.

Santiago tsked. "Nothing for me to worry about? Sure, I'll be chilling on the safe side of the key. But you guys — well, don't get involved with anything you shouldn't. ¿Ya sabes?"[6]

Oliver resisted the urge to roll his eyes. Of course they wouldn't get involved.

Seconds later, Archie and Rasmus arrived, wearing appraising looks.

Archie broke the silence first. *"Rasmus and I will not return with you."*

"Wait, why not?!" asked Emma. "How will we get to school?"

*"Because,"* said Archie, *"we have urgent business to address prior to your arrival at school."*

If Archie thought Oliver would miss how uncomfortable Rasmus looked, he wasn't nearly clever enough as a mythical beast should be. *What are they not telling us?*

*"As for your passage to school,"* Archie continued, *"the directions on your admissions letter will serve as your guide for the time being. Orientation begins this Sunday, the 30th of August."*

---

[6] Translates to "you already know?" but best to think of it as a colloquialized way of saying "got it?"

## * Chapter 5: At the Sign of the Anvil *

Emma glared at Rasmus as he circled around her to say goodbye. *"It was a pleasure meeting you, Santiago and Oliver. Emma, we have an exciting year ahead together at school!"*

"Yeah, yeah," Emma muttered as she opened the doorway with her dark-red key. "I would have expected y'all to *guide* us to Tenochprima seeing as you are our *Guides,* but I guess we'll just see you there!"

Oliver grunted, feeling similarly betrayed, but also embarrassed by Emma's aggression. "See y'all later," he mumbled, stepping towards the oscillating doorway. Emma had already stepped through.

*"I'll see you soon,"* said Archie's voice in his head. It carried a warmer, apologetic tone. *"Just follow the directions on the letter."*

Oliver was about to say thank you, but Emma's hand reappeared to pull him back to the Original Side.

"Can you believe those two?" Emma asked as they stumbled back into an alleyway that now looked drab. The Original Side looked dull and gray after having seen the Other Side.

Emma had her hands on her hips again. "Ugh! They refused to listen! What happened to you in Miyada's shop was *not* normal!"

Having no ability whatsoever to know what it should have felt like when he put on the ring, Oliver wasn't so sure anymore. In fact, since he had spent his whole life being the opposite of special, he had begun to believe Archie and Rasmus were right, and that nothing out of the ordinary happened in the shop at all.

"I don't know …" he said. "Don't you think Miyada just wants me to come back next year and buy something else even more expensive?"

*102*

## NOVA 01

Emma scowled at him and stormed off with her fists tight.

Oliver followed, rolling his eyes. "Emma, now *you're* being dramatic!"

"You'll see at school, Oliver!" she shot back at him, pausing in her stride to glare and point at him. "I'm going to be right, and you're going to be wrong."

"Okay," said Oliver, trying hard to be patient. He found it difficult to care whether he'd be right about the subject or not. "Before you leave, let's at least exchange cell phone numbers so your family can drive us to the airport – is that alright?"

"Oh," said Emma, her cheeks reddening slightly. "Can't Santi drive us?" She scratched her arm just above the sleeve.

"Nah, he works Sundays," Oliver replied. "If your parents can, that'd be great, or we could catch a cab? Also, I'd take off the sleeve on this side. You look a bit silly."

"Fine," she said, stepping forward to stand directly in front of him. After a few twists and tugs, she'd stuffed the sleeve into her back pocket without much difficulty. Weirdly, Oliver thought she looked less sure of herself with it off, but then she held out her hand and motioned with her fingers for him to give her something.

Oliver stared.

"Well?" said Emma impatiently. "Hand me your phone so I can give you my number."

"Oh, right!" said Oliver. It was his turn to blush. She was close enough for him to count out the freckles on her face.

## * Chapter 5: At the Sign of the Anvil *

Before he could say much else, she swiped the phone out of his hand. "Shoot me a text when you're ready to leave. Make sure you also text me your address." She looked at his phone as she spoke, which gave him the opportunity to study her a bit. With a kind face and long, button nose, she didn't look as fierce as the girl he'd gotten to know, but rather more like someone to buddy up with for help on homework assignments. But maybe, Oliver realized, that said more about his preconceptions than anything else.

When she finished adding her number, she handed the phone back to him and looked up into his eyes, startling him. "I had a lot of fun today. Even if Archie and Rasmus didn't listen to us."

"Erm," Oliver agreed awkwardly.

"But don't think this is over yet!" she continued. "You'll see about your ring when we get to school. I'm convinced there's more to you than just a wise, old man."

Oliver started to smile, but Emma had already turned to leave, waving goodbye. In no time at all, she'd disappeared into the crowded main-street, leaving him by himself.

Seconds later, Santiago popped out of the doorway, shuddering. When he saw Emma was gone, he ruffled Oliver's hair. "Making friends before school even started – how wisdomous."

## Chapter 6: The Shadow

*He has this bracelet – says the Peloponnesian's left it behind. He's clearly lying because it looks too shiny and new to be anything that old. I managed to break into his office and put it on last night. What a rush! Never felt that gutsy in my life!*

*16th of September, the first year of the 10th Age*

Unlike the excursion to Davidstown, the wait for Sunday passed by as slowly as a class with Mrs. Caldwell. When they got back home, Oliver couldn't stop revisiting the day's events. Eventually, Santiago calmed him enough to try playing an old kart racing video game to pass the time, but it only made Oliver daydream further about the magic that waited for him at Tenchoprima. The only thing he could distract himself with turned out to be the admissions letter. By Saturday night, he'd combed over every letter hundreds of times.

"Ok," said Santiago, "read it back one more time – the part about how to get to school."

*2) Upon entry to the Other Side, make your way to your nearest Khufu Ship, Trundholm, Sky Disk or Quadriga*

*3) Board the Southern Line towards Tampico, México*

*4) Exit at Charleston, South Carolina (eighth stop on the Southern line)*

*5) Follow signs to Tenochprima Academy*

# * Chapter 6: The Shadow *

*6) Board the Tenochprima Shuttle and arrive on campus where ushers await*

*7) Orientate yourself with your fellow extramen*

"That's not helpful at all, is it?" Santiago grumbled. "What's a Khufu Ship or Trundholm?"

"You're asking me?" asked Oliver, feeling a slight twinge of panic in his stomach. "You're supposed to be my parental guardian!"

Santiago gave him a dry look and yawned. "Well, I'm sure you'll figure it out. You text Emma yet?"

Oliver ran his hands through his hair, momentarily relieving his forehead of his dark bangs. "I texted her about the Khufu Ship stuff, and all she said was Rasmus mentioned something about a 'skydraft.'"

"A skydraft?" repeated Santiago with a hand on his chin. "I've never seen signs for anything like that at the airport. Maybe it'll be behind a magic door or something?"

Accepting that he couldn't prepare for a situation he knew nothing about, Oliver resigned himself to stumble through it. Worst case scenario, his gut feeling told him, Emma would drag them both to school by foot.

At this point, all that remained here was to figure out how to say goodbye to Santiago.

Silence fell over them as Oliver stared at his uncle. His eyes popped slightly when he realized what Oliver was thinking. Scratching one arm with the other, he said, "You ready for a new school, jefecito?"

Oliver's first impulse was to look down at his shoes and not reply. What was he supposed to say? He hadn't broached the subject of his leaving yet because he didn't want to ruin the excitement of the last day. For so long, Santiago had been an aloof presence in his life. But now he sat across from Oliver asking if he was ready for his first day at school. Were they really going to unpack all the thoughts and insecurities he had in his head in one night? His gut guided him on.

"Santi," he said slowly at first, "Emma obviously has a 'Gift' based on the way she talks and acts. And I know Archie and Rasmus joked that I'm Wise, but that sounds so useless compared to Bravery or Power. Even though I did have the most amazing feeling when I put on this ring" —he raised his hand and wiggled his index finger— "I'm not sure it had anything to do with Wisdom? Maybe I was just too weak to experience magic."

Santiago gave him a compassionate grimace. "I don't know a thing about this magic stuff, but, based on what Archie and Rasmus said, I think each Gift has gotta have pros and cons, you know? Like, let's say you have a classmate with Power," —he flexed his arms— "now, Power might be awesome because they can break down a door with their fist. But you, if you're Wise, that might be nice too, because you'll be able to find out how to open the door instead. Their way might be quicker, but you'd save yourself from a lot of splinters, eh?"

Oliver laughed half-heartedly at the analogy. "I guess I'm just not feeling as confident as I thought."

"Don't mention it," said Santiago, ruffling his hair. "Now, about Miyada, I don't know nothing. Ask a teacher when you get to school. Do I think you're a part of a prophecy? Not even a little bit. I think it's more likely you

# * Chapter 6: The Shadow *

bought a super stylish ring and you felt fresh as a cucumber when you put it on."

This time Oliver really did laugh. But then he thought back to what Emma had said. "Emma is convinced something special happened with the ring."

"How would she know?" Santiago suggested. "She's just as inexperienced with all this as you are."

Oliver thought that was a fair argument. "Well, I'll follow Archie's advice and keep that story to myself, so nobody thinks I'm a pretender or anything."

"Smart move," Santiago agreed. "If you ever get homesick or anything," he added with an awkward scratch of his short hair, "just give me a text or call, OK? Even during work hours."

"Yeah, ok," said Oliver, nodding his head.

"I'm gonna miss you, little man."

"You, too."

With a last ruffle of Oliver's hair, Santiago bade him goodnight and turned out the lights, leaving Oliver to his thoughts. For a while, he tossed and turned, thinking about Tenochprima Academy, Archie, his Gift, and even The Damned at one point. But a new, much more comforting feeling eventually brought him to sleep. For the first time in his life, he knew what it was like to be close to his uncle.

## NOVA 01

The next morning, Oliver awoke to the *buzz buzz* of his cell phone vibrating on his nightstand. Two messages waited for him: one from an unknown number and the other from Emma. He opened Emma's message first.

"Hey! Mom had to go to a meeting this morning, so we'll have to pick you up at noon. I got my ticket this morning from somebody called Tolteca … you did too, didn't you?"

Looking at the time, Oliver felt his heart skip a beat. He only had an hour to pack and eat breakfast. In a flurry of motion, he shot out of bed and began throwing every article of clothing he owned into an old green duffle bag Santi had given him years ago. Fifty minutes later, all his belongings were successfully crammed into it. Sweating slightly, he splashed some water on his face to cool down and grabbed a tart from the pantry to make sure he wouldn't be starving by the time they arrived at the airport.

His phone buzzed again – it was another message from Emma, along with the still unread message from an unknown sender. His heart skipped a beat again - he hadn't checked to see if he actually had a ticket yet. He opened Tolteca's message.

"Attached you'll find your ticket for passage to Tenochprima Academy. Kindly refer to your admissions letter for further instructions. I recommend a baggy article of clothing if a skydraft is required to reach your *Air*port."

Still completely oblivious to what a skydraft was, Oliver nervously threw open his duffle and removed an oversized poncho. "Is this baggy enough?" he thought to himself. He shrugged his shoulders and dropped them before opening Emma's second message.

## * Chapter 6: The Shadow *

"We're outside. Road trip time."

"How is she so relaxed about this!" he grumbled out loud. He squatted down to pick up the handle of his bag and then dashed outside where he slowed his stride. Pulled up next to his house wasn't a normal car, but a sleek, enormous SUV. It had tinted windows, extra-large rims, and what appeared to be a personal driver holding a door open for him.

"Mr. García?" the driver asked with a pleasant smile, "may I?"

"Uh, may you what, sorry?" Between having no idea how to get to school and the arrival of a personal driver, Oliver was out of his element.

"He's asking to take your bags!" came an impatient voice through the open door. The driver smiled understandingly.

"Indeed, I am," the driver continued, "so if you wouldn't mind." He relieved Oliver of his duffle and proceeded to load it in the rear of the car. Oliver, still awestruck, hauled himself up and through the open door.

"You have a personal driver!" He laughed at Emma as he entered. "Must be nice. I'd been looking forward to meeting your parents." He didn't know what else to say as the situation was so unfamiliar to him. He even momentarily forgot how nervous he felt about the airport.

Emma stiffened at the mention of her parents. "Oh, boo-hoo, my free ride is even better than I imagined!" Her hair was up in a ponytail today, giving her eyes a fiercer expression than the last time they had seen each other. "My *parents* are always working, so I don't think you'll meet them anytime soon."

## NOVA 01

"Only joking..." Oliver mumbled. He added a smile to defuse her a bit. "I guess what I meant to say was, thanks!" Judging by the way she'd spoken about her parents, he knew not to pursue the subject further.

Emma's eyes softened. "This is Charles, by the way. He's been our butler since before I was born."

"Good to meet you, Charles," said Oliver, nodding his head.

The butler nodded his head back at him curtly through the rear-view mirror. "The pleasure is mine, Mr. García. To the airport, then, Ms. Griffith?"

"Yep, lead the way," she replied, shrugging at Oliver who looked concerned again now that he remembered where they were going. The motor of the car ignited into life as Charles put the car into gear.

"Uh, Emma?" he asked quietly as his house receded in the distance.

"What?" she whispered back.

"You mentioned a skydraft when you texted me," —he began timidly— "and our tickets do, too. You have any idea what a skydraft even is?"

"Not a clue," she replied. "Hey, you want a piece of gum?"

"Gum? What? No. I want to know what a skydraft is."

"You sure? It's the classic bubblegum flavor. I can chew on this stuff for hours." She had already placed several pieces in her mouth.

"No... thank you. About the skydraft... did you bring something baggy like the ticket said?" He brandished the green, black, and cinnabar poncho in his hand.

"What on Earth is that?" asked Emma, trying her best not to laugh but failing spectacularly. She reached into a backpack nestled between her legs

# * Chapter 6: The Shadow *

and the seat in front of her, pulling out what appeared to be a tablecloth. "I figured this fit the description – what did you bring, a cloak?"

"It's a traditional poncho!" said Oliver, blushing slightly.

Emma giggled. "That'll look good at school, no doubt about it."

Oliver frowned at first but then saw Emma widening her eyes as she realized what she'd said.

"Sorry!" she blurted out before he could say anything back. "I'm not laughing because it's a poncho or anything like that." She paused to look into his eyes and emphasize her sincerity. "I'm laughing because it's so baggy, we could both fit in it and still have room for a third. Is it Santiago's or something?" She started laughing again and this time he joined her.

The remainder of the drive passed them by effortlessly. They traded light-hearted insults and spoke about what excited them most about Tenochprima. At first, Oliver was hesitant to mention magic in front of Charles, but Emma insisted he was more family than her real family and rightfully pointed out they gladly spoke about magic in front of Santiago. As it turned out, Charles didn't do much talking anyway, so Oliver and Emma were free to discuss Tenochprima and their upcoming classes without pause.

They slowed to a halt at the "Departures" level of Charlotte Douglas International Airport just before noon. After they hopped out of the car, Oliver gave Charles an awkward thanks as the butler handed him his bag and then waved goodbye with Emma until the car disappeared around an exit ramp.

"Come on then," said Emma, "let's get checked in I guess?"

## NOVA 01

Oliver nodded his head and pulled out his admissions letter for the umpteenth time. "Any clue where the Southern Line is?"

She stood on her tip toes to look at the letter with him. "I come here all the time and I've never seen signs for anything like that." She frowned slightly as passersby began to stare at them. "Let's go inside and ask the information desk."

Oliver smiled as he followed Emma inside past the automatic doors. A blast of cool air hit him as the doors opened, causing him to instinctively close his eyes for a moment. Peering around, he saw Emma already standing in line at an information desk with a friendly-looking woman standing behind it.

When Oliver reached her, she'd already moved to the front. "Do you know where the Southern Line is?" Emma asked the friendly woman.

"Mm-hmm," said the woman with a perfect drawl, "you mean Southwest Airlines, sweetheart?"

"No, not Southwest Airlines, ma'am," Emma said politely, "the 'Southern Line.'"

"Nah-uh," the lady said patiently, "no such thing as a Southern Line. Lemme see your tickets."

Oliver, who didn't feel like showing anybody their tickets to something nobody would have ever heard of, began to worry. But then something strange happened, the feeling of assurance in his stomach returned to him, and a sign he was sure hadn't been present a moment ago drew his attention. Placed below arrows pointing to Terminals A and B was a new sign, and it read "Skydraft" in an altogether different, red font.

# * Chapter 6: The Shadow *

"Psst! Emma!" he said, tugging on her sleeve, "look!" He pointed above the lady's head towards the new sign. Emma gasped.

"Well, that's new!" she said with a smile. "Told you we'd figure it out."

"Ain't nothing new goin' on here," the lady said, "now lemme see those tickets."

"We were being stupid, ma'am," Oliver interjected, grabbing Emma's arm before she could speak. "Our tickets *do* say Southwest Airlines." He began tugging her away from the information desk before the lady could ask them if they needed to be walked to their gate. Looking over his shoulder, he saw her squinting at them suspiciously past the duffle bag he was rolling along behind him. But after a few more moments, she visibly shrugged her shoulders and turned her attention to the next guest. Relieved, Oliver let go of Emma's arm and excitedly pointed at the sign again.

They continued following the signs until they saw "Skydraft" pointing towards a dark, short corridor separate from the other terminals. Before entering, Emma gave him an excited thumbs up and stepped forward. Oliver followed behind her.

About half-way down the corridor, the air felt still around their faces, and the noises behind them muffled out of existence.

"I think we're headed in the right direction," said Emma. "This feels just like Miyada's shop!"

Oliver squinted his eyes. "Yeah … but we're not on the Other Side of the Key yet. Is magic possible on our side?" He felt wary at the possible presence of magic on the Original Side of the Key. But then he remembered the alleyway in Davidson had also been muffled. Perhaps entrances to the Other Side leaked a bit of magic into their own side.

When they reached the end of the hallway, sunlight flooded in as two blacked-out electric doors swung open. After a moment of squinting their eyes, they stepped through, entering a strange clearing of asphalt surrounded entirely by giant concrete walls. Overhead, a communications tower peered over them along with the rest of the airport. Outside of that, only the tall slabs of concrete greeted them.

"Well, this is strange," said Emma. "It feels like a trap or something – OH, look, Oli, there's a door!"

Oliver saw it too but that didn't stop Emma from grabbing his head and pointing it in the direction of the door. On the opposite side from where they entered, another door stood. It looked small and grubby, but if there was a door, surely they'd be able to use their key.

Caught thinking, Emma grabbed Oliver's hand and pulled him towards the door, perhaps more aggressively than he would have liked. "C'mon, Oliver!" she said. But he dug his heels into the ground. A funny feeling had crept up his back and shoulders, one that he couldn't quite understand. All he knew was that something … something felt off.

"Wait!" he said.

"What's going on?" Emma asked rolling her eyes. "The door's right there, genius."

"Something's wrong," he said, motioning for her to stop speaking. He was scanning the sea of concrete. He thought the feeling might mean danger was nearby.

# \* Chapter 6: The Shadow \*

"Oliver, would you stop being so dramatic?" said Emma, trying to grab his hand again.

He slapped her hand away. "I'm telling you there's something or someone watching—," He stopped speaking because his eyes finally locked onto something besides the door. On top of one of the concrete slabs, stood a tall, dark shadow.

"Emma, up there," whispered Oliver, attempting to draw her attention to the danger. Without thinking, he bent his knees and felt a surge of energy beat within his ring.

But as Emma turned to face the unknown with him, the black, automatic doors behind them swung open again, and a bespeckled boy entered the concrete clearing with them. By the time Oliver looked back up to where the illuminated shadow had stood, it was gone.

"Hello," said the boy timidly.

"Who are you?" Emma asked in a confused tone. "Oliver, what the heck is going on? Is this kid dangerous or something?" The boy blushed, drawing attention to his gaunt cheeks. He was somehow thinner than Oliver.

"Oh, don't worry," hummed the boy, "I've never been a danger to anyone." He readjusted his glasses on his face and the bag in his hands.

Emma began to laugh. "Hah! Maybe Archie and Rasmus were wrong after all. If you think this kid is dangerous – no offense, man – then you definitely don't have the Gift of Wisdom."

"How is that not offensive?" said Oliver absentmindedly. He tried relocating the shadow but couldn't see it anywhere. Where had it gone?

## NOVA 01

"Did you see something besides me?" the boy asked Oliver, following his line of sight and ignoring Emma.

"Yeah," Oliver muttered, not fully paying attention to the boy. But then he realized the feeling in his stomach had disappeared, so he shrugged his shoulders. "I thought I saw ... well, a shadow staring at us from up there." He pointed up to the top of the concrete walls where the sun was brightest.

"A shadow of a man?" the boy asked.

"Or woman ..." Emma grumbled.

"Or woman," the boy agreed, blushing again.

"Well, whatever it was," Oliver muttered, turning his full attention to the boy, "it's gone now. What's your name anyway?" Realizing he might be coming off as a lunatic, he threw in a late smile.

"Oh, right," said the boy. "Well, I'm Abraham." He awkwardly placed his bag on the asphalt so he could readjust his light brown hair and offer a handshake. "But everyone calls me Abe."

Oliver took the hand and shook it vigorously. Abe nursed his hand as he withdrew it, only for Emma to crush it further.

"I'm Emma, and the scaredy-cat is Oliver," she said, smiling.

"You two must be extramen, huh?" Abe asked, holding his smarting hand with the other.

"That obvious?" Emma asked, pursing her lips slightly.

"Well, only because Oliver was showing clear signs of being a Wiser and you said you didn't think he had the Gift of Wisdom," said Abe. Oliver drooped his shoulders a bit. *Does Emma really think I don't have wisdom either?*

# * Chapter 6: The Shadow *

"But don't worry!" Abe added, "you'll be tested this fall semester and you'll know for sure."

"There's a test?" Oliver and Emma asked in unison.

Abe nodded, grabbing his bag and heading towards the grubby door across the concrete clearing. Oliver and Emma followed.

"Yeah, but nobody's allowed to tell you about it so don't start with me. Where are you guys from anyway?"

"Davidson," answered Emma.

"Hunterton," said Oliver.

Abe stopped, nearly dropping his bag from his hands. "Did you say Hunterton?"

"Yeah, and I said Davidson," Emma growled, threatening to roll her eyes. "So what?"

"Well, uh," Abe spluttered, barely containing his excitement, "there's a rumor about the next Trinova!"

At the looks on Oliver's and Emma's faces, Abe blustered but otherwise kept going. "Someone who has all three Gifts of magic – Power, Bravery, and Wisdom. This next one, they're called the Prophet's Advent because Augustus predicted their coming from Tenochprima." Oliver's skin crawled at the mention of Augustus. That was the name Miyada had said in the armory. "The prophecy," Abe continued, "says they'll come from a new, feeder school!" He left his bag on the asphalt unattended to look at Oliver more closely. "Your school from Hunterton – you're the first one, right?"

"I think so …" said Oliver sheepishly.

## NOVA 01

"Hah!" Emma exclaimed. "Looks like Miyada was right!"

Abe grabbed Oliver's shoulders and looked into his face inquisitively, causing him to drop the handle of his duffle. "There's no way to tell," Abe murmured after a few, uncomfortable moments. "I've done extensive research at school, but the text was lost centuries ago."

Oliver laughed, not as confidently as he would have liked. "You think I'm a part of a prophecy? I'm not even sure I'm a Wiser. Definitely not Powerful ... maybe a Brave?"

Emma laughed back at him. "Oliver! The blacksmith saw it too! I bet you *are* a – what's it called, Abe? A Trinova!"

"Wow," said Abe, releasing a long whistle. He let go of Oliver's shoulders and looked down at him differently. Oliver didn't like the look – it felt like misplaced reverence.

"C'mon guys," he whined at them both. "Archie and Rasmus had a point. I'm not going to school claiming to be a Trinova! I'll be laughed at!"

"Hmm, that's actually a fair point," said Abe, nodding his head sympathetically. "You'd get bullied mercilessly if we show up and everyone thinks you're calling yourself a near deity that hasn't been seen in one thousand years. The general consensus is an older student will develop into the Prophet's Advent but that it's a one-off event. Only crazy people, like me, believe that Trinova's exist every thousand years to keep the world on track."

"Wait," Emma asked, "how can everyone believe in one thing but not the other? You're telling us nobody believes in Trinovas but then everyone expects them to be an older student."

*119*

## * Chapter 6: The Shadow *

"Well," said Abe, scratching his head, "there's no real evidence of past Trinovas. So, most everybody thinks the prophecy refers to a new being that develops at school just one time."

Emma nodded her head appreciatively. "I gotcha. So, it might not happen to Oliver right away?"

"I'm not a Trinova!" Oliver interrupted, clapping his hands together. He had been feeling sick to his stomach as they traded answers. "Can't we just say I'm a Wiser? There's no way I've got Power or Brave in me. Let's just forget it."

Emma and Abe stared at him for a moment. Oliver could tell Abe had a dozen other questions waiting at his lips, but he also saw Emma's eyes and detected a sliver of sympathy within them. She mouthed "sorry" at him as Abe continued to stare.

"Fine," said Emma, snapping her fingers near Abe's head. "Are we right in thinking we should take that door over there to get to Tenochprima?"

Abe sighed. "Yeah, on the Other Side there's a skydraft. We'll take it up to the Southern Line." He walked ahead, leaving the two of them to mouth the word "up" at each other with confused expressions.

When they reached the door, Abe opened his bag, removing a large, green raincoat, and put it on. This struck Oliver as odd but then again, so did a small gnome statue standing at the foot of the door; its eyes stared at them welcomingly from across a thin nose.

"Y'all brought your baggy clothes, right?" Abe asked.

## NOVA 01

For the first time since he'd met her, Emma looked slightly concerned. "Umm, will this work?" she asked, pulling out the tablecloth she had shown Oliver during their drive to the airport.

"Umm, maybe?" Abe said with a grimaced smile. "You'll have to hold on tight for sure."

Oliver pulled out his extra-large poncho with a smug look on his face, which he unfurled loudly and unapologetically in front of Emma. After seeing Abe's large raincoat, he knew he was much closer to being correct about what to bring than Emma was. She stuck out her tongue at him in reply.

Abe chuckled at them both. "Emma will be fine as long as she has a strong grip."

"Abe, what exactly are we getting ourselves into?" Oliver asked. "Are we taking an elevator up or something?"

Abe smiled at him. "Easier to explain when you're looking at it, I think." Without waiting for either of them to respond, he took out a key from his bag. His was a brilliant gold that dazzled in the sunlight.

"Ooo, pretty key," Emma exclaimed. Oliver raised an eyebrow at her. "Oh, *whatever*, Oli!"

Abe ignored them again, turning his key.

*Whoosh!*

A great gust of air roared through the doorway, ruffling their hair and clothes. Oliver had anticipated it this time but was surprised when it didn't stop.

"GO ON AHEAD!" Abe yelled through the noise.

# * Chapter 6: The Shadow *

But Oliver didn't like the idea of going on ahead. When he peered inside the shimmering portal to the Other Side, an enormous tornado roared at him endlessly.

"ARE YOU NUTS?!" Oliver yelled back at Abe. "THERE'S A TORNADO IN THERE!"

"QUIT BEING A SCAREDY-CAT!" Emma shouted from behind.

Grumbling, he stepped through the portal.

He regretted it immediately.

Next to the tornado, the wind howled around him in every direction, deafening his thoughts and whipping his hair painfully back and forth across his head. As high as he could see, up into the cumulus clouds, the giant cyclone spun, threatening to consume the sun. Surprisingly, however, it did not suck him in.

A hand belonging to Emma touched his shoulder, making him jump. Turning to face her, he also saw the doorway to the Original Side, back to Santiago and his old middle school, close shut.

"EMMA," Abe yelled through the uproar, "MAKE SURE YOU HANG ON TO THAT TABLECLOTH REAL TIGHT!"

Comprehension dawned on Oliver as Abe began rolling his shoulders. He was readying himself to enter the tornado.

"YOU MEAN WE'RE SUPPOSED TO JUMP INTO THIS THING?! YOU'RE CRAZY, MAN!"

Abe shot him two thumbs up. "MAKE SURE YOU GET HEIGHT OTHERWISE YOU'LL SCRAPE YOUR LEGS ON THE

CONCRETE!" Then, with his oversized raincoat flapping around him, Abe sprinted towards the torrent of wind and jumped.

Oliver's eyes wavered, threatening to look away, but he held strong and watched Abe's jacket puff out to its oversized maximum, pulling itself and its owner upwards in a spiraling motion.

Slightly nauseated, Oliver glanced at Emma. "ARE YOU SURE ABOUT THIS?"

He shouldn't have bothered asking.

Emma wasted no time emulating Abe, even opting for a front flip as she jumped into the cyclone. A second later, she too zoomed upwards, circling towards the clouds as the wind caught the cloth in between her hands. "C'MON IN OLIVER," she yelled down at him. Her voice faded into a faint laugh as she disappeared from view.

Unwilling to be undone by "a Brave," Oliver readied himself to take the ascent too.

"This is absolutely crazy," he muttered. "What would Santiago think?"

Steeling himself, he ran at the tornado, jumping as high as he could at the last moment.

As soon as he crossed into the tornado, his poncho expanded like a pufferfish, shooting him towards the heavens. As he spun and rotated, his duffle bag threatened to rip away from his fingers, but he held on with all his might.

And then, no sooner than it had begun, he found himself at the top of the tornado, swirling among white, fluffy clouds and forgetting about the sinister shadow he'd seen below.

* Chapter 6: The Shadow *

## NOVA 01

# Chapter 7: Above the Skydraft

*He trusts me enough to tour the "Other Side" with him. None of his acquaintances know what to do with me. They think I'm some sort of mastermind, his only trusted counsel. Our vision is beginning to take hold. We'll soon bring an end to inequality on both sides of the Key. What a blessing magic is.*

*20$^{th}$ of September, the first year of the 10$^{th}$ Age*

Dazed and blinded by the puffy, bright clouds, Oliver struggled for a moment as he circled at the top of the tornado. A long minute later, he grew accustomed to the motion and looked up. Nearby, Emma and Abe waved at him from atop a floating grey platform. Not entirely sure what to do next, he tried swimming towards them.

Despite feeling like wading through thick seaweed, the motion worked, and after a few strokes, he reached the platform.

"WOOOOO," Emma bellowed at him. "Wasn't that AMAZING?!"

"Really?" Abe asked Emma. "Throwing up one second, and screaming 'amazing' the next?"

"Just like a roller-coaster, eh, Oli?" said Emma, ignoring Abe and pulling Oliver onto the platform. As he stood to gather himself, the noise of the storming winds behind him diminished, becoming no louder than a whisper.

## * Chapter 7: Above the Skydraft *

From the corner of his eye, he saw Abe push together his lips and raise his eyebrows appreciatively. "I have to admit. That's pretty good, Oliver. Most people look more like Emma when exiting the top their first time."

At the scowl Emma gave him, Abe coughed and gestured towards the middle of their cloud formation. "Erm, the Southern Line should have an outbound flight any minute. Let's get going."

For a while, they followed Abe along a path leading away from the skydraft. There weren't any hand-railings or signs to guide them, which alarmed Oliver enough to proceed with caution. But he soon abandoned the deliberation as he took stock of how the platform above the clouds operated.

As Abe progressed to the front of the queue, fluffy clouds whisked to-and-fro in circular motions. With each wisp of cloud, pathways revealed or hid themselves, hinting at additional magic working subconsciously around them. As Oliver studied the movements, he couldn't decide if the pathway beneath them permanently existed, or if it simply sprang into existence no matter where Abe might lead them.

Soon enough, they arrived at a platform much larger than the one above the skydraft. It looked like a regular subway station, only suspended thousands of feet in the air by clouds. The outbound side, on which they stood, had been labeled as the Southern Line. Across the middle, they could see the Northern Line, but Oliver didn't get too close to the gap. One look showed him it gave way to nothing but clear, blue skies and the airport below.

## NOVA 01

While they waited on a bench, Oliver wondered how on Earth planes could fly with a skydraft nearby. Then he realized the planes were still on the *Original* Side. Here, he could see them flying below but they probably couldn't see the skydraft, let alone the platform or him sitting on a bench in a cloud. The absurdity of the situation made his head spin.

After a few moments, Abe stood and approached the gap, peering out into the distance. "This next flight is already late," he grumbled. "I bet it's an old Khufu Ship. Seats are always the worst."

Oliver nodded his head again, still oblivious, but resigned to it. He'd felt that way a lot growing up in a country different from his family's.

Next to him, Emma slid closer. "Hey," she whispered. "I'm starting to feel like I'm speaking a different language than this guy."

Oliver chuckled before whispering back. "No kidding." Then he coughed and raised his voice. "Abe! What's a Khufu Ship?"

"Only the least comfortable type of public transportation ever conceived by man," Abe grumbled. "They've been in operation since the Fifth Age." When he saw Oliver and Emma exchange a look of confusion, he added, "Like 3000 BCE!"

From behind Abe, Emma saw it first. "Oh look!" she said, darting forward to get a better look.

Abe whirled around to see it too, before sighing. "Yep, that's a Khufu Ship alright."

From the gap between the two sides of the station, a magnificent wooden ship approached. At its bow and stern, two plain figureheads jutted up high above, pointing towards the heavens. Amidship, where the boat

## * Chapter 7: Above the Skydraft *

was at its widest, a cabin was situated, stretching from near the rear to just across the middle of the vessel, with enough room to seat twenty people. On the sides of the cabin, long, ornamental oars pointed upwards where they met in overlapping Xs above the cabin, creating an altogether impressive sight.

"This is a *bad* way to travel?" Oliver asked with raised eyebrows. Next to him, Emma gaped as the ship settled and a gangway popped into existence before clattering to a halt on both the ship and the platform.

Abe smiled at their expressions. "I guess they look cool. They're just not as fast as the Trundholms or Quadrigas. C'mon, let's find a good seat."

Oliver didn't care in the slightest if the Khufu Ships weren't as fast as other modes of transportation. As he, Emma, and Abe stepped off the platform onto the creaking wood of the ancient barge, he felt a thrill at the thought of how many people had taken the same step before him.

"Can you believe it?" he shot at Emma, "3000 BCE! This thing probably moved the Egyptians!" Emma nodded her head absentmindedly at him, running her hand on the side railings of the deck. He joined her, attempting to feel the memories within every groove and dent.

"Sometimes," Abe began with a sigh, "I wish I could experience it all again for the first time. Life has this annoying habit of convincing you that amazing things aren't amazing after you've experienced them once or twice."

Emma scratched her head as she stepped away from the railing and towards the cabin. "Man, why're you always talking like an eighty-year-old? You're like sixteen at best."

## NOVA 01

Oliver burst out laughing as Abe's face turned maroon. He began to splutter at her incoherently, unable to find a response. Nonplussed, Emma followed up with, "What year are you anyway?"

Abe took a moment to squint his eyes at her before ducking inside the cabin. "That's just the way I talk," he grumbled, disappearing from view. Oliver and Emma began to follow him inside, but Abe popped his head back out again and sneered, "*And* I'm a junior! Turning seventeen this year, thank you very much."

Inside, two columns of short rows already hosted around a dozen other travelers. While Abe surveyed them, Oliver went ahead and led Emma towards the rear.

Some of the other travelers erred on the younger side, fourteen or so, like Oliver and Emma. Older passengers, however, were some of the most bizarre people Oliver had ever seen in his life.

Towards the front of the cabin, a giant of a man wore not much more than a burlap produce sack over his mid-section. While his head looked clean-shaven, unkempt eyebrows raged in drooping loops on either side of his head. In his hands, he handled an enormous potato with reverence. Every now and then, he licked it loudly.

In the row immediately behind them, an ancient whisp of a woman cooed intimately to a pot of flowers that bobbed around on their own accord. What appeared to be a pet racoon chattered at her for giving the flowers more attention than it. As Oliver turned away, the racoon's chattering increased, and it even began to shake a little fist in fury.

## * Chapter 7: Above the Skydraft *

When Oliver turned back around, he'd hoped to find Abe just as weirded out by the events transpiring around them. But Abe rummaged through his bag, appearing entirely unbothered as he looked for something.

On his other side, however, Emma, stared aghast at the man and his potato, wincing at the sound of every lick.

"Oh, don't worry," said Abe when he caught Oliver's uneasy looks around the cabin. "We only have to take this for one stop."

Before Oliver could even nod his head in reply, the Khufu Ship *lurched* forward without warning, snapping each of the passengers to the back of their seats.

"My potato!" yelled the man dressed in burlap sacks. Oliver had to dodge as a tuber hurtled towards the rear of the cabin and out a window.

"This, is slow?" Oliver tried shouting. But he couldn't. The explosive movement of the Ship had a stranglehold on his lungs. Every time he blinked, clouds disappeared and reappeared. It was almost too much to take in at once. Next to him, he saw Emma bracing herself against the bench with her jaw clenched.

Beneath them the forests of North Carolina turned into flatlands and eventually the Atlantic coast crossed the horizon, bringing a port city along with it.

"That's Charleston," Abe breathed as the ship began to slow down. "Tenochprima's just outside of the city."

Emma let out a light burp and sounded hoarse. "That was quick." Oliver raised his eyebrows at the burp, but then noticed there was a tinge of green in her cheeks that hadn't been there before.

Abe, who also looked a little sick, laughed at Emma light-heartedly. He wrapped his knuckles on the galley's railing as they exited. "I bet the dang boat heard me call it slow! Never seen one this fast."

When they'd composed themselves on the new platform, Oliver turned to watch the Khufu Ship zoom away further south. Then, he noticed Emma had stooped over with her hands on her knees.

"Here," said Abe, stopping beside her. He removed a dagger from a sheath under his shirt and flourished it, muttering *"remasco!"* Immediately, Emma's face recovered to its normal color.

"Loads better!" said Emma, offering a thumbs-up. "But how come Oliver didn't get sick?" She shot him an envious look.

Abe squinted his eyes at Oliver and the corner of his mouth twitched. "Usually, kids with the gift of Power are immune to motion sickness. But Oliver swears he's a Wiser, so I'm not sure."

"Stop it!" Oliver growled, throwing his hands in the air. "You've just invented that!"

"Dead honest," said Abe, crossing an imaginary "x" over his heart. "I got really sick my first time. Threw up and everything."

"Not what I need to hear right now," said Emma, burping again.

Oliver scowled. "Well, maybe I have Power, then." As the words left his lips, he felt a swirling motion stir within him. Was it Wisdom telling him he was gifted with Power as well? The thought made him feel as nauseated as Emma had, so he pushed it out of his mind.

"Hmph!" said Emma. "You're gonna have to come to terms with the facts soon enough."

## * Chapter 7: Above the Skydraft *

"We're only teasing you," Abe added, which stopped Oliver from yelling at them both. "It's very unlikely that —,"

"Hey," interrupted a deep voice. "Have you kids seen my potato?"

They slowly turned to face the voice. It was the tall and rotund man from the front of the Khufu Ship. Unsurprisingly, he smelled like root vegetables.

Abe shook his head slowly. "Nope. We've, uh, *never* seen your potato."

Emma gaped unpleasantly, abandoning any pretenses of politeness.

"Argh," said the man while scratching his leg where his burlap sack met it. "I've lost my potato."

As the potato-less man walked away to the next group of uncomfortable students, Oliver broke out laughing. "You should see the looks on y'all's faces!"

Abe tried laughing too, but it wasn't convincing past the mortified grimace on his face. "C'mon," he managed to stutter, "we've got to catch our carriage next."

"Lead the way!" Emma insisted, still staring at the man uncomfortably.

Smiling, Oliver followed Abe and Emma towards a sign that read "This Way to Tenochprima Academy." Following it, they eventually turned onto a large cloud where dozens of open-faced, purple, and gold carriages waited for them at the far edge.

"Are we taking one of those to school?" Emma asked, squinting her eyes to see better. "Khufu ships again, or something else?"

"Just normal carriages," Abe said, "and yeah, we'll be taking one down."

## NOVA 01

Ahead of them, they heard other extramen ooing and aaing at the sight of the carriages, and soon enough, they understood why.

Tethered to the front of each carriage was a pair of enormous eagles. Some were bald, others were brown, and for the most part, they stood at six, terrifying feet tall. Their beaks and talons shone the same golden yellow as the carriage wheels while their plumage cascaded down their lean figures in shades of brown. When one stretched its wings, Oliver estimated a wingspan of greater than fifteen feet.

As different groups of students drew near, the eagles continuously cocked their heads, causing even the truest Brave to feel on edge. Every so often, one would release an ear-splitting screech and shake with mirth as timid students scurried away like frightened chipmunks. Oliver smiled when he noticed, as their behavior appeared in line with what Archie and Rasmus might do if they were the center of attention.

*"Well, go on then, boy!"* said an impatient voice in Oliver's head, *"enter the carriage before I place you inside like a hatchling!"*

Oliver jumped. "Who said that?!" he shot back, unable to locate the voice's source.

"Mr. Eagle did," said Abe, nudging Oliver's head in the direction of one of the eagles in front of the nearest carriage. It stared at them with its head cocked, looking more like a chicken hunting for grain than a six-foot alpha-predator.

"Really? Your name is *Mr.* Eagle?" Emma asked, placing her hands on her hips. "That's not creative, now, is it?"

* **Chapter 7: Above the Skydraft** *

*"Scrawww!"* was the eagle's reply. A nervous trio of students behind them decided to select a different carriage.

"Emma!" Abe hissed. He grabbed her hand, pulling her away from the giant eagle. "If you don't know a Guide's name, you refer to them as Mr. or Mrs. whatever species they are! It's only polite!"

Emma scowled but before she or Oliver could respond, Abe had pushed them both onto the carriage. Oliver's duffle flew up after them, and Abe followed. Once they were situated amidst white and purple pillows, they could hear the eagles in front chattering about Emma's disrespect.

Emma rolled her eyes. "I didn't know, okay?"

"Bah!" said Abe, waving a hand. "Don't worry about it! But I wouldn't be surprised if it takes a couple years for the eagles to warm up to you."

"A couple years?" Emma asked with raised eyebrows. "That sounds like something I should definitely be worried about."

"Not the type to forget an insult," Abe whispered. "Same with all ancient species like the feathered serpents and osori."

"The oso – what now?" Oliver asked.

"At some point," Abe said, rubbing his eyes and collapsing into the cushions, "you're going to want to discover things for yourself. Osori, feathered serpents, and giant eagles are the three types of Guides we have at school. They call themselves sacred beasts and, this year, the feathered serpents are up for the new class. Then you've got the rising hardmores with giant eagles and my junior class with osori. By the time you reach your senior year you don't really need a Guide so they serve the incoming Extraman Class instead. You get the idea – a rotating basis."

"And what does an osori look like?" Oliver asked.

A broad grin spread across Abe's face. "You'll meet Reggie, soon enough. And, it's osorius when singular. Osori for plural."

Emma growled. "You're really not going to tell us?"

"Nah," said Abe, "it'd ruin the fun."

Emma crossed her arms and fell back into the cushions next to Oliver in protest. Across from them, Abe raised his eyebrows repeatedly, wearing a smug grin. Oliver was starting to get used to the smugness and wondered if he'd ever know enough about magic to return the favor.

Once they were seated, he thought at least three more students could have joined them, but none ever came. He was beginning to feel self-conscious about being skipped by other students until he turned around to check on the eagles in front of them. They scratched at the platform beneath their six-inch talons and cursed outwardly. "*Such impudence! The nerve of that girl! Who does she think she is?*"

Inwardly, Oliver thought he'd always been good at understanding what others were thinking. He often didn't need more than a glance at Santiago to know what kind of mood he was in. Did that make him a Wiser? Goosebumps erupted across his arms as the thought nestled in his heart. *Ok, definitely a Wiser, but didn't Abe say I have Power as well? Or was he pulling my leg?*

Before he could daydream too much, a deep bell tolled in the distance, shooting him and Emma upward like spooked cats.

Abe grimaced as the bell tolled a second time and Oliver couldn't help but notice him tighten his grip on his backpack before sinking further into

## * Chapter 7: Above the Skydraft *

the cushions. "Batten down the hatches," he said in response to Oliver's stare. "We'll be off soon - but don't worry if you fall out - you *usually* get teleported right back in."

"What do you mean don't fall out?!" Emma shrieked. "What are you talking —,"

*Gong!*

After the third toll of the bell, every eagle on the platform began screeching. One by one, Oliver heard batches of students scream as pairs of eagles took off around them. He watched, squirming on the inside, as a nearby carriage descended at a frightening speed. Without warning, their carriage lurched next, tearing them away from platform and into the open space below.

## Chapter 8: A Headmaster's Welcome

*There's a school! It's called Tenochprima, and one of the Founders is Toltecan! Supposedly. They teach everything there is to know about magic! What a farce. Why not admit all children? Why is magic only taught to the select few? Something else we'll be sure to change after we're finished.*

*30th of September, the first year of the 10th Age*

As they plummeted and twisted through open air, Oliver squinted, barely making out the eagles in front of them. Their wings were furled, which explained how they'd reached terminal velocity so quickly. Oliver's stomach lurched as the carriage bobbed them around like an out-of-control jet plane. It didn't take long for Abe to begin shrieking in a surprisingly high-pitch voice, Emma following soon after, albeit in a less embarrassing tone. Oliver, meanwhile, felt too much gravity on his lungs to do anything other than pray for their survival. As they fell, the purple and white pillows around them abandoned the carriage in every direction, only to magically pop back into their laps.

By the time they crash landed to an undignified halt onto a rocky landing strip, Oliver, Emma, and Abe were buried in the respawning pillows. From the cushions, they emerged dazed and confused, watching the eagles taxi them off the landing strip.

"You have to do that every year?!" Emma blustered through a mouthful of feathers.

## * Chapter 8: A Headmaster's Welcome *

Abe began to reply but a *"scrawww!"* from the front of the carriage interrupted him. They could hear the eagles scratching their talons on the ground and clicking their beaks again.

"Perhaps we better get off first," said Abe, peering at the eagles uneasily. He stood up to exit, but tripped clumsily on a pillow, causing him to stumble out of the carriage entirely. A great w*ham!* and a cloud of dust followed.

"Nice," said Emma, looking down at Abe's plastered figure.

Oliver nodded without sympathy. "Good thing his face broke his fall."

They hopped down from the carriage to help him up, but an enormous, terrifying paw beat them to it. With an outstretched claw, the paw lifted Abe from his backpack and onto his feet. While Abe wiped the dirt and dust off his clothes, Oliver and Emma slowly looked up to face the owner of the enormous limb. Without warning, they had managed to find themselves face-to-face with the largest grizzly bear they'd ever seen.

Emma put a hand to her mouth to stifle a scream. "This," Abe said, his voice cracking, "is Reggie! My Guide!"

*"Enchanted,"* Reggie said to them telepathically. His voice was deep, like the babbling of an eddying mountain creek. He licked the blood off of Abe's nose. Oliver worried the nose might come off, too.

*"Indeed,"* added two familiar telepathic voices.

Oliver recognized the unannounced voices at once. "Archie!" he exclaimed. And sure enough, both Archie and Rasmus appeared with a flutter of wings. Their feathers dazzled in the sunlight as they circled continuously around them. Emma reached out a hand for Rasmus to brush his side against.

*"Always showing off,"* Reggie chuckled. Like the feathered serpents, there was a richness to his voice that didn't exist in humans.

*"Preposterous,"* said Rasmus indignantly.

*"Not you, slim,"* said Reggie, shaking his massive sides. *"I'm talking about the eagles! D'you see how hard of a ride they gave our kids here?"* One of the two eagles in the front clicked its beak menacingly. Before hostilities could break out, however, a booming voice rang through all of their heads.

"ALL EXTRAMEN, PLEASE HEAD DOWN TO FOUNDERS TEMPLE AS SOON AS POSSIBLE. DO NOT DILLY, OR EVEN CONSIDER DALLYING, AS YOU'LL BE RUN OVER BY THE NEXT CARRIAGE, AND THAT WOULD MAKE QUITE A MESS. THANK YOU FOR YOUR COOPERATION."

*"Always definitive,"* said Archie, chuckling. *"Leave your luggage and let's get moving!"* Heeding the announcement's warning, they meandered forward, following a line of extramen and feathered serpents towards the top of a staircase near the center of the runway. Behind them, they still heard the occasional batch of screams as the next carriage come to a crashing halt.

When they reached the top of the stairs, Abe turned to toss a buffoonish grin at Emma and Oliver. "Welcome to Tenochprima Academy!"

Though Oliver hadn't realized it, the landing strip they had just crashed into was situated at the top of a very large hill in an otherwise flat landscape. Brick buildings poked their facades and corners into view through the leafy foliage that littered the hillside. Oliver's eyes tracked one of the larger brick

# * Chapter 8: A Headmaster's Welcome *

buildings towards the bottom of the hill when something even larger grabbed his attention. Just where the hill began to flatten out, an enormous, thirty-layered temple towered impressively over the land. At the temple's peak, a statue of a great feathered serpent leered down at them all, passing its gaze from one campus occupant to the next, making Oliver feel like he was being scanned for viruses. After a moment, the statue shook its body, causing the jewels and feathers on its torso to twinkle at them elegantly in the sunlight.

"Wow," said a boy walking next to them as they descended the stairs. He had shaggy, blonde hair and a crooked smile. A wiry feathered serpent circled around him as he spoke. "I thought we didn't have anything like this in America."

*"Come, Lance!"* said the wiry serpent. *"We have to make our way to Founders Temple!"* The boy gave them an awkward look as if he wanted to stay and chat before giving up and following his Guide down the stairs.

"That's actually a good point," said Oliver, whispering in Abe's direction. "I thought we didn't have any temples in the United States – don't only México and South America have 'em?"

Abe responded with a pretentious tap of his nose. "Two sides to every key, remember?"

Fascinated by their surroundings, Oliver and Emma continued down the staircase at a pace Mrs. Caldwell would not have approved. At one point, Emma grabbed his arm and pointed excitedly at a set of lagoons sprawling past the temple. Oliver responded by guiding her sight towards a forest of cypress trees to the left of the pools. On closer inspection, he found the

## NOVA 01

trees began on hard ground, creating a forest, before continuing eastward into the water and turning into a dark swamp. Following the cypress trees, his eyes locked onto a thick fog in the center of the lagoons. He briefly wondered what may lay hidden inside when he felt a strand of the chaos outside his ring lull him towards it. The feeling stopped him in his tracks as it continued creeping up his arm. It went away, however, the second Emma pulled him forward again.

At the temple's base-level, two additional statues supervised the campus: a snarling bear to the west and a flapping eagle to the east. *"Osorius, giant eagle, and feathered serpent,"* Archie hummed, *"we've been friends to the school since the founding fathers first settled here."* Reggie growled in agreement, causing Abe to jump with fright.

Instead of doors, the temple's entrance consisted of an enormous, open entryway. It didn't need doors, Oliver realized, because a circular river guarded the entire temple. He peered down into the churning water as they crossed over one of four mossy, wooden bridges. The other three bridges, he noticed, led to not only brick buildings, but other smaller temples along with an open space surrounded by bleachers. *Must be the soccer field.*

When they reached the temple's entrance, they stopped to appreciate its height and width. Forty feet above them, licks of moss reached towards them, and even if they'd lined up side-by-side, they still would have easily entered. And yet, light only reached a few yards inside, barely revealing stone floors and the corner of a decorative rug.

"You betcha," said a voice behind them. It was the blonde boy from the stairs again. He held out a large map despite the protestations of his

# * Chapter 8: A Headmaster's Welcome *

feathered serpent Guide. "Says here that the big one is Founders Temple and the little ones are Hutch, Tancol, Champayan, and Preston."

"Where'd you get the map?" Oliver asked earnestly. Emma missed his sincerity because he heard her stifle a giggle.

Abe answered quickest. "You can buy them at most bookstores. I'm sure they had some at yours in Davidstown."

"Y'all are from North Carolina?" the blonde boy asked. "That's a relief. I was worried I'd be the only non-Northerner hear. I'm from Atlanta. My carriage was full of kids from Boston or thereabouts and they were making fun of my accent. I don't even have much of one, do I?" The words had come tumbling out of the boy's mouth.

"Yeah, we're from North Carolina," Emma said uneasily. "My name is Emma. This is Oliver, and —,"

*"Yes, we're delighted to meet you too,"* interjected the boy's feathered serpent. The melody in her voice made Oliver's brain feel hazy. *"I'm Merri, and this is Lance. But we're due at Founders Temple! I must be leading us inside for orientation!"*

Laughter rolled through Archie's chest, causing everyone to turn and look at him. *"All too hasty, Merri."*

This wasn't the first time Oliver noticed his Guide rank senior above other feathered serpents. Hadn't he also bossed Rasmus around in Davidstown?

*"Come along, Lance,"* said Merri, ignoring Archie, but looking embarrassed. *"We don't want to miss the Headmaster's Welcome."*

Lance waved goodbye with a goofy smile. "It was good to meet you guys."

# NOVA 01

They followed Lance and Merri inside, where a foyer greeted them, dimly lit by lanterns and mysterious, green light fixtures. The whole room seemed unnecessarily large to Oliver, but then again, it *was* the foyer of a thirty-layer temple.

Towards the opposite side of the entrance, a double-sided, curved staircase led up to a second level and a more reasonably sized doorway. Some students had selected to climb the stairs on the left, others on the right. Oliver and Emma, however, couldn't help but focus their attention on a turquoise and red sundial that hung in the center of the wall in-between the staircases.

Outside of the various torches illuminating the foyer, the sundial served as the main decor. In its center, a grimacing face flicked its round eyes at the students that passed, causing some to step away in fright. Oliver found it difficult not to look away from the face, and just as he was about to comment on its unpleasantness, the grimace turned to a silly smile with raised eyebrows. It even took a moment to blow a raspberry at Lance, who ahead of them, had gotten too close. As Lance stumbled back into a couple of other students, the face changed again, only this time to a completely neutral expression whereupon it began announcing a message in the same booming PA voice they had heard at the top of the hill.

"ALL EXTRAMEN, LAST CALL – HEAD INTO FOUNDERS TEMPLE IMMEDIATELY. LATE STUDENTS WILL BE DRAWN AND QUARTERED BY OSORI CUBS. THANK YOU FOR YOUR COOPERATION."

## * Chapter 8: A Headmaster's Welcome *

"That's Tolteca," said Abe, pointing towards the sundial. It'd resumed blowing raspberries at passersby.

Archie's voice sounded in Oliver's head. *"Tolteca's involvement with the school predates us Guides. We didn't join the school until after all of the founders arrived."*

Oliver thought there may have been more to that puzzling remark, but he was too distracted to follow up on it. They walked through propped-open doors standing twenty-feet-high to join a crowd waiting at the front of an enormous dining hall layered by dozens of oak and mahogany wood tables. Elsewhere, thick stone columns lined with torches stretched from floor to ceiling, providing both structure and light.

As they waited for an announcement, most of the extramen eyed each other nervously. Oliver noticed some students had belts with sheaths for magical dirks, daggers, throwing axes, and even swords. Others, like Emma, wore sleeves or bandanas to channel their magic. None, as far as Oliver could see, wore a ring like he did. Before he could comment on it, Archie zoomed towards the front of the queue where, to Oliver's surprise, Tolteca joined him, levitating ominously in the air in front of the students.

*"Welcome! Yes, welcome to Tenochprima Academy!"* Archie signaled towards the extramen. *"My name is Archie, and I serve as the Chief Guide here at the Academy. Should you ever have any questions about anything, really, please approach your Guide, or any other Guide for that matter. For today, however, please allow me to introduce our PA, Tolteca, who will be addressing a few housekeeping items prior to dinner and the Headmaster's Welcome."*

## NOVA 01

When he stopped speaking, Archie fluttered his wings to circle around Tolteca, causing the floating sundial to spin around a few times. He then resumed his position next to Oliver, Emma, and Abe where a few gazes followed, locking onto Oliver.

Tolteca boomed with laugher as his spinning came to a halt. When he began to speak, Oliver didn't know if he should cover his ears or drop his jaw. Tolteca's voice was unlike anything he'd ever heard, carrying the authority of a Nahuatl accent and the history of another millennium. "YES! THANK YOU FOR THE INTRODUCTION, ARCHIE! AND THE SPIN, FOR THAT MATTER. YES! WELCOME TO TENOCHPRIMA ACADEMY, CHILDREN! AS ARCHIE SAID, I SERVE AS THE SCHOOL'S PUBLIC ANNOUNCER.

"FIRST THINGS FIRST, EACH OF YOU SHOULD ALREADY HAVE YOUR MAGICAL CHANNEL AND SOURCE.

"IF YOU DO NOT, YOUR GUIDE WILL SHOW YOU TOWARDS THE EXIT FOR YOUR INCOMPETENCE—,"

Next to Tolteca, Archie let out a telepathic cough.

"ERM … YES, THE CAMPUS STORE WHERE YOU CAN PURCHASE AN APPROPRIATE SET.

"SECOND! AFTER THE HEADMASTER'S WELCOME, YOU'LL BE TAKEN DOWNSTAIRS TO FOUNDERS DORMITORY WHERE YOU'LL MEET YOUR ROOMMATES."

Oliver's stomach churned slightly at the idea of *roommates*. With just how many strangers was he going to be forced to live? Would they be cold and

## * Chapter 8: A Headmaster's Welcome *

distant like Santiago had been for most of his life? Or more like the new Santiago?

"LASTLY!" Tolteca resumed. He'd somehow raised his already deafening voice to drown out the whispering that had broken out at the mention of roommates. "AFTER THE FEAST, YOU'LL FIND YOUR COURSE SCHEDULES AND ORIENTATION ITINERARIES ON YOUR DESKS. ONCE EVERYONE'S SETTLED, DEAN CHAVARRIA AND PROFESSOR BELK WILL SUMMON YOU FOR NEXT STEPS."

"Roommates?" Emma mouthed silently at Oliver. He shrugged his shoulders and shook his head, feeling just as bamboozled as she looked.

"BUT FOR NOW," Tolteca shouted past a grimace of ruby and emerald teeth, "WELCOME TO TENOCHPRIMA ACADEMY! PLEASE GO AHEAD AND FIND A SEAT FOR THE WELCOME DINNER!"

In the confused din that followed, nearly a hundred pairs of shoes scuffed against the stone floors as the extramen awkwardly jostled towards the dining tables. Ooing and aaing soon followed as dozens of feathered serpents danced and circled their way into the room above them; overhead, light from a chandelier danced off their bodies. Oliver also noticed two giant eagles batting their way through the crowded upper half of the room. Meanwhile, Reggie and two other osori made their way forward by ground, pushing aside extramen like bowling balls to pins.

Each of the Guides eventually sat on large purple cushions that surrounded a large slab of quartz-riddled stone on the far side of the room.

## NOVA 01

Judging by the hissing and growls Lance received when he approached the quartz table, it didn't appear as if the extramen were welcome there.

For the most part, different groups of either boys or girls sat together. Oliver and Emma, however, managed to find themselves in a coed group with Lance, who waved merrily at them. Emma managed to wave back, even if hesitantly, but Oliver's attention was focused on a sharply dressed woman who stood at the center of the Guide's table. Tolteca floated in the air next to her, but somehow, she appeared more interesting than he did.

Thin, wrinkled, and athletic, the woman didn't have to say a word for the room to quiet down. She wore a slim, charcoal grey pantsuit, a white blouse, and a purple bow that matched the frames of her circular glasses. Around her neck, a necklace with jewels of azure blue cascaded over her blouse. The moment every head in the room focused on her, she spoke with a voice that reminded Oliver of fresh maple syrup.

"Welcome!" said the woman, smiling at each corner of the room. "I am Dr. Elodie Lalandra, and I have the privilege of serving as the thirty-third Headmaster of Tenochprima Academy. As Tolteca mentioned, we refer to the start of orientation feast as the 'Headmaster's Welcome,'" she added air quotes with her fingers "but it's really more of a Headmaster's quick relaying of our history and nonsensical school rules."

Whispering threatened to break out, but before it could take hold, Lalandra raised a single finger, stealing the breath from every distracting thought, concern, and complaint.

"But I digress," Dr. Lalandra continued. "For tonight, allow me to remind you that our Founders began this school here in South Carolina as

# * Chapter 8: A Headmaster's Welcome *

refugees from different parts of the world; Augustus from Scotland; Madeline from France; and Cuahtemoc from the Aztec Empire. Their intent was to prepare users of magic for the Tenth of Age of Proximity, in which we find ourselves – let us strive to not disappoint them."

Oliver thought he detected a scarring memory in the Headmaster's eyes as they flickered over the student body. "D'you think somebody else disappointed them?" Emma murmured into his ear, mirroring his thoughts.

"Sounds like it, doesn't it?" he whispered back, turning to meet her eyes. Lance, he saw, was observing them from the other side of the table.

"Now! Onto the housekeeping items!" Dr. Lalandra continued with a clap. "First, the Ceremony of the Gifts will occur on the first of November when the Founders' spirits are most near. For those of you who are unaware, the Ceremony is a series of trials used to determine each new student's Gift! The Founders will determine your Gift and test you accordingly."

This time, whispering broke out like wildfire. "I thought it was a joke!" shot Lance. "We have to take tests?! I wouldn't be able to make a toad croak!" Emma snorted. Oliver, meanwhile, smiled uneasily as he felt more like Lance than Emma. How was he supposed to pass a set of trials in just a couple months if he didn't even know what his Gift was?

"Power, Bravery, and Wisdom!" continued Lalandra, reducing the whispers to embers. "Each Gift has its pros … and its cons! Wouldn't it be nice to have them all! Alas, each of us is relegated to just one. As we approach the Ceremony, however, I recommend you do not become seduced by the idea of who you'd like to be, but instead fall in love with who you are meant to be – no matter its manifestation, appreciate the Grace that's been blessed onto you."

Pausing for a moment, Headmaster Lalandra surveyed the room cryptically. Nobody dared speak. When her eyes passed over Oliver's, they stopped and came back to lock with his for a moment. There was a fire within her eyes that made it difficult to meet them but also impossible to look away. Just as he began squirming in his chair, she glanced elsewhere and resumed speaking.

"To the rules! Students are permitted to enter the lagoons only during school field trips or for supervised beach volleyball, skiing, or wakeboarding. A word to the wise, the Bald-Cypress Havens is a sacred place to the Eagles. As such, they will not hesitate to grievously injure anyone foolish enough to enter without permission." She paused to give the Giant Eagles a reproachful look from above her glasses but resumed speaking soon after. "On a more positive note, I'm delighted to announce the Swampy Woods is now open for Magic and Monsters field-work under faculty supervision!"

Nearby, Oliver heard Abe and a few older-looking students cheer excitedly.

"Yes, yes," said Lalandra, waving a finger at the older students, "but I must stress that it is forbidden to go in alone, as the swamps and woods are chock-full of monsters who'd relish the idea of a lost student in their midst."

"Monsters?" mouthed Lance towards Oliver and Emma with wide eyes.

## * Chapter 8: A Headmaster's Welcome *

"I don't know if I like this kid or not," Emma whispered into Oliver's ear. Oliver shrugged his shoulders and shook his head, not wanting to interrupt the Headmaster.

"For now," said Lalandra, smiling again, "enjoy the feast!"

She stepped down from the quartz table, amidst a chorus of excited hissing, roars, screeches, and applause from the feathered serpents, osori, eagles, and students, respectively. The moment her trailing foot left the table, enormous chunks of meat began to plop into existence in front of the Guides. The ripping, squelching, and gulping noises that followed were downright disgusting.

Elsewhere, chairs groaned as the extramen adjusted to better position themselves for supper at their own tables. The only problem was, there wasn't anything to eat.

"What are we supposed to be digging in to?" asked Emma. She frowned at Oliver, looking for advice. He looked around to see what the other extramen were eating but only saw the feathered serpents, giant eagles, and osori chowing down on their smorgasbord of meat.

"Oh! I know what we have to –," Lance began, but Abe interrupted them, leaning over a plate of buttery potatoes and meat Oliver thought might be venison.

"I told y'all, you're gonna want to start figuring things out for yourselves." He brandished his fork disapprovingly at them – Lance hungrily eyed the potato speared to it. "Quit being stupid and tap your channel on the table to order!" He rolled his eyes and resumed a conversation with an older student next to him.

## NOVA 01

"I'm sorry, what?" asked Oliver, looking around with furrowed eyebrows. "You mean like at a restaurant?"

From across the table, Lance began to hit the table with what appeared to be a two-foot warhammer. The thump of wood against metal was everything but graceful and brought a lot of attention to their table.

"We have to order – my sister mentioned it to me before!" he said excitedly before tossing the warhammer back onto the table. It clanged noisily to a halt. "Mr. Table," he said, "I'll have a pepperoni pizza!"

They all stared at Lance's plate, waiting for a pizza to appear, but instead a cloud of brown dust and a drab piece of parchment appeared.

"What's it say?" said Oliver, trying to peer at the text on the parchment. Lance picked it up.

"Oh," he said, both ears turning red.

"Go on!" prodded Emma, "what's it say?"

Lance coughed before reading the message as quiet as he could. *"With the whole world of cuisine in front of you, you ordered a pepperoni pizza? Try again, peasant,"* A couple of extramen laughed, pointing at the card and the cloud of disappearing smoke as Lance looked miserable. Oliver turned to the voices and glared, registering their faces.

Emma laughed with the others but stopped when she saw Oliver's glare. "Ah, don't worry about it, Lance, they must be trying to keep us healthy for sports and stuff!"

Lance nodded his head timidly. "How about a turkey sandwich and tomato soup, instead?" he countered.

*151*

# * Chapter 8: A Headmaster's Welcome *

This time, a piping hot bowl of creamy red soup appeared, accompanied by a turkey sandwich with lettuce, tomato, pimento cheese and thin, sourdough bread.

The sight of Lance dunking his sandwich into his tomato soup wiped the smug look off Emma's face. She pulled her magical sleeve on so she could tap the table too, ordering a grilled salmon fillet with roasted bell peppers over brown rice.

Oliver, meanwhile, couldn't help but notice everybody but him was clumsily hitting the table with daggers, knives, axes, or large sleeves. One strong looking boy in the rear was even slamming the butt of an enormous battle axe on the table.

Quickly, he tapped his ring on the wood, and in a low voice, ordered the first thing he could think of: "If you please, I'd like eggs over medium with hash-browns, buttered toast, and grits."

With a puff of green smoke, the food appeared, steaming deliciously into his face. To his astonishment, a message was written in the hash-browns. "*You could use the carbs, string bean.*"

Smiling, he scrambled the note and looked up to check if anyone had noticed. Emma's attention was caught by the slurping noises emanating from Lance's tomato soup. Nearby, Abe's conversation continued with the student to his right. And Dr. Lalandra, well she was staring right at him.

Taken by surprise, Oliver choked on the bite of toast he had just taken.

"Oh nice!" said Emma, gesturing at his plate with her fork. "I tried to think of something my parents would make on the weekend, but that looks loads better!"

## NOVA 01

"*Desasuffo,*" came Abe's voice. "Try not to choke to death on your first day, eh, Oliver?"

Oliver gave Abe a thankful thumbs up as the toast dislodged itself from his throat. He chanced a look towards Dr. Lalandra. Though he saw a pinch of a smile on her face, her attention was now focused on an athletic professor speaking stoically to a group of faculty members.

"What're you staring at Dr. Lalandra for?" Lance asked, peering in the direction Oliver faced. Tomato soup dribbled down his chin.

"I wasn't staring at Dr. Lalandra! She was staring at me!"

Lance shrugged, returning his face to his soup. "Maybe," he continued amidst a chorus of slurps, "she might have wondered why your channel is a ring when all of us have stuff like this?" He picked up his warhammer and shook it before putting it back down. Its handle now had tomato soup on it.

Emma looked from Lance to Oliver and then back to Lance. "Ooooo, you're smarter than you look, Atlanta! But keep it down. We're not trying to draw attention to his ring or Gift."

Lance shrugged. "Good luck with that — that's the first thing most everybody's gonna notice. 'Specially the older students. Oh thanks, Mr. Table." Lance had finished his soup and the dishes were disappearing with faint *pop*s, leaving behind naught but clean dishes and linens.

"Seriously, though," said Oliver, leaning over his own disappearing dishes. *Pop pop pop.* "Not a word to anyone."

Lance solemnly traced an imaginary X over his heart, "cross my heart and hope to die."

*153*

## * Chapter 8: A Headmaster's Welcome *

"We got our channels in an armory in Davidstown," Emma began. Oliver shot her a warning look, not wanting her to divulge the conversation they had with Miyada. "Calm down, Oli. Where'd you get yours, Lance?"

Lance straightened in his chair at the question, excitedly telling them how it had been in his family's basement for generations. Evidently, his great-great-great-great grandmother first attended Tenochprima Academy during the Civil War back when Nova, and magic, hadn't even returned yet.

Oliver wondered what it would have been like for magic to suddenly be "turned on" one day. "Greatest day of their lives," said Lance, dreamily. "Mom and dad said they'd grown up hearing about it, but never had any evidence. So, there was always a bit of doubt. Then, one day,"—he snapped his fingers— "boom, magic was turned back on."

Soon thereafter, Tolteca floated to the center of the quartz table in a spiraling motion, bringing the excited conversations around the room to a close.

"YES! The first dinner is always a hit – I hope none of you tried wasting an order on a pizza or cheeseburger! It goes against the chef's code!" Oliver and Emma smirked at Lance who smiled back unapologetically.

"And thank you Dr. Lalandra for the kind words. Now, students, please follow your Residential Advisors to your dorm below."

In the commotion that followed, Oliver made sure to wave goodbye to Archie as he zoomed away with Rasmus through a hidden hole in the ceiling. The rest of the feathered serpents followed, ebbing to-and-fro until only humans, osori, and giant eagles remained in the room.

## NOVA 01

"Alright squad," came Abe's voice. "Y'all ready to be residentially advised?" Emma and Oliver looked at one another and then Lance.

"Nah," they said.

Abe chuckled. "Well, you don't really have a choice, so y'all better get used to it." Several extramen had gravitated towards them while Abe spoke – his head towered above most of them.

"Hey, Abe!" came a voice Oliver didn't recognize. "Alex is just herding up the rest of them near the southern staircase."

Abe nodded before addressing the thirty or so extramen standing near him. "All, my name is Abe, this is Katie, and we are two of your twelve RAs here in the Main Temple. Once we're downstairs, Dean Blackwood and Professor Zapien will briefly speak, and then we'll get orientation started!"

They followed Abe and Katie past the quartz table where Reggie still sat, his great bear lips dripping red from dinner.

"Alright there, Reg?" Abe asked with a soft chuckle. Several extramen backed away timidly from the osorius. The blood-matted fur around his lips made him appear extra dangerous.

"Never better," Reggie growled. Flecks of dinner fell from his muzzle as he shook his head.

"Just as y'all have feathered serpents for Guides," Abe said to the twenty or so extramen behind him, "the Junior Class has osori for Guides." After a few more steps, he led them to the northern most point in the room. His body began to disappear down a white marble spiral staircase Oliver hadn't previously noticed. "Only problem is," Abe continued, "they're not much use for anything outside of eating and sleeping."

*155*

## * Chapter 8: A Headmaster's Welcome *

Reggie growled.

"Just kidding, Reg," said Abe, his voice echoing up the staircase. Oliver wasn't sure if Reggie had heard him, but it didn't seem to matter as the great bear began to trudge towards the front entrance, teetering as he went.

Grinning, Oliver followed Abe down the steps looking forward to what he'd see next.

## Chapter 9: The Dean's Threat

*Tenochprima tests the newest children for their Gift on the Day of the Dead. A Trinova theoretically exists for every Age but then there's also a legend of a Prophet's Advent – but that is specifically tied to the school. I think it's superstitious nonsense – all three Gifts in one individual? If you ask me, Power is the one to pray for. The Power to implement your will.*

*1$^{st}$ of October, the first year of the 10$^{th}$ Age*

In the Founders Dorm lobby, Oliver took stock of his surroundings. To the east and west, enormous glass panes loomed well above their heads, creating a barrier between them and murky waters of black, green, and blue. "We're under the lagoons!" Oliver heard Lance whisper.

Outside the windows, trout and bass of all sizes flitted between long cattail roots, blocking the rare strands of sunlight making it through the thick water. Northward and southward, Oliver could see two off-center hallways leading to what he presumed to be the dormitory rooms.

Preceding the eastward glass wall, a wrought iron balcony welcomed anyone to look down below onto three additional floors from a half-dome outcrop. The bottom floor stretched from glass wall to glass wall, taking up the entire space, whereas the floors above only went as far as their respective half-dome balconies; together, the floors formed a giant's short staircase.

# * Chapter 9: The Dean's Threat *

Abe, Alex, Katie, and nine other older students ushered the extramen towards a marble fireplace on the opposite side of the top balcony. Atop the fireplace's mantle, gilded flora twisted and turned, catching the eager eyes of many extramen, including Oliver's. Light spread from the crackling fire, stretching across most of the room. Where its light turned into shadow, standing candle fixtures stood, leaving only the furthest corners of the room absent of light.

"Right," said Abe, "can everybody hear me?" The group of students that descended the southern staircase had joined them around the fire. "OK great! Hi everyone! My name is Abraham Cole, and I'm not going to waste anyone's time with another welcome to the school." Several of the other RAs chuckled. "We're your RAs. If you have any problems, come to us. There's no such thing as a stupid question – we're happy to talk about anything. There are twelve of us, two for each wing of each floor. Questions?"

"Yeah," said a tall, stocky boy with a slight accent Oliver couldn't place. "When do we find out who our roommates are?" Though Abe didn't notice, Oliver saw the boy roll his eyes and shake his head to a thin-nosed girl next to him. Oliver quickly recognized them as two of the extramen who had laughed at Lance over dinner. He whispered this to Emma, who in turn, began to scowl at the boy openly.

"Excellent question," said Abe, clapping his hands together. "I've got a list with everyone's names and room assignments. We're going to display them on the mirrors here." He pointed to two enormous, rectangular mirrors, hanging on either side of the fireplace. They were framed by the same gilded flora found on the fireplace's mantle.

Right on cue, the surfaces of the mirrors began to shimmer until a list of names appeared in alphabetical order. "Perfecto!" Abe continued. "To my right, you'll find A-L and to my left you'll find M-Z." Before he finished speaking, pushing and shoving had already begun towards the mirrors. "Alright everybody! Form a queue in an orderly fashion! Once you know what your room is, head to it!"

In all the pushing and shoving, Emma emerged, half-dazed, but smiling. She walked towards Oliver who had not participated in the uproar. "I'm on level B2, Room Four! You?"

"No clue yet," said Oliver, grimacing at the chaos unfolding in front of him. Abe walked over to join them too.

He grinned at Oliver. "Definitely a Wiser, waiting back here. C'mon, you're in my hall, anyway. Room 10 on B1. And your roommate is –,"

"Me!" came Lance's voice as he emerged from the pile-up in front of the mirrors.

Emma and Oliver grinned.

"I know I talk a lot," Lance began, "but I'm super tidy and relaxed. I'll make a great roommate – I promise!"

Emma playfully punched Lance on the shoulder. "No doubt about it," she said. "And besides, if you're ever talking too much, I'm sure Abe can teach us a spell to make you shut up."

Fortunately for Emma, Abe hadn't been listening. He stood on the tips of his toes, easily peering over everyone's head. After exchanging a few

# * Chapter 9: The Dean's Threat *

thumbs-ups with the other RAs, he led Oliver and Lance to the southern wing. Meanwhile, Emma waved goodbye confidently before striding off to the northern wing below to meet her new hallmates on B2. Oliver felt a pang of sadness as she walked away.

"Ah, cheer up," said Lance, following his gaze. "We'll hang out with her all the time."

Oliver nodded before replying. "Yeah, you're right. She's just the first friend I've made on This Side of the Key, that's all."

"Well, now it's time for the *fellas*," said Lance, dropping his voice playfully. Laughing, they briefly introduced themselves to the other boys on their way to their hall.

In addition to Abe, their other RA was a hardmore named Brantley. He and Abe were as close as brothers, it turned out. Oliver knew Abe well enough by this point, but he did find out he was from Charlotte, North Carolina. Brantley, meanwhile, was from Oxford, Mississippi, and he spoke in the deepest southern accent Oliver had ever heard.

"Now, y'all best be behaving," he told them with a wink, "otherwise Abe and I finna open up a can of whoop-a—,"

"Whipped cream," Abe interrupted. "Thanks, Brantley."

Their fellow extramen, meanwhile, were Dub, Trey, Tom, Jorge, Marshall, Ogden, Se'Vaughn, Grayson, JT, and Bobo. All the boys seemed friendly enough, but Oliver wasn't sure if he'd be friends with all of them.

After brief introductions, they broke out to find their rooms. To his left, Oliver saw a short staircase leading upwards and, to his right, a shorter staircase led to a visible green door with the words "RAs only" emblazoned on it in gold lettering. Brantley made sure to point out this was an *extra-large* room belonging only to him and Abe. Last, but not least, a main quartet of rooms lay just at the end of the main hallway past two sets of bathrooms.

At Abe's direction, Oliver and Lance dashed up the staircase to find room 10. Tom, Bobo, Trey, and Se'Vaughn followed, as they occupied rooms 11 and 12 in the upstairs nook.

At the top of the stairs, they skidded to a halt in a cylindrical foyer with three blue doors left, right, and center. Oliver and Lance entered the one on the left next to Trey and Se'Vaughn.

Rather than finding twin bunk beds in a shabby room, Oliver and Lance entered a large room with enough space for two full size beds, wooden desks, walk-in closets, armchairs, and nightstands. While Oliver marveled at the mahogany headboards and fluffy down comforters, Lance guffawed at the size of their closets. "Honestly don't think I could fill up a tenth of this," he said, standing inside his unit with his hands on his hips as he looked around.

Oliver laughed and hollered at him to join him as he'd noticed each of their desks had a rectangular object wrapped in brown paper waiting for them. He picked up the one on his desk and carefully ripped off the brown paper, revealing a thin mirror, or so he thought. The mirror was slightly larger than the size of a nine-by-eleven piece of paper and was surrounded by an ornate wooden frame similar to the ones on the enormous mirrors in the B1 common room

## * Chapter 9: The Dean's Threat *

"I think it's a mirror," said Oliver. "Hang on, I can't see my reflection in it. D'you know what this is?" He brandished the non-reflective mirror for Lance to see.

Lance squinted his eyes before joining him next to his desk. "Oh! Right, you grew up not knowing about magic, or anything at all really," —Oliver raised his eyebrows at him— "That's a notebook."

"A notebook, huh?" Oliver frowned. "So, like a computer tablet?"

"Like a computer tablet, he says," came a mocking voice from the door. It was Brantley. "Come on y'all," he said impatiently, "we're meeting in the B4 common room for some words from Professor Zapien and Dean Blackwood."

"This isn't a notebook," said Oliver indignantly. "How can you write in this?"

Brantley sighed as he yanked the notebook out of Oliver's hand. "You've got magic now, son. No more writing." With a double tap on the non-reflective surface, the "notebook" began to shimmer, revealing a blank canvas. Smiling, Brantley tossed the notebook back to Oliver who fumbled it once before grabbing it securely with both hands.

"See?" said Brantley. Oliver couldn't help but shake his head at the careless handling of the notebook. His face quickly changed to dull surprise, however, because the previously blank notebook now bore a message.

*"Dear Diary, I'm getting so tired of explaining how to use you. Please notify Oliver that all he needs to do is think strongly enough and you will do the writing for him. Yours impatiently, Brantman."*

"Upstairs crew!" boomed Abe's voice, "we're leaving in 30 seconds!"

## NOVA 01

"Come on y'all," Brantley agreed, "we'd better head down before Abe lays an egg."

Lance and Oliver followed him out. As they did, Oliver was surprised to see his notebook jotting down his thoughts.

*"This is really, really strange – oh, neat! It does punctuation and stuff automatically!"*

"Did you see our schedules yet?" Emma asked Oliver a moment later. She had joined him and Lance in the northern staircase on their way to the B4 common room.

"I still can't believe we have to take freaking math!" she added. "All the magic in the world and we still have to suffer through algebra?!"

Oliver thought back to class with Mrs. Caldwell in what felt like a lifetime ago. "As long as there's no world history," he grumbled.

"How'd you check the schedule?" interrupted Lance. He tried jostling his way between them in the crowded marble stairwell.

"Everything's on that notebook thing!" said Emma. "Just swipe to the left or right until you see it."

Oliver followed Emma's advice and swiped his finger across the surface of his notebook until he found a class schedule. He groaned when he saw *World History* on a list of eight courses, which also included *Destruction 101, Shielding for Novices, Regeneration through Potions & Embalming, Channeling 101, An Introduction to Magical Political Systems, Biomes of the Magically Inclined,* and *Pre-Algebra.*

## * Chapter 9: The Dean's Threat *

"At least some of these sound exciting," he said, shoving his notebook in Emma's face. "Destruction 101 oughta' be cool, right?"

Emma pushed the tablet away, as it had nearly smacked her nose.

"My brother, Elton," Lance interrupted again, "said that's his favorite subject! The professor is supposed to be—,"

What the professor was supposed to be, Oliver didn't find out. When they reached the bottom of the stairs, a shove in his back sent him flying. Lance caught him so he wouldn't fall.

"Watch where you're going, ring boy!" the pusher said in a cruel voice. He, along with two others flanking him, snickered and made faces at Oliver, Emma, and Lance as they walked past.

"Ring boy?" snarled Emma. "Lance did you tell anybody about Oliver?!"

"I crossed my heart, didn't I?" Lance hissed back. "I did warn you – people are going to notice! Look around. Everyone else is carrying a weapon or wearing sleeves like you and me!"

Oliver ignored them. Instead, he kept his eyes on the three figures disappearing in the crowd ahead.

"Those three laughed at Lance earlier at dinner, too" he said, brushing the wrinkles out of his jeans.

"Yeah," said Emma, still scowling. "They also just nearly pushed you to the floor!" She instinctively began tightening her magical sleeve.

"He's just jealous," said Lance dismissively. "Did you see the sword he had on his belt? Looked like a scimitar – what kind of absolute moron brings a scimitar to his first year at school?"

# NOVA 01

Emma smiled with an evil glint in her eyes. "You know what, Lance? I think you're right. I'm sure Oliver could take him down with Wisdom in a dueling match."

"Dueling match?" Oliver asked. He watched the scimitar bounce off the boy's retreating figure uneasily. The boy stood at nearly six feet tall, on pace to be well above six foot by the time they graduated. He had medium length, black curly hair that bounced up and down in sync with the sword on his belt.

Emma rolled her eyes. "Really, Oliver?" she said impatiently. "It's all in your *notebook*. Extracurriculars, page 8." She set off to join the crowd again down the last flight of stairs.

Oliver's cheeks reddened slightly, but he took the hint and kept going through the landing pages on his notebook while following Emma and Lance down the stairs.

It didn't take long for him to find the extracurriculars. Each activity featured a brief description of the rules, season of play, instructional images, and tips. Leafing through the different landing pages, he quickly realized that Tenochprima Academy liked its sports.

Though Oliver had no idea what Coatlball was, Dungeon-Simulation piqued his interest immediately. Image after image showed students solving the kinds of puzzles one might find in Santiago's old video games. One moving image showed a boy falling into a pit of lava after stepping on the wrong platform. Another one zoomed in on a girl being shocked for lighting a series of torches in the wrong order. He smiled absentmindedly

## * Chapter 9: The Dean's Threat *

as he flipped through the pages. Santiago, no doubt, would be very good at Dungeon-Simulation.

Before he could begin reading too much into Coatlball, they reached the B4 common room where two professors stood, speaking to the rest of the extramen. Evidently, they were the last to arrive, having dallied for too long at the bottom of the stairs.

"And remember," whispered Lance before they sat down, "it's pronounced 'Co-ah-till-ball.'"

"Shush!" hissed Oliver. He didn't want to be reprimanded for being late and chatty.

They had taken their seats next to Brantley, who smirked and shook his head at them. "Y'all get lost in the stairs or summat?" he chided. Abe agreed with Oliver and made a shushing gesture.

The common room was large and spacious down on the bottom floor. Like B1, large tables offered spaces in which students could spend time studying, chatting, or playing. Almost every study table featured larger mirrors within elegant frames. Oliver wondered if the mirrors were magically enhanced artifacts like his notebook, or if they were just normal mirrors. Seeing how one of them caused his reflection to wink at him, he was willing to bet on the former and not the latter.

From the rear of an aquatic viewing dome, the two professors continued speaking. Oliver hadn't noticed the viewing dome from the top floor, but it, and an identical one on the other side of the room, extended out past the glass walls. Some of the students, including the boy with the scimitar, sat on tufted sofas or wingback armchairs within the viewing dome. Everyone else, however, found space on the floor.

Oliver, Emma, and Lance sat in the rear just as one of the two professors – a short and stout woman – finished speaking. She bore curly, silver hair and a friendly facial ensemble featuring a wrinkled nose, a set of dimples, and a charming smile.

"And now," she said, "I'll turn things over to our Dean of Discipline, Professor Blackwood."

Tall, broad, and bald by choice, Dean Blackwood looked capable of expelling a student for turning in an incomplete essay. He reminded Oliver of photographs of Santiago's old drill sergeants but with fierce, blue eyes. Somehow, they complimented his bald head and sharp angles.

"Thank you, Professor Zapien," said the Dean with a voice like deep, crunching ice. "Yes, orientation, such an exciting time for us all." As he spoke, he rolled up his sleeves, revealing hairy forearms as wide as Oliver's thighs.

"Tomorrow at 2:00 PM Zulu, your RAs will provide short introductions on each of the subjects taught at the Academy. If you're lucky, they may also grace you with tips on how to succeed - Lord knows you will need them." He paused, surveying the room with palpable disappointment. Lance and Oliver shared a wordless look with one other, agreeing Dean Blackwood was not to be trifled with. Emma, however, kept her eyes on the Dean's.

# * Chapter 9: The Dean's Threat *

"Following those introductions," Blackwood continued, "your afternoon will feature lessons on the noble extracurriculars offered at this school."

A murmur of excitement broke out. "Coatlball" clearly meant something to a lot of the students because Oliver traced it being whispered from one side of the room to the other. The boy who had pushed Oliver grinned lazily from his spot on the couch after whispering something to his friends.

Blackwood formed enormous fists with his hands and shook them emphatically. "Dueling, Dungeon-Simulation, and, yes, the world-famous Coatlball! These are the extracurriculars in which you will find yourself competing during the Magical Five tournament every year – so named for the five dormitories on campus! Hutch, Founders, Tancol, Preston, and Champayan! As the Extramen Class, you all of course sit in Founders. Serve your dorm well, and your colleagues will treat you like a hero!"

"Or heroine!" interrupted Emma. The boy on the couch sighed and shook his head, making Oliver's blood boil.

"Indeed," said Professor Zapien, smiling at Emma.

Dean Blackwood, meanwhile, shot the boy a quick look and waved his hand dismissively at Emma. "Hero or heroine," he continued with a slight snarl, "each of you must understand that to succeed in both academics and extracurriculars is a rare feat at this school. I don't expect many of you to pull it off, but I've been told to encourage each of you to do your best so you can be invited to join your dormitory's team."

Rolling her eyes, Professor Zapien interjected. "Yes, yes. Well, y'all have that intensity to look forward to if you join Dean Blackwood's dorm next year. Here in Founders, however, I am your Dorm Head, and I welcome everyone to try out!"

A ripple of nervous laughter broke out from the extramen. It was quickly extinguished, however, by the cruel smile on the Dean's face – his only real smile so far. When he spoke again, the deep ice from earlier crept back into his tone. "Last I checked, Professor Zapien, it was *my* dormitory, Champayan, holding the Magical Five title eleven years running!"

Oliver glanced from one professor to the other. Though smiling, Professor Zapien's cheery disposition now looked about as convincing as one of Mrs. Caldwell's fake smiles. Blackwood, meanwhile, skipped ahead to an all-out sneer.

Leaning forward, Oliver began to whisper in Emma's ear. He paused when he saw Lance lean in, too, but then shrugged. He'd have a hard time keeping secrets from his roommate, and Lance seemed trustworthy enough, even if he was a little *too* eager. "There's more than Coatlball making these two hate each other."

Emma grinned, flicking him on the head. "Doesn't take a Wiser to see that."

Back in front, Zapien and Blackwood cleared their throats as Oliver and Emma hadn't been the only two to whisper. "Well, then," Blackwood boomed, not even pretending to keep the contempt out of his tone. "I'll take my leave. It's been … well, let's just say it's been a pleasure speaking to you all." His final stare lingered on Oliver, catching him by surprise. Blackwood looked him up and down, shaking his head and chuckling, before leaving with a swish of his cloak.

## \* Chapter 9: The Dean's Threat \*

"And off he goes," said Professor Zapien watching the Dean's shadow disappear up the northern staircase. She turned back to look dolefully at them all. "Oh, don't mind the Dean!" she added with a motherly smile. "He does this *every* year. Professor Watkin and I think it's a tactic to keep the Founders team from competing properly. He's just trying to hold back OUR extramen talent!"

*"Hmph!"* agreed Emma.

Zapien took a moment to smile at several batches of faces, even crinkling her eyes when washing over Emma's. "But! I've got a good feeling about this year's group! Let's go ahead and get our icebreakers going."

At the mention of icebreakers, Oliver stood up a little straighter. Ever since he began worrying about the strength and existence of his Gift, he'd become curious about what advantages his peers might or might not have against him. As far as he was concerned, growing up on the Original Side put him at a significant disadvantage against anyone like Lance, who'd grown up on the Other Side.

"Don't worry," whispered Abe, mid-way through the icebreakers. He caught Oliver frowning involuntarily after a set of twins introduced themselves as novas from an exclusively magical town called Goodwin Forest in Oregon. "I didn't come from a nova background either and I'd like to think I'm doing fine."

Oliver nodded his head back stoically in thanks, making a mental note to maintain more neutral facial expressions going forward.

The next set of icebreakers required the students to form into groups and take turns predicting which Gift they possessed and why. Emma,

## NOVA 01

Oliver, and Lance broke out in a group led by Brantley. Emma wasted no time standing up to declare she was in fact a Brave and looked forward to leveraging her Gift to help Founders win the Magical Five tournament. Oliver smiled, agreeing wholeheartedly.

The boy on the couch with the curly, black hair, however, made sure to snort as soon as she finished speaking.

Unable to help himself, Oliver gestured impatiently at the boy. "Go on then. What's your Gift? Arrogance?"

Brantley, the RA supervising their group, slapped Oliver on the back of the head. "Respect each other," he said firmly. "That goes for you too, uh, what's your name again?"

The boy stood, delaying his reply by readjusting the scimitar on his belt and running a hand through his hair. "Beto Warren. I'm from Greenwich, Connecticut, and I have the Gift of Power." He cracked his knuckles menacingly before glowering at Oliver.

"Well, then," Brantley said jovially, "you and Oliver should get along famously because he's likely a Powerhead, too."

"No, he's not," interjected Lance, "he's a Wiser!" Oliver started waving at Lance to stop talking, but Lance couldn't see him past the fire in his eyes. He and Emma were both trying to bore holes into Beto.

"I have to agree," replied Beto, lifting his chin disrespectfully at Oliver. "No way somebody that skinny has Power."

"But you didn't get sick going up the skydraft," Brantley muttered, looking confused. "Abe told me."

## * Chapter 9: The Dean's Threat *

"I'm sure more than just Powerheads can get through skydrafts," Oliver hissed dismissively. He and Beto locked eyes at each other, neither willing to look away.

"No, they can't," Brantley said, laughing. "You're a Powerhead, get over it. Unless you're trying to claim you've got two gifts rolled up your sleeves."

"He's going to be the next Trinova!" Emma said quickly, looking fierce. Oliver's heart dropped. This was exactly what Archie had warned him about.

Right on cue, Beto bent over, laughing. Oliver turned to shake his head at Emma, but she ignored him, continuing to glare at Beto unapologetically.

Between bouts of laughter, Beto faked wiping a tear from his eye, making Oliver's blood boil even more. "A Trinova? Better yet, the Prophet's Advent? Only a dumb *sinova* would think we'll get another one."

Evidently, Beto had gone too far, because Brantley crossed the gap between two of them, and smacked him hard on the back of the head.

"It's Beto, right?" he said, dropping his usually whimsical tone. The room appeared to close in around their group and the lighting began to fade. "You best leave prejudices behind in the dark ages, ya hear?"

He turned next to Oliver. "And you! Shut up about being a Wiser – fact of the matter is, you got through the skydraft no problem, so you're a Powerhead, OK?"

He flipped back to face Beto again with balled up fists. "Listen here, Greenwich, if I so much as think you hold an elitist prejudice against anybody, your entitled butt is going to be in detention every Friday for the entire year. Got it?"

## NOVA 01

Beto cracked his neck and glowered in response, only chewing on a reply Oliver was sure was rude.

"Lance," Brantley barked.

"Yes, sir?" said Lance, straightening his back and shifting his glare away from Beto.

"I've always thought this icebreaker was terrible. But for the love of all things pure, can you go next? What's your Gift? Emma's probably got Bravery while Beto and Oliver have Power."

Lance looked at the faces around him, swallowing. Oliver returned his gaze, mentally imploring him not to make things worse. "Well, my brothers and sisters tell me I'll be a Brave or a Powerhead," he said, letting out a nervous chuckle. "No chance I'm a Wiser, though."

The rest of the extramen followed Lance's lead without further interruption from Beto. Soon enough, Oliver also learned the names of the skinny girl and short boy who snickered at him after Beto's push on the stairs.

Cristina was from Monterey, California. She stood taller and thinner than most, wearing her jet-black hair in a ponytail that extended past her shoulder blades. Her face was angular, bearing thin lips, a thin nose, and focused, brown eyes. She shot reverent stares at Beto whenever she could sneak one in and smugly declared she knew she was a Wiser as early as five years old. The way she surveyed the room, Oliver believed her.

Short with neatly trimmed, blonde hair, James looked the opposite of Cristina. His blue eyes never seemed focused at all. Instead, they drifted aimlessly around the room except when laughing at anything coming out of

## * Chapter 9: The Dean's Threat *

Beto's mouth. "Born and raised on the Upper East Side," he said when his turn to break the ice arrived. After some prodding from the rest of the room, he guffawed in disbelief at having to explain that the Upper East Side was a neighborhood in New York City. He claimed he possessed Bravery, and Oliver was sure that would be closer to the truth than Wisdom.

By the time their breakout group had finished, Oliver counted fifteen out of twenty had identified as Powerheads or Braves, which Cristina had evidently noticed, too. "Only five Wisers, eh?" she said haughtily. "I guess that's not a surprise, not a lot of talent in this year's class by the look of it."

Beto chuckled in agreement. "Look at these three," he said, blatantly pointing at Oliver, Emma, and Lance after Brantley left to notify Zapien they'd completed their icebreakers. "You," he directed at Lance, "grew up on the proper side of the key and don't even know your Gift? Sinovas, for sure."

Before they could retaliate, Brantley returned. "Come on, y'all," he said. "We're wrapped for the evening – lights out in fifteen."

Too angry for words, Oliver stormed to the nearest staircase with Emma and Lance right behind him.

"Can you BELIEVE that James kid?" Lance growled when they were free of the crowd. "Looks as Brave as a turtle!"

Oliver stopped mid-way up the stairs. "What about, Beto?! Thinking he's more of a Powerhead than anyone else?!" He ground his teeth in frustration as Emma interrupted.

"But what was that he was calling us? Sinova?"

# NOVA 01

Lance's eyebrows rose as footsteps sounded behind them. They took the rest of the stairs quickly to distance themselves again. "Yikes!" he said when they reached the top floor. "I don't really know what it means to be honest – just don't go saying it out loud like that! It's a slur of some sort!"

Oliver was stumped at that, if not surprised.

"Listen," Lance continued, "I've never actually heard someone say it out loud. But Elton, my brother, swears mom and dad beat the tar out of him when he said it one time."

Emma's face had soured too much for words. Instead, she glowered at Cristina, whom they could see on the bottom floor from their vantage point on the balcony. From the staircase, Abe emerged, joining them immediately.

"Making friends already, then?" laughed Abe, following Emma's glare to the floor below.

Emma and Lance threw up their wrists to complain. "He called us sinovas!" hissed Lance.

Abe's jaw dropped. "He called you *what?*"

"You heard me," said Lance. "Just ask Brantley!"

"But what does it mean?" interjected Oliver.

Abe almost looked too shocked for words. But after shaking his head in disbelief, he added. "I'll talk to Brantley about it. I'm really sorry you're hearing that classist crap so early in your time here."

"Classist crap?" whispered Emma. "Did he call us peasants or something?" Only now did she cease glaring at Cristina.

## * Chapter 9: The Dean's Threat *

"Yeah, that's exactly what he called you," whispered Abe in a hollow breath. "That word was a slur from, well, when *The Damned* was in Power. But that's all I know. Lord knows the adults won't tell us a thing about it. Every single one of them buttons up the second you bring up the topic."

Shaking her head with fury, Emma stormed off to her room on B2 without properly saying goodnight. "I'll show those three ... the nerve!"

Oliver, who had been internally lambasting himself for showing his emotions to Abe, watched her disappear down the stairs before tapping Lance on the shoulder. "C'mon," he said, "she's got the right idea. If we run into Beto again we might start a fight, and I'm not getting expelled for a fight with that moron!"

Lance agreed, hoisting his hammer over his shoulder with two hands. Before they could take a step, however, they both flinched as they heard a group of voices echo up the stairs.

"Did you hear? That Beto kid said one of the boys introduced himself as the freaking *Trinova*. Who does that?" A combination of laughter and excited questions followed, but Oliver was too disgusted to keep listening. Resisting the urge to tap into the storm he felt outside his ring, he charged ahead to their room instead. He didn't want to say anything he might later regret.

## Chapter 10: An Introduction to Coatlball

*The Power he wields just by looking at all these people – it makes everyone else look like a joke. Only the Whig party puts up a fight, but for all their Wisdom, they lack vision and, most importantly, the Power to implement their will.*

*15<sup>th</sup> of October, the first year of the 10<sup>th</sup> Age*

The next morning, Oliver felt a pang of anger every time he thought of Beto, Cristina, or James. Rolling out of bed, he shook aside his violent thoughts and dashed upstairs with Lance to the Dining Hall. Lance had a bowl of yogurt with extra walnuts to make sure the table wouldn't poke fun at him again. Oliver, however, decided to follow Emma's lead by loading up on eggs, bacon, and oatmeal so he wouldn't tire during the day's introductions to Coatlball, Dungeon-Simulation, and Dueling.

While they ate, Oliver noticed several students had changed into athletic gear. He peered around and saw boys and girls wearing compression pants, breeches, sleeves, and shirts of all colors and varieties. Some, like Beto, also had on tall leather boots of either black or brown with pronounced heel caps.

"Mine are made from box calf imported from Italy," he bragged loudly.

"You best hope we don't import *you* to Italy," grumbled Emma.

"Should we be changing into other clothes?" Oliver asked Lance, gesturing at the khaki shorts and frayed polo he was wearing.

# * Chapter 10: An Introduction to Coatlball *

"Nah," replied Lance between bites of buttered toast. "It's all for show. At our level none of that makes any difference."

Emma nodded her head appreciatively. "It's just like soccer from back home. Is the kid with the best cleats really going to be better than you? No chance! He's just paid for a brand."

"If you say so," Oliver replied with a grimace. "In that scenario I'd have cleats, though. I'm wearing sneakers, and people are out here wearing half a cow on their legs. What are they for anyway?"

Lance snorted his drink. "Oh right! You have no clue what Coatlball is, do you?"

"Isn't it just magical football?" Emma asked.

"Magical football?" came a sneer voice from behind her. "Did she really just say that?"

Beto's hands flanked his hips as he smiled down at them from the vantage point his heel caps provided.

"Oh, Beto, is that you?" said Lance. "Could barely recognize you with all that gear on."

"Go on then," Beto jibed, his smile cruel, "get your jokes in. We'll see who's laughing out on the field."

Oliver turned his chair so he'd be face to face with Beto. He glowered at him, hating that he had no knowledge of Coatlball or any of the other extracurriculars.

"Rumor has it," sneered Cristina, "Oliver here is from a new feeder school."

"What of it?" snarled Emma, turning her chair, too.

## NOVA 01

"It means we've got a Trinova among us," said James, guffawing. "A Trinova, can you believe it, Beto?"

They burst out laughing. As other students began to take notice, Oliver's blood reached a boil. He stood up to meet Beto's face, coming up just short owing to the height provided by Beto's shiny, new boots.

This only made Cristina and James laugh harder.

"Don't worry," Beto said loud enough only for Oliver, Emma, and Lance to hear. "You and I both know the truth, Mr. Trinova. Whatever Gift you do have, it's so weak, none of us can even tell what it is."

Emma stood now, too, revving up to punch Beto right in the face.

"What's going on here?" came an older voice before Emma could follow through. Abe and Brantley had noticed, standing up to join them from their seats with the other RAs.

Beto shrugged carelessly, never flinching at Emma's motion. "Just wishing these three good luck in orientation today."

Before any of them could counter, Beto, Cristina, and James headed towards the exit. "See you on the field, García," he added with a lazy flick of his wrist over his head.

Brantley shook his head at the retreating figures. "I'm willing to bet nice odds they said anything *but* good luck to you three."

"Forget about it," sighed Oliver, collapsing back into his chair. "How are we supposed to do well at a sport we've never played with a Gift we don't even know how to use?" As much as he hated to admit it, Beto had known exactly what was making him feel insecure.

# * Chapter 10: An Introduction to Coatlball *

"A Gift you don't even know how to use?" Abe asked, bemused. "Of course you don't know how to use it, nobody does at the start!"

"Look," continued Brantley, "you'll have a much better idea of what you are after today's intros. Abe here has put down twenty ameys that you're a Wiser. Easiest twenty bucks I'll ever make, if you ask me. Take it from Powerhead to Powerhead,"—he pointed from himself to Oliver several times— "just take on challenges with the rage of a charging bull and you'll know what you are by the end of today."

Despite still feeling insecure, Oliver half-smiled, appreciating the pep talk.

Emma ruffled his hair. "You've got nothing to worry about. We'll outplay them *without* the extra gear."

"On that note," said Abe, checking his watch, "we better head down to the trench. Dean Blackwood won't appreciate anybody being late."

Lance frowned. "Stevie told me Professor Watkin teaches the orientation lesson?"

"He usually does. But –,"

"FOUNDERS HALL," Brantley's voice boomed, interrupting them, "WE'RE MOVING OUT!"

Chairs all around them groaned and scraped as the Extraman Class stood to abandon their breakfasts. Oliver, who didn't much like the idea of Blackwood leading anything, let alone an introduction to the school's premier sport, navigated through the masses to scooch near Abe. "Hey," he muttered as quietly as possible, "why isn't Watkin doing the lesson this afternoon?"

"Said he had to check on something," Abe replied, keeping his eyes on the mass of students around them. On his hands, he counted out a number before nodding and turning to Oliver. "You can ask him when he's back. Still hasn't returned to school yet."

Oliver slowed, rejoining Emma's side before turning to Lance. "Are professors usually this late to the start of a semester?"

"Doubt it," said Lance, matching Oliver's quieter tone. "We can ask Stevie for the inside scoop tonight!"

"Stevie?"

"One of my siblings! She's at school, too," replied Lance. "She and Elton will be coming in tonight with the rest of the older students."

"Oh, I forgot you said you had siblings at school!" said Emma, excitedly. "What are their Gifts?"

"Stevie's a Wiser, but Elton is a Powerhead," continued Lance as they skipped down the double-sided staircase in the main foyer.

"GOOD LUCK TODAY, EXTRAMEN!" interrupted Tolteca from his station between the staircases. "YOU WILL NEED IT!" He wore his grimace of rubies and emeralds as he laughed.

"That's cheery," said Emma, maintaining a wide berth from the sundial.

"THE CHEERIEST, IF YOU ASK ME!" Tolteca replied, winking with an eyelid of heavy stone.

As they made their way outside, the light blinded them while the stiflingly muggy South Carolina air filled their nostrils.

"Never going to get used to that," grumbled Lance, doing his best Tolteca impression at the bright sky.

# * Chapter 10: An Introduction to Coatlball *

"*Iuxtairis*," murmured Abe, who'd stopped ahead of them. "Much better," he added as he blinked his eyes. From past his own squinting eyelids, Oliver noticed Abe sheath his dagger.

"More magic, eh?"

"Hah!" said Abe, looking smug again. "Yeah, that's a popular one here since we go in and out of these temples so much. Helps your eyes adjust."

"Iuxta-iris?" Emma repeated.

"You can go ahead and try it, but without a Channeling lesson, I doubt you'll be able to do it yourself."

"*Iuxtairis!*" Lance shouted with his eyes squeezed tight. "I can't tell if it worked."

"Try opening your eyes, genius," muttered Brantley. He walked past them, towards the eastern wooden bridge, munching on an apple.

"Oh," mumbled Lance, opening his eyes. "Gah! Nope, didn't work."

"*Iuxtairis!*" tried Emma.

"Neither of you tried to channel anything," said Abe, "you just said the words. That'll never do you any good, but you'll learn. One way or another Professor Zapien will get it out of you."

Thinking over Abe's words, Oliver felt for the sun's warmth permeating through the humid air. He relished the thought of the heat, feeling it on his neck, and then down to his fingers.

He stopped, shocked by the feeling in his ring.

Not only could he feel the warmth on his ring finger, but he could practically *see* it. There, amidst the chaos outside his ring finger, he felt a tendril of stable warmth, waiting to be plucked.

## NOVA 01

*"Iuxtairis."*

He yelped and shook his hand as the ring grew hot. Only when he inspected his finger for burns did he notice he could see as clearly as ever, unencumbered by the sun's glare.

"Hey-oh!" yelled Abe, slapping Oliver on the back a little too enthusiastically. "Oli, Oli, Oli! You're a Wiser for sure! What'd you use, the sunlight or the heat already in the air?"

Oliver blushed as he twisted the ring impulsively on his finger. "A bit of both, I think."

"*Nice* one," said Emma, raising her eyebrows at him in quick succession. A wisp of a smile sat on the corner of her mouth.

Oliver couldn't stop a smile from forming on his own lips. "I know what you're gonna say, but that's looney-tunes. I just went after y'all with Abe's advice, that's it. Nothing special."

"Uh-huh," she replied, "came a little easy to you, didn't it?"

"Are you kidding me?" said Lance, jostling closer with a hand still over his own eyes. "Some guys have all the luck."

Oliver rolled his eyes. They were past the eastern bridge now, following Brantley on a pathway that ran adjacent to a smaller temple. A sign at its base bore the word, *"Preston."*

Abe swaggered next to Brantley. "Whatcha think about that, *Brant*-man? My boy, Oli, here, just Wised his way through his first spell! Not starting to worry about our bet, are you?"

Brantley tossed his apple core at him. "More like brute-forced his first spell. That money's finna be the easiest I ever made."

… Chapter 10: An Introduction to Coatlball …

After a bit more poking fun at Oliver, the group passed through a thicket of jungle brush and a shallow creek before arriving at an enormous clearing. Past the clearing on their left, they could see the campus lagoons in the distance. Oliver peered at the fog that still covered the central portion of the waters, wondering if it might ever dissipate.

A new sight, however, distracted him soon enough.

"This is Coatlball?" Emma asked, unconvinced.

Oliver wasn't sure what to think. Was this really where Coatlball was played?

They'd arrived at two sets of brick and stone bleachers overlooking a long trench. He assumed the sport was played in the trench, but he couldn't see how that might be compelling. It was as wide as a soccer field and as deep as a house but what sport could be played on uneven stone? It almost looked like a bumpy racetrack.

Next to him, Lance sniffled. "I've waited my whole life to see this."

Oliver resisted the urge to laugh, but Emma didn't.

"Greatest sport there is," came an unfamiliar voice, that shut up Emma immediately. It belonged to a tall girl Oliver hadn't noticed the previous night. She wore a ponytail, like Emma did now, and reminded Oliver of the kind of the girl who'd show up to a pickup game of soccer for twenty minutes and outscore everybody.

"That's Elizabeth Korzelius," Emma whispered, "she's one of my RAs."

"Didn't think you'd be the hero-worship type," Oliver whispered back.

Emma punched him on the shoulder as he snickered.

## NOVA 01

"I think that's all of them," said Elizabeth. She grinned at Emma as she noticed them squabbling. "Hey, Emma. Didn't see you there."

"Hey," Emma started, but Elizabeth had already bounded ahead.

Oliver watched her go, admiring her posture and athleticism as she jogged down a staircase leading to the middle of the trench. There, Oliver noticed the rest of the RAs and extramen forming a circle around a fluttering mass of feathered serpents.

When they followed, Reggie approached them from the middle of the trench, booming telepathically for them all to hear. *"I have sufficiently digested in time for the Founders' sport."* His throat hummed pleasantly, making him look more like an enormous cat than a bear.

Once they'd joined the mass of people and beasts, a familiar fluttering of wings caught Oliver's ear. The noise relieved some of the nerves he felt in his stomach, so he allowed himself a smile as he saw Archie descend from the sky and circle around him.

*"It's good to see you,"* Archie's voice rang in his head.

His smile dropped, however, at the sight of Blackwood's glower from the middle of the trench. "Glad you could join us," spat the Dean.

"Sorry, sir," said Abe. "We stayed back to make sure nobody had been left behind in the Dining Hall."

But Blackwood didn't look at Abe. Instead, he focused on Archie fluttering around Oliver. At first, the Dean narrowed his eyebrows and cocked his head, as if he were trying to solve a difficult puzzle. But then, he smiled and pointed at Oliver while shaking his head. "*This,* is what brought the great Archie out of retirement?"

# * Chapter 10: An Introduction to Coatlball *

Before Oliver could ask Archie what Blackwood meant, the dean shifted gears. "Whatever. Hey! Ronnie! You're up!"

Ronnie, as it turned out, was one of the RAs. His presence proved popular among the girl RAs, who whooped and cheered as Ronnie's tall and athletic frame stepped to the middle of the watching crowd; Brantley even wolf whistled.

"Settle down y'all," Ronnie yelled, grinning sheepishly. Next to him, a bald eagle let out a terrible screech, quieting the crowd much more effectively than he had. "Thanks, Espie. Okay, everyone, listen up. Objectively speaking, Coatlball is the greatest sport there is."

The RAs cheered.

"The objective of the game is simple. All you have to do is launch what we affectionately refer to as the pigskin," – he caught an American football thrown to him by Blackwood – "into the opposing team's backboard." He gestured north and south towards wooden backboards before launching the "pigskin" as high as he could into the air. With a launch of scratching talons, Espie took off to catch it.

*Scraawww!*

As the crowd marveled, Espie dove towards the southern backboard. "Now," Ronnie continued, pointing towards the sky, "if you'll direct your attention to the mirror."

There was a clamor as each student put a hand over their eyes to peer past the sunlight. Sure enough, the largest replay screen Oliver had ever seen in his life floated above them. From it, a feed of Espie was shown hurtling towards the Earth. Seconds later, she released the ball, whereupon it clattered to a halt within a net occupying the middle of the southern backboard.

"Nice one," said Ronnie as the RAs clapped. "You get one point for hitting the backboard or three points for hitting the net. But that looked like it may have been past thirty yards so it may be worth double – ah, thought so!" Beneath the live feed of Espie's return flight, a set of numbers read 6 – 0.

"So, that's about it, I think?" said Ronnie, looking around confidently.

Blackwood, however, shook his head, unimpressed. "And the movement? The passing?"

"That's right!" Ronnie replied, snapping his fingers. "Can't believe I forgot. Your Guide can't actually score points, Espie was just demonstrating for us. Only humans can score. That's why the points double and triple if you hit the net from past thirty and fifty yards, respectively."

Blackwood growled, crossing his enormous forearms. "The movement, Mr. Zimmer!"

"Right," Ronnie continued, blustering slightly. "Well, everyone has the honor and privilege of riding their Guide during the game. If you are paired with an osorius, you can move in any direction you please, with or without the pigskin in hand." Reggie hummed deeply behind them all. "If you're paired with an eagle or serpent, you play in the sky!"

"Quiet!" yelled Blackwood as the crowd broke out into whispers. Some, like Lance, had even cheered.

# * Chapter 10: An Introduction to Coatlball *

"Don't get too excited," Ronnie yelled at the crowd. "If you're holding the ball in the sky, your movement is limited to up, down, left, right, or back, but never forward. Let's watch a quick video."

On the jumbo mirror, a video of an offensive movement began to play. Riding a roaring osorius, Elizabeth Korzelius barreled down the trench. As they watched, the RAs heckled the real Elizabeth, pointing between her and the mirror with sarcastic wonder. Before long, her mirror twin passed the pigskin high in the air towards a rider on a feathered serpent.

"Mr. Zimmer forgot to mention, you can only hold the ball for five seconds!" said Dean Blackwood. "And don't think you can bend the rule, there's a magical timer in place so there can be no cheating. This is the most frequent cause of turnovers."

The video above continued, where an unrecognizable student caught the ball. He moved sharply to the left and then backwards to dodge an enormous fireball. Oliver wondered if a dragon was about to enter the feed, but it paused, capturing a comical look of horror on the rider's face.

"Forgot to mention," said Ronnie, scratching the back of his head, "almost all magic is allowed during the game. Literally anything you can think of is legal. You just can't directly attack a player's body or mind."

Oliver smiled at Emma and Lance, raising his eyebrows quickly at the possibilities.

"For example," said Ronnie motioning towards the mirror, "you can launch a fireball at someone, but you can't directly light someone's skin on fire." He resumed the video whereupon the rider passed the ball to Ronnie. Amidst the heckling that followed, Ronnie yelled out, "as the person being attacked, it's your decision whether you want to defend yourself with magic, dodge, or pass!"

As if prompted, his mirror-version passed the ball to Katie Sanders, Emma's other RA. A moment later, Ronnie joined her side as she magicked a brick wall into existence in front of them. Nodding, they began passing the ball back and forth in short, forward movements. The brick wall took a battering as they progressed down the trench.

"This is a really common move every team can use. Off screen, the other team is double-teaming Elizabeth, our only teammate on an osori who can move forward with the ball. Seeing the trap, Katie and I used the 'hot-potato' tactic to move forward. Even though we're on winged Guides, technically, neither of us is moving forward with the ball in hand. And then, once you get close enough," – the video feed zoomed in on Espie, who cut sharply right to dodge a murder of crows, and then Ronnie, who launched the pigskin directly into the backboard's net in slow motion – "you score!"

The girl RAs cheered, and Brantley fluttered sarcastically into Abe's unamused arms, knocking him back several feet.

Blackwood's deep voice interrupted the outbreak. "Yes, yes," he said, pushing Ronnie into the crowd where Brantley caught him, "thank you, Mr. Zimmer. Champayan will miss you this year."

He glowered at the extramen for a moment, as if Ronnie leaving his dorm was their fault, before eventually curling his lip into a sardonic grin. "Since 1692, we've played Coatlball on these grounds. Only now, with Nova's return, can it be played at its fullest potential. The easiest way to learn, however, is to get out there and actually play." Pausing, he clapped

# * Chapter 10: An Introduction to Coatlball *

his saucer hands together and rubbed. "Let's do the half to my right as the northern team, and the half to my left as the southern team."

Thankful to look at anything else but Blackwood's bald head and rippling forearms, Oliver turned to see who else besides Emma and Lance might be on his team. He felt better when he saw Katie, Alex, Brantley, and Abe separate from the throng of RAs to join his team.

"Alright everybody," Brantley drawled. "Mount up!"

Still somewhat awestruck by Archie's mere existence, Oliver watched him touch down onto the stone. Around them, the other feathered serpents followed Archie's lead until the trench felt eerily quiet at the lack of fluttering from their wings.

On the ground, Oliver thought Archie looked more like a horned python covered in feathers. Before he shared the comparison, however, he caught himself. No sense in accidentally insulting one of his only friends.

Making sure not to cause any injuries, Oliver proceeded cautiously to where Archie's wings connected to the upper third of his body. After a quick breath, he clambered on, squeezing his knees hard on either side of Archie's frame.

"*If you ever begin to fall,*" Archie hummed reassuringly, "*hold onto the longer feathers. Those can't be pulled out.*"

Oliver reached forward and grabbed two handfuls of feathers. They felt coarser than expected, but he didn't have much time to think about it. In a whirlwind of fluttering wings, Archie took off.

## NOVA 01

Flight on a feathered serpent, Oliver discovered, felt like an out-of-control roller coaster ride. One moment, his stomach would lurch against his diaphragm, making him feel sick, the next, he'd begin to slide off until he remembered to squeeze his legs and grab onto rough feathers that left light cuts in his hands. With every twist and turn, the nausea in his stomach mounted. As he began to feel sick, he closed his eyes and pressed himself close to Archie's back.

Within his fingers, static electricity jumped from one set of plumage to the next, reminding him of the stable strand of energy he'd felt from the sun when using *iuxtairis*. Instinctively, he thought back to when Abe removed the nausea Emma felt after riding the skydraft back at the airport.

*"Remasco!"* he cried.

Even though Archie continued to circle in the air, the world immediately stabilized in front of him. When he felt comfortable enough, he straightened his back and smiled at his ring finger. Casting magic was far easier than he thought it'd be.

Archie stopped to bob in place with large slow beats of his wings, causing Oliver's thighs to smart. *"That was an impressive piece of magic for one so young. Look around, your classmates continue to struggle."*

Sure enough, all around them, extramen and serpents wrestled to conquer flight together. Emma flew around on Rasmus overhead in out-of-control spirals. *"Hold still!"* they heard Rasmus yell. Lance, meanwhile, kept jumping off as soon as Merri began to flutter her wings – "Sorry!" he

*191*

# * Chapter 10: An Introduction to Coatlball *

grumbled, "I'll stay on this time." Nearby, Trey and Se'Vaughn both kept pulling their Guides' feathers so hard they shot straight up into the air.

Oliver almost began to laugh at the sight of his struggling classmates, but then he locked eyes with Beto twenty or so yards away. He had wrangled his feathered serpent and currently bobbed in place just like Oliver did, only he looked far more the complete package with riding boots and breeches. While Oliver's thighs began to feel raw at Archie's movements, Beto undoubtedly had enough padding to keep his legs comfortable for hours.

They maintained eye-contact for a moment, Oliver from Archie's back, and Beto from the back of his ruby-red Guide. Oliver was just about to hurl a comment at him, but Archie surprised him with a sudden dive towards Rasmus and Merri.

*"Do not look to make enemies so early into your tenure."*

"Hey!" Oliver snorted back. "That kid started it! He pushed me for no good reason last night and has been insulting Emma, Lance, and me, ever since!"

Archie stopped just short of the cobblestones on the surface of the trench where he exhaled steam. *"At least you've made a friend to cancel out the enemy."*

Olive waved the steam away, grumbling. "Fine. I won't call him an enemy. But he's definitely not a friend!"

Archie surprised him by laughing, which felt disconcerting under his legs. *"Humans can be so haughty. I often stress they try to look at the bigger picture. Then again, I'm not overly fond of his Guide either."*

## NOVA 01

Unsure of how to reply to an ancient being's observation on its own species, Oliver opted to focus on Abe instead, who was barreling over to them from the vantage point of Reggie's back.

"How's this group doing, Reg? Oh-ho! Oli, I see you had the WISDOM to fix yourself up already. Nicely done. The rest of you however …"

With a flurry of his blade, Abe cantered Reggie forward and fixed up the surrounding group in quick fashion. Beyond their nearby cluster, similar scenes unfolded as Brantley, Katie, and Elizabeth yelled *"remasco"* at struggling students. After a few moments, the entire congregation of students and Guides bobbed up and down, ready to play.

The next thirty minutes demonstrated little about the sport of Coatlball. Having never played before, most of the extramen seemed ecstatic to simply put together a dozen consecutive passes. Oliver and Emma were even able to try out the hot potato maneuver to great effect, but Beto and James blocked them before they traveled more than thirty yards down the trench.

More often than not, the new students struggled with the movement-based rules. For anyone who had grown up playing football or soccer, the instinct was to move forward, not sideways when catching the ball. This led to turnover after turnover being called from a frustrated Dean Blackwood, who surveyed them from the back of a wizened giant eagle.

"No, no, no, Mr. Kemper," he yelled at Trey. "You cannot *move* forward! You can only *pass* forward! It's really not that complicated!"

By the end of the thirty minutes the Dean's voice grew hoarse from all the yelling. His critiques turned soft, and his exuberance died down, which

# * Chapter 10: An Introduction to Coatlball *

allowed the game to dissolve into a group of ten or so students on each side who felt more invested than the remaining forty.

On the southern team, the remaining players included Oliver, Emma, and Lance, and on the northern team, Beto, Cristina, and James. Once Dean Blackwood realized the majority of the students had stopped playing, however, he blew a large whistle, calling an end to the proceedings.

"Well, there you have it!" he yelled. "As is tradition, your dorm head will determine your team. But rest assured, I'll be having a word with her about who would be a good fit,"—he motioned towards Beto, making Emma scoff audibly— "and who wouldn't," he added threateningly towards Oliver, Emma, and Lance.

As they dismounted their Guides on the ground below, Oliver asked Archie why the Dean had mentioned his coming out of retirement.

Archie didn't immediately respond, and Oliver thought he saw Rasmus bolt away as soon as the question left his lips. So had all of the other serpents, for that matter.

*"Well,"* Archie sighed, *"truth be told, Dean Blackwood was right. I retired nearly fifteen years ago and hadn't planned on coming back into service until Dr. Lalandra approached me over the summer."*

"Why'd you retire?" Oliver asked.

Archie turned his head, staring solemnly at Oliver, but Oliver didn't look away. For the first time, he wondered just how old Archie was.

*"Maybe someday, I'll tell you. But for now, enjoy the rest of your orientation. I must lead the feathered serpents to our staff meeting."*

## NOVA 01

As Archie zoomed away to join the rest of the feathered serpents, Emma pulled her hair out of its ponytail and turned her hands into fists. "That *Dean* has it out for us. We played better than Beto! Why'd he give us a look?" By the time she finished speaking, she grabbed Oliver by his polo shirt and shook him emphatically.

"Geez, alright!" said Oliver, slapping her hands away. "The Dean's got it out for us. But never mind that, did you hear me talking to Archie?"

Lance chuckled. "You mean your telepathic conversation with your Guide? Of course we didn't hear that, ya bum."

"Right ..." said Oliver, "well, do you remember what Blackwood said when we got to the trench?"

"I love Beto?" muttered Lance. "Maybe we should get some breeches, too, my legs are killing me."

"No!" said Oliver. "Oh, well yeah, maybe about the breeches, but no about Blackwood! He laughed at Archie for coming out of retirement for me. What do you think that's about?"

"Who knows?" said Lance. "Maybe he just wanted to settle down and enjoy his golden years?"

Oliver thought back to the moment, remembering the Dean's curling upper lip.

"I don't think so ..." he said. "There was something the Dean was satisfied about."

"Well!" Emma interrupted, "we're not gonna find out now, are we? They've all gone away to their feathery staff meeting."

*195*

# * Chapter 10: An Introduction to Coatlball *

Not wanting to belabor the point, Oliver dropped the conversation as they followed the RAs to a giant, brick building standing closer to the landing strip at the top of the ridge than Founders Temple.

Strangely, the building had no windows. As far as Oliver could tell, the only way inside it was through an ornate archway facing the lagoons at the bottom of the ridge. Above the entry, a large sign read "Simulation Room," which made him think back to the extracurriculars listed on his magical notebook. Hadn't Dungeon-Simulation been one of them?

"That's right!" Abe told nobody in particular as the extramen congregated around the windowless building. "This is where boys are turned to men, where legends are forged, and where mortals attempt to break my record: the Simulation Room."

"Geez, Abe," muttered Brantley, shaking his head. "Humble much? You earn one trophy and suddenly you're a king?"

The rest of the students followed, none too curious about Abe's record in the Simulation Room.

"But I did it faster than anyone before," Abe faltered.

"We know," said Brantley, putting a hand on his shoulder. "A record we'll never remember."

As it turned out, the Simulation Room magically expanded on the inside, occupying an even larger space than Oliver realized. When they settled into the observation deck above the dungeon, Brantley asked the extramen to spectate the RAs while they attempted to navigate the current dungeon below. It didn't take long for every angle of the glass perimeter to be monitored by the eager extramen.

## NOVA 01

As far as Oliver was concerned, Dungeon-Simulation was a severely underrated activity. It may not have had the glamor or reckless pace of Coatlball, but he found it fascinating to watch the RAs advance from room to room, looking for keys or clues. In the second to last room, they fought off giant spiders and poison-fanged bats as Abe tried solving a riddle in front of a sinister, black door with claw marks on it. By the time Abe figured it out, only he, Katie, and Clay remained. The rest had perished in either embarrassing or spectacular fashion, teleporting onto the observatory deck after elimination.

"Oh, this should be good," said Brantley from behind Oliver's shoulder after one of the spider's had eliminated him. Below them, Abe gave Katie and Clay an animated pep-talk before they crossed the threshold of the black door.

As soon as Abe's leading foot crossed into the room, a skeleton of a humanoid lizard emerged from a pile of bones, banging a broadsword against an oaken shield. It bellowed silently at them before charging. After a few tense minutes of dodging, ducking, and weaving, Abe and Katie emerged victorious over the skeleton's crumpled remains. Clay had been eliminated after the simulated broadsword contacted his torso. Had they really been fighting a seven-foot lizard, he would have been cleaved into two. Instead, he teleported from the dungeon and joined the watching crowd, looking slightly delirious as Brantley goggled at him mercilessly. "Why didn't ya duck?"

*197*

## * Chapter 10: An Introduction to Coatlball *

Moments later, Oliver, Emma, and Lance were still trading animated retellings of Abe's heroics when they arrived at their third and final venue of the morning: the Dueling Strip.

This time outdoors, the Dueling Strip exuded a simplistic elegance. Here, short bleachers of black marble flanked either side of a narrow strip of white marble, where contestants would face off. Flames from in-ground light fixtures licked the surface of the white marble, creating shades of pink and blue.

"Imagine kicking Beto's butt in front of a crowd," said Emma dreamily.

To orientate the extramen, the RAs held a tournament amongst themselves. Among them, Katie and Elizabeth proved to be the best. Each of the duels didn't take long as all it took was for one of the duelists to yield or fall out of the marble strip for a winner to be declared.

At one point, Abe shot backwards, propelled by a spring-trap spell in a match against Katie. Oliver winced as Abe flew through the air, anticipating a rough landing, but smiled as he saw him decelerate onto fluffy cushions that appeared from nowhere.

By the time the RA tournament finished, the sun beamed down at them all, prompting Brantley to direct them all back to Founders Temple for lunch.

"Amazing," said Emma through a mouthful of lemon-herb chicken. "I want to try out for all of them. Coatlball, Dungeon-Simulation, Dueling, you name it. We're gonna do them all."

"Thank goodness we don't have to try out to join Blackwood's team," grumbled Oliver.

# NOVA 01

"Yeah, I've been wondering about Blackwood," pipped Lance. "Any idea why he looks at you like a bowl of maggots?"

Emma and Oliver exchanged looks. He nodded his head at her, indicating they could now trust him. She nodded her head back and leaned in so only they could hear.

"Something happened when Oliver first got his ring," she said, giving her best impression of Miyada the Blacksmith.

Lance raised his eyebrows and scooted his chair in. "And you hadn't told me? I'm the one from This Side of the Key, aren't I? What happened?"

"Well, Oliver went all rigid when he put the ring on his finger," Emma continued in barely more than a whisper. "It looked like he got shot with lightning and then the blacksmith in the shop went ballistic. He said Oliver was something called the Prophet's Advent and he had to contact the school about it. Maybe Blackwood knows."

Lance dropped his fork.

"The Prophet's Advent?" he mouthed, paler than the rice on his plate. "I thought Emma had been joking."

"She was!" said Oliver, a little too loudly.

"Look, you three," said Abe, causing all three of them to jump. Oliver hadn't realized he'd been snooping on their conversation, but to his relief, Abe mirrored their stooped shoulders and hushed tones before looking around cautiously to make sure nobody else was also eavesdropping. "Don't go sharing that story in public ever again! You never said anything to me at the Airport about something crazy happening when you first touched magic!" He paused to take an open chair next to Lance. "Look, the

# Chapter 10: An Introduction to Coatlball

last person people thought was the Prophet's Advent turned out to be the second coming of the devil himself. If anyone hears you're calling Oliver that, you're in for a world of attention you do *not* want."

"Archie said the same thing!" Emma whispered excitedly. "Remember, Oliver? At Jacque's Joint in Davidstown? He said *The Damned* was supposed to be the Prophet's Advent when he was at school and then became eviler than evil or something."

Abe's jaw dropped. "Your *Guide* told you this? That's irregular."

"He didn't want us to be unprepared coming in to school after what we saw in Miyada's armory!" Emma said impatiently.

Abe squinted his eyes and motioned towards Oliver's right hand. "Let me see your ring."

"What?" hissed Oliver. He scrambled to put his hands under his legs.

"Fine! Fine!" shot Abe, raising his arms in peace. "Look, all I know is that Augustus left a scroll for the Prophet's Advent to find. But, if you ask me, it's likely just a legend, like the Holy Grail! Don't waste your time talking about it, or the Advent, in general, unless you want everyone to think you're a lunatic!"

"Too late for that …" moaned Lance. "Beto's already started telling people that Oli is the Prophet's Advent. He threatened that yesterday remember?"

Abe closed his eyes and shook his head. "I'll talk to the RAs about it, but I'm not sure how much damage control can be done." He stood up to leave with a grimace on his face. "In the meantime, drop all conversations about anything special from now on, okay? If anybody asks, Oli's a Wiser.

## NOVA 01

I'll make sure Brantley says the same. He can keep the money." He stood up to leave, concern etched across his face.

Emma, meanwhile, grinned devilishly at Oliver.

"How are you smiling at a time like this?" Oliver shot impatiently.

"He just gave us some spicy intel," said Emma, looking haughty. "Looks like there's a hidden scroll on campus for us to find."

\* **Chapter 10: An Introduction to Coatlball** \*

## Chapter 11: Shadows of the Past

*I'm spending a lot of time reading about long-dead people these days. He seems to think it's important to learn from them. But everything I'm researching is about where they died, not where they lived. He's withholding some key information and I'm going to find out what it is.*

*17th of November, the first year of the 10th Age*

As Oliver mulled over the idea of a potentially hidden message left behind by Augustus, the older students began to arrive.

Most came from the platform above the clouds, screaming as their carriages descended at reckless speeds. Others arrived by regular, old cars, their families opting to distrust the sky pillars or barges on their way to school. For the parents and siblings with previous exposure to the Academy, cheerful goodbyes ensued, along with wistful retellings of their own time at the school.

The extramen, meanwhile, were allowed a few hours break before the Start of Year Feast.

After washing off the sweat and grime from their introductions to Coatlball, Dungeon-Simulation, and Dueling, Oliver and Lance changed into a set of the school uniforms they'd found in their closets.

Oliver felt stuffy while wearing boots, breeches, and a collared shirt, but there wasn't any point in complaining about it. Beginning with the feast, the uniform would be required for all meals and classes.

# * Chapter 11: Shadows of the Past *

Still thinking over Augustus' scroll, he stepped out their room, heading towards the circular staircase leading to the rest of their wing below. Before he took his first stair, however, Lance stopped him with an outstretched arm. With his other, he placed a finger to his lips and pointed down.

"I spoke to Professor Zapien about it," they heard Brantley grunt, "but she said, 'don't worry about it.'"

"What do you mean, don't worry about it?" spluttered Abe. "If some of these kids start texting their parents about a Trinova being in their class – or worse, the Prophet's Advent."

Oliver felt his heart drop. They were talking about *him*.

"He can't be a Trinova," Brantley hissed. "They're just a myth! You've always said it yourself – no real evidence!"

"Every single Age of Proximity has someone or some *thing* fitting the bill!"

Brantley scoffed. "Pshh! You're just making things fit your narrative."

"Genghis Khan! The founding of Carthage! Sumerian city states! There's nothing to force, it's all there!"

Beginning to feel nauseated, Oliver crept back into their room, unwilling to hear the rest of the conversation. Behind him, Lance followed, shutting the door.

"You alright?" Lance asked.

"I think Emma's right," Oliver muttered. He peered around the room, feeling antsy, until his eyes stopped at their window. Sunlight trickled through the glass panes invitingly. Now that he thought about it, their room might be the only one with a window above water level.

"If," he continued, "there's a scroll left on campus for the Prophet's Advent to find, maybe we should take a peek just to prove it's not me."

Lance swallowed. "What makes you think we could find it? I bet every student since the 1700s has looked around."

Oliver ignored the question because he didn't have a good answer. Instead, he gestured at the window. "Think we can get this open?"

With a loud *crack*, they managed it open, ruining a fresh coat of paint in the process. Shrugging at the damage, they clambered outside, finding themselves in between the southern and eastern bridges.

Lance grinned, looking down at their now-closed window. It looked as innocuous as a ventilation grate. "That'll come in handy more than once."

Ignoring the temptation to stay outside and enjoy the sun, Oliver led them back around the temple to reenter from the main entrance. As they crossed into the double-staired foyer, however, they came face to face with Tolteca.

"CHILDREN!" announced the sundial. "I DON'T REMEMBER SEEING YOU LEAVE."

Oliver stammered as he felt his heart skip a beat. Had they already ruined their secret escape route?

"Well, Mr. Tolteca," he began.

"The thing is," added Lance.

"I MUST HAVE MISSED IT." Tolteca finished, winking. "BACK INSIDE YOU GO."

\* Chapter 11: Shadows of the Past \*

Not wanting to give the sundial an opportunity to change his mind, they sprinted until they reached the eastern viewing dome at the bottom floor where Emma waited for them.

She'd also changed into boots, breeches, and a collared shirt, but while Oliver had attempted to comb his hair, she'd left hers in a messy, red bun on the top of her head. She pulled off the look much better than he did.

Lance laughed at the sight of her. "You look like my sister, Stevie, wearing a bun like that. Are you rebelling against the establishment, too?"

Emma pushed together her lips appreciatively as she sat on one of the armchairs. "Maybe. Any luck with the research?"

Oliver shook his head, taking the arm on her chair to look at her notebook. "No, and sorry we're late. We had to sneak out through our window. Couldn't go down the stairs because Abe and Brantley we're talking about me."

Emma raised her eyebrows. "What'd they say?"

"Nothing we haven't already heard. More Trinova rumors."

"Hmm," said Emma, handing him her notebook. "Not much in there other than our course syllabi, a map, and this glossary I just started going through. I was just reading an entry on the feathered serpents."

Amongst a sea of words on the notebook, Oliver saw Quetzal occupy a single entry. *Quetzal: The Quetzal, or feathered serpent, is a species of large, heavy-bodied, nonvenomous snake. Despite weighing up to one thousand pounds, the species is capable of flight at birth, featuring (i) coarse feathers from head to tip, (ii) long, thin wings, and (iii) a sharp upper mandible resembling a beak more than the nose of a snake.*

# NOVA 01

*First encountered in North America during the fourth millennium BCE, the Quetzal is thought to predate humanity.*

"Interesting," Oliver mused, "but not exactly helpful." He scrolled up absentmindedly to see if anything else might catch his attention.

Before long, he shot up, his stomach twisting.

Not far above *Quetzal*, the words *Prophet's Advent* shone innocently up at him.

He sputtered. "Emma! Right above it!"

Without a word, she pulled the notebook out of his grasp and read aloud. *"The Prophet's Advent refers to the prophecy of a $10^{th}$ Age Trinova. Though purportedly issued by Augustus Henderson during the $9^{th}$ Age of Darkness, no records of a formally issued prophecy exist. The legend persists verbally to the present day, indicating a student from a previously non-magical background and school will rise as a Trinova during the $10^{th}$ Age of Magical Proximity to maintain the balance of man."*

"The balance of man?" Emma wondered aloud. "What do you think that's supposed to mean?"

"Haven't got a clue," said Oliver, deep in thought.

Emma looked at him, a wry smile on her face. "Oli, there's too much smoke here for the legend not to be true. Miyada knew something about it, Archie and Rasmus certainly do, and even the school has it in their public glossary!" She shook the notebook emphatically. "I'm not saying you're guaranteed to be the Prophet's Advent or anything ridiculous like that, but shouldn't we at least try to find the scroll?"

Lance butted in quicker than Oliver cared to reply. "He's already decided to find it – only to prove it isn't him."

# * Chapter 11: Shadows of the Past *

Oliver tired not smiling back at their eager faces when he did reply. "Alright, y'all. If we start making it obvious we're looking for this scroll, that's only going to make rumors of me being obnoxious spread even faster. And to be honest with you, that terrifies me. I still haven't ruled out that I might show up to the Ceremony of the Gifts and find out I have *no* Gift."

"Don't be silly," said Emma, settling down on the coffee table. "Between you, me, and Lance, you're the only one who could use *iuxtairis*, remember?"

Oliver thought that was a good point and resisted the urge to add he'd already performed *remasco*, too. "If we search for this thing, not a word to anyone but Abe and Brantley, okay? You should've heard them. The subject gets everybody on edge!"

"How many times do I have to cross my heart?" muttered Lance as Emma nodded her head vigorously. "Can we at least ask Stevie and Elton if they've heard of a scroll since starting school? They're bound to have heard something while at school before us and they should be moving into Hutch right now."

Emma looked at Oliver and raised her eyebrows. "Well, we don't have to tell them anything about you specifically. We can play it cool and say there've been rumors floating about it and we just want to learn."

Before replying, Oliver deliberated inside his own head.

On the one hand, he didn't want people to hear him talking about trinovas, prophets, or anything else that might get him labeled as a nutjob. On the other hand, if he felt he could trust Lance, maybe talking to his siblings for more information wouldn't be too risky.

## NOVA 01

Still somewhat hesitant, he eventually agreed, causing Lance to cheer and lead them outside again. Instead of turning west as they had done to reach the Coatlball trench, this time Lance led them east across one of the bridges he and Oliver had seen earlier. Moments later, they arrived at a smaller temple. A plaque on its façade bore the word, "Hutch."

Unlike Founders, all of Hutch stood above ground. Even more surprising was the amount of noise that greeted them on the second floor.

From one room, lights and hip-hop music overwhelmed their senses. Inside another, they glimpsed a cheering crowd congregated around a cardboard box. "Go on! Pick it up!" someone from the crowd yelled. An unidentifiable squelching noise followed, making Oliver's stomach churn, but Lance shook his head until they reached a larger room towards the end of the hall.

"This," he said cautiously, "should be Elton's room."

Curious to see what a dorm room for older students looked like, Oliver peered inside.

"STOP!" bellowed a voice. "IS THAT SIR LANCE-A-LOT?"

"Oh no," muttered Lance, attempting to back up.

But it was too late.

From the room, a barrel-chested boy emerged, hurtling towards Lance in a blur of pink and yellow. A second later, Lance's eyes popped as the boy crushed him within a hug.

"You found the pain cave all by yourself!" the boy growled. "I'm so proud."

# * Chapter 11: Shadows of the Past *

"Cut it out, Elton," Lance gasped. "Meet my friends, Emma and Oliver."

Elton dropped Lance, and offered his hand to Emma – "Enchantée" – and then Oliver – "so you're the kid Brant-man messaged us about, huh?"

Oliver's hand went limp inside Elton's mammoth paw as they continued shaking.

"Don't worry," Elton added as Emma flared her nostrils. "Your secret is safe with us. Step into my office." He pushed them into the room before any of them could say a word.

Inside, a thin purple fabric draped underneath the over-head lighting, giving the room an atmospheric and hazy look. In the corner, a girl with long blonde hair sat playing a bass guitar. Her hair was wrapped together in an unceremonious bun.

"What's good, my extramen?" she said, continuing to pluck at the guitar's strings.

"Cheese and rice," grumbled Elton, "if you're gonna play that dang thing, do it in your own room!" He grabbed the guitar out of the girl's hands and tossed it onto his bed.

"Whatever, dude," she said, running a hand through her hair to fix her bun. "Y'all are Brant's kids too, right?" She gestured at Oliver and Emma inquisitively.

They nodded their heads.

"Right on!" she said, leaning forward in her chair and clapping. "Let's get to it then." She pointed at Oliver. "You, you're Oli, the Powerful Wiser who may or may not be a Trinova, right?"

"Umm," said Oliver, looking at Emma for help.

"He's just a Wiser," said Emma, coolly.

The girl grinned knowingly in reply. "Yeah, that's the memo we got from Brantley too. Listen, my name's Stevie, and I'm the oldest of the lot, so naturally, that also means I'm the smartest." She paused to gesture at herself theatrically. Oliver didn't know whether he should laugh or not, so he opted for an awkward smile instead.

"Yikes," said Lance. "Look, we just wanted to ask what y'all have learned about trinovas since starting school."

"Well, that's what's interesting, isn't it?" said Stevie waving her hands about. "We've hardly learned anything at all. Ask a professor and they'll tell you it's a myth, nothing to know! Only Professor Watkin briefly mentions it as an old legend during his World History classes."

"Sometimes," chimed in Elton, "it feels like everyone older than us is hiding something. Too many hints and whispers and smoke – hey! Easy there!" Lance had picked up a pigskin and tossed it towards him.

Stevie ignored the ball that now went back and forth between the two brothers. Instead, she raised her eyebrows and nodded suggestively at Oliver and Emma. "Where there's smoke, there's fire, you know?"

"What kind of smoke are we talking about?" Emma asked, giving Oliver an I-told-you-so kind of look.

"Well, for starters," said Elton, "nobody ever teaches a thing about *The Damned*."

# * Chapter 11: Shadows of the Past *

Stevie slapped him on the back of the head and gestured towards the open door where the squelching noises grew louder. "Wait until the door's closed next time, egg-head," she scolded.

"Mom and Dad never talked about it," Lance agreed, shutting the door quietly, "but I thought it was always just them being scared."

Stevie looked at him with a smug expression. "Scared? Or embarrassed."

"Embarrassed?" Oliver repeated inquisitively.

"Hey, you can talk!" Elton cried, slapping Oliver's back, nearly breaking him in half.

Stevie rolled her eyes. "You'll have to forgive, Elton. He's part gorilla."

Elton grinned. "Why, thank you." The pigskin flew overhead again.

"Yes, embarrassed or in denial," Stevie continued. "Not many of the professors will tell you this, but they don't teach modern day history right for a reason." She stepped towards Oliver with wide eyes and raised hands. "One after-hours session, Abe got Watkin to spill the beans, you see." Oliver, Emma, and Lance stared at Stevie, transfixed. "Apparently, *The Damned* convinced not just a few, but pretty much everyone to do some terrible stuff."

"What kind of stuff?" Oliver asked.

"Oh, that we don't know," said Stevie, dropping her hands. "But I'd guess it'd have something to do with politics."

The door flung open with a bang, causing them all to jump.

A group of eight or so students barreled in with the squelching cardboard box, pushing Oliver, Emma, and Lance to the rear of the room. "WE'RE TAKING BETS," yelled a tall boy carrying the box. He shook it with strong arms as he stepped around the room. By standing on the tips of their toes, Oliver, Emma, and Lance could see two enormous slugs charging at each other in the box – one red and the other blue. "I've offered two to one odds on the red one here – OHHHHHHH!" The crowd yelled and gagged. The red slug had just slammed onto the blue slug causing goo to splatter the purple cloth overhead along with the boy's long dreadlocks.

"C'mon," said Lance. "I don't want to get in trouble on day one."

"But the slugs!" said Emma, continuing to peer excitedly into the box even as Oliver dragged her out of the room.

Dashing back down the stairs, they soon found themselves outside where the sun had begun its descent. Hungry, Oliver directed them straight back to the Dining Hall.

"D'you think Stevie was right?" he asked as the eastern bridge passed beneath their feet.

"About what?" said Lance, scratching his ear.

Oliver rolled his eyes impatiently. "About the professors and adults. And probably our Guides, for that matter. Do you think they're hiding something?"

"It kinda fits what Archie and Rasmus were saying, right?" said Emma, furrowing her eyebrows. "They told us to never mention the Prophet in public because *The Damned* had told everyone he was a Prophet. What if it's bigger than that? What if everyone believed him?"

Oliver's skin crawled at the line of questioning. Could everyone in the country really have been party to a movement started by a man so evil his name had been erased?

# * Chapter 11: Shadows of the Past *

"Only one way to find out, really," said Lance, shrugging. "We've gotta find that scroll and see if it's real! Maybe this Watkin guy could tell us more. Stevie said Abe got him to talk."

In agreement, they entered the foyer and headed upstairs for the Start of Year Feast, with a convoy from Hutch not far behind.

Before the Dining Table would listen to Lance's requests for food, Headmaster Lalandra spoke again, welcoming back the older students and reminding them of the rules with a wry smile. At one point during her speech, Oliver thought she met his eyes for longer than usual, but he couldn't be sure.

When she finished speaking, a chorus of orders bounced around the high ceilings as hungry students requested their meals.

Plates of beef bourguignon proved popular, along with braised short-rib, and elegant ratatouille for vegetarians like Stevie. Then, before long, they switched over to ice cream, pie, cake, and decaf coffees to enjoy while discussing what lay ahead in the new year.

Though Oliver stayed mostly quiet, he enjoyed listening to the others talk about what excited them. Emma, for instance, couldn't wait to get up to speed on dueling so she could feel the rush of defeating her competitors. Other Braves, like Se'Vaughn, nodded along with her as she spoke but only Oliver knew she daydreamt of crushing Beto, Cristina, and James, specifically.

In all the excitement, the minutes quickly turned to hours and before long, the RAs began shepherding the extramen back down to their dorm rooms. Elton surprised them then, giving Lance an aggressive rub of the head before he could escape down the stairs. After the brief exchange, that left Lance glaring, Elton departed with Stevie, who waved goodbye lazily.

With his belly full, it didn't take long for Oliver to fall asleep after he and Lance crashed to a halt in their beds.

At first, he dreamt about the trip with Emma to the platform above the clouds. Then, his mind wandered to less pleasant memories, like Blackwood's cruel laugh. Was Oliver too skinny for the Dean's liking? Did all Powerheads have the same kind of body type? Did it mean he definitely wasn't one?

He turned in his bed, dragging his sheets with him.

Next, the weight of Dr. Lalandra's stares pressed down on him. This too made him feel uncomfortable. Did she think he was a Wiser like Abe? Wouldn't she have introduced herself instead of stare if she thought well of him?

Finally, his dreams turned more vivid.

He'd arrived at a sunny concrete clearing, momentarily blinded. As his vision adjusted, he realized he stood in the same airport clearing just before the skydraft. Only this time, Emma and Abe were nowhere to be seen, and his forearms tingled.

Panic-stricken, he looked up. At the top of the westward wall, the same shadow as before peered down at him. From its vantage point, it jumped down and approached him.

Oliver wanted to run, but as the figure drew closer, its stare immobilized him. The world began to shrink around him as the shadow stepped closer and closer, forcing the air from his lungs and burdening his legs with an

## Chapter 11: Shadows of the Past

unmovable weight. He couldn't move. He couldn't shout for help. All he could do was face his attacker.

Before the figure could strike, the vision faded, only to be replaced by a sea of blinding white light.

"*Iuxtairis*," Oliver muttered, bringing three unfamiliar people into focus. Two men and a woman turned to face him from the foot of a small temple enshrouded by trees. They were oddly dressed, with furs over linen shirts and cotton breeches. Where their eyes might have been, cold, white spheres blinked creepily, but from them, Oliver felt no imminent threat.

"Who are you?" he asked bravely.

The closer of the two men dropped something and gestured a shaking palm towards Oliver. "Shadows of your past," it rasped.

But Oliver had already drifted back into the future.

## Chapter 12: The History Professor

*While I'm researching, he's rising in the polls. The Free-World Coalition is gaining members by the day after his speech on society enrichment and equality. Next, we'll roll out the rehabilitation centers in New York and New Jersey while the Federalists and Anti-Federalists squabble over the best way to repeal the 3rd Amendment for Magic.*

*20th of November, the first year of the 10th Age*

The next morning, Oliver, Emma, and Lance met in the Dining Hall before heading to their first ever class at Tenochprima Academy. Oliver hadn't slept well but couldn't remember why, leaving him in a more irritable state than he would have liked. He thought he may have had a bad dream, but every time he came close to remembering, it slipped away from his conscious like smoke in the wind.

After a quick breakfast of eggs and hash, he felt somewhat better. A moment later, they exited the Dining Hall, finding themselves scrambling through their schedules and syllabi.

"OK!" said Oliver swiping through his notebook. "First up—,"

"Shielding with Blackwood," Emma growled.

"You're kidding!" said Lance, yanking the notebook out of Oliver's hands. They walked past Tolteca who hovered in the Founders Temple foyer.

"GOOD LUCK, CHILDREN! FIRST DAY OF LESSONS IS ALWAYS –," he yelled.

## * Chapter 12: The History Professor *

"Yeah, yeah, not now Tolteca," grumbled Lance with a wave of his arm. "Are you telling me that every Monday morning we get to look forward to that old fart telling us about how terrible we are at everything?"

"Good morning," came a familiarly deep voice. All three of them jumped.

It was Blackwood. He stood just outside Founders Temple, hidden underneath the shadow of the osorius statue.

"I hope I didn't interrupt," he threatened, stepping out from the shadow. In the morning breeze and light, his scalp shone bright.

"Nope," said Oliver, recovering quickest. Emma and Lance still stared up at the enormous man.

"You will address your professors as Professor, Sir, or Ma'am," Blackwood snarled without looking at them. He kept his eyes on the foyer. "And you will address me as *Dean*."

"Uh, yes, Professor Dean, sir," he spluttered, still dazed.

Blackwood surveyed Oliver more fully this time, watching his collared shirt billow around in the breeze; its uniform design wasn't exactly fit for his slim build. Chuckling at him, Blackwood cracked either side of his neck, drawing attention to the powerful muscles visible beneath his own collared shirt. "Careful, Mr. García. I will put you in detention quicker than your brain can synapse if you don't improve your tone."

Fuming, Oliver almost returned an earful, but Emma elbowed him hard in the ribs.

"Let's not make enemies day one," she hissed in his ear.

## NOVA 01

With his ribs smarting and his temper flared, Oliver glared at Blackwood through a red haze while the rest of Founders B1 and B2 stopped to assemble around the Dean.

"Since I am a kind man," the Dean continued, insufferably oblivious to Oliver's escalating rage, "I guide my Extramen Class to the Academic building for their first lesson every year. If you'll follow me."

Angry for having been insulted by the Dean for a third time –"and for no reason!" he muttered to Lance – Oliver barely noticed Beto, Cristina, and James join them on their walk up the hill.

High up the ridge, Blackwood led them past palm trees and toucans. But not even the jungle around them could distract Oliver's attention from the back of Blackwood's bald head. He grumbled mutinously every step of the way until they eventually made it to the Academic Building, which stood past the Simulation Room.

Made of brick and mortar, the Academic Building looked more like a structure on Oliver's original Side of the Key than the magical temples and statues peppered across campus. Four floors could be counted from the outside – Dean Blackwood assured them a fifth also existed in the basement.

Each level of the Academic Building staggered higher and higher into the hillside until the fourth floor stood level with the feathered serpent statue at the top of Founders Temple. It peered at them as they walked through open-faced hallways past rows of classrooms with roofs of orange clay tile.

## * Chapter 12: The History Professor *

By the time they reached Blackwood's classroom on the third floor, most students were breathing heavily, including Oliver and Lance.

Beto, who didn't look even remotely winded, shook his head as he walked into the classroom past Oliver, wearing a frock coat. "You think you can make the Coatlball team when you can't even climb a flight of stairs?"

Already furious about Dean Blackwood, Oliver followed Beto, into the room, and slammed his bag of books on the chair immediately next to him. "What? No ridiculous leather boots for class?" he chided aggressively. "Frock coat just jerky enough?"

Beto narrowed his eyelids but decided not to escalate the situation further while Blackwood walked in with the rest of the class. Instead, he stood up slowly, wiping off imaginary dust from his coat. "Sorry, I don't sit next to *sinovas*," he whispered. Then, with an arrogant simper, he joined Cristina and James at a different table.

Oliver was lucky Lance grabbed him by the shoulder and pushed him back into his chair, otherwise he certainly would have ended up in prison, let alone detention.

Half an hour went by, and he hadn't listened to a word Blackwood had said. Instead, he imagined himself knocking Blackwood's bald head against Beto's curly-haired one.

That is, until Lance poked him in the ribs where Emma had elbowed him.

"What?" he hissed.

## NOVA 01

From the front of the classroom, Blackwood growled. "What indeed? If you are done daydreaming, Mr. García, you will kindly answer my question."

"What question?" Oliver answered with a light sneer.

He regretted it immediately.

Silence followed his outburst. Though he didn't check, he felt Beto's arrogant stare on the side of his face.

With a step that moved loose stone, Blackwood descended from his pulpit and marched towards him, rolling up his sleeves. By the time he reached Oliver's desk, he snarled like a boar.

"That is the second time you've neglected to refer to your superiors by their titles, García. You'll stay behind after class so we can schedule your detention. Really, on your first day ... what will Archie think?"

Angrier than he could ever remember, Oliver focused on grinding his teeth for the remainder of the lesson, keeping his jaw shut. At the end of the lesson, when his cheekbones were sore, the rest of the class filed out while Blackwood approached him again, smiling like Mrs. Caldwell. He leaned on Oliver's desk, taking out a small, black-framed mirror as the wood groaned under the weight of his muscles.

"You're lucky I oversee Coatlball tryouts with Professor Watkin, García, otherwise, we'd be booking this for the afternoon of September the $26^{th}$." I'm usually not this lean on punishment – we'll settle for hard labor the same morning."

# ✱ Chapter 12: The History Professor ✱

Though he wanted to yell at Blackwood, Oliver kept his mouth shut, refusing to fall into whatever trap the dean might be laying. He felt a bit of pride tingle within his upper back for maintaining eye contact.

Blackwood shrugged. "I'd been *joking* about same-day labor, but I can't argue if you think it's the best course of action. Very well."

Standing before Oliver could protest, Blackwood muttered into the black mirror. *"Mr. García to serve detention on September 26th, 7:00 A.M. Kitchens."*

Oliver took a deep breath as the words scribbled into existence on the notebook. Recognizing there still might be a trap waiting for him if he spoke, he bowed stiffly and backed away, never turning until he was safely out the door.

Seething, Oliver caught up with Emma and Lance on the floor below just in time for the start of *Destruction 101*.

"Did he really give you detention?" Emma whispered when he slammed into a chair next to her.

Not wanting to face further disciplinary action, he made a shushing noise and pointed at Belk instead. If she was anything like Blackwood, he planned to stay quiet.

To his relief, Belk proved much more amenable than Blackwood. Instead of sneering from behind a pulpit, she moved around a tall room, destroying scarecrows and dummy enemies with all the grace of a roaring rhinoceros. Two enormous gold bracelets clicked and clacked on her wrists as she wowed them.

"PHYSICAL DESTRUCTION OFTEN GETS THE MOST ATTENTION!" she yelled, slamming her firsts into the ground. A wave of tile and Earth followed, pulverizing a nearby scarecrow, but she'd already moved on to close her eyes and place a finger against her temple. "MENTAL DESTRUCTION, HOWEVER, WORKS JUST AS WELL AS ANY AMOUNT OF BRUTE FORCE."

With a noise like a silenced pistol, a concentrated beam of wind shot through the air from her forehead, cleaving another scarecrow's head in two.

"IT ALL DEPENDS ON WHAT YOU'RE COMING UP AGAINST. SOMETIMES PHYSICAL ATTACKS WILL WIN THE DAY. OTHER TIMES, ONLY MENTAL WILL DO."

An hour later, despite having learned no actual magic, Oliver felt energized enough to take on Reggie himself.

"Did you see the way she moved the ground?" Se'Vaughn said to Trey and Lance as they walked back to the Dining Hall for lunch. Oliver joined in the conversation, too, appreciating that both Se'Vaughn and Trey didn't seem to care about any of the rumors being spread about him.

"Aww," sneered Beto, passing them, "you'd think it's their first time seeing magic!" Following him, James guffawed, and Cristina snickered.

"Watch it ..." said Oliver, raising his hands in front of Emma's and Lance's faces. Emma tightened her sleeve while Lance placed a hand on the hammer hanging from his belt.

## \* Chapter 12: The History Professor \*

Beto smirked at them before turning towards the Dining Hall.

"See," Oliver growled. "He made that same *stupid* face at me right before I lost my temper in Blackwood's class."

"Now I get why you were so mad," said Lance. "That face is enough to strangle a –,"

"Please don't finish that sentence," Emma interrupted. She relaxed her sleeve and continued walking. "You're right, Oli. He's probably *trying* to get us into detention."

Oliver scratched his chin. "To his credit, he's already a third of the way there. But I wasn't about to fall for it a second time."

Emma laughed. "So much Wisdom."

"The wise-iest, ain't there no mistake," agreed Lance.

"Y'all are the worst," said Oliver, unable to hide a smile. He stormed ahead, leading them to lunch.

After some grilled chicken sandwiches, they climbed back up the ridge towards the Academic Building for *World History Throughout the Ages*.

Legs searing, they paused to catch their breaths at the top of the stairs only to find they weren't alone. Next to them stood a man they hadn't yet met.

He was tall, if a bit shorter than Blackwood, and where Blackwood chose to be bald, this man wore long, brown hair in a tight ponytail that reached his upper back.

"It always takes a few weeks for extramen to get used to the ridge," the man suddenly said, startling them, "but I think you three will master it in just two, don't you?"

Unsure as to whom the question was directed, Oliver, Emma, and Lance looked at each other, nonplussed, and then back at the man.

He stared right back, a twinkle in his green eyes. He wore salmon-red pants under a white linen shirt and a navy-blue frock coat. Though he wasn't as wide as Blackwood, his clothes fit properly around his athletic frame, impressing Oliver. He'd even managed to match a frayed, sash belt of silk to the rest of his ensemble.

"Where are my manners?" the man finally said, bowing. "I am Professor Cato Watkin, and you three are extramen in my history class."

"Yes!" said Lance, recovering quickest. "My name's Lance Wyatt."

"Indeed, you are, Mr. Wyatt!" said Watkin. "I should be very surprised if you do not end up being a Powerhead. I see you've selected a warhammer, a solid choice."

Lance patted his hammer awkwardly. "Thanks!"

Watkin turned, locking eyes with Emma next. She piped up before he could say anything. "I'm Emma Griffith and I'm –,"

"A Brave," Watkin interrupted, surprising her. He scrunched up his chin as he surveyed her. "A sleeve? Excellent touch of sophistication, I'd say. You should do well, too."

"Which means," Watkin continued, "you must be Mr. García." He shifted his weight to face Oliver directly, looking him up and down. Oliver thought for a moment that Watkin looked puzzled. "You were selected by Jeff Hamilton, correct?"

# * Chapter 12: The History Professor *

"Yeah!" said Oliver, feeling a rush of old emotions. "He was my school counselor before Tenochprima. He helped me apply. Took a bit of convincing to be honest."

Watkin laughed. "Rest assured, Jeff required even more convincing than you."

Oliver couldn't help but smile at Watkin. Despite his pretentious presentation, the man was inescapably likeable.

"So, you knew him?" Oliver asked. "Now that I think about it, he did mention someone from Tenochprima had visited him. Was that you?"

Watkin nodded, gripping a staff Oliver hadn't noticed was perched behind him. A large, green jewel was embedded into its handle. "Oh, that was me alright. Eventually got through to him. Adults tend to have a harder time accepting a new paradigm since they've spent longer acclimating to their existing one." He paused to raise his left arm to check an upside-down watch under the sleeve of his frock coat. "Regardless, I'm sure we can expect many accomplishments from the three of you over the next four years. For the time being, however, if you'll follow me." He turned halfway and ushered for them to walk with him between the sun-lit classrooms on the first floor.

Oliver marveled at the way Watkin moved as they walked from one tile-roofed classroom to the next. Unlike Blackwood's heavy footsteps, or Belk's bounding leaps, Watkin appeared to glide across the floor, seemingly wasting no energy.

When they reached a semi-open staircase leading up to the building's second floor, Watkin coughed politely. "If you don't mind my saying, I also heard you acquired your magical channel from my own procurer of choice, Blacksmith Miyada."

Oliver's marveling stopped at that. With Watkin's back to them as they ascended the stairs, he exchanged a wide-eyed look with Emma.

"Yeah," he replied, straining to keep his tone casual. "We both did, actually. Who um, mentioned it to you?"

"Did he say anything else?" Emma interrupted. Oliver grimaced. He would have approached that question with more subtlety. They didn't know if they could trust Professor Watkin.

Watkin looked down from the top of the staircase. Following his gaze, Oliver heard the scuffling of shoes, indicating the rest of the class drew near.

"Yes, he did," said Watkin, raising an eyebrow, surveying them. "He also told me Oliver purchased a ring, which, according to him, is very unusual for a fourteen-year-old. So much so, that Oliver is the youngest client to whom he's ever sold one." His head had drawn closer to Oliver as he spoke.

Emma grabbed at her shoulder while Lance scratched his head.

"Oh?" said Oliver, alarm bells tolling in his head. Even though he liked Watkin, Archie's advice had been to not mention what happened in Miyada's shop to anybody else and, so far, Watkin hadn't mentioned Oliver's reaction to the ring.

"Oh, indeed," said Watkin. He looked directly at them in turn – raising his left eyebrow, and then his right. "As you know, I'm Tenochprima's history professor. As such, I'm happy to spend time after classes discussing any *additional subject matter* with my students. I would encourage you three to

# * Chapter 12: The History Professor *

do so, should you ever feel the need to discuss historical figures or events related to your *extracurricular* interests."

Unsure of how to respond, Oliver bowed awkwardly for a second time that day.

"Anytime at all," Watkin reiterated, returning the bow. When he straightened, he entered the nearest classroom, beckoning for them to follow. Bewildered, they complied.

"What do you think he means by additional subject matter?" hissed Emma a little too loudly.

"Oh, anything at all, really," interrupted Watkin, causing Emma to jump when they passed him. "If you see anything on campus your Guide can't explain, it may be of historical significance. Let's have a chat if that's the case."

Nodding their heads and exchanging looks, Oliver, Emma, and Lance claimed the nearest desk by placing down their notebooks. Then, they took stock of their surroundings.

Unlike most classrooms with chalk boards and small, uncomfortable desks, Watkin's classroom resembled a cozy library more than anything else. Tables of rich mahogany and books bound by leather, pipe-reed, and sheepskin fought for space between rows of shelving lining the front, left, and right walls of the room. Up a short staircase, the door to Watkin's office stood open, filled with even more books.

Towards the rear of the classroom, an open-faced terrace lent in a breeze past a wrought iron railing. In the distance, the bejeweled feathered serpent atop Founders Temple flexed its muscles. Closer yet, a green, keel-billed toucan ruffled its feathers lazily from atop the railing.

"Out of the way, goof squad," came an interrupting snarl. Turning quickly, Oliver found himself face to face with Beto.

Though he wanted to say something rude, Beto did have a point. He, Emma, and Lance had blocked the door when gawking at the classroom, leaving their peers stuck outside. From the rear of the hold-up, Se'Vaughn and Trey waved cheerily towards them.

"Do have a seat," said Watkin, gesturing towards the mahogany tables.

*"Caw-caw!"* agreed the keel-billed toucan. It flew into the classroom from the terrace and landed on the desk on which they'd placed their notebooks, pointing enthusiastically at the six chairs behind it.

Red in the ears, Oliver took a seat without another word. Emma and Lance followed while the rest of the class filed into the room. Beto made sure to grin at them arrogantly, brightening Oliver's ears further.

He quickly forgot about Beto, however, when the toucan hopped over to stand in front of him and jerked its head sideways.

*"Caw-caw!"* it surmised.

"Nice to meet you, too," said Oliver. He raised a hand to softly pat the toucan's side. It flew away before too long, however, landing on a gnarled bird stand next to Professor Watkin's podium. Watkin stared for a moment at the Toucan and then Oliver before moving on to address the class.

"Welcome to *World History Throughout the Ages; Dawn of Magic through the Seventh Age!*" boomed Watkin. His teaching voice carried more loudly than his speaking voice did. "I am Professor Cato Watkin, and, though I can't

# * Chapter 12: The History Professor *

promise this course will be your favorite, I *can* at least guarantee it will provide you with *Wisdom* we can only glean from the past."

Beto scoffed audibly enough for most everyone to hear. Emma turned to look at him, disgusted.

Watkin turned, too, surprising Oliver.

"Mr. Warren. Did you have something to say?"

"Uh, no, *sir*," Beto replied, smiling sleazily at Cristina and James.

"I thought not," said Watkin, smiling back. "At any rate, should you find this course too boring for your entitled presumption of self-worth, please do not hesitate to leave my classroom and collect your F for the year."

Beto stammered, straightening up in his seat while Oliver exchanged impressed nods of the head with Emma, Lance, Se'Vaughn, and Trey. Next to Beto, Cristina scowled while James thought hard.

"That won't be necessary, Professor," Beto finally managed.

"I thought not, Mr. Warren," said Watkin. "Tenochprima Academy does not tolerate rude behavior, and neither will I." He turned to face the rest of the class "While you all are in my classroom, you will raise your hand to speak. Understood?"

A chorus of "yes, professor" and "yes, sir" followed.

"Good!" said Watkin, still smiling. "Let's begin! Notebooks out on your desks for your mental notes. No need to touch it, Lance, just leave it on the desk – thank you."

Oliver, Emma, and Lance made sure to turn towards Beto and simper at him sarcastically when Watkin walked past them towards the terrace.

## NOVA 01

"We'll start the year," Watkin continued, "learning about the Cradles of Civilization and the Sumerian City States, eventually making our way to the Founding of Carthage in the Seventh Age."

For a very brief moment, Oliver worried the class might resemble Mrs. Caldwell's dull lessons on Venice and Tenochtitlan. Again, however, Watkin surprised him. After introducing the subject matter for the year, he jumped right into a lesson on the Cradles of Civilization. Instead of simply lecturing them to sleep, he used a large floating board he brought in from the terrace to simulate the Earth's surface in 3D. Oliver stared in wonder as miniature humans built houses and roads in an area of the world Watkin called the "Fertile Crescent" during the First Age of Magical Proximity. As the tiny humans used their even smaller tools, more and more buildings were erected until sprawling towns formed under the guidance of wizards and witches who held simple staffs with glowing rocks. Watkin promised that for any battle they covered during the year, the simulation board made for excellent viewing.

As they packed their bags to leave an hour later, Oliver, Emma, and Lance thanked him for the lesson on their way out.

"Anytime, you three," said Watkin, waving goodbye. His toucan nodded its head next to him. "But I'd recommend taking the staircase past the terrace." He pointed towards the rear of the classroom. "If I were as angry as Mr. Warren, I'd be waiting right outside my door to give you three an earful. Jaiba will show you the way. Ta-da!"

Smiling at the thought of Beto waiting for them to never show up, they followed Jaiba until he landed on the railing outside. *Caw-caw!* With his beak

## * Chapter 12: The History Professor *

he pointed to a descending, circular staircase they hadn't seen from the tables in the classroom.

After thanking the bird, they hurried down, only stopping once they were out of earshot.

"Okay," said Oliver at the bottom of the staircase, "don't get me wrong, I like Watkin, but what on Earth was he talking about when he said we should stop by and chat about 'additional subject matter'?"

Emma placed a hand on her chin, pretending to think hard. "Let's see. What would our history professor want to talk to us about after admitting he knows what happened to you at Miyada's? What historical artifact related to the Prophet's Advent might he want to study?"

"Augustus' scroll!" Lance yelped.

Emma exhaled, rolling her eyes. "Of course it's the freaking scroll! Sarcasm a foreign language to you?" She turned to Oliver, crossing her arms. "Do we really want to talk to Watkin about it, though? I thought we weren't trusting anybody."

Oliver opened his mouth to speak but then stopped. Emma had stumped him. Even though Watkin could likely be a big help in finding the scroll and clearing Oliver's name, they had agreed not to trust anyone. So, why did he feel compelled to do so anyway?

*Because my gut tells me I should. Only I don't know why.*

"Listen," Oliver finally replied. "Something in the back of my mind is telling me he'd be able to help us. Maybe in more ways than one."

"What do you mean?" Lance asked, mirroring Emma's crossed arms.

## NOVA 01

Oliver focused on the handrailing, looking up to make sure Watkin or Jaiba weren't eavesdropping. "It feels like my mind is warning me that it's all connected somehow. Remember what Archie and Rasmus said about *The Damned?* That he 'ticked all the right boxes' for being the Prophet's Advent?"

"Yeah," said Emma, "and Stevie said maybe a lot of people bought into it, right? What's that got to do with you?"

Oliver shrugged. "I'm not sure it does or doesn't, but maybe we should ask Watkin about it. See if the scroll is connected to *The Damned* or anything."

Lance laughed, giving his best impression of James. "You're kidding, right? If you think Watkin is going to spill the beans for us on day one, you're insane. My parents don't even talk about what happened with *The Damned.*"

"Maybe not day one," Oliver murmured, thinking out loud more than anything else, "but if we find the scroll and offer him a chance to study it, maybe we can exchange it for information on *The Damned.*"

Emma smiled, uncrossing her arms and leaning towards him. "Now *that's* crafty! Didn't know you had it in you, Oli – I'm all in." With a tilt of her head, she lifted her chin at Lance. "What about you?"

"Don't really have a choice, do I?" said Lance, looking over his shoulders with wide eyes. "Already crossed my heart, didn't I?

* Chapter 12: The History Professor *

# NOVA 01

## Chapter 13: Beneath the Swirling Fog

*I've just found out all my research was to prepare me for some extended traveling. I'm to explore the sites using a tool that detects protective barriers and stuff like that. Even though I would have liked to know the full plan before I started researching, it's for the best.*

*20$^{th}$ of November, the first year of the 10$^{th}$ Age*

When their first weekend finally arrived, Oliver, Emma, and Lance collapsed, exhausted, onto their favorite couch cushions in the eastern viewing dome.

"Nobody said we'd be this busy!" Emma groaned, rubbing her eyes.

Oliver felt tempted to laugh but resisted. He didn't want to sound insane.

Only four days prior, they'd agreed to use their evenings for researching Augustus' scroll. It seemed, at the time, a perfect plan. But that was before they knew their professors would *drown* them with homework.

Nothing satisfied them.

Between hundred-page reading assignments, hour-long spell practice sessions, a thousand-word essay on the best applications for medical remedies, and *math* problems, they barely had time to eat or shower, let alone snoop around to investigate the whereabouts of a dead man's hidden prophecy.

## * Chapter 13: Beneath the Swirling Fog *

When neither Oliver nor Lance replied, Emma snapped her fingers above her head. "I still can't believe you *like* pre-algebra."

She'd directed the comment jovially at Lance who grunted like a zombie, too tired to scoff or sneer. "You just wait," he said, yawning. "One day, I'll save your life with one of those shapes …"

In his head, Oliver agreed with Emma more so than Lance. Though he was sure shapes *could* matter for magic, the wizened man who taught the subject, Victor Euclid, bored him to tears. He seemed cheery enough behind his long, white beard, but it was hard to care about studying shapes when other classes offered him the actual opportunity to *use* magic. Only Lance sat upright, taking copious notes while the rest of them kept their heads up with sore wrists.

Emma, for her part, much preferred *An Introduction to Magical Political Systems*, which everyone just called "poli-sci", along with *Channeling 101* taught by Zapien. Oliver, too, relished Zapien's channeling lessons. He found it fascinating that one subject could form the basic building blocks for the five branches of magic they'd study for the next four years.

But he did wish Zapien would tone down her praise a bit.

"Clear as day a Wiser," she told the class on Tuesday, winking. "It's rare to master *iuxtairis*, the sun acclimation spell, so quickly. Yep, Oli's shaping up to be a Wiser, just like me."

After a repeat of the compliment on Thursday, Trey and Se'Vaughn began addressing Oliver as kingly, wise men with pretentious bows whenever they saw him. Others, like Beto, however, genuinely resented the praise, opting to grumble and flash red eyes at him instead.

Professor Chavarría's regeneration course, meanwhile, fell in the middle of Oliver's list. Short, broad, and stoic, Chavarría didn't exactly inspire the same way Watkin could, but at least his lessons taught them life-long skills.

During their first lesson, he whipped up a potion made of water, mango juice, and sluffed feathered serpent skin, curing everyone of light headaches induced by the presence of an open jug of chupacabra venom. Then, in their second lesson, he embalmed a kitchen sink before offering each student the chance to destroy it with a sledgehammer. Nobody could scratch it.

Last of all, they had *Biomes of the Magically Inclined*.

Based on the classroom alone, Oliver expected to love the course. Everywhere he looked, bizarre plants of red, green, and yellow bobbed in place to a rhythm he couldn't emulate. One plant, which followed Lance's every move, suspiciously looked capable of *eating*, or at least slowly digesting, any of them within a bulbous sack underneath its bell-shaped head.

But then Professor Desmoulins waltzed into the room ... over five minutes late.

"Sorry, sorry," he said, grinning lazily as he made his way to the front of the class. "Lost track of time doing my research."

Instead of diving into their coursework immediately like Watkin had, Desmoulins spent their entire first lesson stepping through their syllabus, line by line, with frequent pauses for smiles, lazy jokes, and pointless observations. Though Oliver was sure Desmoulins intended to come across

## * Chapter 13: Beneath the Swirling Fog *

as aloof and cool, the charade didn't work, making it obvious he was just plain lazy.

When they weren't reading theory or writing essays, Oliver, Emma, and Lance attended Coatlball and Dungeon-Simulation practice sessions. Tryouts for the Founders teams were only a few weeks away, and if they wanted to participate in the Magical Five Tournament, they'd have to attend as many practices as they could, exhausted or not.

When late September did approach a couple weeks later, however, all the late nights began to feel worth it.

With the tryouts only days away, a palpable thrum of excitement began to hang on the air. Older students now wore frock coats commemorating past Magical Five titles — they bore gold-stitched lettering on the front lapels, highlighting dorm names and years won.

"We're getting one of those," Lance breathed hungrily when they passed yet another batch of Champayan students wearing jackets covered in gold.

Oliver couldn't help but agree. Not so much for personal glory, but mainly to wipe the smirks off the Champayan faces. Given the dorm's success over the last decade, almost every coat they saw celebrated Champayan's titles. Only rarely did they see hand-me-down jackets commemorating titles from before Champayan's nine-year streak.

One of those came from Watkin. He surprised them the week of their tryouts by wearing a coat commemorating his extraman year title with Founders Hall three decades prior. When prodded, he revealed he played a key role in winning the trophy and even confirmed a rumor that indicated he went on to play Coatlball professionally after school for a year or two.

# NOVA 01

Blackwood, in turn, made sure to grin smugly at them when donning his own frock coat the very next day. Oliver's blood boiled at the sight of *Champayan Hall – Nine Years Undefeated* overcrowding his front pocket. Beto, however, took the opportunity to praise Blackwood at the end of class.

"Hard to believe any dorm will have a chance to beat Champayan this year, sir."

Emma made a retching face as Blackwood replied.

"You're quite right, Mr. Warren." Oliver marveled at how his deep, crunching voice somehow sounded warm whenever he spoke to Beto. "But you'll be winning with us when you join our dorm next year. If you're as good as your cousin, John, we'll have a real talent on our hands."

In his seat, Beto leaned back, tossing a grin at Cristina. "I look forward to it, sir."

"I look forward to whacking you on the head," whispered Lance, gripping his warhammer's handle with white knuckles. Thankfully, only Oliver heard him.

On the day of the tryouts, Lance insisted on accompanying Oliver to his 7:00 AM detention in the kitchens. With half-open eyes they made their way to the Dining Hall, nearly running into Emma, who'd set up shop at the top of the white-marble staircase, snoring.

Smiling, Oliver poked her a couple times on the shoulder until she woke up.

## * Chapter 13: Beneath the Swirling Fog *

"Was' goin' on?" she said in between yawns. "Oh, it's y'all. Thought you might want some company during detention, Oli."

Oliver felt elated as they trudged up the stairs, appreciating both her and Lance's loyalty.

Truth be told, none of them knew where the detention was supposed to take place – Blackwood had only mentioned the *kitchens*. But, as Lance put it, "there's magic food in the Dining Hall, so there's gotta be a magic kitchen nearby."

Upstairs, the Dining Hall remained enveloped by the quiet brought about by the previous evening. None of the overhead lanterns were lit, which meant the only sources of light came from the staircase they had just exited and Tolteca's foyer on the other side. Long shadows danced from their feet as they walked forward, sniffing around for the kitchens like an inexperienced pack of wolves.

Emma, still yawning, began tapping on a nearby wall, whereas Lance approached the foyer to check for a hallway they might have missed. Oliver ignored them both to take a seat at one of the dining tables.

"Kitchens," he said, rapping his ring on the wood, "I'm here for my detention!"

Just as Lance was about to cross into the foyer and risk waking up Tolteca, the wall Emma had been knocking on slid right, making a terrible scraping noise. At the same time, the overhead lanterns turned on, blinding them.

"*Iuxtairis!*" Oliver mumbled.

## NOVA 01

"All three of you named Oliver or something?" shouted a woman's voice. As Oliver's eyes reacted to the spell, the voice's owner came into focus, revealing a tall, slender woman with short, black hair. She couldn't have been older than thirty, and Oliver nearly blushed just looking at her cheekbones.

"Mhmm," she continued, "Blackwood warned me you might try and pull a fast one. Y'all best believe these dishes are going to be cleaned by our detentionee, *alone*." She pointed at Oliver with a soup ladle.

"Ah," said Oliver, realizing what lay before him. "Dishes."

"Yes, dishes," said the woman, placing her wrists against her hips. "Nothing quite like manual labor to punish a budding nova! Finna be the cleanest dishes any of us have ever seen!" She laughed at her own joke and sauntered back through her hidden door. "Come here, Oliver. My name's Joan. But everybody calls me Ms. Joan, so you better do the same. You and I are going to become the *best* of friends." More loudly she added over her shoulder, "y'all other two best stay outside. Entering my kitchens is a privilege you haven't earned yet."

Mouthing "sorry" to Emma and Lance, Oliver followed Ms. Joan with a perplexed smile on his face. It fell the moment he saw a *mountain* of dishes waiting for him inside an enormous white sink. He looked at Ms. Joan and then a ruby necklace on her neck pleadingly.

"Nope," she said tossing the dirty ladle to the top of the mountain. "No magic, just your sweat, tears, and maybe blood – careful with those knives, they're sharper than most of your classmates. If it makes you feel any better, I could clean all these in a second, but Blackwood made sure I left last

## Chapter 13: Beneath the Swirling Fog

night's dishes caked and dirty. Now you'll think twice before disrespecting your elders."

"I didn't disrespect anybody," Oliver replied, grumbling.

Ms. Joan winked. "Of course, you didn't. Just like *I* didn't wash all these dishes."

Frowning, Oliver stepped past her only to be stopped by a heatwave. As he covered his face, he saw it emanated from a small doorway to the left of the sink, leading deeper into the kitchens. He wrinkled his nose at the waves of hot air before doubling back to approach the sink from the right lest he burn off his eyebrows. Unsure of where to start, he grabbed the dirty ladle at the top of the mountain and began scrubbing with some steel wool he found next to the waterspout.

After starting, he expected Ms. Joan to leave him alone to tackle the mess like Santiago would. To his surprise, however, she spent the next two hours chatting with him while he scrubbed, washed, and dried. Every now and then an order for breakfast would distract her, but otherwise, she sat on a stool next to him, keeping him company.

As it turned out, Ms. Joan led a fascinating life.

Born just outside of Charleston, she grew up working jobs to support her family. When she was thirteen, she caught none other than Headmaster Lalandra passing through from the Other Side of the Key in the alleyway behind her restaurant. For her silence, Lalandra offered her a spot at Tenochprima.

## NOVA 01

"But the coursework bored me to *tears*," she said, continuing her story with a dramatic hand over her forehead. "The only things worth studying here were the people and the kitchens."

After graduating, she returned to the Original Side to travel across the culinary world, training in Paris, New York, Tokyo, and even Johannesburg before returning to Tenochprima to take over the kitchens.

"Before I got back here, some crusty, old man served only the deepest of southern food. The craziest he ever got was a big bowl of gumbo or jambalaya. What a waste!" She threw a dish towel emphatically. "With me in here, y'all can now eat anything from sashimi to gratin dauphinois whenever, *however*."

Ms. Joan was so personable, she even got Oliver to talk about his childhood. She told him she was sorry when hearing that his parents died in México when he was too young to remember. But she also reminded him to spend more time writing Santiago because he was more a father than a lot of boys ever had growing up.

When a grandfather clock with no hands chimed nine times, Ms. Joan placed a hand to her necklace, causing the remaining dirty dishes to shoot into the air and land in neat, clean stacks nearby. With a second touch of her channel, the dish grime on Oliver's hands and arms disappeared, too.

"Thanks," he said sheepishly.

"See? That wasn't so bad, was it? But don't think you'll get so lucky every time. You caught me in a good mood today!" She gave him a wink and a crushing hug before sending him on his way with a hearty breakfast sandwich.

## * Chapter 13: Beneath the Swirling Fog *

With no time to spare, Oliver ate the sandwich on the go, barely arriving at the Simulation Room in time for the start of tryouts. To his dismay, none other than Dean Blackwood oversaw the team selections.

"Looks like he's split us up on purpose," Emma muttered mutinously as they surveyed the list of teams – each featured four extramen and one RA, and according to Zapien, the teams with the two best times would form the Founders squad for the upcoming season.

Entering the dungeon, Oliver found himself in a simulation with more enemies than allies. Not because of the *walking* snakes or ink-shooting octopi he came across, but because his team included Beto, Cristina, and James. His representative RA, Katie, appeared oblivious to the looks of hatred exchanged between them.

Although Beto and his cronies couldn't blatantly push him into a poisonous vat of water or anything, they could slow down the team's progress by disagreeing with every idea Oliver put forth.

Fortunately, however, both Beto and Cristina fell into a pool of piranhas in the second room they entered. Oliver made sure to wave a sardonic goodbye as they were chomped into oblivion, even making eye contact with Beto as a piranha went for his nose. Turning back to his team, he grinned at James like a tasty snack. James took thirty seconds to understand anything whatsoever. He and Katie could just move forward before James could synapse an alternative.

An hour later they reached the dungeon boss room unscathed. Although Oliver and James couldn't perform any useful magic, they both managed to scavenge large shields and wooden spears from tombs of lizard people. Katie, meanwhile, had scavenged a bow and arrow.

In the boss room, Oliver stared at their enemy, aghast. As tall and wide as one of their classrooms, there stood a sickly looking toad. When they entered, it croaked and viewed them with seven bloodshot eyes. While Oliver and James blocked jets of scalding water from the toad's mouth, Katie loosed arrows at its eyes. A few burns and dozens of arrows later, the amphibian croaked its last before disappearing in a puff of smoke. Seconds later, so did Oliver, James, and Katie, reappearing in the observation deck.

A blast of cheers deafened him as several hands grabbed onto his shirt.

"You did it!" he heard Emma shout. "Three hours and seventeen minutes! Y'all got the second-best time!"

At first he felt elated. But then he actually locked eyes with Emma and the emotions there told him everything he needed to know.

"We didn't make it," said Lance not looking up. "The room with the snakes … they took us all out, even Brantley."

Emma shrugged, tossing Abe's team a jealous look – his team was the other one to qualify, which included Trey, their hallmate. "It's good that Abe's team qualified – we're gonna need him for the Emerald Trophy. It's just baloney that Blackwood separated us."

As they made their way to the Dining Hall for a quick lunch, Oliver spent the walk ignoring everyone's congratulations to instead talk up Emma's and Lance's chances at making the Coatlball team. He only stopped when Emma put a finger on his lips.

## * Chapter 13: Beneath the Swirling Fog *

"Oli, we don't need your sympathy. We know what we have to do to make the team."

Red in the ears, he whispered an order for lunch, making sure to thank Ms. Joan in the process. He smiled when his gumbo arrived – she'd sent it up with the shrimp and sausage shaped into a grin.

Down at the Coatlball trench, Oliver's excitement from having made the Dungeon-Simulation team began to wear off. Though his Coatlball connection with Archie had grown considerably after all their practice sessions, they still weren't communicating as effortlessly as the RAs did with their Guides. And even though Emma and Lance assured him Rasmus and Merri were the same way, it only made him worry that none of them would make the team.

By the time Ronnie and Katie blew their whistles, the butterflies in Oliver's stomach threatened to orchestrate a prison break. Taking a deep breath, he calmed himself before joining his classmates in two lines.

For their first drill, Ronnie and Katie split the extramen into pairs for long-range passing drills. When Oliver reached the front of his line, he looked over and saw Se'Vaughn grinning. Oliver smiled back, thanking the heavens. They didn't drop a single pass.

Next, Emma and Cristina managed to do the same – even if they glared at one another the entire time.

Lance, however, wasn't so lucky.

As Oliver rejoined the back of the line, he saw Beto grinning at Lance from the back of his Guide like a hyena might a dying gazelle. At Katie's whistle, Beto's pass hurtled at Lance like a shooting star. As the ball streaked through the air, Oliver wondered if Beto was actively imbuing a spell into the ball or if his Power was just that strong.

Unsurprisingly, Lance ended up fumbling most of Beto's passes, looking more and more crestfallen by the minute. Thinking fast, Oliver wondered if the morning sunlight was blinding him, so he muttered *iuxtairis* to try and help.

The drills continued for nearly two hours, ranging from full-field defensive drills to one-on-one penalty shoot outs. Oliver's favorite test came when Zapien asked them to cross the length of the entire trench while dodging dozens of obstacles thrown at them by the RAs. A fishnet proved to be James' undoing, stopping him and his Guide abruptly as a pass from Ronnie sailed overhead, uncaught. Similarly, Trey ran into a brick wall, which required a healing spell from Professor Zapien to bring him back to consciousness. Lance, of all people, crossed the trench quickest, grimacing with concentration under his blonde bangs even after he finished.

During their final test, Oliver and Emma pulled off the "hot potato" technique Ronnie taught them during orientation. Emma winked at him as she offered him the final pass before allowing him to score. Oliver didn't need any second invitations.

He finished the move by lobbing the ball over James' helpless, stubby arms.

As the ball nestled in the net, Oliver heard a snarl behind the backboard. It came from Blackwood.

He glared at Oliver openly as Archie twisted them back around towards the pack of extramen. Glaring right back at Blackwood, Oliver prodded

## \* Chapter 13: Beneath the Swirling Fog \*

Archie to zoom high into the sky to celebrate instead. To his surprise, Archie didn't hesitate, leading them higher and higher.

For a moment, time stood still as Oliver breathed in the euphoria of scoring in front of Blackwood. Unless he was mistaken, he'd just made the team and there was nothing Blackwood could—

An unnatural, cold breeze interrupted his thoughts, freezing him in place. When it finally circled past him, a familiar, tingling sensation settled in the back of his head.

Squinting, he kept his eyes on the gust of wind as it careened towards the lagoons. It didn't look natural when it danced on the water's surface, so he tried viewing it from the perspective of his ring, as if he might cast a spell.

He regretted the shift in perspective almost immediately.

From his ring, a tempest roared, *begging* him to get lost in an ocean of wiggling, black strands of ... lines? Rivers? Wisps? He didn't know what to call them, but they attacked his conscious like foreign influences, demanding he channel them into action through the heartbeat he felt on his finger.

Just when he felt as if he had no option other than to cut off the connection, a new influence stopped him. Amidst the chaos of black and grey channels, a golden strand of ethereal thought stood out, wriggling to a stabler rhythm than its infinite counterparts.

Goosebumps exploded across Oliver's arms as he watched the new strand. Its movements *mirrored* the wind he'd just seen in the real world. Was he viewing the wind itself through his ring?

Feeling frantic, he snapped his perception back into his own eyes where it felt strangely quiet after the din he'd heard from his ring—

The wind turned, catching his eye, and shot towards the wall of fog obscuring the center of the lagoons.

To Oliver's astonishment, the permanent fog *lifted,* revealing a small island he'd never seen before. Around its perimeter, a host of overgrown willow trees stood guard with long, creeping branches covered in moss and lichen. But it was the center of the island that caught his eye. There, he saw a single, golden tree that shone brightly from the top of a crumbling temple.

Oliver's goosebumps went past his arms now, covering his entire body. "Archie!" he cried. "Archie! Look at the lagoons! Now!"

But even as the words crossed his lips, he watched the fog scramble back into place, as if pulled by invisible hands.

*"Why the sudden care about lagoons, dear boy?"* Archie replied with amusement. *"Dark, dreary things. How about that goal? I dare to think you've just made the team."*

"Never mind the goal!" Oliver shot back. "Out in the lagoons, I just saw a golden tree and a temple! Have you ever seen—,"

Archie dove, cutting Oliver off. As they descended towards the dismounting extramen at the bottom of the trench, his frame rolled with laughter. *"Never mind the goal? What are you talking about? A golden temple? Preposterous! I've been here since the sixteenth century and no such thing exists."*

"Not a golden temple!" said Oliver out loud, feeling frustrated. "A golden tree on *top* of a temple!"

## \* Chapter 13: Beneath the Swirling Fog \*

"What's going on?" said Emma, walking over with Lance. Rasmus and Merri circled above them, giving Archie satisfied looks.

"What were y'all doin' up there?" Lance asked.

*"Indeed,"* hummed Rasmus.

*"Celebrating, of course,"* sang Merri.

*"But not gloating,"* mused Archie.

"Would y'all quit it?" said Oliver, adopting a tone of urgency so they'd listen to him. "I just saw something out in the lagoons!"

"*Did* you now," interrupted a growling voice. It was Blackwood. He'd somehow managed to zero in on Oliver amidst the ruckus of descending extramen. Next to him, Watkin and Zapien handed out water bottles to their classmates.

Sneering, Blackwood continued. "Tell us, Mr. García, what did you see while you showed off up in the skies?"

"Nothing, sir," said Oliver, kicking himself for garnering the Dean's attention. Why did he have to zoom off and gloat when Blackwood was watching? Unbelievably stupid to have—

A snarl from Archie made Oliver jump in place. It shook the air around him and garnered attention from more than a few.

*"I would never presume to show off, human."* His tongue flit in and out of his mouth as he surveyed Blackwood.

Somehow, Blackwood didn't even flinch, flourishing into a deep bow. "Of course not, honored sacred beast." When he righted himself, he ignored Archie entirely, continuing to glare at Oliver. "Go on then, Mr. García. What did you see?"

"Nothing, *sir*," Oliver repeated. "Just a funny looking tree on an island out in the lagoons."

Nearby, Watkin began choking over his own water bottle, coughing loudly. Zapien slapped him on the back, but he waved her away, eyes locked on Oliver as he continued coughing.

Blackwood frowned at them all. "A funny looking tree, eh? On an island in the lagoons? Really, Mr. García. I, for one, refuse to humor such a desperate plea for attention."

Fire escaped Archie's nostrils, frightening Oliver, but when he spoke again, his tone felt softer than before. *"Corruption's effect on man,"* he directed towards Oliver, *"will never cease to amaze me. I take my leave before I say anything I might regret. You stand a great chance of making the team, Oliver. No matter what this purported adult maintains."* With a shake of his head, Archie turned to the skies and departed, followed by the remaining feathered serpents, as if summoned.

A moment of silence followed as only humans, osori, and eagles were left behind.

Watkin, who appeared to have recovered from his choking fit, spoke first. "Great work today, everyone!" he said, clasping his hands together as he addressed the confused crowd. "Professor Zapien and I will confer with Dean Blackwood before announcing the team in the Dining Hall just before dinner. Carry on."

Blackwood snorted at the words and stormed off. His scornful expression had creased all the way into a snarl as he shouted back. "Any

## * Chapter 13: Beneath the Swirling Fog *

more lies, García, and you'll find yourself in detention every Saturday for the rest of the year!"

Anger boiled up in Oliver's chest as he watched Blackwood lengthen the distance between them. He felt like shouting back but then Watkin surprised him by trotting ahead to walk side-by-side with the Dean. What did he want to talk to Blackwood about so urgently? The team selection? And what had Archie meant by corruption affecting man?

He kept his eyes on Blackwood's back as Zapien mobilized the rest to follow. A tug on his shirt, however, brought his attention back to himself.

On his right, Lance stared at him with wide eyes. "Did you really see an island out in the lagoons?" he whispered.

"Of course he did," shot Emma from his left. "Didn't you, Oli?"

He nodded, returning his eyes to Blackwood and Watkin.

"What do you think they're arguing about?" Lance asked.

For a quiet moment they watched Blackwood shake a fist at Watkin before disappearing into Tolteca's foyer. Curiously, instead of following Blackwood inside, Watkin angled to the eastern bridge, headed towards Hutch. As he crossed the infinite river, a green dot in the sky dove towards him. For one, strange moment, Oliver worried Watkin was under attack, but then he realized the green dot had settled onto the man's shoulder. It was Jaiba, the toucan, and unless Oliver was mistaken, the bird now spoke into Watkin's ear.

"Well, that's weird," said Emma as they lingered just outside Founders Temple to watch. "Can birds talk?"

## NOVA 01

"Wouldn't surprise me," Oliver replied, shrugging. "But I'm pretty sure I just found us a starting conversation for Watkin."

Lance scratched his head. "The bird?"

Emma rolled her eyes, stepping inside Founders Temple without them.

"No," said Oliver, resisting the urge to slap Lance on the back of the head. Santiago would have. "The secret island in the lagoons!"

"Do you think it's related to the scroll?" Lance hissed in his ear as they approached their favorite table in the Dining Hall. Before Oliver could answer, Elton dashed towards them, lifting Lance like a doll and shaking him with his hands. "DID YOU MAKE THE TEAM?!"

"We don't know yet," Emma replied as Lance tried speaking while his ribs were crushed into his lungs.

"Oh," said Elton, dropping his brother, disappointed. "That's weird. Normally they let you know down at the trench."

"Thank you," Lance wheezed towards Emma.

Stevie ignored everyone but Oliver as they settled down. She gave him an appraising look before glancing towards the Founders RAs whispering with Zapien at the faculty table. Blackwood was nowhere to be seen.

"What," she asked while shaking her head, "did you three do?"

Emma popped a quick look at Oliver, her mouth open to answer, but then Brantley joined them from the throng of RAs.

"Oliver! Emma! Lance! And you, too, Se'Vaughn. Congrats! You've made the team!"

"Never mind that," said Stevie, punctuating her words with a dismissive wave of her hand. "What's gone on at the trench? Blackwood stormed

## Chapter 13: Beneath the Swirling Fog

through here and went straight upstairs to the faculty apartments. Then y'all showed up without the teams announced? Did someone pants him at the tryouts or something?"

"Since when do you care about Coatlball?" Brantley asked chuckling. As he caught her up on Oliver's distraction at the end of practice and Blackwood's rant, Oliver ignored Elton's reactions to watch Ronnie instead. Even though he was out of earshot, his approach towards Beto and Cristina could only mean one thing.

A moment later, Beto's smile confirmed the bad news.

"Looks like Beto and Cristina made the team, too," Oliver said, interrupting Brantley and Stevie. Their entire table turned to watch when a tall, athletic boy with dark-brown hair approached Beto after Ronnie. Though Oliver couldn't see the boy's face, he saw Beto's.

For once, Beto didn't smirk as he clasped hands with the dark-haired boy. No words were exchanged but Oliver learned quite a lot by the interaction. The surrounding tables had gone quiet when the boy stood. They'd only resumed speaking when he sat back down.

"Who's that?" Emma asked, squinting her eyes.

Oliver answered first, putting two and two together. "Beto's cousin, right?"

Stevie's eyes widened as she nodded. "Yep – that's John Tupper. And you better hope you never see his nasty side. He's the reason why Champayan has won the last three years. Nobody – and I mean *nobody* – can duel like him."

# NOVA 01

Oliver opened his mouth to ask what made him so good, but Stevie shushed him. A second later, he understood why.

"Well done today, you four!" said Zapien from behind. On the table, she dropped four pairs of leather riding breeches and long-sleeve jerseys with weaves built into the arms. "Lance, you'll be number 9, Oliver 10, Emma 11, and Se'Vaughn 12! I'll go and give Beto and Cristina 7 and 8. First game is in November!"

When Zapien left, Oliver looked over the riding breeches with awe. They weren't as nice as Beto's, but he didn't care. Outside of his ring, nothing else made him feel like a part of the Other Side. This was a start.

An elbow in his ribs distracted him. It came from Elton.

"You should be thankful your first game isn't against me," he said bringing his head close to Oliver's. Above a maniacal grin, he rose his eyebrows in quick succession. "When we do meet – your tiny, twig frame – I will break it."

Lance shook his head as Elton boomed with laughter. "Ignore him, Oli. He can't help being part lizard."

"I thought it was gorilla," Emma whispered in Oliver's ear.

Stevie joined their huddle. "It's a combo, really. You see, when a gorilla and lizard person love each other very much—,"

"Okay!" shouted Lance. "That's enough family for today! Oli, Emma, let's go celebrate with Se'Vaughn, yeah?"

\* Chapter 13: Beneath the Swirling Fog \*

# NOVA 01

## Chapter 14: The Ceremony of the Gifts

*Something's happened — and I don't know how he'd take the news. It'll be good to be away.*

*$2^{nd}$ of December, the first year of the $10^{th}$ Age*

Oliver, Emma, and Lance's elation at making the Coatlball team fizzled over the coming weeks. Now that they were actually on the team, they began to appreciate the difference between tryouts and actual practices.

Ronnie pushed them. And he pushed them hard.

Foolishly, Oliver thought practice would consist of airborne defensive maneuvering and scoring formations. But Ronnie surprised him with an absurd amount of conditioning and cardio on the ground. More than once, Oliver was forced to take a break to throw up with exhaustion. His only comfort was that he knew he wasn't the only one.

"First game isn't even until November," Se'Vaughn growled mutinously at dinner one October evening.

Emma nodded with him while glaring at the other extramen in the Dining Hall. While the Coatlball team had just entered, covered in mud, most everyone else was already enjoying dessert.

"It's unfair!" Lance nearly shouted. He dropped his hammer on the table with no attempt at cushioning its impact. "Anyone doing chess or debate should have to practice as long as we do! What if Ms. Joan runs out of food!"

# * Chapter 14: The Ceremony of the Gifts *

Oliver, who was more acclimated to meals coming late in the day, shrugged. "I doubt Ms. Joan will ever run out of food. Order the craziest thing you can think of!" But he knew Emma and Lance weren't really upset about late dinners. That was only part of the problem.

What really had everyone on edge was the upcoming Ceremony of the Gifts. As members of the Coatlball team, they had the least time to prepare for it.

Even though their Professors and RAs kept promising they'd pass whatever test they faced, it was hard to ignore the rumors that spread.

"Every year, I swear!" they heard Valerie, Emma's roommate, hiss to Ogden and Grayson further down the table. "My cousin told me. Apparently, three of us are doomed to be *expelled*. No telling who it's going to be this year." They began looking around the Dining Hall suspiciously when Valerie finished. Before they got to Oliver, he looked away.

Every time he heard one of these conversations unfold, he felt his hands get sweaty. Despite what anybody said, he still couldn't tell if he was a Wiser or Powerhead.

Beto didn't help either.

"All bow to the King of Wisdom," he routinely jeered in the hallways. This was always accompanied by snickering and ironic bows from James and Cristina. Thankfully, however, Se'Vaughn and Trey took the sting out of it by doing the same thing with jovial, ironic expressions.

"He's not even listening, is he?" said Lance. "Hellooooo, Oliver?"

"Sorry," said Oliver, shaking his head, "what's up?"

# NOVA 01

Emma growled from across the table. "*What* do you think we'll face at the Ceremony? You're the Wise one here."

"Yeah!" agreed Lance. "Give us some wisdom, will ya?"

Oliver's heart sank. How was he supposed to know?

Just the previous week, Professor Belk asked him to step to the front of the class and fire off a brick of Earth using the physical side of destruction. He managed to lift a blob of dirt after kicking into the ground, but when he punched out to fire, he shattered his knucklebones in the process. After getting fixed up in the infirmary, he skipped the rest of the lesson, too mortified to return and give Beto the opportunity to call him "the King of Broken Knuckles," or worse.

"I bet that's what the Test of Power will be," he muttered back to Emma. "To attack something with Earth."

"Hmm," Emma replied, "maybe we should practice near Hutch. Get some tips from the older guys."

Agreeing, Oliver pushed back his chair and stood up, thanking Ms. Joan before he left.

A few moments later, they approached Hutch where groups of students practiced several different levels of magic. Nearest, they saw Elton practicing his shielding against Stevie.

"Howdy!" said Lance, waving at them.

"Don't you howdy me!" bellowed Elton. "We're practicing over here! Go find your own space!"

Lance's smile faltered under his blonde hair. Oliver, on the other hand, laughed, before suggesting an open space nearby.

## * Chapter 14: The Ceremony of the Gifts *

First, Emma practiced lifting globs of Earth into the air. None of them had mastered this piece yet, often lifting muddy Earth instead of dry, crispy chunks of rock like Professor Belk. Oliver and Lance followed, both kicking up dripping globs to chest level.

"Stop!" came a voice.

*Thud, thud, thud* sounded as their globs fell back down.

"Abe, you ruined our concentration!" said Emma, frowning.

"I know," he said, scratching the back of his head. "Has Belk taught you about the theoretical side of elemental magic, yet?"

Oliver, Emma, and Lance exchanged confused looks.

Abe sighed. "Did she tell you *how* to move the Earth? Was any reading assigned?"

Emma laughed. "Who's got time to read?" Lance nodded along while Oliver scratched the back of his head sheepishly.

Abe pushed his lips together, unamused. "What you would have learned in the *reading* is the underlying theory. Belk doesn't need theory because she can brute force her way to the end result. That can sometimes work for Powerheads, but for a Wiser like me, it's never worked."

He kicked into the ground, popping up a perfect chunk of dry rock. Then, he punched it, *hard*.

It flew towards Elton, who yelped and magicked a wavering, purple shield to block it. "Hey! Watch where you're launching!"

Abe waved a hand dismissively. "Look y'all. I'm not your parents. But do the reading assignments. It'll up your game."

## NOVA 01

Oliver looked down at the ground, kicking loose bits of dirt. Out of the corner of his eye, he could see Emma and Lance doing the same.

"For now," Abe sighed, "I'll fill you in. Elemental magic doesn't require a magical word of prompting because energy already exists *inside* the elements. No need to channel Nova when you're already flush with heat or kinetic energy."

Oliver stared at Abe, dumbfounded. He could almost feel a veil lifting off his head. He didn't need to use magic through his ring to move the Earth, he just needed to ask the energy itself to move for him.

Reflexively, he kicked into the ground, lifting a new clump of Earth. He laughed as he held it in place.

A perfect, dry square.

Grinning, he punched hard, like Abe had. Elton yelped again as the missile flew towards him. This time, he lifted a rock wall to block it.

*Wham!*

Emma and Lance's shots followed, splattering bits of mud at Stevie as they exploded.

"Would y'all, stop?" Elton growled.

"Sorry!" yelled Oliver. When he turned back to Abe, a big smile waited for him.

"Told you. Do the readings."

# * Chapter 14: The Ceremony of the Gifts *

Since the Ceremony of the Gifts was only a week away, the campus began decorating itself accordingly. From the Swampy Woods to the west of the lagoons, skeletons emerged to dart across the grounds, pranking students as often as they could. One walked into the Dining Hall over breakfast the next morning and managed to start a food fight before Ms. Joan emerged from the kitchens roaring. At the sight of her, it cackled through unhinged jaws before bolting towards the lagoons, covered in eggs, hash browns, and syrupy pancakes.

Elsewhere, jack-o'-lanterns chased innocent pumpkins across the grounds, adding them to their midst whenever they caught one. Oliver never grew tired of seeing one of these chases unfold. Surprisingly high paced affairs, the hunts typically ended in seconds. Whenever a pumpkin was caught, the jack-o'-lanterns would descend upon it, whooping madly before creating eyes, a crooked smile, and a removable head cover to place a candle inside their newest member. By the next weekend, the campus was covered with pumpkin innards and a small army of jack-o'-lanterns that bobbed up and down across the grounds, searching for the last surviving pumpkin. Emma had spotted it hiding on top of the roofs of the Academic Building, shaking with fright.

Even the lagoons weren't exempt from the campus traditions. A deadly spirit called *Xihuacota* [7] stalked the edges of the water, wailing like a banshee during the evenings. Oliver, who was frightened to death of her, was surprised to hear she rarely drowned anybody, but mostly kidnapped

---

[7] Phonetically pronounced as "Chee-wah-coat-ah" in English.

students who came too close and forced them to spend time with her in her house at the bottom of the lagoon knitting or playing cards. She would only reluctantly return students by direct request from Headmaster Lalandra and, according to her, it could often take a week for *Xihuacota* to "process the paperwork." Any student that did manage to return inevitably took years to recover.

But even *Xihuacota* felt like a cheap appetizer by the morning of the Ceremony of the Gifts.

"Look," said Lance for the dozenth time after lunch. "Belk's had us practicing the Earth elemental move like crazy, so we probably have to attack something for the Test of Power."

Oliver nodded his head absentmindedly, not wanting to risk speaking in case he got sick.

"And Zapien keeps making us channel energy from stuff she's set up in the classrooms," Lance continued. "No clue how we'll get tested on that. But then Chavarría keeps quizzing us on the smells and shimmers of embalming fluids."

"Maybe we'll have to pick between an embalming of frost and a poison for one of the Tests," said Emma. Her head was on the table as she swiped through pages of Belk's reading assignments on her notebook.

"Blackwood keeps making us shield with elementals until we're ready to channel a forcefield shield," said Oliver. "Maybe we'll have to block attacks, too."

## * Chapter 14: The Ceremony of the Gifts *

"I can't handle it!" said Emma suddenly. She stood up and motioned back up the common room. "I'm going outside to practice. All this reading and worrying isn't helping any."

"Yeah, I think you're right."

Standing up, they exited the eastern viewing dome, heading straight for the stairs and fresh air.

But they didn't get that far. In the short hallway between the viewing dome and the main common room, Beto, Cristina, and James blocked the way out with crossed arms.

"You three look stressed," said Beto, looking at them pityingly. "Don't worry, the school charters direct flights back for everyone who fails."

Pushing Oliver aside, Emma put her face directly in front of Beto's. "Give me a reason," she growled, flexing her sleeved arm. Beto didn't flinch; his smile only grew wider.

Cristina stepped forward and pushed Emma hard. Oliver and Lance managed to catch her before she hit the floor. Just as Lance unbuckled his hammer from his belt, Brantley's voice boomed around them.

"HEY!" he yelled, appearing at the stairwell. Oliver felt an invisible force hold him from moving any closer to Beto. From B2, Oliver saw Abe looking down, his eyes narrow. "Cristina, Lance! Both of you! Detention next weekend!"

"What did Lance do?" shouted Oliver.

"Don't talk back to me!" growled Brantley pointing a finger at Oliver. The world seemed to darken around them as Brantley's voice grew in their heads. "Brandishing a weapon can get you expelled! Both of you report to Blackwood after the ceremony to schedule your detentions."

Beto smiled as he walked away. James followed, looking smug. Cristina, to Oliver's pleasure, had an ugly frown on her face.

"Listen here, you three," said Brantley. "Can't you tell a setup when you see one?"

Lance balked. "You mean you expect us just to smile back at them and take their abuse?! He said we'd fail the Ceremony!"

"Yes," said Abe. He had joined them downstairs. In the common room, a cheer came from a group of students watching a Coatlball game. "He knows none of you will fail the Ceremony! He just wanted to bait you into doing something stupid. Really, Lance. Were you going to bash his head in with your hammer?"

"No," said Lance, sighing. "Thought his ribs could have used a good whack, though." At the look on Abe's face, he quickly added, "just kidding!" Abe continued to frown, but Brantley grinned.

"Don't worry about the Ceremony," he said, grabbing Lance and ruffling his hair. "Elton passed, and he's dumb as a post!"

"Is it true people are expelled every year for failing?" asked Oliver, unable to help himself.

"That's for y'all to find out," said Brantley, releasing a disgruntled Lance.

"Y'all are the worst," muttered Emma. "Actually, that's not true. That Cristina girl is the worst."

"She just pushed you because you got closer to kissing Beto than she ever has," laughed Lance. Oliver raised his eyebrows at that.

## * Chapter 14: The Ceremony of the Gifts *

"I expected him to flinch," she said, pulling at a strand of hair, "but he didn't move a muscle."

"Yeah, well," said Abe, "that kid's clearly got the same Powerhead genes as his cousin. I'm sure you'll continue to be friends for *years* to come."

"Just like us and his cousin," muttered Brantley.

Oliver scratched his head at the mention of Beto's cousin. "Blackwood keeps mentioning him. And we saw him in the Dining Hall a couple times. Is he really just as bad as Beto?"

Brantley nodded his head. "An absolute treasure of a human being."

"Well, it might have been easy for you to ignore John," said Emma, matter-of-factly, "but I'm not going to just sit there and take abuse from Beto, Cristina, and James. Now, if you don't mind, we have to practice before the Ceremony!" She began to walk off towards the stairs.

"You don't know what John is like," said Brantley, looking stern. "And besides, I hate to break it to y'all, but the Ceremony starts in fifteen minutes."

"AAAARRGH," yelled Lance. "If Beto hadn't distracted us!"

"You'd still pass one of the Tests," said Abe, shaking his head.

With their hearts in their stomachs, Oliver, Emma, and Lance stared at each other for a moment before joining the throng of students marching out of Founders Hall. Before long, they were on their way to the Dungeon-Simulation Room, too worried to open their mouths lest their stomachs betray them.

As they ascended the ridge with their classmates, hardmores through seniors jeered at them from either side of the path. The shouts from

# NOVA 01

Champayan students proved to be the most egregious with phrases like "wouldn't be surprised if the whole class is expelled this year!" and "there won't be any left by dinner!" ringing clearly in the air through the ruckus. Blackwood, who led the extramen, grinned at the worst of the insults.

Emma walked with her shoulders back, staring down anyone who dared throw an insult at her. Those who did, quickly looked away, unable to match the steely resolve in her eyes. Lance, meanwhile, kept reciting all they'd learned so far to anybody who would listen. Oliver, however, already had enough of his own thoughts reverberating noisily in his head.

Although he felt Brave, like Emma, he couldn't rid himself of a nagging anxiety. Any number of traps might lay ahead, and it didn't help he had no idea what they might be. Emma was sure to receive the Test of Courage and Lance the Test of Power, but what about him? Brantley was convinced he was a Powerhead before Abe forced everyone to call him a Wiser. Would they give him the Test of Wisdom only for him to be sent home? Would he have to beg Lalandra for another Test if he failed?

By the time they reached the Simulation Room, the world around him had slowed down. He heard everything, including Lance's running monologue, as if through thick sheets of wool. As he blindly followed the others into the Simulation Room, he saw James and Cristina snickering at something Beto had said. There was no doubt in his mind the joke featured him front and center.

"Oli! Oli!" said a girl's voice. A concerned face appeared before his.

It was Emma. Why did she sound so different?

# * Chapter 14: The Ceremony of the Gifts *

She snapped her fingers in front of his eyes. "Hey! Remember Miyada's shop?"

Whether it was Emma's hand in his face, or the memory of Miyada's shop, all of a sudden Oliver heard the noise around him grow loud again.

"Remember the power you felt?" she continued, shaking his shoulders. "I saw it happen. No matter what test they throw at you, you're gonna pass — you got that? You're gonna pass."

Oliver nodded his head, still somewhat numb. He managed to shoot her a weak smile and she grinned back, breathing more life into him.

"Worst case scenario," growled Lance, "just blow everything up with shots of Earth. That's my backup plan if I can't—,"

Just what Lance's plan was, Oliver never found out, because his voice was drowned out by Tolteca.

"MY BELOVED EXTRAMEN!" boomed the sundial. "TODAY WE GATHER TO TEST YOU FOR YOUR GIFT. IN THE OBSERVATION DECK, THE ENTIRE STUDENT BODY WATCHES, READY TO CELEBRATE WITH EACH OF YOU THAT PASSES." The sundial took a moment to zoom around the top of the room. Instead of a dungeon, like normal, they stood in an enormous foyer with nothing but a turquoise blue door waiting for them. A soft, yellow light flooded the room with light no shadows could obfuscate.

Tolteca continued to float overhead, grimacing through ruby and emerald teeth. "THE RULES ARE SET. ONE BY ONE, YOU WILL PASS THROUGH THE DOOR. INSIDE, AN INDIVIDUAL TEST AWAITS – DETERMINED BY THE FOUNDERS' SPIRITS AND

## NOVA 01

COMMUNICATED TO YOU VIA THE FOUNDERS' FLAME. FLASH OF GREEN, YOUR COURAGE MUST BE SEEN. SPARK OF RED, YOUR POWER MUST BE SPREAD. DANCE OF BLUE, TRUST YOUR WISDOM TO SEE YOU THROUGH. LET THE CEREMONY OF THE GIFTS BEGIN!"

A drum sounded from above.

*Boom!*

Oliver quickly wondered if they were supposed to form a line to go through the door, but then it creaked open and the Headmaster's voice was heard.

"Harrison, James."

The extramen collectively gaped at James as he shuffled forward nervously. Instead of his normal, buffoonish grin, he scowled at the room at large. When he made his way through the door and it shut behind him, another beat of the drum echoed around them.

*Boom!*

*Randomized agony*, Oliver thought. And then the door creaked open again. *That was quick.*

"Kirk, Se'Vaughn."

"Good luck," Oliver heard Trey say as Se'Vaughn approached the door without hesitation. *If he isn't a Brave, I'll give up my spot on the Coatlball team.*

*Boom!*

Butterflies threatened to burst from Oliver's stomach. Nearby, he saw others sit down to put their heads between their heads and mutter.

A few moments later, the door burst open again.

## * Chapter 14: The Ceremony of the Gifts *

This time, Oliver noticed a floating list on the right-hand side of the room next to Tolteca. On the list were Se'Vaughn's and James' names in one column, and *Test of Courage* and *Test of Power* in the next column. He didn't see any indication of a pass or fail. *Where did they go after taking the Test?* He looked around the room for a second door but couldn't find one. *Ah, the Observation Deck.* His eyes flickered above where the older students watched, unseen and unheard.

"Fleishman, Dub."

Oliver watched as name after name went before him, each time adding to the floating list next to Tolteca. After a dozen names, he was forced to begin pushing his black hair off his forehead, where sweat had begun to percolate.

*Boom!*

Oliver held his breath.

"Griffith, Emma."

He exhaled and tried nodding his head at Emma reassuringly. She met his eyes and nodded back appreciatively, rolling her sleeved arm in a few circles as she stepped forward. He certainly expected her to pass.

The door shut.

*Boom!*

Emma's name popped up next to *Test of Courage*.

"No surprises there," whispered Lance.

"Warren, Beto," rang Lalandra's voice.

# NOVA 01

Smirking, Beto stood up and unbuckled the scimitar on his belt for everyone to see. He shook his head to adjust his curly hair before proceeding forward and kicking the door open.

*Boom!*

"What an absolute clown–," Lance began.

But the door swung back open. Beto's name was already up on the board next to *Test of Power*.

"Wyatt, Lance," said Dr. Lalandra.

Lance's jaw dropped.

Oliver, still standing, pulled him up and clapped him on the back. With a scowl on his face and his warhammer in both hands, Lance approached the turquoise door, his lips tight.

A boom and a few moments later, the next name was called, and *Test of Power* shone next to Lance's name on the list. Oliver felt very much alone looking at Emma and Lance on a list that didn't include him. With each additional beat of the drum, he winced or cringed, but still, his name didn't come.

"Thompson, Leah."

*Boom!*

"Lauderdale, Bobo."

*Boom!*

"Yang, Grayson."

*Boom!*

"Adams, Valerie."

*Boom!*

# * Chapter 14: The Ceremony of the Gifts *

"Smith, Alexis."

*Boom!*

After an hour, only he and Cristina remained in the waiting room. Feeling nauseated, he put his head in his hands.

*Boom!*

Oliver's heart skipped a beat.

"Morris, Cristina."

His hands shook as he met Cristina's eyes. Even though they detested each other, they now shared the bond of having had to wait the longest.

"They really ought to have us all go the same time in different rooms," he said, smiling weakly.

She looked away quickly, reproachful eyes behind her thin nose.

*Definitely not a Brave.*

The door shut, and Oliver closed his eyes, waiting for the drum.

When he opened his eyes again, he stood, shocked. The waiting room had gone, leaving him in world of shifting greys and whites. When a voice spoke nearby, he held back a scream.

*"The vision has escaped me, Cuahtemoc,"* said a man's voice. *It belonged to an eerie silhouette with white spheres where eyes should have been. He dashed up the steps of an overgrown temple towards a willow tree at its peak.*

*"So, that's it, we stop our efforts?"* boomed the voice of another man speaking in his non-native tongue. *"What of the boy, Augustus?"*

*"We leave him this,"* said the first man, brandishing a scroll of parchment.

*"Others will find it,"* challenged Cuahtemoc.

## NOVA 01

"Not if we scrub all memory of it," said a third voice belonging to a short woman with a thick accent. "And leave clues only discoverable by him."

"Stop!" yelled Augustus, nearly tripping on his way up the stairs. He looked back down directly at Oliver. "He's here, now! He watches us!"

Boom!

"García, Oliver."

Oliver stood quickly, *drenched* in sweat, as the vision receded in his mind. Had that been his test? It had felt like he'd been peeking into another part of the world from a different set of eyes, not his own. Unless he was mistaken, he'd just seen the Founders conversing – and they'd somehow sensed *him*.

"García, Oliver," repeated Dr. Lalandra.

Remembering where he was, and the importance of the next few moments, Oliver ambled forward, nearly tripping over himself. What would he be tested for? Wisdom, Power, Bravery? It was nearly impossible to focus with ghostly visions of Augustus, Cuahtemoc, and Madeline still popping up in his eyes.

Stepping through the door, he flexed his ring hand and surveyed his surroundings. Against the far wall, a torch crackled yellow. The Founders Flame – just as Tolteca promised. It'd turn to blue for Wisdom at any moment—

Red. The Founders Flame shot a wave of red across the room. *"TEST OF POWER!"* rang Tolteca's voice.

# * Chapter 14: The Ceremony of the Gifts *

Next to the torch, a door began scraping open. As it ascended, Oliver cracked his neck and exhaled. He could unpack the vision with Emma and Lance later.

He almost laughed as more and more of the door slid away, revealing the largest person he'd ever seen. Out stepped an eight-foot humanoid, covered from head to toe in black, seamless armor. In one hand, it brandished a claymore large enough to cleave an oak tree from its roots. With the other, it pointed at Oliver before letting out a howl.

*Definitely not a human.*

Oliver watched torchlight catch the blade as he scrambled to think of a way to defeat his foe. When it finished howling, however, his priorities shifted because the beast *charged*.

Panicking, Oliver pictured Elton creating his elemental Earth wall. With a release of his breath, he emulated the movements, shifting his weight onto his right foot.

A wall of rock and stone, far larger than Elton's, rocketed into the air until it crashed into the ceiling. The lights went in and out as the room shook, and, for a moment, Oliver thought he heard the student body screaming and shouting from the observation deck.

A second later, he ignored the thought because the portion of wall directly in front of him had *dented* towards him. Pebbles crumbled as Oliver wasted time inspecting the damage. Then, when he heard a muffled howl from the other side, he punched the wall like he would a regular rock in one of Belk's lessons. The wall of rocks obliged, firing across the room with the monster stuck to it.

# NOVA 01

*Boom!*

Pieces of armor shot from either side of where wall now met wall and before Oliver even realized it was over, the observation deck came into view.

Relief swept over him as noise engulfed his ears. From among the cheering crowd above, he saw Elton shaking Lance in the air. Next to them, Emma and Stevie jumped up and down, cheering. Even Lalandra applauded, smiling regally at him with a warm expression.

But then, her smile shifted.

With shock in her eyes, she exchanged words with Watkin, and after rushed whispers, they looked back towards Oliver, or rather, past him. Nervous his foe hadn't been defeated, Oliver turned to follow their gazes.

It wasn't the monster. It was the Founders Flame.

Only, now, it flashed *green*.

"*TEST OF … BRAVERY!*" said Tolteca's voice, faltering slightly. The noise from the cheering crowd faded away again, blanketing him in silence.

"Hang on!" shouted Oliver, "I just passed the last one! I didn't fail! Why … do …"

But as he spoke, he realized what was happening. The torch, no, the Founders were testing him for a second Gift! A memory from Miyada's shop flashed in his head, unprompted, as the silhouettes of Augustus, Cuahtemoc, and Madeline flitted in and out of his vision. *"You're the Prophet's Advent!"*

# * Chapter 14: The Ceremony of the Gifts *

Goosebumps erupted across Oliver's arms. But a feeling in the back of his head calmed him as the room changed in front of his eyes. *Is that Bravery I feel back there? Or Wisdom?*

He disregarded the thought to focus on his task.

In front of him, the room turned into a long, empty hallway. *That's suspicious.*

Cautiously, he took one step forward.

He heard, and *felt*, a whistling noise above him.

He rolled back, just in time, to avoid a thin, wide blade. It had swept through where his head had just been.

For a moment, Oliver blanched. A hallway full of traps? How was he supposed to navigate through it?

And then the answer slapped him in the face. *What would Emma do?*

Grinning, he sprinted forward as fast as his legs could take him.

More than once, he felt something narrowly miss his legs, or nearly reach his neck; but that was as close as any of the traps got to him. When he reached the other side next to the torch again, he caught his breath with his hands on his knees and laughed. Behind him, torn ropes still wiggled, while swinging blades, poison-tipped arrows, and even a giant rolling boulder kept attacking the different areas he'd sprinted past.

With his heart pounding, he looked up and around the room, waiting for the observation deck to appear again. But it didn't come. Instead, sparks cracked and popped merrily from the Founders Flame as a wave of royal blue dispersed around the room.

"*TEST OF WISDOM!*"

## NOVA 01

*About time.*

In the back of his head, a voice wanted Oliver to feel proud that he'd already passed two tests. That the Founders had determined he was a Trinova. That he had proved them all wrong. But he wasn't done yet. One test remained – the one he'd expected to get all along.

*No sliding door this time. That's weird.*

He turned to look around the room and groaned, realizing what was happening. Next to him, the torch light began to fade, eventually turning to nothing more than a handful of embers and across the room, a door scraped open. For a moment, he felt tempted to dash closer to the torchlight – at least what was left of it – but his subconscious tugged against the urge.

"*Iuxtairis*," he said in the dark. His subconscious was right. He'd have a better chance of fighting his enemy if he knew what it was. Standing with a flame to his back wouldn't be of any use.

He grinned into the dark. *Wisdom.*

Snickering laughter followed, dropping his smile and making the hair stand on the back of his neck. *What creature made a noise like that?*

He fired a rock in the direction of the noise. A second later, it crashed against the far wall. Light footsteps echoed across the room, along with more snickering laughter.

Taking a breath, Oliver fired off a handful of rocks in every direction. His heart skipped a beat as the projectiles forced a shadow to step close enough to the torch.

A leathery, green creature came into view, making Oliver feel as frightened as he could ever remember. It had four legs and could have been

## * Chapter 14: The Ceremony of the Gifts *

mistaken for a dog if it weren't for the patches of leathery sinew and quills on its back. Crouching low, it hissed at the torch, quills quivering.

*It's blinded by the light!*

Oliver shifted his weight, popping up another rock. As he decided what to do, he held it in place.

In front of him, the creature continued hissing at the Founder's Flame, ignoring him entirely. Still, Oliver held onto the rock, refusing to believe the challenge could be this easy. Was he supposed to launch the rock and end it already? Or was he missing something else entirely – something like the sound of another pair of feet scampering towards him in the dark!

He nearly screamed as a second set of quills clinked together on his right. Ducking, he rotated with a twirl towards the torch.

Not a moment too soon. As he ducked, a creature twice the size of the first sailed past him, having leapt for his throat. Fear threatened to consume Oliver as he locked eyes with the beast. Where the first could have passed for an abused street dog, the second screamed at him like a monster from the depths of hell.

Channeling his fright into a guttural roar, Oliver launched a projectile of hardened rock towards the creature's flank.

It connected with a sickening *crunch*.

Before he could even inspect the damage, cell-shaded smoke enveloped the simulated beast, leaving nothing behind. Ignoring it, Oliver kept his focus and turned towards the remaining monster.

*Great.*

# NOVA 01

It had vacated its post near the Founders Flame, nowhere to be seen. From the dark, no more laughter echoed, only a low growl.

*Look who's scared now. I'll have to force you out.*

This time, Oliver rose half a dozen spheres of Earth before punching each one in turn towards everywhere the light didn't touch.

*Where are you hiding?*

Finally, the smaller of the beasts reappeared near the Founders Flame, forced to do so as rock after rock burst shrapnel across the room.

Sensing his opportunity, Oliver charged. Before the dog-like monstrosity could dart away, he kicked into the Earth beneath him, reflexively scooping his right foot beneath the surface. The motion worked, launching a sphere like a soccer ball. It connected with the beast so quickly that it disappeared in a cloud of smoke before the rock even connected.

This time, Oliver allowed himself to succumb to the relief nagging his soul. It swept over him like a warm blanket as the lights flooded back on and chaos ensued. Above him, the observation deck exploded into sound, deafening his ears. Elton, who frothed at the mouth from yelling himself hoarse, slammed his hands into the ground while Lance jumped up and down. Nearby, Emma looked down at him smugly with her arms folded, *I told you so* was painted across her lips with the least subtle brushstroke Oliver had ever seen.

After a moment, he too disappeared in a cloud of smoke before reappearing next to Lalandra in the observation deck.

## ∗ Chapter 14: The Ceremony of the Gifts ∗

Only then did he notice the student numbers had thinned. In fact, even though a majority of the extramen celebrated, at least half of the older students looked to have left – he didn't see a single Champayan frock coat.

Now that his heart had slowed down in his chest, he even saw Lalandra's face contradicting itself. Though a hint of a smile rested on her lips, a shadow of concern creased her brows.

With her voice magically loudened, she stepped forward and interrupted the remaining celebrations.

"Yes, yes, congratulations to all extramen!" she said. "Please head up to the Dining Hall for the celebratory feast where we will celebrate each of your victories in full. And maybe," she added, giving Oliver a poignant look, "much more!"

Grinning, Abe and Brantley led the charge out of the Simulation Room. Oliver started to walk with the rest, but a hand on his shoulder stopped him. It was Professor Watkin.

"You better stay put for a moment," he said. Oliver's jubilation fell at the grim look on his face. *What is going on?*

Emma and Lance walked up, looking determined to wait with him, but Watkin dismissed them with a wave of his hand. "Sorry, you two. Just Oliver."

Emma glared with crossed arms. Lance, however, still jumped up and down in between running his hands through his hair.

"I never *actually* thought—," he shouted. Emma began dragging him away, still glaring. "You're a TRINOVA! A REAL TRINOVA! What are Mom and Dad going to say?"

## NOVA 01

Out of the faculty, only Professor Euclid went with the students, but even his wizened face looked at Oliver with concern.

After he left, nobody said a word. Oliver looked around at the faces remaining, shocked to find nearly a third of them surveying him as they might a bomb in a town square. Only Watkin, Zapien, and Lalandra gave him comforting nods of the head, albeit with grim expressions.

Last of all, he met eyes with Blackwood, who openly seethed at him with clenched fists and tightened lips. Desmoulins, next to him, looked simply stunned.

A nearby cough snapped Oliver away from Blackwood and Desmoulins. It was Watkin who'd broken the silence.

The usual mischievous spark in his eyes was absent, replaced by some of Santiago's steel. "Oliver," he began, "you should know, you are the first confirmed Trinova in recorded History."

"BAH!" shouted Blackwood. "You inflate an already inflated ego! Do not—,"

"That is quite enough, Broderick," interrupted Dr. Lalandra. The finality in her tone wilted Dean Blackwood, which was a first. He stepped back, fuming even more than before.

Oliver stared around, bewildered. The others looked from him to Blackwood and then to Lalandra. Was that fear on their faces? Fear of what?

"We tell you this," Watkin continued, "not to make you feel Powerful, Wise, or Brave, but to warn you that you are now the most dangerous tool in the world."

## * Chapter 14: The Ceremony of the Gifts *

*They're afraid of me.*

"Now is that really necessary?" interrupted Professor Zapien, her curls bouncing as she stepped forward. "He doesn't need to know about any of that! Just let him be a normal student at school!"

Desmoulins let out a false laugh and shook his fingers at Oliver, his palms up. "He'll never be a normal student. The press is going to have a field day with this."

They all began to argue with one another, their voices growing louder by the second.

Still stunned, Oliver watched in silence as they insulted or challenged each other, almost forgetting he stood there among them. Nearest to him, Zapien and Watkin continued squabbling in undertones. Just past them, Lalandra and Blackwood entered a shouting match, cracking any illusions Oliver had of harmony among the faculty.

*Shouldn't they be proud of me? Why does it matter?* Even just thinking about his position gave him a thrill of energy. He wanted to yell out, to tell them they were all being fools. He wasn't evil. He was just a boy. Maybe if he told them about his visions of the Founders they'd worry less?

Just as he was about to pipe up, a terrifying thought flooded his brain.

*Do they think I'll become like The Damned? What aren't they telling me?*

The door to the Observation Deck blasted open, followed by Archie, who shot inside with fire leaking from his mandibles.

His voice tore through the air like a pointed sword, causing everyone but Lalandra to wince. *"HOW DARE YOU? YOU ALREADY PLAY YOUR GAMES? YOUR PETTY POLITICS? ON A HATCHLING?!*

## NOVA 01

*AUGUSTUS CREATED THIS SCHOOL TO STAY THIS MADNESS, NOT ENCOURAGE IT!*

*"THE BOY WILL RECEIVE HIS EDUCATION AS INTENDED – ABSENT OF YOUR SELF-SERVING DELUSIONS!"*

Archie didn't finish there, but the language he spoke shifted to Nahuatl, leaving only Tolteca to understand.

Although most shirked away from Archie's tirade, diverting their eyes, Blackwood and Desmoulins mirrored the anger right back at the feathered serpent.

*"Come,"* Archie directed towards Oliver. *"I'm taking you to the Feast."*

In his heart, Oliver desperately wanted to hear what else the faculty had to say. But he wasn't about to disagree with a raging, thousand-pound sacred beast. Without a further word, he ducked his head and stepped outside.

With one last look behind his shoulder, he saw the adults were nowhere near finished arguing. How could they be? One of their students had just become a walking myth – a potentially dangerous one.

\* Chapter 14: The Ceremony of the Gifts \*

##  NOVA 01

## Chapter 15: The Prophet's Advent

*We held a New Year's Eve fundraiser last night and some sycophant called him the Prophet's Advent. He laughed it off, but I could tell he was loving the attention.*
*Before Congress broke session, they officially repealed the 3rd Amendment for Magic, which will make rolling out the rehabilitation centers easier.*
*Not that it matters for me. I'm headed out for Chichén Itzá – and not a moment too soon. Starting our research with the Mayans before moving on to the Khmers.*

*1st of January, the second year of the 10th Age*

"Really? The skinny kid? I thought ... well, he'd be bigger, you know? More Powerful?"

"Lighten up, he's just an extraman."

"Kinda cute though, right?"

"Sure, in a little brother kind of way. You're three years older than he is for crying out loud!"

"..."

"I think he can hear us!"

"Of course, he can hear you!" Emma shouted at a gaggle of senior year girls on the second floor of the Academic Building. "We're not even six feet away from you!"

Blushing and giggling followed.

They always giggled.

Oliver sighed. He'd had a difficult time ignoring these conversations since they'd broken out like wildfire after the Ceremony of the Gifts. Every

## Chapter 15: The Prophet's Advent

walk to class, every meal at the Dining Hall, and every lesson in the Academic Building was now interrupted by students shamelessly staring at him as if he were a piece of cheesecake at a bakery.

At first, he enjoyed the attention. A *lot* more girls now stared at him. If it weren't for daily reminders from Emma – "they're only batting their eyes at you because they think you're a demigod!" – he might have allowed himself to enjoy the sea of stares and soft expressions. But a voice in the back of his head, which he now recognized as Wisdom, implored him to listen to Emma.

Still, it wasn't entirely possible to ignore the shift. Elton, for instance, now walked down the hallways ahead of him with his chest puffed out shouting "make way for the King of Wisdom! Make way for Founders' pride!"

By the third week, the extra attention made Oliver sick to his stomach. When a hardmore girl asked him out on a date just after a dull lesson on triangular magnification with Professor Euclid, all he could manage to do was press his lips together awkwardly and shake his head. After a bout of laughing and teasing from Lance and Se'Vaughn, Oliver made straight for the eastern viewing dome, where he barricaded himself to work on his ever-growing pile of homework and research. There, only Emma and Lance could bother him, allowing him to tackle a strain of anxiety he never knew he'd had. Others still peered at him from the main common room, but he always chose a seat facing the murky waters of the lagoons to avoid their faces.

# NOVA 01

Oliver's mind often strayed outside of the viewing dome, however, to worry about the looks some pockets of older students and a growing majority of faculty members now gave him. On those faces, he didn't see smiles of approval, let alone slow, batting eyelashes. Instead, he saw grimaces of anger, eyes dusted by fear, and eyebrows furrowed with curiosity.

The night of the Ceremony of the Gifts, Oliver pulled Emma and Lance into the same viewing dome to tell them what happened in the Simulation Room.

"Watkin really called you a dangerous tool?" asked Emma, her eyebrows raised.

"Well, he said it in a warning kind of way, not a mean way."

"Pshh!" Emma dismissed. "Warning or not, there's something behind that. Did he say what kind of tool?"

Oliver had to think before answering. "No, not really. But when Archie stormed in, he was angrier than anything I've ever seen. Absolutely scary stuff – full on *fire* was coming out of his mouth and everything. He accused them of using me for politics before pulling me away. He straight up told me not to trust any of the faculty and to only listen to what the Founders left for me to find."

"Hang on," interrupted Lance. "He told you we can't trust any of the faculty? Not even Watkin? Weren't we planning on talking to him about our 'additional subject matter'?"

Oliver took turns staring into each of their eyes, imploring them to remember his every word. "In my vision, Madeline said they would *scrub* all

# ✷ Chapter 15: The Prophet's Advent ✷

memory of whatever they left behind. So, whatever, they hid, they had a reason to do in secret."

"Why?" Lance asked.

"Why what?"

"Why keep it a secret?"

"Because," interrupted Emma, "they knew they couldn't trust anybody else with it! Aren't you listening?"

"I get that," said Lance, reddening slightly, "but why couldn't they trust anyone with the secret? They could have just passed down word through the Headmasters or something, but they decided to *scrub* all memory of it? What does that even mean? Seems strange to me. What secret was so important that absolutely nobody else could know about it? None of the professors know about it. And I bet you Archie doesn't either. It must be one hell of a secret, Oliver."

That had been a very good line of thinking from Lance, and Oliver had been agonizing about it every day since. He knew they needed to find the scroll, and *fast*. But they had nowhere to start looking other than the mysterious, golden willow and temple in the lagoons. But he'd been stupid enough to mention it to Blackwood, Zapien, and Watkin after Coatlball tryouts all those weeks ago. Was it possible Blackwood secretly believed Oliver and would go looking for the willow too?"

When the viewing dome thinned out so that just he, Emma, and Lance remained, Oliver slammed shut *Lycene's Lance; the Lost Treasure of the Peloponnesian War* and stood up.

"We have to find that scroll!"

## NOVA 01

"*Finally!*" muttered Emma, dismissing the essay on her notebook.

"*Excellent!*" said Lance, throwing his notebook to the side. It clattered into the glass wall, indestructible. "Now how do we find an island that can't be found in the middle of a lake covered with fog?"

"I've been thinking about that," said Emma. "Now that *Xihuacota* has disappeared for the year, it shouldn't be too difficult to swim—,"

"Okay, ain't nobody going swimming in the lagoons," interrupted Lance. "Have you seen the size of the catfish in there?" A twelve-foot catfish bumped into the glass in front of them, as if prompted. With annoyed whiskers, it glared at them through the glass. Lance smugly pointed at it with two open hands and outstretched arms.

"Fair point," said Emma, showing her palms for peace. "We could build a raft?"

Lance sighed, sitting down. "We're wizards and witches, not medieval peasants."

"*Fine!* You can think of a better idea!"

"What about our elemental magic?" said Oliver, ignoring their arguing. He thought about the Earth spheres they'd been working on in Belk's class.

Emma and Lance stared at him, nonplussed.

Given his exhaustion, it took a lot of effort *not* to roll his eyes. "Earth's just one of the elements. When are we supposed to start on water? Or non-elemental magic?"

"What are you getting at?" said Lance. "You want to create a tunnel through the water until we find the island? I'm pretty sure only Moses has ever done that. We can barely throw rocks!"

# * Chapter 15: The Prophet's Advent *

"Maybe," said Oliver, smiling, "but there might be an easier way. What if we could just freeze the top, or bring the mud in the water to the top so we can have a bridge to run across?"

"That sounds like some seriously advanced stuff," said Emma, pensive. She retrieved her notebook and began to scroll through Belk's course syllabus. "It doesn't look like we move past Earth as extramen. We could ask Abe when we'd start Water?"

"No chance," said Lance. "We can't give anybody any clues as to what we're doing."

Emma glared at him. "What about the bookstore? We could buy a textbook for one of Belk's more advanced classes?"

"No use," said Oliver, "I bet Blackwood's monitoring bookstore purchases after he heard me mention the willow. Won't want me researching anything." He threw up his hands suddenly, feeling a burst of anger. "Why did I open my stupid mouth? All I had to do was not mention the willow."

They sat for a moment, thinking hard.

"Did you still want to speak to Watkin about it?" asked Emma. "We were ready to talk to him about the scroll weeks ago but that was before you saw the willow, your visions, or became the Prophet's Advent."

Oliver winced as she spoke. It was a question he'd been expecting, and yet, he still didn't have an answer. "He did offer to help us before all of this even happened. But if Madeline *scrubbed* it from memory, I'm with Lance. Can't exactly trust anyone, right?"

# NOVA 01

Emma nodded, looking resigned. "That still doesn't leave us with any way to get to your island. We know nothing about water magic or non-elemental magic yet, and they're probably patrolling the lagoons now."

They collectively sighed as the catfish behind them let out a long, slow bubble.

"We could *borrow* one of Abe's textbooks," said Lance, breaking the silence.

Emma frowned. "What? You mean steal your RA's textbook. 'Cause that's not suspicious or anything."

"No," said Lance, "I mean borrow it. We'll only need it for a night so we can open it, take any notes we need, and put it back. He'll never even know it was gone."

Emma's frown creased upward into a grin. "*Excellent*. Bend the rules a bit since we don't have a choice, really. When should we snag it?"

"Tomorrow afternoon we've got Coatlball practice," said Lance, rubbing his hands together. "I'll let Zapien know I have a headache and can't make it. She won't like it, but I'm the only defensive player we have so she can't exactly drop me from the team before our game on Saturday. It'd be too obvious if you don't go, Oliver."

"You're better at lying than you look," said Emma.

Lance chuckled. "Sometimes, y'all make it obvious you don't have siblings. You can't survive 'em without getting your hands a little dirty."

Grinning for the first time in several minutes, Oliver nodded his head. "Okay, then. Show us the way. Make sure you take notes on everything related to water, yeah? While you're doing that, Emma and I will keep an

# * Chapter 15: The Prophet's Advent *

eye out for the island during practice. *And* let's start spying on Watkin a bit. We've got to see if he's trustworthy. Maybe we can ask him questions after we find the scroll?"

As Lance exited with a mock salute, Oliver felt his heart pump quicker than normal. After weeks of wondering about the willow tree, it felt exhilarating to finally have a plan in place, even a rudimentary one. All they had to do was get through their Friday classes without incident.

The following morning, Blackwood had a surprise for them, however.

He brought a cage with him when he entered the classroom after the students arrived. It was covered with a thick black cloth.

At the front, Blackwood shook the cage which prompted a yelp and rattle from behind the cloth.

Oliver jumped at the noise, wondering if he recognized it.

Blackwood narrowed his eyes at his interruption. "Frightened, Mr. Trinova?"

"No, *sir*," said Oliver, his face tight. "Just caught by surprise, that's all."

The cage rattled again.

"Sir," said Valerie from the rear of the classroom. "What's in there?"

"A chupacabra, Ms. Adams," said Blackwood. With a flourish of his wrist, he removed the cloth, revealing a monster. Scraping noises followed as most of the class pushed their chairs back to get as far away as possible from the cage. From inside, a dog-like figure hissed at them all.

Oliver and Cristina recognized it right away, exchanging a quick look. It was the enemy from the *Test of Wisdom*.

# NOVA 01

As the beast hissed and shook its quills against its green, leathery skin, the crowd gasped. Curiously, Oliver noticed most of the light that touched the skin, didn't reflect back, making it hard to see, even in the fully lit classroom.

"Most of you," Blackwood jeered, "will recognize this animal from the Test of Wisdom. We'll begin shielding lessons against it next week."

A murmur broke out.

"Did I *ask* any of you to speak," Blackwood snarled.

"Professor," said Se'Vaughn, "I thought we didn't start shielding against animals until our second year?"

Blackwood smiled as much as his pursed lips could. "I daresay Mr. Kirk, your *advanced* year is ready for the challenge. We'll start with Mr. García on Monday and the rest of you as necessary."

Oliver glared at Blackwood, determined to not let the evil man get under his skin. It was difficult not to with Beto throwing a smug look at him and the chupacabra scuttling in the nearby cage.

By the end of the lesson, Blackwood had assigned almost two-hundred pages of reading for the weekend and stressed that elemental magic wouldn't be allowed for their next few lessons. Instead, they were to cast magical shields using the word "*defenderis*." He demonstrated the proper use of the spell for them once, letting the chupacabra loose and then immediately pushing it back into its cage with a force shield. Red sparks flew whenever the beast touched it, causing it to snarl. After a few tries, it hissed at Blackwood before scurrying back into its cage.

## ✱ Chapter 15: The Prophet's Advent ✱

When the bell tolled, Oliver immediately stood up to leave so Blackwood wouldn't have a chance to harass him further. With his head bowed, he ducked out the door and left everyone behind, reaching Belk's classroom unscathed. He fumed through her entire lesson, thinking about Blackwood's insufferably bald head and evil blue eyes. Belk's lesson ended up covering Earth refinement, which she explained was the practice of ensuring the Earth you employ be perfect rock instead of mud. Since Oliver had already perfected that, he didn't feel bad about dreaming about letting a pack of chupacabras loose on the Dean instead of listening.

By the time he settled down in Watkin's library of a classroom, he'd calmed down enough to focus. They had completed their lessons on the Fertile Crescent and moved on to cover the early Sumerian City States. Watkin liberally used his demonstration board during the lesson, allowing the students to visualize what the cities looked like long ago and what the ruins looked like today. As always, Watkin was able to keep them on the edge of their seats. He told them of ancient magical artifacts, which allowed the first witches and wizards to create the two sides of the Key and found civilizations. Only at the end of the lesson did Watkin acknowledge there was no proof of the existence of the artifacts. "If they did exist," he said with a wistful look at the miniature wizards on the demonstration board, "magic would be accessible at all times – even during an age of darkness."

Eventually the bell tolled, and the usual shuffle of students packing their bags ensued. Just as Oliver stood, Jaiba landed on Oliver's desk and squawked at him.

*Caw-caw!*

# NOVA 01

"Hello, Jaiba," Oliver said, noting Watkin staring at him. He made to leave just as Watkin opened his mouth. Not wanting to be rude, Oliver hesitated.

"Good luck with the game this weekend, Mr. García," said Watkin. "I hate myself a little more every time I say this, but I did play professional ball after school. I am happy to provide pointers should you ever decide you need them – not that you do. From what I hear from Professor Zapien during staff meetings, you're a great offensive talent for the team. She actually thinks Founders can challenge Champayan this year."

Beto scoffed audibly as he exited the room.

"Thank you, sir," said Oliver, trying his hardest to ignore Beto and decide whether Watkin was someone he could trust. He opened his mouth to speak some more, but Emma grabbed his arm.

"Come on, Oli," she said, loudly, "don't want to be late to Biomes class."

"*Certainly* not," agreed Watkin. "Carry on, you three."

Oliver's heart rocketed in his chest as they made their way to the fourth floor for their final lesson of the day with Desmoulins.

"I almost told him," he said, hands shaking. "Did Jaiba put a spell on me?"

"I don't know," said Lance, "but I'm glad Emma grabbed you and pulled us out of there. We gotta find the scroll before we can talk to—,"

"There you are," interrupted Professor Desmoulins from outside his classroom door. They'd already made it to the fourth floor and hadn't been paying attention to their surroundings. "Bell rang two minutes ago, come on in so we can get started."

# Chapter 15: The Prophet's Advent

"Sorry, Professor," they muttered.

Inside, Beto laughed at them. "Nice of you to join us, García."

A chorus of snickering followed from Cristina and James.

"Settle down, y'all," said Desmoulins, shutting the door behind him. "First things first, quick announcement for everyone. Our field trip next Friday is being moved to the lagoons instead of the Swampy Woods. Professor Watkin spotted a gang of *escorpi* in there."

Alarm broke out among the extramen. "Escorpi?!" Cristina asked, dropping all pretense of being calm and collected.

"Nothing to worry about," said Desmoulins, waving a dismissive hand to them all.

Oliver thought that was a stretch. Not three weeks ago Desmoulins had covered a lesson on escorpi. Somehow, he had a hard time believing that eight-foot-long, fire-breathing scorpions weren't an issue.

"How did they get onto campus?" asked Trey. "Didn't you tell us they're native to volcanic areas?"

"No clue," said Desmoulins, "but our focus in the lagoons will be catfish and caimans, so forget about the escorpi."

Oliver found it difficult to care about catfish and caimans, but he exchanged looks with Emma and Lance all the same. If they had a field trip into the lagoons, couldn't they use that as an opportunity to find the island with the glowing willow tree?

At the end of the lesson, just as Oliver was about to leave to debrief with Emma and Lance, Desmoulins surprised him by asking him to stay behind. Curious, he obliged. Lance stood to leave but Emma grabbed his arm and sat him back down next to Oliver. Desmoulins gave them a look, his chiseled face curious, but then shrugged and let his shoulders drop.

"I know y'all are best of friends, so, by all means, feel free to stay." He paused to smile lazily at them in turn. "So," he finally continued, "Blackwood told us during a faculty meeting that you saw something out in the lagoons, is that right?"

Lance's jaw dropped. Emma stifled a gasp.

Oliver grimaced.

"Yes, sir," he said, thinking hard for the lie he and Emma had rehearsed. "It was a long practice, so my tired brain *thought* I saw something move in the foggy side of the lagoon." He laughed unnaturally, adding, "probably was just the fog moving about."

"Hmm," Desmoulins mused, a light wrinkle on his nose. He stood up grabbing an apple and sat on the desk in front of them with one leg still on the tile floor. "What do you know about Tenochprima's Founders, Oliver?" he asked, ignoring the panicked looks on Emma and Lance's faces.

"What?" said Oliver, his stomach dropping. He hadn't expected the conversation to turn to the Founders. Did Desmoulins know about his visions too?

"The Founders, good man, what do you know?"

"Not a thing, to be honest," he said, not so honestly.

"My great-great-great, I can't ever remember how many it is, grandmother was Madeline Desmoulins, one of the three Founders."

## \* Chapter 15: The Prophet's Advent \*

This time, *Oliver's* jaw dropped. The woman at the temple, Madeline, who'd recommended scrubbing all memory of the scroll, was Professor Desmoulins' ancestor.

*Crunch.* Desmoulins took a bite from his apple. "I only bring this up because my family has never left this school. We've dedicated ourselves to passing on the knowledge of our forefathers for generations. I'll freely admit, I never expected a Trinova to exist, but now that I know she was right … well, it finally makes sense."

"What makes sense?" asked Oliver, unable to stop himself from asking. Desmoulins looked pleased as he took another bite from his apple. *Crunch.*

"My family has passed down some knowledge that may help you, Oliver. A myth, from father to son, from mother to daughter, from generation to generation, claiming that a Trinova would reveal himself – or herself – at school and that my great-great-grandmother or whatever left some information on campus for him or her to find."

Oliver shifted his weight from one foot to the other. Behind his somewhat calm facial expression, his heart pounded in his chest. He could almost hear Emma hissing in his ear, *don't trust any of them!*

"*So*," Desmoulins continued, "if you did see something in the lagoons, do yourself a favor and don't ignore it. I can help you find it. After all, my past and your present are intertwined. It's the least I could do."

*This sounds too rehearsed,* he thought. Where the voice in the back of his head urged him to trust Watkin, it screamed at him to run away from Desmoulins.

"Thank you, sir," said Oliver, giving his best Beto-inspired simper, "but I really do think I imagined it. I get hungry at the end of long practices, you see, and I really think I imagined the whole thing."

"Of course," said Desmoulins, smiling everywhere but in his eyes. "Well, should you ever discover something on campus, don't hesitate to let me know. I'm happy to follow through on the knowledge passed down through my family.

"Now get a move on. Last practice before the big game tomorrow, right?"

Not wanting to skip the opportunity to leave, they issued hurried goodbyes and made their way to Founders Temple without stopping.

"What *on Earth* was that about?" hissed Emma when they reached the bridge before the Dining Hall. "It sounded just like Watkin telling you to talk to him after lessons!"

"You thinking they're working together?" asked Lance.

"No," said Oliver, squeezing his eyes closed for a moment. "Watkin asked before I saw the tree or became a Trinova. I think Desmoulins is trying to use me as a 'dangerous tool' after discovering what I am. Did either of you know?"

"That he was related to Madeline?" said Lance. "Of course not! They've kept that a secret, haven't they?"

"I think you're right," said Emma, ignoring the question, "if his family had known something was hidden on campus for the next Trinova to find, why wouldn't he have told anyone?"

## * Chapter 15: The Prophet's Advent *

A memory came to Oliver unbidden. *Blackwood was asking him what he saw in the lagoons at the end of tryouts. "Nothing, sir," the memory of Oliver replied. "Just a funny looking tree on an island out in the lagoons." Nearby, Watkin choked and Zapien slapped him on the back. "You alright, Cato?"*

Oliver froze, stopping them at the end of the bridge. "Watkin knows, too!" he said, putting a hand to his forehead. "That day, just after tryouts, I said I saw something in the water to Blackwood and Watkin nearly choked to death when he heard!"

Emma's eyes grew wider. "I noticed that, too!"

"He knew the whole time," said Oliver, realization dawning upon him like water cascading over rocks. "It all fits! Jaiba looked at me funny, maybe he could tell I was a Trinova. Watkin was already trying to help me find whatever the Founders left behind! He already knew I was the Prophet's Advent!"

"Are we sure, though?" asked Lance, looking grim, if a little unsure. "What if he was just trying to help himself? If he knew you were a Trinova before anyone else and wanted something from you, it makes sense that he'd offer to help! How can we know who's actually being honest and who isn't? It could be Desmoulins or Watkin."

Oliver's lips tightened. He wanted to trust Watkin, but was the professor really just using him to find what the Founders left behind like he suspected Desmoulins was?

"Does it even matter?" Emma growled, forcing them to keep walking towards Founders, "we have a plan for practice today. Lance, you need to start having a headache, now! We can worry about who to trust later!"

# NOVA 01

"Right," said Lance, putting a hand to his head and wincing. As they walked to the Dining Hall, he walked up to Zapien muttering about a migraine nobody was able to magic away. Oliver watched with his breath held, but he needn't have worried. Only seconds later, Lance walked past them heading straight for the dormitories below. He gave them a thumbs up with his free hand before disappearing down the circular staircase.

Oliver chanced a look at Abe, who sat nearby eating a light snack before practice. He laughed at something Brantley said, completely unaware of their plan.

"Well," Emma whispered into his ear, "the only thing now is to hope Abe doesn't lock his room."

"And that his book isn't in his bag," said Oliver, eyeing the backpack resting on the back of Abe's chair. It seemed like a lifetime ago when Abe walked into the clearing at the airport with that same backpack.

Oliver shook himself into life, ate a small portion of pasta Ms. Joan whipped up for him, and made his way towards the Coatlball field with Emma and Se'Vaughn.

In addition to their extramen teammates, most of their RAs were also on the team, including Elizabeth, Clay, Ronnie, Katie, Brantley, and Abe. To encourage first-year participation, however, only two RAs could be fielded at any given time during a game.

As the practice was the last one before the season opener the following evening, Professor Zapien and Ronnie guided them through lighter drills than usual while keeping the tone serious. "Can't be having any injuries before a game," Brantley said, imitating Ronnie to great effect. Captaining

# * Chapter 15: The Prophet's Advent *

the team, Ronnie wore the #1 jersey. Since joining the team, Oliver had learned the #1 jersey was *the* number to have in Coatlball. Secretly, he preferred his own #10 because all of Santiago's favorite soccer players wore it.

Given his off-field troubles, Oliver didn't have his best practice that afternoon. At first, he thought he'd be able to ignore his concerns about Desmoulins and Watkin, but it proved to be impossible with Archie floating between his legs, serving as a constant reminder of the Founders, the school, and the secret temple hiding in the lagoons. Not wanting to draw any unnecessary attention to himself, Oliver kept Archie flying low for most of the practice and avoided staring out into the lagoons.

After falling for the same feint from Beto twice in a row while playing a defensive drill, however, Archie vibrated beneath him, slightly annoyed.

"*Oliver,*" he said, "*what burdens your mind? Do not bear the world's responsibilities on your own. Is everything alright?*"

"No," confided Oliver telepathically. "You remember the glowing tree I told you about in the lagoons?"

"*What? What are you talking about? Glowing tree in the lagoons? This is the first time you've mentioned this.*"

This time Oliver did block Beto, forcing him and his feathered serpent to take a wide route where Katie waited for them.

"Haha, very funny, Archie. I get that you don't want me drawing unnecessary attention to myself or anything, but I figured now that I'm the Trinova, you'd be more supportive of this."

Archie huffed beneath him, jets of steam issuing from his nostrils.

# NOVA 01

"Unnecessary attention? More supportive? What are you talking about?"

Oliver gasped as for a second time that day an unbidden vision swarmed him.

*"Not if we scrub all memory of it,"* said Madeline. *"And leave clues only discoverable by him."*

"Archie," said Oliver, choosing his words carefully, "what do you know about memory scrubbing?"

Archie rumbled between his legs, laughing. *"Stark change of subject, but I'll oblige. Memory scrubbing is one of the most difficult pieces of magic to perform, as far as I am aware. It involves maintaining a secret between a 'secretor' and 'secretees.' Only a secretor can pass on the secret. Without direct knowledge transfer of the secret, it cannot be known."*

Oliver tried to understand what Archie said but couldn't. "What? Any chance you can dumb that down for me." *Why did he always have to speak so differently?*

*"If something has been scrubbed of memory, only people who have been entrusted to the secret can retain any memory of it."*

"So, anybody who doesn't know about it would forget it immediately?"

*"Yes, exactly. But how did you hear of this? This magic cannot be performed by humans."*

"Archie, I know something that's been scrubbed from memory, and every time I tell you about it, you forget it."

Archie stopped mid-air, forgetting about the practice session entirely. *"Are you certain?"* he asked, sounding almost frightened.

"Yes."

# ✱ Chapter 15: The Prophet's Advent ✱

*"Does it have to with the Founders?"*

"Yes."

*"Troubling, most troubling. This is quite extraordinary. I'm sure I'll forget this conversation, too. What did you find on campus?"*

"An island in the lagoons," said Oliver, "with a glowing tree, left behind by the Founders for me to find."

Archie hummed. *"An island? I have no memory of an island or tree hidden by the Founders."*

"We just covered this," said Oliver. He could almost feel the tension in Archie easing away as something came over him.

*"Covered what?"* asked Archie. *"You're really not making any sense today."*

Oliver sighed, realizing the conversation was hopeless if Archie would keep forgetting it every time he mentioned the island.

"Archie," he repeated, "I know something that's been scrubbed from memory, and every time I tell you about it, you forget it."

Almost exactly as he had before, Archie stopped mid-air.

*"Are you certain?"*

"Yes."

*"Does it have to with the Founders?"*

"Yes."

*"Troubling, most troubling."*

"You said that already," he sighed. "And don't ask what it is because if I mention it, you forget the whole conversation."

*"Have I really?"* said Archie, turning his head to face him. *"Extraordinary. I suppose it's foolish of me to think I know all of Augustus, Madeline, and Cuauhtémoc's*

secrets. Should you decide to investigate the matter further, be careful to whom you do mention it as any information withheld from me by the Founders will have been by design, not accident, and that troubles me. What, pray tell, did Augustus foresee requiring ultimate secrecy? Nothing good, I fear. If feathered serpents could not have known then, they certainly should not know now. Keep the secret to yourself. Keep it safe."

It took a moment for Oliver to understand what Archie meant.

"Are you saying not to trust you, either?" he asked as he situated himself on Archie's back.

*"I'm saying to trust in your forefathers,"* Archie implored with a tone of warmth. *"And, if you imagined the whole thing, then I need not have ever worried!"*

"What if others on campus already know about the secret?"

Archie vibrated beneath.

*"Have you already entrusted people outside of your closest friends with this knowledge?"*

"What?" said Oliver, almost emulating the vibrations of frustration Archie gave him. "Of course not! I'm a Wiser, not some thick Powerhead!"

*"So, somebody else on campus may know the secret already without having been shared the knowledge by you? Who?"*

"Watkin, I think," said Oliver, "and Desmoulins for sure."

Archie's feathers bristled beneath Oliver painfully.

*"I'm going to trust you with some information,"* Archie replied after a moment's hesitation. *"But I must stress to you that what I'm about to share is not a unique issue."* Twisting and turning through the air for a new drill, Oliver held his breath, waiting for Archie's reply.

## \* Chapter 15: The Prophet's Advent \*

*"Both Professors Watkin and Desmoulins ... they attended this school at the same time as The Damned."*

Oliver's stomach couldn't help but twist at the name. He suddenly pictured younger versions of his professors at school next to the hooded figure he'd seen at the *airport.*

*"While Watkin openly admired the evil man during his time at school, I'm certain they were not friends after graduation."*

Oliver felt nauseated. He'd almost shared information with Watkin without even researching his history yet. Even if Archie was confident that Watkin and *The Damned* had not been friends after school, how could Watkin have admired a monster in the making when he was younger?

*"Desmoulins, however,"* continued Archie, oblivious to Oliver's private thoughts, *"along with a few other professors at school, mind you, contributed to a disastrous political movement led by The Damned after he graduated."*

"Political movement? What does that mean?"

*"I can honestly say you're too young to understand, and that I'm too biased as a different species to comment. What I can emphasize, however, is Desmoulins' involvement in the movement was not unique to him. Many other people contributed to it, as well — many of whom still teach at this school."*

"Did Watkin?" asked Oliver, dreading the potential answer.

*"No."*

"Are you sure? Can he be someone I trust?"

*"To be honest, Oliver, you're the first human I've trusted since Augustus."*

Oliver laughed out loud at that, a pass from Emma sailing right past him. "Sorry!" he yelled.

# NOVA 01

Archie completely ignored the drills now and stopped to turn and face him. *"I don't know whom you can trust, but I do trust you to make the correct decision. Do not do so hastily."*

Oliver nodded, appreciating the kind words. "I bet Blackwood was also friends with *The Damned*," he said, unable to stop himself from grimacing.

Instead of chortling back, Archie surprised him by furrowing his eyebrows. It was a long, appraising moment before he replied. *"Remedying the sins of your forefathers requires that you employ greater principals. To create a better future, you must understand the scope of their sins, remaining agnostic of their mistakes. Do not stoop to their pettiness."*

Oliver's cheeks reddened. Though he couldn't quite understand what Archie meant, he knew he'd been properly scolded.

"Well," he said, unable to maintain eye-contact, "I'll let you know if I do end up trusting someone. But I've got a lot of catching up to do during these drills if I'm going to be asked to play tomorrow."

This time, Archie did laugh. *"It may be too late for that,"* he chortled. *"But let's see what we can do."*

For another hour the drills continued, with Oliver putting in a much better performance than before. In a build-up offensive drill, he ducked, weaved, and passed with great effect, committing zero fouls and scoring every shot for three points down the middle of the net. He even managed to score once from past thirty yards, earning six points and nearly injuring his arm in the process. Last of all, during a defensive drill, he stopped everyone but Se'Vaughn from getting past him with the help of Archie's shepherding.

## * Chapter 15: The Prophet's Advent *

By the end of the practice, Zapien and Ronnie gathered the team for a pep-talk in the locker room beneath the western bleachers.

Unsurprisingly, and yet still painfully, Oliver's name was not mentioned among the starters when Zapien announced them. Beto's name was called last, and when it was, he made sure to run his hands through his hair before tossing a cruel grin in Oliver's direction. He wasn't the only one to look at Oliver; each of the RAs did so as well – but where Beto wore cruelty in his brow, they wore anxiety.

After stepping through the formation, Ronnie pulled Oliver to the side. "Need to see you more focused before we can start you, García. Half of practice today it looked like you had other things on your mind." He put an arm around Oliver's shoulder, pausing to look around and lower his voice. "Zapien *also* told me it'd be good to have you as a secret *weapon*, if you know what I'm saying. We saw the scoring you were capable of at the end of practice there – that six-pointer was top class, man! If we can get you off the bench to score a flurry of points, that'll be a huge help!"

Oliver tensed. His first impulse was to point out he didn't need coddling, but one look into Ronnie's eyes stopped him. Confidence swam within those irises, born about by a lifetime of success with limited hurdles. *He genuinely thinks I'm buying into his every word.* Sighing, Oliver held up his hands for peace. At the heart of it, Ronnie was a good person – a snide remark from Oliver would be unfair. At the end of the day, he simply hadn't done enough in practice to deserve a starting spot.

"Thanks, Ronnie," he said. "I'm happy to do whatever the team needs."

# NOVA 01

Ronnie smiled handsomely and clapped his hands together. "Atta boy, Oli! That's the mentality you'll need to succeed around here." To the rest he added, "OY! Dinner! Showers! Bed! In that order!"

Trying his best to ignore the shame that banded around his throat, Oliver focused on what really mattered. No matter how many times he mentioned it, Archie would never be able to *remember* the willow tree or temple hiding within the lagoons. The memories were actively scrubbed from his brain every time they entered. What kind of magic had the Founders pulled off to perform this continuous *scrubbing* from centuries prior? And why could Emma and Lance hold onto the memories with no issues? Had the original secretor predicted their comings as well, and not just his own? On and on questions cascaded through his mind – none with answers.

A strong push to his left side interrupted his thoughts, knocking him into the thicket surrounding the pathway between Founders and the Coatlball trenches.

It was Beto. Strangely enough, he wore a look of shock on his face and offered Oliver a hand.

"Sorry," he said. "Didn't see you there, García." Begrudgingly, Oliver took the hand, suspecting a trap.

"You should just quit the team," the taller boy whispered as he pulled Oliver to his feet. "You know you're not good enough."

Blood boiling, Oliver clenched his right fist, mustering Power from the chaos outside his ring. Just as he was about to launch Beto off into the

## Chapter 15: The Prophet's Advent

stratosphere with a direct punch, Emma put a hand on his shoulder. He stiffened at the touch.

"Oli," she said, "let's *go check on Lance.*"

"Yeah," said Beto loudly as they walked away, "make sure he's not crying about not starting tomorrow either." Oliver turned, disgust on his face. Further behind, the RAs laughed at something Zapien had just said, unable to hear Beto's taunts.

"You're not fooling anyone, Beto," sneered Emma, "you're just jealous you're not a Trinova."

"Jealous?" shrieked Cristina. "Why would he ever—,"

The rest, Oliver didn't hear, because Emma pulled Oliver forward aggressively before anyone could escalate the situation further. "What were you doing today during practice?" she hissed, ignoring Cristina's huffing as they walked past the thicket. "You and Archie were stop and go the whole time!"

"I'll tell you in a minute," he grumbled. "I don't want to have to say all of this twice."

A few moments later, they'd taken their dinners to-go into the eastern viewing dome where Lance sat in a chair, focused on his notebook.

"Lance?" whispered Oliver.

"Oww, sorry I have a headache, it's so painful, please go away."

Emma sat down, rolling her eyes. "Lance, it's us!"

"Oh! Right!" He shot up from his seat and grinned at them.

"Well? What did you find?" asked Oliver.

# NOVA 01

"What did I find?" repeated Lance, maintaining the smile, "your boy found *exactly* what we needed." He slammed his notebook down on the coffee table but, given his Power, it ricocheted right back off the wood and into the glass wall. The catfish they'd come to know wrinkled its snout in disgust at the commotion. Retrieving the notebook, Lance tried again. "I left Abe's book exactly where I found it in his room. The idiot had a copy of *Advanced Water Elementals* just sitting on his desk for anyone to see."

"Really?!" said Emma, snatching the notebook before Oliver could. "What did you find?"

Lance leaned back in a winged armchair, impersonating a lazy king on his throne. "Oh, nothing too big. Just a spell to turn water to ice."

"This is huge!" said Emma, scrolling through the pages of notes Lance took. "You even took a copy of a visual in here. Look!"

She brandished the notebook in front of Oliver's face. Sure enough, Lance had logged a visual of a girl running on water with footsteps of ice trailing behind her.

"Good stuff," said Oliver, leaning back into the sofa he'd sat down on and closing his eyes. He embraced the heat wafting in from the fireplaces in the main common room just outside their enclave. "What are the words for the spell?"

"Looks like, *conjelareth*," said Emma, squinting at the notes.

"*Conjelareth*, eh?" repeated Oliver.

"Woah!" shouted Lance, "Do less! Do less!"

Oliver snapped his eyes open, realizing his ring finger felt warm to the touch. Frantically, he looked around to see what he'd done until he locked

## * Chapter 15: The Prophet's Advent *

eyes with the horse-sized catfish. It blinked slowly, but otherwise kept perfectly still. It wasn't until Emma stepped up to tap the glass where the catfish floated when Oliver realized he'd frozen the water around the viewing dome entirely.

"Sorry!" he said. "I swear I didn't try to do anything!"

"Shhhh," said Emma, waving a hand impatiently at him. She tapped the glass where the catfish blinked at them, still frozen in place. "This is going to be a heck of a lot easier than I thought!"

"Yeah," agreed Lance staring around the entire viewing dome. "We just gotta make sure you don't freeze us in the lagoon by accident because I didn't see anything about a counter-spell!"

## Chapter 16: A Word to the Wise

*The Whigs are such a pain. I ran into one of their leaders in the middle of the Cambodian jungle! I'm not sure how he found me or even got here, but he won't budge on their opposition campaign. Says we're going about things the wrong way, and even had the nerve to say, "I suggest you visit the rehabilitation centers yourself upon your return." As if we're doing anything wrong. We're fixing centuries of negligence.*

*15th of January, the second year of the 10th Age*

After much squabbling over when to search the lagoons for the golden willow, Oliver, Emma, and Lance finally decided on Christmas break. Emma had initially argued over searching right away, but after several heated debates, Oliver convinced her a slower approach would suit them better. Between Blackwood hating him for no good reason, Lalandra staring at him every time she saw him, and Watkin and Desmoulins offering to help, they needed to pretend to focus on school for a while.

"We don't have to *pretend*," said Lance, sighing. In his right hand, he frowned over a schedule Valerie had put together for them. She'd begun floating around Emma a lot more now that Oliver was a Trinova. Even if Oliver didn't trust her, she still proved helpful as far as *normal* schoolwork went. Thanks to her schedule, for instance, he now knew he had sixteen training sessions, four games, and eight exams to worry about before the semester was over.

# * Chapter 16: A Word to the Wise *

During their debates on timing, Oliver explained the memory scrubbing symptoms displayed by Archie during the previous day's training session. Both Emma and Lance had been stunned to hear Archie was incapable of remembering the willow tree every time Oliver mentioned it. Lance blanched when Oliver also revealed Desmoulins and other professors on campus likely worked with *The Damned* during his political movement. The only thing Oliver didn't share was the fact that Watkin had admired *The Damned* when they overlapped at school. At first Oliver didn't know why he didn't want to share that particular piece of information. But then it hit him. He *wanted* to trust Watkin.

Logically, it made no sense to do so. He knew nothing about the man except that he dressed well, possessed the Gift of Wisdom, and used to play Coatlball professionally.

And yet, for some reason, the warm touch of Wisdom kept imploring Oliver to trust the man anyway.

The next morning, however, he didn't have any time to focus on the scroll or worry about whom to trust, because the rest of campus had woken up with only one thing in mind.

Coatlball.

The commemorative frock coats they'd seen during tryouts in September made a resurgence, with more students than not wearing one. When Oliver, Emma, Lance, and Se'Vaughn joined the RAs, Cristina, and Beto at their team table for breakfast, cheers and claps came from several other students, including many from Hutch.

# NOVA 01

Professor Watkin even stopped by to wish them good luck. "If I could drag my fellow extramen to a title, *nothing* can stop you six from doing the same!" Oliver and Emma managed to smile weakly at him. Lance, however, was too nervous to do much else than open his mouth and groan.

After a quick breakfast, they made their way past the now familiar thicket to the Coatlball trench for light warm up drills. Even though the game didn't begin until twelve o'clock, Ronnie had promised that getting to the trench early would set them up for success. By the end of the drills, they were buzzing with a mixture of excitement and dread, which they saw mirrored on the faces of the students filling the bleachers. Among them, Blackwood stood out like a redwood in an oak forest. He wore his extra-large Champayan frock, glaring at anyone who dared look up at him.

The dorm they were up against was Tancol. In recent years, Ronnie warned them, they'd grown as a defensive powerhouse. What Ronnie hadn't warned them about, however, was their *fans*. As Oliver exited the locker rooms, an explosion of noise slapped him in the face. The chants, the yelling, the shouting – he'd somewhat expected those, even if not to the scale he heard now. What he never could have predicted, were the drums.

From both sets of bleachers, the drums reverberated, rattling his body and numbing his mind. Peering east and west, Oliver spotted the drums and the students playing them. When one side played, the opposite banged back in perfect synchronization. Some of the drummers were dressed to honor the feathered serpents, with colorful feathers and painted bodies dancing to the rhythms of their enormous instruments. Others wore more subdued quills or rounded ears to look like their eagles or osori. Even Beto

# * Chapter 16: A Word to the Wise *

looked apprehensively at the two sets of bleachers where the madness ensued.

In hushed silence, Oliver and his team walked up with Ronnie to their bench on the eastern side of the channel. Cheers emanated from the crowd as the starters' names were announced. Emma's smile shone brightest when her name was called. Only she seemed impervious to the uproar going on around them.

Since Oliver and Lance weren't starting the game, they stayed at the bench wishing the rest of the team good luck. After exchanging handshakes with the opposing team, Emma, Se'Vaughn, Beto, and Cristina took offensive positions in the air while Abe and Ronnie, the two starting RAs, took defensive positions – Ronnie on Espie in the air, and Abe on Reggie on the ground.

From the din of the crowd, Oliver could just make out the voices of two students in a commentator's box at the top of the eastern bleachers.

"Interesting tactics from the Extraman Hall this year, wouldn't you say, Joel?" said a familiar voice. It was Elton.

Joel, meanwhile, looked like the boy Oliver had seen carrying a box of dueling slugs ages ago on that first weekend in Hutch.

"Agreed, Elton. Although, it's no surprise with Ronnie leading the team. He's tinkered with interesting line ups for years to great effect."

"Still, only one osorius on the field? Even for a Founders team that's unusual. It'll be difficult for them to move the ball forward, if at all."

"I guess we'll find out the answer to that question and *more* as Headmaster Lalandra takes to the trench to kick off the game!"

# NOVA 01

Oliver shifted his gaze back to the trench and saw Lalandra with the pigskin in her hand. She wore her usual pantsuit and blouse combo with an added frock coat for the colder weather. After saying some words to Ronnie and then to the Tancol captain, a skinny but athletic girl on an osorius, she leaned back and tossed the ball straight into the air, beginning the game.

It was complete and utter chaos to start. Although Ronnie had trained the team with game-starting drills, the noisy crowd made it impossible for any of the airborne teammates to communicate with one another, causing them to move around with little structure in a mad dash to get the ball first.

Emma and Rasmus emerged from the throng of initial players with the pigskin in hand. They shot left to dodge oncoming players and an enormous net hurtling through the air. Though he couldn't be sure, Oliver thought it had been summoned by the skinny captain, who stuck to Emma closely from below, waiting for a dropped ball.

Beto quickly appeared nearby, allowing Emma to pass the ball and the accompanying pressure from enemy defenders. Shooting back the opposite way, Beto turned quickly enough for the skinny captain to be left behind, her osorius too slow to follow. Abe shouted for a pass from below, free to catch the ball and move forward. Beto ignored him for a moment, looking for Cristina, but saw she was unavailable, so he passed it to Abe with a growl. Oliver winced when a brick wall popped up from the ground in front of Abe – nearby, a Tancol player grinned at the wall cruelly. To Oliver's surprise, however, the wall crumbled, and Reggie jumped through it with a great roar, revealing Abe with one hand holding the ball close and the other on the hilt of his dagger. Oliver and Lance cheered in unison with large

# * Chapter 16: A Word to the Wise *

sections of the crowd as Reggie and Abe barreled forward, gaining more and more momentum with every step. A moment later, Cristina swooped low in front to receive a pass and shot left to pass back and forth quickly to Beto on the left channel. As they approached the goal, Se'Vaughn made a smart move to the opposite side in a perfect position for an easy goal. Beto, however, decided not to pass, instead opting to shoot from past thirty yards.

"Ohhhhhhh," shouted the crowd as the shot sailed narrowly past the backboard.

"Good movement, team," shouted Ronnie, "but pass the ball next time, Beto!"

"Slim chance of that," Lance growled from the bench. "Se'Vaughn was wide open!"

"Looks like John's curly-haired cousin has a good shot on him" said Joel over an unseen intercom. "But he'll have to work on his aim."

"You can see his teammate berating him now," added Elton, "not good for team dynamics, but he really should have gone for the assist there instead of the points."

"His decision making will improve over time, no doubt," said Joel.

Se'Vaughn and Beto exchanged a few words and scowls as they went back to position. Katie and Alex on the bench exchanged concerned looks before whistling to get Ronnie's attention. He waved a hand at them dismissively, pointing at Abe, who was yelling at Beto to get back to the left wing because he'd left a hole that the Tancol players were now exploiting. With two osori players able to move forward without restriction, Tancol easily progressed down the left side. Abe tried boxing them out but had little luck. In a desperate defensive move, Emma summoned an Earth sphere and shot it at the back of the skinny Tancol captain. Focused on Abe's boxing out maneuvers, the captain didn't see the sphere coming. Just as it was about to knock into the back of her head, a midfield Tancol boy pointed his staff at the sphere, turning it to mud.

*Splat!*

Jeers ensued from the crowd as the girl fell off her osorius, mud covering her back. She'd dropped the ball as she fell.

"Turnover, Tancol!" announced Tolteca's voice over the crowd. "Founders' ball!"

Without hesitation, Espie and Ronnie swooped down, picked up the ball and moved back towards their own goal. Oliver wondered what Ronnie was doing but then, out of the corner of his eye, he saw a blur shooting down the right flank. It was Se'Vaughn and his feathered serpent, Xhak, hurtling, unmarked, Emma hot on their heels. After freeing up space for himself, Ronnie launched the ball, a distance nobody else on the team could throw, leading Se'Vaughn by a dozen yards. With a fingertip catch, Se'Vaughn pulled in the pigskin, just ten yards away from the goal. Xhak stopped quickly to not cause a turnover and moved towards the western bleachers. Emma then appeared, making a supporting move forward in the opposite direction. Tancol's only remaining defender chose to follow Se'Vaughn instead of her, allowing him to lob an easy pass. The ball descended onto where Emma and Rasmus waited in what felt like slow-motion to Oliver and the gasping crowd.

## * Chapter 16: A Word to the Wise *

For one agonizing moment, Emma fumbled the ball from one hand to another, and then –

"GGGOOOOAALLLLLLL," boomed Joel, over the intercom as the crowd erupted, muffling the noise of the now desynchronized Tancol drums. The Founders team swarmed her, celebrating with fist pumps, roars, and slaps on the shoulder. Even Beto high-fived her as he and his serpent shot past. They didn't have more than a moment to celebrate, however, as Tancol had already initiated another run, this time on the eastern side of the cobblestone trench. While play resumed, Oliver took a moment to watch the replay on the mirror above. Se'Vaughn's pass had been perfect, and it deserved as much if not more credit than Emma's finish. Smiling, he returned his sight to the live play in front of him, itching for his own chance to score.

The game continued at the same breakneck speed. Tancol's captain scored on their next two runs, both times down the middle of the net. Then, after several runs without a score from either team, Beto redeemed himself somewhat by hitting the backboard from twenty yards out to bring the score to 4-6. With the team down, Ronnie took a time out with five minutes remaining in the first, twenty-minute half, taking the opportunity to substitute in Brantley, Alex, Lance, and Oliver.

When Elton announced Brantley's, Alex's, and Lance's substitutions, the crowd gave out cheers to welcome the new players onto the trench. When he reached Oliver's name, however, hushed whispers spread like fire on oil.

"Yes, yes," Joel said to Elton over the intercom, "Oliver García takes the field for the first time this season. Many students have debated the appropriateness of the Trinova being allowed to compete but, c'mon, Elton, he's just an extraman – Tancol shouldn't worry about him *too* much, right?"

Boos, jeers, and even some tomatoes were pelted at Joel from the stands, indicating not the whole crowd agreed that Oliver shouldn't be allowed to play.

With a blast like a gunshot, the game resumed. Brantley now led them from the rear, taking a slow, possession-based approach to get the new players settled. After a couple minutes, Cristina shot forward from the midfield, unmarked. It was an easy pass for Brantley to make, and Cristina wasted no time getting Se'Vaughn the ball on the right wing a half-second later.

But a Tancol player read the play and intercepted the pass. From his left-forward position, Oliver saw the interception coming as soon Cristina made to throw the ball. He pushed Archie quickly towards the center of the pitch to meet the intercepting player who shot straight towards the western stand, looking for a Tancol player to pass to. Bulky like Elton, the interceptor barely acknowledged Oliver's presence as he continued westward. He almost slipped past Oliver after feinting a pass to the middle, but Oliver shot up a wall of Earth all the way from the ground below – nearly thirty yards – to force the boy wide.

The crowd gasped as the wall ascended with a sound like crunching gravel. Looking at the wall, Brantley gave Oliver an appreciative thumbs up. "That'll come in dead useful, García," he shouted, "can't wait until you can do more than just the elementals!"

# * Chapter 16: A Word to the Wise *

After being forced back, Tancol came forward again on two osori-based players. With no osori on the field for the Founders team, Brantley and Alex used every piece of magic they could think of to slow them down. They shot fireballs, conjured brick walls, and even a wave of water.

*A wave of water!*

Without thinking Oliver raised his right hand, the one bearing his Red-Beryl and chestnut ring, and muttered *"conjelareth!"*

The wave of water at the osorius' feet froze entirely, locking all but one enormous leg into place.

"Oooooooo," gasped the crowd, including Joel and Elton from the commentator's box.

"Not sure which RA performed that freezing charm," said Joel, "but great, great application of magic right there."

"I think that may have been Oliver," said Elton.

"The extraman? No chance, Elton. No chance at all. Water elementals aren't taught until your junior year."

Thinking quickest, Se'Vaughn swooped down and grabbed the ball from the struggling players on the ice. "Don't mind if I do!" he shouted before chucking the pigskin at Oliver. He then urged Xhak onwards down the right flank, pulling a defender with him.

Looking back at the frozen osorius, Oliver saw a player de-icing them, leaving an opening on the left. "Cristina," he yelled, "hot potato on the left!" She eyed Beto on the bench uneasily before nodding her head and joining him for the move.

## NOVA 01

With fewer than twenty seconds remaining in the half, Oliver and Cristina passed the ball in quick succession down the left flank, never moving forward while holding the ball directly. Applause broke out from the crowd as the move brought them closer and closer to Tancol's goal. With desperation on their eyebrows, the three remaining Tancol players congregated near their goal. Instead of stopping the attackers directly, they formed a perimeter zone defense, hoping to stop any shot from going in.

With less than ten seconds left, Oliver stopped the hot-potato maneuver and shot eastward, more than thirty yards out.

"Five!" shouted Joel.

The goal was almost directly in front of him. Lance made a run from midfield towards the right side of the goal, a defender went with him.

"Four!" screeched Elton, his fingers laced over his eyes.

Se'Vaughn made a second run, getting into a semi-contested area near the left side of the goal. A defender followed him, too.

"Three!"

Oliver feigned a pass to Lance.

"Two!"

He shot straight at the goal.

"One!"

The net rippled.

"GGGGOOOOOOAAALLLLLLLLLLLLLLL!! García scores!"

Oliver let his passion for the competition consume him entirely as he rushed to the extraman crowd to celebrate the goal. He raised his arms, shaking them wildly at Trey, Ogden, and his other hallmates, yelling himself

## * Chapter 16: A Word to the Wise *

hoarse at the foot of the bleachers. A moment later, three other serpents and two eagles barreled into him.

"NICE ONE, OLI!" shouted Brantley, clapping him on the back. Katie ruffled his hair at the same time.

"We're up 10-6!" came Se'Vaughn's voice. He managed to cross biceps with Oliver. "They had me pretty well covered. Nice shot!"

"YES, OLI!" screamed Lance. He'd joined the celebrations last as he'd wheeled off to celebrate in front of the wrong bleacher first.

In more subdued fashion, Cristina shot Oliver a thumbs up. "Good idea with the hot potato move," she said, not looking him in the eye.

They fist pumped towards the crowd some more as they retreated to the bench for a ten-minute half-time.

When they arrived, the RAs ruffled Oliver's hair some more while Emma offered him a fist bump. "Nice shot!"

Unsurprisingly, Beto ignored Oliver entirely, instead focusing on Ronnie for his half-time speech.

"Alright team," said Ronnie, "great job all around. Just like in practice, we want to be shooting high percentage successful shots. And that means?" He raised his hands and closed his eyes.

"Fewer than ten yards out," chorused the team.

"Exactly!" agreed Ronnie, pointing a finger at them all. "Oli, that was a great play at the end there. Six points will do us a load of good, no doubt about it. If we find ourselves in a similar situation in the second half, hold onto the forward move a bit longer to make your shot more and more likely to go in. Got it?"

# NOVA 01

An evil grin returned to Beto's mouth and Oliver wasn't surprised to see it. Despite scoring, had Ronnie been upset with the way Oliver had done it? *I just doubled our score – he should be more grateful.*

"Which one of you did the freezing charm?" Ronnie eventually asked Brantley and Alex.

"Alex," said Brantley.

"Brantley," said Alex.

They looked at each other, confused.

"Well, it had to be one of you because the field blocks magic from the bench or crowd."

"Maybe I did," said Brantley after an awkward pause. "Abe and I've been struggling with it in class – I must have done it without thinking."

"Yeah," said Abe. He looked at Oliver directly who tried to pretend something on Archie's back was interesting.

"*It was the boy,*" said a voice Oliver hadn't heard before. It clearly belonged to a serpent, but which one?

Oliver's eyes narrowed when they met Beto's red and black steed. Thicker but shorter than Archie, the serpent was an impressive specimen. It glared right back at him.

"*Unequivocally false, Musfati,*" Rasmus huffed.

"*Indeed,*" agreed Archie with a tone of finality only centuries of practice could muster.

Musfati growled but didn't speak again.

# * Chapter 16: A Word to the Wise *

The RAs looked at the serpents uneasily. The eagles appeared to operate in isolation when compared to the structure of the serpents. As far as Oliver was aware, the eagles didn't have a leading representative like Archie.

Espie flapped her wings breaking the silence.

"Yeah, good point, Espie," said Ronnie. "Ok, everyone, good stuff out there. More of the same – head on a swivel! High percentage shots only. Beto and Emma, you're both on for Se'Vaughn and Cristina."

The second half had Tancol begin with the ball. They made good use of it, driving forward with *three* osori before rippling the net for three points, bringing the score to 10-9. After scoring, they called a time out to substitute two of the osori to defend with more airborne players.

After Oliver's six pointer, the wiry captain man-marked him for the first ten minutes of the second half. Based on the magic she displayed, Oliver guessed she was likely in her senior year, like Ronnie. She shot stones, earth, nets, packs of birds, and even clouds of poison smoke at him.

With the Tancol team changing tactics to defend with mostly airborne players, the Founders team struggled to move forward. The Tancol players sat in two horizontal lines of three players, pressing hard whenever anyone approached the front line. If Founders did ever manage to progress to the back line, they were rushed to take shots early, resulting in misses from everyone but Beto, who managed to clip the backboard once from within thirty yards, bringing their score to 11.

The Tancol team, on the other hand, counter attacked explosively whenever Founders turned over the ball. More often than not, Beto didn't urge Musfati back into defense quickly, giving Tancol the upper edge to

# NOVA 01

attack before they arrived. This allowed them to score six points over three different moves, making the score 11-15.

After lots of back and forth, several substitutions, and good defense from both teams, the two-minute warning sounded, giving both teams a time out. The final changes left Ronnie, Katie, Beto, Se'Vaughn, Emma, and Oliver on the field. Lance looked hurt, and Cristina outraged, but they needed their best goal scorers to make up the four points.

"High percentage shots!" yelled Ronnie at the team taking the field. "We'll get enough opportunities!"

Oliver looked at the score floating above and saw only two minutes left on the clock. He wished he shared Ronnie's optimism. With so little time left, they'd be lucky to take more than one shot. The Tancol drums drowned out the noise of everything but his heartbeat.

Lalandra's whistle sounded, though he couldn't hear it, and the play resumed with Founders' possession of the ball. For a few precious moments, Ronnie and Katie passed the ball back and forth as they exchanged positions on the eastern and western side of defense. With time dwindling down, the Tancol players pressed Founders' midfield and attacked hard to make sure the RA couldn't pass the ball forward to the extramen.

With only a minute left on the clock, Oliver made a run to the western flank of the trench the same moment Emma went east. Two Tancol players followed Oliver, one followed Emma. Seeing the opening, Ronnie passed the ball to Katie, who'd moved up to the vacated midfield, and hurtled forward faster than Oliver knew was possible.

# * Chapter 16: A Word to the Wise *

"Oh," said Elton over the intercom, "Ronnie Zimmer's seen an opening!"

Espie shot like a peregrine falcon down towards the base column of the goal – it now loomed above him. As he descended, Katie launched the ball. Less than a perfect pass, it wobbled in the air. Thankfully, however, it sailed through the hands of a would-be intercepting Tancol player before arriving safely in Ronnie's hands. At twenty yards out, he and Espie zoomed up and then back slightly, to dodge a desperate brick wall and a congress of hooting owls, before throwing a perfect spiral into center net.

"GGGGOOOOOOOOAAALLLLLLLLLLLLLL," rang Joel, over the intercom. The team began to celebrate with him, the score now 14-15, but Ronnie waved them all away angrily.

"Get back in position!" he yelled. "We still need a point!"

Chastised, Oliver assumed his position on the left of the midfield. Tancol resumed play passing the ball from one defender to another, looking to run out the clock. Desperate, Emma joined Se'Vaughn and Beto to hassle the Tancol players, hoping to cause a turnover through a rushed pass. Oliver faked a run forward to help the cause, leaving an opening in the midfield behind him. But then he pulled Archie back hard. One of the Tancol players attempted to lob the ball over Archie to where one of them had made a short move to the midfield. Oliver reached up and caught the pigskin with both hands.

"GARCÍA'S INTERCEPTED THE PASS," shouted Elton, "GAME ON!"

## NOVA 01

Desperate to not force a turnover, Oliver rushed back and tossed the pigskin to Ronnie before hurtling back into position.

With fifteen seconds left, Ronnie and Katie abandoned the defense and used the hot potato move to progress forward on the right-side of the trench. Emma dropped deeper to provide an outlet for a pass, and good thing too because an exhausted senior Tancol player attacked the RAs with an enormous wave of fire. Panicking, Ronnie threw the ball back to Emma, and dodged the fire.

"Ten!" shouted the crowd.

Oliver and Se'Vaughn were well defended, but Beto wriggled free of the Tancol player marking him after a tight turn by Musfati. With a frown, Emma passed Beto the ball.

"Oh no," Oliver groaned, though nobody could hear.

Catching it and turning, Beto launched a blind shot at the goal.

"Five!" boomed Joel.

The pigskin flew through the air. Both teams stared at it, transfixed and immobile.

"Four!" replied the crowd.

It was going to miss left, Oliver knew it.

"Three!" shouted Elton. "But hang on!"

Like Oliver, Se'Vaughn had also seen the pigskin wasn't destined for the goal. Closest to it, he urged Xhak slightly forward while every other player was caught watching him and the ball.

Leaning as far forward as he could, Se'Vaughn stretched his hands and caught the ball. With no time to spare, he leaned back in the opposite

# * Chapter 16: A Word to the Wise *

direction and shuttled the pigskin towards the goal from only five yards out. Everyone watched, almost as if in slow motion. The ball wavered in the air, spinning uncontrollably before clipping the board and finally nestling into the back of the net!

The crowd exploded.

"GGGGOOOOOOOOAAALLLLLLLLLLLLLLL," rang Elton and Joel. "FOUNDERS WINS THE GAME!"

Abandoning all pretenses for politeness, the Founders team rushed Se'Vaughn with screaming, pushing, shoving, back-slapping, and forehead kissing. So exuberant were their celebrations, Brantley managed to knock Se'Vaughn off Xhak. Quick as fire on oil, Espie swooped to catch him with her talons before tossing him back onto his steed where he continued to fist bump. The bench cleared to celebrate with them, hurt feelings forgotten.

Around them, the Tancol players seethed or hung depressed shoulders. Their drum-players continued to beat, although perhaps more solemnly. Or was that what Oliver heard now that they'd won the game?

Once the celebrations finally quieted down, they exchanged handshakes with the Tancol players still remaining in the trench or in the air.

"Good game," they said, one after the other, their expressions flat to not flaunt their victory. The Tancol players Oliver managed to shake hands with looked either depressed or angry.

As Oliver shook the wiry captain's hand last, she crushed his grip, forcing him to wince.

"Good game," she said, turning her grimace into a legitimate smile.

"Good—," Oliver tried replying, but something in the distance caught his watering eyes.

Shining from atop a decrepit temple situated on the eastern side of the lagoons, sat a golden willow tree.

"Good game, Mr. García," said another voice, taking his attention momentarily away from the temple. It was Professor Watkin.

"Thank you, Professor," Oliver replied, unsure of what else to say. He chanced a look at the temple again but only saw thick rolls of fog circling over the lagoon.

"*Thank you, Cato,*" agreed Archie.

He crinkled his nose at them both. "And excellent use of magic, I might add."

Oliver felt his stomach twist. Could Watkin have known he performed the freezing spell during the game? *Does he know I'm trying to hide something?*

"Yeah, thanks again!" said Oliver, simpering like Beto. "I'm getting better and better with Earth walls and spheres."

"Indeed," said Watkin. His eyes continued to stare at Oliver, almost forcing their way into his brain. For once, he didn't wear a smile.

"Er," said Oliver awkwardly, "thanks again, but we've gotta join the team in the locker rooms. So, Archie and I will just be on our way …"

"Yes," replied Watkin, looking towards the lagoons. An additional reply looked ready on his lips.

Oliver prodded Archie to turn but he did not.

"*By your leave,*" he said.

# * Chapter 16: A Word to the Wise *

"You need not ever wait for my leave, honored sacred beast," Watkin mused. "Nonetheless, just this once, I appreciate your courtesy as it has allowed me to finish a thought.

"Oliver, I do not fully understand why you seek to advance your elemental magic so early into your education, but I implore you do not betray your advanced positioning any further unless absolutely required."

Oliver began to sputter, ready to deny any accusations.

But Watkin cut him off with a raised finger. "Don't. This is a rare opportunity for me to speak to you unheard. Even now, the rest watch as this greeting is running long for a post-game congratulations.

"Understand, Oliver, the faculty watch you with keen interest. A word to the wise, master spells of concealment prior to commencing any rule-breaking – I cannot promise the others won't notice your next move."

"Rule-breaking?" said Oliver, attempting to pretend he didn't have a clue what Watkin meant.

"For now, let us hope I am the only faculty member who's connected Mr. Wyatt's borrowing of *Advanced Water Elementals* to your demonstration of today's freezing charm. For the future, try reading a book in the Research Lab, *without* checking it out."

He finished speaking abruptly, not allowing Oliver time to react or deny having done anything wrong.

"Until, next time," he concluded. With a cheery wave that didn't match the tone of their conversation, he pulled his eagle away, heading to Founders Temple.

## NOVA 01

"*What on Earth?*" said Archie, watching Watkin disappear. "*Are you breaking rules, Oliver?*"

Oliver smacked his lips, taking a moment to recover before replying. When had his mouth gone dry?

"I wouldn't say *breaking* rules," he eventually muttered. "We just borrowed one of Abe's books so I could read up on more advanced magic."

"*And why do you need more advanced magic?*" He circled them down to the locker rooms unbidden.

"I don't," Oliver lied. He didn't want to have to relive the conversation about the Founders with Archie, only for him to forget again.

"*Does this relate to the secret you can't tell me about?*"

"Yes."

"*Very well, I won't press the matter. It would appear Cato is helping you avoid the attention of the other faculty. Though we cannot know his intentions, we at least know he certainly does not align himself with the teachings of The Damned. Embrace his Wisdom to conceal your future 'borrowings' from the rest.*"

"I will," Oliver grumbled. He still winced at the conversation – how did Watkin know they'd borrowed the book? How had he noticed he performed the freezing charm in a field full of moving bodies and older students?

When they reached the locker room, most of his teammates had already dismounted their Guides. As he began doing the same, Archie turned to face him. Between the tendrils flanking his mandibles and the feathers on the side of his face, Archie had somehow put together a smile. "*Regardless of your other pursuits,*" he said in a much warmer tone than before, "*job well done*

# * Chapter 16: A Word to the Wise *

*today. I can't remember the last time Founders won a season opener, so make sure you take time to properly celebrate with your friends, eh?"*

A pair of coughing throats interrupted them. Before Oliver could turn to see who'd interrupt a conversation with a sacred beast, he felt a pair of hands begin pulling him away.

"Excuse us," said Emma, dragging Oliver into the locker room, "but Oliver's got some celebrating to do."

A second pair of hands grabbed Oliver's other arm. They were Lance's.

"Either that," he said, "or a *lot* more training sessions. Next week we play Champayan! Can't be losing to those jerks!"

Oliver couldn't stop himself from grinning as they tugged him away.

# NOVA 01

## Chapter 17: Light Refraction

*Just finished surveying the Siamese Temples. Not a peep from the cloaking device the entire time! I'm starting to think anything worth discovering inside a scared ground is long gone.*

*19th of January, the second year of the 10th Age*

As December's final exams loomed closer, the days grew shorter and the weather colder, moving most activities indoors. This shift, Oliver was surprised to discover, also applied to every osori and feathered serpent that called the campus home. The rafters in the cavernous Dining Hall now served as the serpents' den, and according to Elton, it was only thanks to Lalandra's magic that the students weren't being covered with loose feathers, shed skin, or worse while they dined in between lessons and studying. The osori, meanwhile, fought over spots in front of every fireplace spread across the grounds. Every now and then a study session would be interrupted by Reggie dueling with another osorius for the fireplace in Founders B4. Only the Eagles remained outside, banking their wings on gusts of wind to float pleasantly in place, seemingly unbothered by the below freezing temperatures.

The lagoons had changed the most. Blocks of ice now floated amidst wilted cattails and shriveled lily pads, ridden like rafts by stubby, winter rocks that had emerged from the lagoons' deepest recesses. They brandished little arms with crude, wooden scimitars like silent, stone pirates.

# * Chapter 17: Light Refraction *

Oliver had been surprised to hear the RAs groan at the arrival of the rocks, or "golems," as he'd heard Ronnie say. After a few weeks, however, he began to share their reservations. Capable of creating frigid temperatures, the rocks bothered more than they charmed. Oliver and Lance, for instance, woke up one freezing night in early December to see the outline of a small boulder just outside their above ground window, tapping at the glass with a stubby arm to create a flurry of snow in their room. Their only redeeming quality, according to Ronnie, was that their arrival meant the skeletons would be forced to return to the Swampy Woods. Sure enough, after one last batch of pranks and food fights during the final weekend in November, the skeletons made their escape, cackling merrily as they fled to the woods, dodging the golems that swung out at them.

Also making their seasonal debut were red and blue flightless birds the seniors called pinguinos. They emerged from the woods, standing four feet tall and carrying sacks full of mediocre Christmas presents. Compared to the golems, the birds were downright charming in Oliver's eyes. They waddled around the academic building or any of the dorms at irregular hours, squawking at anyone who would listen. If you squawked back, as Lance demonstrated during a late-night study session, the birds would charge up excitedly, rummage through their bags, and present a rusty fork or other useless present before waddling away. During a late-night studying session, Oliver couldn't resist squawking at one of the birds in the Founders B4 common room. It approached him with glee on its face before presenting a narrow piece of driftwood. He fully intended to turn it into a walking stick.

# NOVA 01

One week later, Oliver, Emma, and Lance emerged from their end-of-semester exams exhausted and cranky. When Lance asked Emma how she'd answered Chavarría's prompt on creating basic healing salves, she glared at him until he wilted and apologized for the stupid question.

Though Oliver was sure he survived with mostly Bs, there was no guarantee Blackwood wouldn't bend the rules to give him an F for something ridiculous like incorrect spacing in between words or missing his footwork during a shielding exercise. In fact, he was sure the latter would happen because after he'd pulled off a perfect shield summoning using *defenderis,* he'd let his guard down, allowing a chupacabra's quill to scratch him across the forearm. Afterwards, he saw Blackwood scribble something down with a manic smile on his face.

But he had to admit, it was better to think about his exams and even the Chupacabra scratch instead of Coatlball. Only a week prior, Champayan had flattened them without mercy. They'd been led by Beto's older cousin, John, who scored twenty-seven points without ever smiling or celebrating.

Wincing at the thought, Oliver returned his mind to the Research Lab, where he, Emma, and Lance had been spending much of their time during the first half of Christmas break.

"There isn't anything in any of these books on how to conceal magic!" groaned Emma. Like Oliver, she had dark semi-circles under her eyes from all the extra time they'd spent researching on top of their end-of-semester studying and training. She and Lance had taken Watkin's advice to heart, agreeing they should learn how to conceal any troublemaking before engaging in it. They worked in a private research room, as Watkin had

## * Chapter 17: Light Refraction *

recommended, where a large, interfaceable mirror lay hung against the wall. It allowed them to pull up any book stored in the World Magical Database, or WMD, which Oliver was fascinated to hear served as the inspiration for the internet on the Original Side of the Key. The door to their room squeaked open as Lance arrived with half a dozen more hardcover books. He dropped them unceremoniously on the table in the middle of the room.

"We'll just have to keep looking," Oliver sighed. He rubbed at the chupacabra scratch on his arm. It *shimmered* greenish purple whenever aggravated.

"You should get that checked out," said Lance, peering uneasily at the wound. "Didn't Blackwood say some chupas are venomous? I wonder which type he would have put in front of you, hmm?"

"Forget about it – I'm not giving him the satisfaction of knowing I've been to the infirmary."

Lance shrugged. "Did I tell you I saw him while I was in detention?"

Oliver shook his head, looking away from the mirror, where images of a decrepit book titled *Illusion-making for Beginners* hung. Truth be told, he'd forgotten about Lance's detention altogether. Their near-fight with Beto felt like it had occurred in a separate lifetime. Now that he thought on it, it kind of was a lifetime ago – he hadn't even been the Trinova yet.

When Oliver didn't respond, Lance kept talking, wringing his fingers around the handle of his hammer. "He's *evil*, that man. Genuinely wants others to suffer. Cristina and I had to clean all of the hallways and staircases up and around the faculty apartments above the Dining Hall. When we thought we were done, Blackwood's bald head showed up and told us to clean the lounge, too! When we were in there, he just sat reading some little book called *The Prince*. But he wasn't really reading it – he kept looking up with this stupid smile on his face. I thought about bashing his head in with my hammer when he told me to repolish the frame of some ugly temple painting. Complete waste of time! He could have done it all by himself in a second! Cristina doesn't like him nearly as much as Beto does."

As Lance spoke, Oliver resisted the urge to cut him off, or tell him none of it mattered, but he was glad he didn't, because he appreciated the jab at Blackwood *and* Beto.

Emma shook her head, reburying herself into a hardcover book so old Oliver wondered how it hadn't fallen apart. "Listen, you two," she said, slightly muffled by the dusty pages. "We can't worry about Blackwood or Beto right now." When she reappeared and caught Oliver's eye, she stood and put the book on a green pedestal next to the magical mirror. In a swirl of motion, *Illusion-making for Beginners* was replaced by *Duels of the Ages, by Desaix Ogden*.

Emma flipped through the pages until she landed on a page towards the rear of the book and began reading aloud.

*"Although no official record exists from known wizards or witches of the time, Genghis Khan's successful ventures on and off the battlefield point to the career of a man wielding magic leftover from the Ninth Age of Magical Proximity. A capable duelist, more than one clash with a rival Khan ended with reports of Genghis' complete disappearance from sight mid-battle. Only with the luxury of hindsight can we infer the Great Khan possessed the ability to perform Light Refraction."*

## \* Chapter 17: Light Refraction \*

Echoes of Mrs. Caldwell's dry history classes bounced around Oliver's head. "Genghis Khan?" he asked. "The Mongolian Empire guy?"

"Who cares?" dismissed Emma. "What's important is the bit at the bottom here. It's been capitalized like it's an official name, see? *Light Refraction.*"

Feeling a rush of excitement, Oliver saw the words stick out in the text as if they glowed. He tapped at the bottom of the mirror and mentally implored it to run a search for *"Light Refraction."*

To their astonishment, only a few dozen line items showed up on the list. Every other time they'd searched for something, hundreds, if not thousands of search results appeared.

Huffing at Oliver and Lance's gaping mouths, Emma launched the first result. When the cover page appeared, they collectively gasped.

"You've gotta be kidding," said Lance, pale light shining off his face.

*Light Refraction; Sifting through the Lies, an Essay by Elodie Lalandra*

Emma flew through the essay – "just looking for the spell itself," she said, despite Oliver's protests – until she reached the forty-ninth, and final, page.

*"In conclusion, with the summoning words lost to the sands of time, it is impossible to conclude whether a Light Refraction spell ever existed, let alone could be cast again during the Tenth Age of Magical Proximity."*

"Well, that's a bummer," said Lance, shaking his head. "When I saw Lalandra's name on the front, I thought we'd struck gold."

## NOVA 01

"What about the other results?" said Emma.

Oliver took control now, commanding the screen back to the search. His eyebrows furrowed as he looked.

Past a list of dusty sounding books such as, *History's Most-Accomplished Spell-Weavers*, the remaining ten or so line items all appeared to be newspaper clippings. He opened the first one.

*Tenochprima Academy denies rediscovery of Light Refraction.*

*Shocking scenes at Tenochprima Academy earlier today as reporters found the school in an uproar over one student's alleged disappearance during the Magical Five Tournament's Dueling Finale.*

*"Look uhh, it was just a trick of the light," claimed Headmaster Highbury to a group of the press restricted to the school's landing strip.*

*Reporters were hurried away when asked who cast the spell, but our sources can confirm the student in question is none other than ~~~ ~~~ of the ~~~ family. Headmaster Highbury all but confirmed this to be true when he banned the press from the grounds after being directly asked about the boy.*

*Light Refraction, or Invisibility, of course, grants the user the ability to disappear from sight. Regrettably, however, the spell has been lost over the ages.*

# * Chapter 17: Light Refraction *

Oliver, Emma, and Lance didn't speak for a moment as they reread the news clipping.

"Why is the name of the student blurred out?" Oliver asked, breaking the silence.

"Probably the school just protecting the privacy of the kid," said Lance, dismissively.

"Either that or his parents sued to make sure his name was removed," said Emma.

Oliver sighed. "It would have been nice to have a name. We still have nothing to go on. Even if somebody did cast a spell in – when was this written?"

"Nearly thirty years ago," said Emma, sitting down in a chair.

"I think we're going about this the wrong way," interjected Lance. "Watkin told you to look up ways to conceal, not be invisible."

"Alright then," said Emma, her tone sassy, "you go through these books and find something – anything – on concealment! Go on! I've been searching since before break, when you two were working on Belk's final essay on Fireball Theory!"

Lance raised his hands for peace. "Didn't Watkin say we just need you to not do magic in public again? Why can't you just perform the freezing spell late at night when nobody's watching? All we need to do is walk on the ice and then we'll be on our way!"

Oliver grimaced as he repeated his conversation with Watkin. "He said he'd known about you borrowing Abe's book. That means the faculty can track any rule-breaking. We need to find a way to remove trackers or something, because I've got a feeling that the second we get close to the lagoons—,"

Emma interrupted him with a loud clap of her hands. "Say that again!"

"What?" said Oliver, frowning.

"Not you! Lance, say that again!"

"Walk on the ice and then be on our way?" suggested Lance, wincing in anticipation of another clap of Emma's hands.

"You're a genius – and you too, Oliver!"

"Naturally," agreed Lance, "but I don't follow."

"All this time we've been searching for a way to *use* magic undetected, but what if we just don't use magic?"

Lance and Oliver stared at Emma dumbfounded.

"Look, let me just show you. Y'all just made me remember something when you mentioned the lagoons!" She stood up to clear the search on the magical mirror. "I researched the lagoons and cypress trees a couple weeks ago and found an article. Let's see here …"

After clearing the search, she implored the mirror to pull results for "Tenochprima lagoons," and opened a news article from more than two decades prior. "Listen to this," she said.

> *"At the Dawn of the Tenth Age of Magical Proximity, Tenochprima Academy bans students from its famed Eastern Lagoons and Swampy Woods. When asked by reporters about the new policies, Headmaster Highbury insisted the changes were designed to protect the student body. No doubt the Board, however, will be wondering why the Headmaster*

## \* Chapter 17: Light Refraction \*

*instilled the measures without any supporting legislation or discourse with parents on privacy rights, as the Headmaster used magic provided by Nova's moon, Aurora, to place tracking spells on the forbidden areas. Does the Headmaster have the right to track whether students are performing magic in restricted areas? Is he going too far, invading student privacy? Or is he simply ensuring the safety of his students? Let us know what you think in the comments below."*

"Let me get this straight," said Lance, shaking his head. "You want us to go into the cold lagoons, in the dark, covered by fog, with *Xihuacota* liable to pull us down to the depths at any moment, and just swim on over to the island?"

"Man, why'd you have to mention *Xihuacota*?" said Oliver, shaking his head as the back of his neck tingled.

"Not swim," said Emma, rolling her eyes, "just like you said, Lance – we'll walk on the ice."

"How are we going to walk on ice if Oliver can't turn the water into ice without being caught? Didn't Desmoulins say there are crocodiles in there?"

"Because we won't be using *our* ice – the golems have a fleet of ice rafts out there! Listen to the article – *does the Headmaster have the right to track whether students are performing magic in restricted areas* – don't you get it? Lalandra, Watkin, Blackwood, none of them will know we're out there as long as we don't perform any magic."

Lance raised his eyebrows.

"Okay, I'll admit, that's a great idea."

Emma raised her hands and shook them. "Obviously!"

They looked at Oliver.

He grimaced before speaking. "I don't know, y'all. Watkin knew Lance borrowed Abe's book … how's he going to miss us borrowing an ice raft?"

"That's a good point," said Lance. "Let's see what the rules have to say."

He stood up next to Emma, clearing the search again, and entered "Tenochprima Rules." The surface of the mirror swirled as the news article disappeared and was replaced by a lengthy list.

"Yikes," said Emma, "page 1 of 256."

"Run a search for ice or golem," commanded Lance.

*Displaying 0 out of 0 results.*

"There you go, Oli, zero results!"

"C'mon," pleaded Emma, pushing and pulling Oliver's arm impatiently. "If we get caught, we can just say we wanted to get up close to *Xihuacota!*"

Oliver stood up, looking over his shoulders uncontrollably. "Stop mentioning her!"

Emma laughed. "You're the Prophet's Advent, and you're afraid of a little old lady?"

Oliver glared at them both.

"Fine," he said. "Let's go for it. But if we do see *Xihuacota*, I'm throwing fireball after fireball at her because no chance I'm getting dragged to her house to knit for the rest of the year!"

Emma and Lance shared a fist bump to celebrate.

"Okay," said Emma, "when are we going?"

## * Chapter 17: Light Refraction *

"Tomorrow's Christmas Eve," said Lance, "Elton told me there's a cocktail hour with the faculty. We could make an appearance, and after the faculty have had a few drinks, scram to the Lagoons."

"Works for me," said Emma.

They looked at Oliver. Inwardly, he thought they weren't prepared enough, but if the plan wasn't to perform magic, what was stopping them?

After another few seconds, he nodded his head.

The next day Oliver woke early. He quickly wondered if his ability to rise without an alarm on important days was tied to him being a Trinova, but then dismissed the arrogant thought with a smile after noticing Lance was already up brushing his teeth at the sink in the corner of the room.

Kicking his covers away, Oliver made to rise out of bed, but stopped halfway and collapsed as a sharp pain shot from his arm.

With nausea riding up his throat, he glanced down at his arm, following the pain to its source.

His chupacabra rash had turned a shade of green he didn't know existed, and his arm felt as if it had its own heartbeat.

Lance shook his head at him through the mirror. "Health Center will be closed this time of day, but let's see if Ms. Joan can do anything about it."

Wincing, Oliver nodded, doing everything he could not to scream from the pain.

# NOVA 01

With as little motion as possible, he pulled on a polo, khakis, and boat shoes, before heading to the Dining Hall and tapping on the wall that hid the kitchens, Lance right behind him.

The door scraped as it began to open, but then stopped an eighth of the way, leaving little to no room to enter. Ms. Joan's voice floated towards them from clouds of steam and smoke.

"For the last time! You'll have to wait until the cocktail hour before I serve any of my eggnog! I know it's delicious, but *dang* – stop being impatient!"

"We don't want your eggnog," Oliver shouted through the opening. "We just want your help!"

"Oh!" came back Ms. Joan's voice. Her tone shifted from bristly to sweet as honey. "I'm sorry, kids!"

The door opened up some more, allowing them inside. Lance's stomach growled involuntarily as the smell of bacon met their noses.

"What can I do for you two?" she asked, barely looking away from the many things she was cooking. "You need to misbehave again and help me clean all this mess, Oliver – WHAT IS THE MATTER WITH YOUR ARM?"

With one hand on her ruby necklace, she raised the other to freeze all the activity in her kitchen in place. Though they could hear bacon sizzling, eggs frying, and the oven baking, everything appeared locked in time.

"You need to go to the Health Center, right away," she said, grabbing Oliver's hand and twisting it lightly to get a good look at the wound.

# * Chapter 17: Light Refraction *

"Chupacabra venom, hmm? You too proud to go get this checked? Where in the heck did you run into a Chupacabra?"

"That's why we're here," said Oliver. He pulled his hand out of her grip, wincing at the motion. "Health Center is closed, and it just started turning white, so we wanted to see if you knew how to fix this."

"Let me get Blackwood," she replied, frowning. "He knows Chupacabra venom better than anyone."

"Don't!" said Oliver, almost shouting.

"You got something to tell me, Oliver? Because you're not making any sense. Blackwood will be able to heal this immediately."

"Blackwood's the reason he has the rash!" said Lance defensively. "He made Oliver fight one off during our finals. He's had an agenda against him since he became a Trinova."

"Hmmm," said Ms. Joan, narrowing her eyes. "Is this true, Oli?"

"Yes."

"Boys are the definition of stupid. Now you're too proud to ask him for help? If we weren't in an Age of Proximity, that kind of stupidity would kill you."

Oliver's blood boiled a little bit, mostly because he knew Ms. Joan was right. He wouldn't have been in this mess if he'd just gone to the Health Center right away. His Wisdom needed practice.

"But," she continued, "as my friends in México City like to say, *ni modo*." She put her hand back on her necklace and pointed at a mirror over the sink, "Jaime, calling in a favor. Bring your toolbox, if you don't mind."

# NOVA 01

Puzzled, Oliver and Lance stared at the mirror. It fogged over, and cursive letters came back one motion at a time. *On my way.*

After a few moments, Professor Chavarría entered. Oliver and Lance were finishing up plates of eggs and bacon when the hulking figure of a man walked in.

"Well, Joan? What's going on?" He looked from Oliver to Lance, nodding at them in turn. "Gentlemen." Oliver always thought he looked a bit like Santiago, but friendlier, with well-trimmed hair and a neat mustache.

Ms. Joan froze the food again, turned to face Chavarría, and shook his hand. "Thank you, Jaime, for coming," she said with a take-your-breath-away smile she'd never given Oliver or Lance. "Our Trinova here has gotten himself into a mess."

"What's wrong with him? He looks fine to me—,"

Oliver raised his arm, bringing the green and white rash to everyone's attention.

"Chupacabra?"

He nodded.

Chavarría grunted and placed his toolbox on a marble countertop. It opened on its own accord, revealing dozens of small vials, scales, feathers, stones, and small notebooks. Chavarría grabbed one of the vials – it bubbled ominously with white liquid inside it.

"Best antidote to Chupacabra venom is Chupacabra saliva," said Chavarría. He took a knee next to where Oliver sat and grabbed his arm, twisting it over until he could see the extent of the rash. When he removed the vial's rubber stopper, the contents hissed slightly. If Oliver hadn't been

## * Chapter 17: Light Refraction *

in so much pain, he might have noticed the vial had grown to the size of a pitcher. Taking a brush, Chavarría applied copious swaths of the saliva onto the wound before then wrapping it in gauze. "The pups, you see," Chavarría lectured, "often wrestle with each other, scratching themselves with their own poison. Over time, they evolved to have antibodies in their saliva to heal their self-inflicted wounds as they licked them."

Oliver winced as the skin beneath the gauze felt like it was boiling. He raised the arm and closed his fingers, feeling better already. "Thanks, Professor."

Chavarría stood and nodded down at him. "No problem. Next time don't wait until it gets that bad before asking for help."

"Professor?" inquired Lance before Chavarría had left. He stopped and turned.

"Yes, Mr. Wyatt?"

"What's a good healing spell we can practice for next time?"

Chavarría laughed and shook his head. "A healing spell? That's advanced magic, son. You best stick to the common ointments I had you all practice this semester." He turned again to leave.

"But what are the words?" pleaded Lance. "At least let us practice!"

Chavarría paused at the door, a frown at the corner of his mouth. "Well, you can always try *'vulna recuperet,'* but don't expect to accomplish anything until you've practiced the theory for at least a year."

"What was that about?" hissed Oliver as Ms. Joan gave Jaime a breathy goodbye at the door.

# NOVA 01

"I thought it'd be worth having in your back pocket in case one of us gets frostbite, or worse, from a golem tonight!"

Oliver pushed his lips together, impressed. "Good thinking."

After rushed goodbyes to Ms. Joan who seemed to barely notice them, Oliver and Lance exited the kitchens to find an anxious looking Emma shoveling down breakfast, surrounded by Stevie, Elton, and Joel.

"Hey there, Oli," yelled Elton, "and you, too, Lance – forgot you existed to be honest – have a seat."

Lance gave Elton a hand gesture a faculty member would not have approved while Oliver peered at them with a wary expression.

"Yeah," said Stevie, her eyes unfocused, "we've just been talking to Emma here, wondering about some rumors."

"Rumors," piped in Joel, "that you three have been spending quite a bit of time in the Research Lab."

Stevie shook her head, pain etched across her face. "That's what the rumors say. A sin punishable by death according to the rumor spreader himself, Lord Blackwood."

Oliver's skin crawled at Dean Blackwood's name.

He took the open seat next to Joel and looked at Emma with his best sarcastic smile. "You mean to tell me – Blackwood is saying nasty things about me? No chance!"

A chorus of laughter boomed from Elton and Joel.

"Good one," said Elton clapping him on the back, nearly forcing Oliver's face into a bowl of porridge.

# \* Chapter 17: Light Refraction \*

"Nah-uh," said Stevie, shaking her grinning head slowly. "You can't wriggle out of this with charm and sophistication — I've got enough for all of us combined."

Joel raised his eyebrows and whispered to Oliver, "I don't think she does, do you?"

"Uhhh …"

"The reason why we're bothering you at this ungodly time of day," Stevie continued, still looking pained.

"It's already nine-thirty!" hissed Emma.

"Is to ask you, why you've been holed up in the Research Lab?"

Lance crossed his arms and growled. "That's none of your business."

"None of our business, he says," Elton laughed, elbowing Joel's ribs with fake exuberance.

Stevie sighed and lowered her head into a solemn shake. "Quit being so stupid, Lance." She raised her nose and placed her fingers on her forehead. "We don't care what you've been doing in the Research Lab, just that you haven't majacked your notebooks before snooping around."

"Majacked?" Lance asked.

"Yeah, majacked," concluded Stevie. "Here, Emma, gimme your notebook."

"What are you gonna do to it?" Emma growled as Elton snatched her book.

"Lighten up, girl. We're just gonna remove some of the school's rules. Joel, you've got watch."

# NOVA 01

Joel straightened up, his dreadlocks bouncing off the small of his back, before looking around to make sure no faculty were present. After a brief moment, he snapped his fingers.

At the cue, Stevie took out a wizened looking stick lined with emerald and gold rivulets. She handled the wand with reverence as she tapped Emma's notebook. "This has been in Hutch since the first year of the Tenth Age," she said with her eyes closed, "we owe everything to our forefathers."

"Two kids by the names of Jon and Justin," said Elton, "bless 'em."

"What shall we give 'em, folks?" said Stevie, her fingers at work on Emma's screen. "The Lab? What else?"

Oliver could barely register what they were talking about.

"The map?" asked Elton.

Stevie snapped her fingers. "Genius, beautiful brother of mine. Map's in now too, what else?"

"List of spells?" said Joel.

Stevie shook her head. "Strict policy on that one. They might mess up something permanently if they take on advanced magic too early."

"Yeah, but Oli's a Trinova," said Elton, shrugging his shoulders. "Triple the ability."

"Or triple the danger. I'm Wise you're Powerful, that's my final word, big man."

"Fine," said Elton, crossing his gorilla-sized arms. "At least give them the points of interest mod for the map."

"Good looks," said Stevie, "I'll do that. Anything else?"

# * Chapter 17: Light Refraction *

"Wrap it up," said Joel, sitting down, "Bald and Brash has just entered from the south."

With a motion like water, the wizened wand Stevie had brandished was hidden from sight, and Emma's notebook was back on the table. Stevie leaned back in her chair to complete a picture of innocence.

"Hey Elton, why'd the chicken cross the road?" she asked.

"I don't know, Stevie, why *did* the chicken cross the road?"

Stevie leaned in dramatically and quieted her voice. "To get away from Lord Blackwood, that's why. Sheesh, what a creep!"

This time they all roared with genuine laughter.

Unable to help himself Oliver looked at the Dining Hall's southern entrance to see Dean Blackwood approaching them. "Your code name for Blackwood is Bald and Brash?" he whispered to Stevie.

"Yeah, we used to call him Browntree, but he caught on and wasn't amused."

As Blackwood joined Professor Chavarría at a faculty table, he shot a reproachful stare at Joel and Elton, who still kicked with laughter. A second later, his eyes flicked to Oliver, at which point his expression turned to pure disgust, his lips almost nonexistent behind a thin line of blue.

"He really does hate you, huh?" said Elton as Chavarría began an animated conversation with Blackwood.

"You're telling me?"

After Blackwood's entry into the Dining Hall, Stevie refused to allow anyone to mention the "mods" they'd made to Emma's notebook. She did, however, insist on Oliver, Emma, and Lance joining them for the Wyatt snowball fight scheduled to begin sharply at "elevensies" outside Hutch. They gratefully accepted the request, and a moment later, Oliver, Emma, and Lance were dashing down the stairs to change into warmer attire.

On their way back up, Emma shouted at Oliver and Lance to join her in one of the observation rooms on B4. When they arrived, she showed them the changes Stevie had made to her notebook.

It reflected the same modules as before, but if you swiped even further right, two new modules now gave them access to the Research Lab's WMD and an interactive map of the campus grounds.

"This is amazing!" said Emma, looking down at the map.

At first, Oliver thanked the heavens for the virtual access to the WMD — they wouldn't have to hole away in the Research Lab anymore. No wonder none of the older students were ever in there. But then he started paying attention to the map from past Emma's shoulders. When he realized what he was looking at, he grabbed the notebook from her hands in a rush of excitement.

"Oh, that's OK," said Emma haughtily. "I wasn't using that or anything."

Scribbled in different handwriting, thousands of notes could be opened for practically every area on campus. If he touched one of the notes, a rating appeared, giving him the option to contribute with a helpful or unhelpful vote. The notes with the most helpful votes appeared largest on the screen. Oliver resisted the urge to check the thousands of notes across campus and zoomed in on the lagoons. Seconds later, his excited grin faded off his chin.

# * Chapter 17: Light Refraction *

There weren't any notes in the lagoons themselves. Only a few on the shoreline.

*"Tried exploring out here but got caught – do not use magic when near the shore or past it!"*

*"Got thrown into detention just for firing a melting spell at a golem on a block of ice!"*

*"Almost got taken by Xihuacota but managed to block her with a brick wall. Lalandra was ready to throw me into detention until I explained it was self-defense!"*

"Holy smokes," said Lance, reading along with Oliver. "Let's get these mods on our notebooks too so we don't have to beg Emma for hers anytime we want to research."

They didn't stop perusing through the map's scribbled hints until they'd joined Stevie, Elton, and Joel outside Hutch for the snowball fight. When they arrived, they were forced to put it away in Lance's small backpack because the snowball fight had already begun in earnest. Grinning at the opportunity to push away the anxiety he felt, Oliver ducked and weaved to join the fray with Emma right behind him. They barreled into Elton to dodge a well-placed missile from Joel, collapsing into a heap behind Elton's thick wall of snow. He looked down at them past askew, blonde hair, his eyes red with Power, and gestured rudely towards Lance, who'd just slid into safety within a rickety fort hiding Joel and Stevie.

"So that's how it's gonna be, little bro?" he said, his voice low. Then, he crouched low to pick up and lift Oliver and Emma up as if they were ragdolls. "Do as I do, yes?"

# NOVA 01

Oliver's jaw dropped as he watched Elton's hands operate like a windmill, creating snowball after snowball that he fired off just as quickly. The constant barrage of white blurs kept Stevie and Joel from being able to peer over their lopsided wall. Unaware of the danger, Lance made the mistake of sticking up his head, allowing a snowball to connect with his forehead. Dazed, he stumbled backwards, where Stevie caught him, howling with laughter.

"Snowballs!" Elton commanded towards Oliver and Emma. The power behind each of Elton's throws made Oliver understand why he had stood a man down before they'd arrived.

After loading up on more ammunition, Elton popped his head through an opening in their roof to resume his barrage. "Uh-oh," he said, ducking down and shielding himself into a ball. "Incoming!"

"What's incoming?" shouted Emma, alarmed. She made to stick her head over the wall, but Oliver grabbed her arm to stop her lest she stumble backwards like Lance.

A whooshing noise sounded overhead as two dozen balls obliterated the wall just behind where Emma sat.

"What the—," began Oliver.

"Stevie's putting together wind tunnels!" Elton bellowed. "Oliver! Strengthen our walls, I'll cover you!"

Helicopter noises ensued as Elton upped his firing rate, forcing Stevie back into hiding.

Smiling and laughing, Oliver stepped outside the fort and looked to the sun for energy before pulling in the surrounding snow as he might have

# * Chapter 17: Light Refraction *

done to raise a wall of Earth. A moment later, he'd doubled the amount of snow packed into their fort's defenses. Satisfied, he rushed back to the other side of the fort to continue making Elton more ammunition.

By the end of the fight, Stevie, Joel, and Lance had managed to create a snow mortar that caught Oliver's team unawares. They ended up buried in snow after their roof collapsed from the pressure of repeated mortar bombs. Stevie and Joel high fived as they emerged from their fort, victorious. Lance smiled, too, but quickly found himself frowning after Elton pointed out the welt he'd left on his younger brother's forehead.

They capped off the afternoon with hot chocolate from Ms. Joan, who didn't pay them much attention even though the kitchen wall was open. She waved a hand dismissively at anyone who approached, but Oliver chanced a glance inside. She stooped over a large cauldron of creamy liquid which he guessed might be her world-famous eggnog.

As they drank their hot chocolate, Stevie revealed she and her siblings were staying on campus for the holidays because their parents were in Paris celebrating their 20$^{th}$ Anniversary. Oliver managed to awkwardly ask Stevie to pass along his congratulations before taking a heavy sip of hot chocolate. The news slightly surprised Oliver as he'd just assumed both Emma and Lance had stayed behind to help him find clues about the Temple. It never occurred to him they had their own reasons for staying behind.

Nearby Emma laughed. Oliver wondered if she had stayed behind to help him with the clues or if some other reason left her here just like Lance. Had he been selfish with her, too? He rubbed his shoes together under the chair subconsciously before deciding he'd be better at learning more about his friends' family lives and not just focus on solving his problems.

Realizing, he'd dozed off, he brought his attention back to the Dining Hall. From the kitchens, Ms. Joan had just emerged with a cauldron waddling behind her on four wooden legs. Its contents sloshed back and forth, releasing fumes of nutmeg, cinnamon, and a thinner smell Oliver couldn't quite place. Beneath the cauldron's rim, a label read "Faculty Eggnog."

Though the rest had gone quiet at Ms. Joan's approach, Stevie stood to applaud and bow dramatically. Elton, Joel, and Brantley soon followed suit, licking their lips.

"Nah-uh," said Ms. Joan, wagging a finger at them. "This is for adults *only*. Doesn't matter how much you try and exploit my vanity – you won't be getting any of it! Can't y'all read?" She whistled loudly, and a stubbier cauldron exited the kitchens to join them. This one read "Student Eggnog" under the rim instead. "You can have as much of this batch as you want."

Stevie smirked. "Of course. *Of course.*"

Over the next hour, the faculty members and their families descended from their apartments to join the Christmas Eve cocktail hour and dinner. Most of them stopped to introduce their loved ones to the students who'd stayed behind on campus. Professor Zapien's husband, for instance, turned out to be a warm, portly fellow with a bustling mustache.

"And you must be our Trinova!" he said to Oliver causing his heart to sink. "Oh, don't worry about me. I'm Sabrina's husband – couldn't care less about politics outside the school. I do hear, however, that you shop with

# * Chapter 17: Light Refraction *

Mr. Miyada. Should you ever want to expand your collection of magical artifacts with more – erm – *elegant* pieces, do not hesitate to let me know."

As Oliver met more and more of the families, he couldn't help but feel self-conscious about the snow and mud-splattered clothes he had worn to the event. Where the faculty and their loved ones wore stylish dresses, coats, slacks, and jewelry, he and his fellow students wore dirty khaki pants and quarter zip pullovers. Looking from side to side, he pulled up the collar of his wrinkly polo to make sure it was visible beneath his coat.

Next to Blackwood, a thin, brooding woman caught Oliver's attention. She matched his gaze when he did, scowling momentarily before resuming conversation with Blackwood, Desmoulins, and another thin woman.

"Have you ever seen a scarier bunch?" whispered Emma, following his line of sight. "They might take fashion tips from *Xihuacota*."

"Hey, when are we making moves?" whispered Lance, joining them at the end of the students' table. Nearby, the older bunch from Hutch focused intently on Stevie who held an enormous mug of eggnog.

"Hush!" hissed Emma, looking over Oliver and Lance's shoulders.

"Good evening, you three," came a friendly voice.

It was Professor Watkin. Unlike the others, he hadn't dressed up more than usual – perhaps a reflection on the quality of his day-to-day dress.

"Hey, Professor!" said Oliver, smiling genuinely. Not too far away, Stevie's mug had vanished.

"Enjoying yourselves, I hope?" He took the seat next to Emma, handing her his walking staff to hold.

"Most definitely, sir," said Lance, not making eye contact.

"Fun party this," added Emma, nodding, "do y'all do this every year?" Oliver let out a sigh of relief – at least Emma was able to act calmly when rule-breaking was imminent.

"Oh, this tradition is as old as the school itself! The faculty have always lived on campus – in the apartments on the upper floors of the Temple where we now sit. Lance, you recently served detention up there, am I not mistaken?"

"Uh, yes, sir," said Lance.

"I suggested it to Blackwood, if you don't mind my saying. The staff room in particular needed some blood, sweat, and tears on the floors. Wouldn't you agree?"

"Uh, yes sir," repeated Lance. Oliver almost smacked him on the back of the head. Couldn't he think of anything else to say?

"Yes, very interesting room," continued Watkin. "You know, I don't think the décor has changed at all since it was created. The paintings *in particular* are said to have been created by the Founders themselves." He paused to point at Professor Desmoulins. "Madeline, whom you know was Professor Dionysus' ancestor, was renowned for her painting."

"That's cool," said Emma, nodding her head.

"Cool, indeed," agreed Watkin, standing up. "Well, I'm off for some more eggnog. Speaking of which …" He motioned for Emma to give him his walking stick. She obliged, handing it back to him. Without pausing, he tapped it against the stone floor causing the mug of eggnog hidden behind Stevie to shoot straight into his open hand from its hiding place beneath the table. Smiling, he took a sip and nodded at Stevie, who gaped at him in

# * Chapter 17: Light Refraction *

response, no clever words forming on her lips. "Merry Christmas," he concluded with a final nod of his head towards Oliver. Without another word, he walked away to join Blackwood, Desmoulins, and the two women they'd not met.

Once out of earshot, Elton and Joel pounded on the table, thoroughly enjoying the fact there was someone in the world Stevie couldn't outwit.

"Well, that was weird," muttered Lance.

"What else is he supposed to talk to a bunch of teenagers about?" returned Emma. Lance shrugged his shoulders.

"You know what I think?" whispered Oliver, looking at his watch. "I think it's time *we went to bed*."

"Yeah," said Lance, looking around. Most of the faculty looked to be laughing boisterously amongst themselves, their cheeks flushed, and eyes glazed. None turned to spare any attention to the students anymore.

Emma looked confused. "Go to bed? What are you talking about? How are we going to—,"

But Oliver placed a hand over her mouth. She just as quickly slapped it away.

"We'll sneak out the window in our room," he hissed before she could blab again. "Can't exactly walk out the main door, can we?"

"Fair enough," she said, slightly flustered.

With Stevie, Elton, and Joel hatching another plan to acquire eggnog from Ms. Joan's cauldron – it now continuously waddled in place, bumping into her – they made their way towards the circular staircase to the dormitory just below. Oliver managed to catch Lalandra's eyes just as his head ducked beneath the final stair. He winced, hoping she didn't realize what they were up to.

A few moments later, they found themselves hesitating on the windowsill in Oliver and Lance's room. Despite the bundles of clothing they'd put on, the dark and wintry mix that awaited them roared like a blizzard.

"We're sure about this right?" asked Oliver. "I appreciate y'all staying behind for the holidays, but I won't blame you if you don't want to do this."

"Unbelievable, this one," said Emma, shaking her head. Most of her red hair was stuffed in the back of the puffy hoodie she'd donned for their trek across the lagoons, making her freckles more pronounced than usual.

"We're going with you, Oli," said Lance almost laughing. He, too, wore an outrageously large, down-feather coat. "We didn't waste all that time researching in the Lab just for you to tell us we shouldn't come."

Oliver blushed. "Of course not! I just didn't want y'all to think I didn't appreciate—,"

This time Emma put her hand over his mouth, flustering him instead. "Let's just go, alright? We've got your back."

Without another word, she hopped over the windowsill and began the trek down to the lagoons, her boots crunching against the snow. Lance quickly followed, leaving Oliver alone to close the window behind them.

# Chapter 17: Light Refraction

NOVA 01

## Chapter 18: Under the Willow Tree

*The Whig leader showed up again! This time at the Great Wall. He shouldn't be able to see me since I've been holding onto the light refraction staff Tío loaned me since Cambodia. I can't afford anyone seeing me at this point. It was weird, though — he just stood there with a bunch of tourists, listening to some tour guide, and then he looked right at me and winked!*
*My tired mind is starting to play tricks.*

*24th of January, the second year of the 10th Age*

Down by the lagoon's edge, the wind howled, bringing a bite of cold not felt in South Carolina on the Original Side of the Key. It nicked and gnawed at their faces wherever their skin wasn't covered.

"Now what?" shouted Lance through the blustering weather. "Just wait for a golem to appear and take his raft?"

Feeling stupid, Oliver ignored him. Back up the hill, warm light drifted towards them invitingly. He did his best to ignore that, too.

"If only Watkin had told us how to conceal magic!" Emma growled. "What was the point of telling us what to do but not how to do it. Sometimes I wonder whether—,"

What Emma wondered, however, they didn't find out, because a terrifying screech reached their ears from the far side of the lagoon. It echoed off chunks of ice and water, arriving at different desynchronized crescendos.

# * Chapter 18: Under the Willow Tree *

"*Xihuacota,*" thought Oliver, grimacing. "*What would Santiago think of me now? He'd be half-way back up the hill already.*" Shuddering, he managed to turn his grimace into a grin at the thought of his uncle.

"How are you smiling right now?" shouted Lance. He'd positioned himself behind Oliver when the scream came. Emma, meanwhile, looked out over the water, seemingly trying to spot the noise's source.

"Sounded pretty far off – I think we're good to keep going!"

"What's our exit strategy if it begins to sound closer?" Lance asked in a whimper.

Emma shrugged. "Pray she really does just want to force us to knit with her. And, you know – not kill us."

"Shush!" said Oliver. Behind them, he'd heard crunching snow.

Just barely visible in the dark, a short figure hobbled towards them. As it neared, the ground around them stiffened into crackly ice.

"That's a golem, alright," said Lance, next to him. Oliver felt inclined to agree. "What do we do?"

The golem walked right past them.

"Oli?"

"I think we just follow it," he said, almost trance-like. He didn't know why, but something urged him to stay close to the rock-like creature.

"If *Xihuacota* catches us, I'm never talking to you again," Lance grumbled.

"Yeah, me neither," Emma agreed.

# NOVA 01

Resigned to their task, they followed the shuffling golem towards the shoreline. When it reached the water, liquid turned to solid until a small raft formed beneath its stubby feet.

"That won't hold even one of us!" shouted Oliver to the golem more than anybody else. "Can't you make it bigger?"

The golem rotated slightly at Oliver's voice.

"Can you hear me?"

It nodded its whole body.

"Are you here to help me?

More nodding.

"Did Watkin send you?"

Incapable of shaking, the golem waved its arms around.

*"Then who did?"* Oliver thought to himself. His vision of Cuahtemoc, Madeline, and Augustus came unbidden to his mind.

"Did Augustus?"

Vigorous head-nodding.

Lance whistled. "Well, I'll be. That rock is three hundred years old – at least!"

More arm flailing.

"Well, can you make your boat bigger?" Oliver asked. "We can't fit on that."

The golem looked from the raft back to Oliver and back to the raft. It pressed a stubby foot into the ice, forcing it to grow larger. After a moment, the vessel could fit all three of them somewhat comfortably. The golem

# * Chapter 18: Under the Willow Tree *

even managed to create two paddles for rowing. It used one and handed the other to Emma, who had gloves.

"Proper geniuses, those Founders," Emma muttered, shaking her head. She hopped onto the ice raft, nodding at the golem as she did, and prepared to paddle on the starboard and port sides. As they shoved off, the golem used its own paddle for steering, the wind continuing to howl around them, somehow feeling colder and colder with every yard they delved deeper into the lagoon.

"Are you sure about this?" asked Lance. They were nearing the wall of circling fog. "We won't be able to see squat once we're in there."

Oliver gulped, keeping his insecure thoughts to himself. "We have to trust Augustus. In my vision, he'd left me something to find. He wouldn't have gone to the trouble of hiding it if it wasn't important."

"Again, all these clues," sighed Emma. "Watkin, Augustus, who cares? Why can't they just give you real answers?"

Oliver found himself agreeing with Emma as they crossed into the fog. In the blanket of dense air, the wind ceased to howl, giving way to an eerie silence. It pressed against them uncomfortably, dampening the swishes of their paddles along with their moods.

As they progressed, Oliver had to stop himself from looking behind his shoulder every few seconds – he felt like somebody, or some*thing*, was watching them.

Every now and then, a log, or clump of frozen lilies would appear as a dark shadow breaking the surface of the water, causing them to panic, but as the minutes trickled on, no obstacles slowed them down.

## NOVA 01

After a few moments in silence, however, a second, murderous scream sounded through the muffled waters.

Oliver's skin prickled at the noise. Lance nearly fell of the raft.

"That sounded a lot closer this time!" stammered Lance

"Hmmm," said Emma. Even she, a Brave, shifted uncomfortably.

Oliver squinted his eyes to try and see further.

His heart skipped a beat.

Just ahead, a looming figure broke through the fog. Just in time, he covered Lance's mouth to stifle his scream.

Emma flicked him on the forehead for good measure. "It's a tree, you coward!"

Sure enough, an enormous willow tree stood tall and proud through the icy water. It loomed over them, appearing almost threatening with weeping branches cascading into both fog and water.

Without a fuss, the golem steered them past it. With the threat of *Xihuacota* imminent, however, Lance sat down and put his head through his arms, too frightened to speak or see.

More trees began to appear in the dark as they progressed through the eerie and cold waters. The crowded space forced the golem to take rounding paths instead of a direct line to wherever it led them.

The feeling of being watched prickled on Oliver's neck again, making him turn suddenly to look behind them.

Only swirling fog met his eyes. But not too far away, he thought he heard ragged breathing. It made his skin *crawl* behind his neck.

## * Chapter 18: Under the Willow Tree *

"We need to move *faster*, Mr. Golem," he said to the rock-creature. "I think she's getting closer." Though he felt terrified at the thought of *Xihuacota,* he focused on the mission at hand. "Can you make me a paddle, too?"

Nodding, the golem handed Oliver its paddle, and began to shake side to side, creating a rocky ruckus. Two splashes followed nearby, forcing another whimper out of Lance.

From where the splashes sounded, two ice rafts approached, bearing four golems. The stubby creatures made growling noises with their slit-like mouths, and, for a moment, Oliver thought they meant to attack. Rather than sink their vessel or throw their spears, however, they fused the three ice rafts together to create one, larger one.

"Welcome aboard," said Emma, patting one on the head.

It saluted her silently before manning the front of the boat with a spear held outstretched in its arms. The other three did the same, forming a perimeter around their makeshift boat while Oliver paddled on the left and Emma the right, increasing their speed.

Soon more and more trees loomed overhead, however, forcing them to slow down again. Just as Oliver heard a swish of fabric over water, an entire wall of trees rose from the fog in front of them. Ragged breathing followed the swishing noise, causing Emma to pull out her paddle and brandish it like a weapon in the center of the raft. Oliver, meanwhile, paddled even harder. Sweat trickled down his arms under his coat as he tried to move them away from the wall of trees, but the golem behind him paddled just as hard on the other side of the raft, pushing them forward at a breakneck speed again.

Just as a blood-curling scream sounded directly behind Oliver's shoulders, the raft struck something in the water, launching them all forward, hard.

Bracing himself to fall into icy water, or worse, Oliver flexed his muscles.

*Wham!*

A yelp escaped his lips. They hadn't fallen into water – they'd fallen onto land.

Feeling damp soil beneath him, Oliver pushed himself up, reflexively feeling for the energy in his ring. It arrived almost immediately, washing away any aches or sores he'd momentarily felt after the fall.

A nasty site waited for him at the water's edge. Screeching and wailing, the lagoon's creepy specter, *Xihuacota*, rustled over the ice rafts they'd just abandoned. She darted back and forth manically, desperately trying to reach them, to take them with her. But she wasn't able to.

Either a spell protected the land where they now found themselves or *Xihuacota* was unable to step onto land altogether, because any time she darted forward, an invisible wall pushed her back, reminding Oliver of the shields formed by Blackwood's *defenderis* summoning. Red sparks flew every time the specter or her tattered white dress met the invisible force, bringing a dull light to the surrounding area and illuminating the decomposing nature of her pale, blue skin. Just then Oliver noticed the land where they'd beached was not enshrouded by fog.

# * Chapter 18: Under the Willow Tree *

Comfortable that *Xihuacota* could be ignored, he turned around, lowering his arms. In a pale mist, standing serene and warm, a golden willow reflected moonlight down at him from atop an overgrown temple.

"How are we supposed to get back onto the rafts?!" shouted Lance. *Xihuacota* continued to wail – she'd taken to bashing her hands – or what was left of them – against the invisible barrier.

"No need," said Emma, pointing at the temple. "We're here."

Ignoring them, Oliver darted up the steps, recalling and reperforming Augustus' climb from his dream – a climb made over three-hundred years prior.

*"The vision has escaped me, Cuahtemoc," said a man's voice. It belonged to an eerie silhouette with white spheres where eyes should have been. He dashed up the steps of an overgrown temple towards a willow tree at its peak.*

*"So, that's it, we stop our efforts?" boomed the voice of another man speaking in his non-native tongue. "What of the boy, Augustus?"*

*"We leave him this," said the first man, brandishing a scroll of parchment.*

*"Others will find it," challenged Cuahtemoc.*

*"Not if we scrub all memory of it," said a third voice belonging to a short woman with a thick accent. "And leave clues only discoverable by him."*

*"Stop!" yelled Augustus, nearly tripping on his way up the stairs. He looked back down directly at Oliver. "He's here, now! He watches us!"*

Oliver stood on the same spot where Augustus had stopped. Did he imagine it, or did Lance stand where Cuahtemoc had crossed his arms – and Emma where Madeline had suggested the scrubbing?

# NOVA 01

"I've seen this all in my vision," said Oliver, at first in a whisper, and then a yell. "They were here – Emma, Lance – don't you get it? We found it!"

"Of course, we get it," said Emma shaking her head impatiently, "golden willow and temple right in front of us – OH WOULD YOU JUST SHUT UP?!"

She had directed her shout at *Xihuacota*.

To everyone's surprise, *Xihuacota* did shut up. With one last screech, she changed tactics, floating away to just outside the small island's visible perimeter. Far from gone, however, they could still hear every swish of her dress and ragged breath whenever they listened carefully.

Lance shuddered.

Shaking his head, Oliver continued up the stone stairs, jumping over one of the roots of the willow tree. Below, the stone golems did not follow, opting to stay near the base of the temple, their spears in hand.

Emma's and Lance's footsteps echoed behind him when he reached the top where the remaining willow roots congregated into the tree's main frame.

"We didn't see an entrance near the base," said Lance, slightly out of breath. He brandished his warhammer with both hands, rotating it like a lacrosse stick every so often.

Oliver kept his eyes on the tree. "Something tells me it's right here."

Drawing closer, he swept his ring hand's fingertips over the tree's rough bark. At first, they met scaly resistance but when they reached the middle,

## * Chapter 18: Under the Willow Tree *

the bark gave way to nothingness; allowing his hand to enter through the wood entirely.

"Right here – this is where we enter. Look, there's a hidden opening in the middle."

"How did you know that?" said Emma.

Oliver shrugged. "Instincts, I guess?" He didn't feel like explaining that the Wisdom in the back of his head was usually right. Motioning for them to follow, he stepped through the bark and into the tree's base.

Inside the tree, the world deafened to a silence only interrupted by the tinkling of an unseen lantern. Its light flickered up to where Oliver stood, at the top of a circular, wooden stair. Not wanting Emma or Lance to run right into him, he took the first couple steps down and waited. Soon enough, Emma passed through the barrier, pulling in a tentative Lance from behind.

"What if Oli's instincts can't get us back out?" he groveled.

She stuck her arm back outside, shaking her head apologetically at Oliver. "See? We can get back outside no problem."

"Fair enough," said Lance, entering slowly. Once inside, he rolled his warhammer in his hands again. "We can always force our way back out anyway."

The tree shuddered.

Lance's skin grew pale. "Maybe not, then."

"Definitely not," said Oliver, giving the wooden walls a friendly pat.

## NOVA 01

They made slow work of the descent in case a trap or unwanted trespasser waited for them at the bottom. Oliver winced at every scuffing noise their feet made, echoing loudly on either end of the stairs.

After longer than expected, they reached the bottom. Oliver jumped out front and Emma right, ready to cast defensive shields. Lance, meanwhile, barreled down the left with a yell, his hammer raised high.

After a few steps, however, he stopped, lowering his hammer back down clumsily. "Area looks secure, Oli."

Oliver didn't respond. Instead, he took stock of his surroundings.

They stood in a large, stone-laden room, shaped like a hollowed-out, circular pyramid. The walls stretched twenty-five feet from floor to ceiling, meeting in a concave point at the room's peak. Torches that flanked the walls left little to the imagination, illuminating moss and bugs that crept on the walls, ceiling, and floor indiscriminately. Where the moss didn't grow, weeds and roots dangled down from cracks in the ceiling's foundation; one of the larger ones curled up into a ball when Lance got too close.

"Gross," said Emma, grimacing.

"What's that up ahead?" asked Lance.

A wide, stone table waited for them at the back of the room. On its surface, lay a small skeleton, no longer than two feet, with the bulk of its length coming from a long tail.

Oliver stopped and raised a hand for Emma and Lance to copy.

"It's just a long, dead lizard or something," said Emma, ignoring him. "An iguana, maybe?"

## * Chapter 18: Under the Willow Tree *

"Don't you remember the dungeon sims?" hissed Oliver. He wondered if the skeleton might come to life and attack them.

But the skeleton didn't even so much as twitch its tail when Emma neared it.

"Any idea what those mean?" said Emma pointing to glyphs carved on the front of the stone table.

"Isn't it obvious," said Lance. He seemed to have found his voice after charging into the room. "There's a feathered serpent, an osorius, and an eagle—,"

"Not the animals," sighed Emma, "the glyphs underneath them! I think I recognize the eagle's one but not the others."

Oliver crouched lower to get a better look at the glyphs. Beneath each of the school Guides, a glyph had been etched. The serpent's was fluid, the osorius' rigid, and the eagle's a combination.

"Wisdom, Power, and Bravery," he murmured.

"What?" said Emma.

"I think the glyphs are symbols for Wisdom, Power, and Bravery – didn't we see them during the Ceremony of the Gifts?"

"You might have," laughed Lance. "All I saw was that first glyph, under the osorius."

"What does that make this thing then?" said Emma. She'd pointed at the skeleton on the table. Underneath it, a fourth glyph had been etched. "It kinda looks like all three, doesn't it?"

## NOVA 01

Oliver felt goosebumps looking at the fourth and last symbol. "That's probably my symbol," he mumbled. "The Trinova's symbol." He felt a blast of nostalgia as he looked at the symbol. It somehow looked familiar.

Lance snorted. "Ooo, you get your own special symbol? Aren't you cool?"

Oliver growled. "Oh hush."

Just then, he noticed a scroll of parchment nestled in the skeleton's skull. Heart racing, he removed it and began to unfurl its corners.

"There's writing on it!" he said.

"Don't be selfish!" huffed Emma. "Read it out loud!"

*When the Gifts of the Three,*
*are encompassed within thee,*
*look to Tenoch's Temples*
*to master your fundamentals.*

*Speed is of the essence,*
*to defeat an evil presence,*
*that has lusted for release,*
*since the dawn of divine peace.*

*Begin with the Forgotten Wood,*
*for there, your Gift has stood,*
*the entrance lies within our grounds,*
*Good luck – it cannot be found.*

# * Chapter 18: Under the Willow Tree *

"What a bunch of garbage!" said Emma. She stepped towards Oliver and grabbed the parchment from his hands. "What's all this supposed to mean? It's even ripped at the bottom and, hang on, there's more on the back!"

*What is gone cannot be lost,*
*balance and order come at great cost.*

"It's a riddle!" said Lance, reading over her shoulder. Oliver kept his eyes on the skeleton as he thought over what he'd just read. "The first bit," continued Lance, "that's obviously talking about Oliver – three Gifts – and they want you to find Tenoch's temples."

"What are Tenoch's temples?" said Emma, handing Lance the scroll.

"No clue," sighed Lance, "that's part of the riddle, isn't it?"

"What worries me," interrupted Oliver, "is the second part. Read that over, Lance?"

"Speed is of the essence, to combat an evil presence ... that has lusted for release ... since the dawn of divine peace?"

Dreading the question he was about to ask, he did so anyway. "Didn't Archie say *The Damned* was only placed in a purgatory?"

Emma put a hand to her mouth.

"What?" said Lance, his eyes wide. "No chance! Didn't that happen years and years ago? What's he been eating all this time?"

# NOVA 01

Oliver stifled a laugh. "A man so evil a higher power erased his name from memory, and you're concerned about what he's been eating for a decade?"

Emma smacked his arm. "This isn't funny! I think you're right – 'lusted for release, since the dawn of divine peace'?! What if the divine peace was his imprisonment? We need to talk to Archie and Rasmus right away!"

Oliver grabbed her arm to hold her back. "Archie said if the Founders hid something from them – it was hidden for a reason! We can't tell anyone!"

"Are you kidding me? We're just kids – have you tried reading up on *The Damned*? There's *nothing* – absolutely nothing – on the search results. Whatever he did, it was so bad nobody has the guts to tell us about it!"

"I know!" said Oliver, gripping either side of the stone table hard. "But remember what Stevie said – everybody was in on it, not just *The Damned*. He was just the leader! Archie's right, if we tell anybody about this, even him, people will start talking about what happened, and it might restart whatever stopped when *The Damned* was imprisoned."

Emma huffed. "So, what are we supposed to do? Just wait for him to release himself from his prison and kill us all? He's not going to like a Trinova being around if he was saying he was the Trinova last time around – especially if you're against his movement."

Oliver raised his hands in frustration. "I don't know—,"

"Yes, we do!" interrupted Lance, waving the parchment above their heads. "Look to Tenoch's temples! Begin with the Forgotten Wood!

# * Chapter 18: Under the Willow Tree *

Augustus, Cuahtemoc, Madeline – they left you a Gift by the looks of it. Something to help you – us – defeat this guy!"

Emma and Oliver traded an uncertain look, but what Lance said made sense. Oliver grabbed the parchment back from Lance's hand.

"Its entrance lies within our grounds, good luck – it cannot be found," he repeated. "That doesn't give us much to go on."

Emma shook her head. "No, that gives us *nothing* to go on."

"Sure, it does," said Lance. "We've got some homework to do – what are Tenoch's Temples and what is the Forgotten Wood? Maybe we'll find something using the WMD module Stevie gave us."

"Or in other books in the Research Lab," agreed Oliver.

Emma crossed her arms.

Oliver grinned. "Hah! Tell you what – even though we can't talk about the scroll to anyone, if we're sly, we can ask around about Tenoch's Temples or the Forgotten Wood. Deal?"

Emma kept her eyes narrowed for a moment, but then relinquished, offering a hand to Oliver. "Deal!"

"Terrific," said Lance, placing his hand awkwardly on top of theirs as they shook. "Now what about the writing on the wall?"

"What writing?" said Oliver.

Lance pointed with his hammer. "Up behind the iguana skeleton."

Following the direction of Lance's hammer, Oliver looked to the back wall. Words had been etched into the wall, smooth and barely visible.

*Take Roli with you – he's the last of his kind.*

# NOVA 01

Then, in different set of handwriting, a second message had been scribbled beneath the first.

*~~~ was here. Sorbelux.*

Puzzled, Oliver looked back down at the skeleton and then the scroll. "The handwriting on the second message is different than Augustus' scroll."

"I think ... I think another student beat us here," said Emma, stepping closer to the letters on the wall; they glistened in the torchlight. "A name was written in, but it's been scratched out – it says '~~~ *was here*', doesn't it?"

"Yeah, but what is *sorbelux?*" asked Oliver. The torches flickered as he said it.

"No clue, but I'm not sure how I feel about somebody else getting here before us – Lance, what on Earth are you doing?"

Lance stopped, halfway done shoving the iguana's skeleton into his backpack. "What?" he asked, a torn expression on his lips. Beneath his mop of blonde hair, it looked like a mix of unconvincing confidence and guilt. "The message said take Roli, so that's what I'm doing."

Oliver laughed loudly. "I think Roli has been dead for centuries. What's the point?"

When Emma turned to grin with him, she jumped, and began looking left and right with concern. "Oli? Where'd you go?"

# * Chapter 18: Under the Willow Tree *

Lance looked behind the stone table even as he zipped his bag shut, with Roli secured. "Are you playing a trick on us? Quit hiding?"

"What are y'all talking about—,"

"GAHH, where is that coming from?!" shouted Lance. Emma had jumped back with nerves in her eyes, too.

"I'm right here!" yelled Oliver.

"No you ain't!" said Lance, shaking his head and holding his hammer high again.

"Oliver?" said Emma, smiling again, "I think you've just figured out what *sorbelux* is. We can't see you anymore – try releasing your spell if you're holding onto some magic."

Looking down at his ring hand, Oliver realized he couldn't see any part of his body. He tried waving his arms and legs around and only saw light shimmering when moving quickly enough.

"*Light refraction,*" Lance breathed, dumbstruck. "Are you moving now? I feel like I can see waves in the air sometimes."

Oliver tip-toed until he was behind Emma.

"BOO!" he shouted, giving her a slight shove.

Emma jumped several feet into the air, disappearing for half a second. "NOT FUNNY, OLIVER!"

Releasing the flow of magic in his ring finger, he brought the spell to an end, popping back into existence. He laughed mercilessly at Emma, who'd put a hand on the table to brace herself. Lance howled along with him.

"*Sorbelux!*" tried Emma, staying entirely visible.

Oliver laughed some more.

"You enjoying yourself?" she growled.

"Here let me try," said Lance. *"Sorbelux!* Hey, I thought I felt something!"

"No use," said Emma, "wouldn't be surprised if Oliver's the *only* one who can do it."

"I didn't even disappear for a second?"

"Nope," said Oliver. "But Emma did, when I pushed her. Here let's try it – *sorbelux!*"

In a half-second, light no longer reflected off him naturally. Instead, he saw it refract or absorb into his body, casting him invisible. When he stepped towards Emma again, Lance pointed forcefully. "Oh! Oh! I can see a shimmering if I know where to look – and I can hear your footsteps if you're not careful."

"Good to know," said Oliver. He grabbed Emma's hand and held onto it. This time Emma stayed invisible with him.

"Woah!" said Lance. "Let me try too!"

Pulling Emma with him, Oliver grabbed Lance's hand next. Without a sound, Lance disappeared, too.

"This might just give us a chance to sneak back into Founders Temple!" he said.

"Forget about getting into Founders!" said Emma, letting go and popping back into light. "We have to figure out how to get back onto dry land first – *Xihuacota* is still out there!"

## * Chapter 18: Under the Willow Tree *

Oliver dropped the spell and went pale in the face. "And I've just realized! Won't the faculty get a warning someone performed magic out in the lagoons?!"

Emma put a hand to her mouth and Lance's eyes popped.

"We're idiots!" said Emma.

Lance darted towards the stairs, pausing when he reached them. "We've gotta get back to Founders Temple and fast! Oli, can you make us invisible again? Maybe we'll be able to sneak onto the raft without *Xihuacota* noticing!"

Oliver nodded. Stuffing the scroll into his pocket, he went invisible for a third time and grabbed their hands. With the three of them having to remain in contact with each other, going up the narrow stairway proved tricky, but a moment later they were readjusting their eyes to the foggy darkness above.

Ragged breathing made Oliver's neck prickle. His hands had also begun to hurt from just how hard Emma and Lance were squeezing.

"Psst," Oliver whispered to the golems near the water's edge. "We're going to get onto the rafts, can you take us back to school?"

At first the golems raised their spears and poked in the direction where Oliver's voice had come from. They looked none-too-pleased at an unidentifiable source of noise. After some back and forth growling between the lead golem and the other four, however, they all began to nod their frames at different intervals.

Relieved, Oliver led Emma and Lance onward, but as they stepped onto the raft, *Xihuacota*'s breathing grew sharper, forcing even Oliver to squeeze his hands hard. With a sound like rustling leaves, she appeared before them, revealing rotting skin and visible bones beneath the torn gaps of her dirtied, white dress.

Just as Oliver felt like releasing his hands to defend himself, the specter floated right past them, renewing her assault against the invisible barrier on the shore. Red sparks flew as the golems stepped onto the raft and began paddling the ice raft away from the temple.

Gradually, the screams began to muffle, and their grips lighten, but they dared not speak for the risk of being caught was too great.

But as the fog around them began to thin and the shore came into view, words drifted across the water's surface, causing the hair on their necks to stand on end.

"I'm telling you Dionysus," came Blackwood's voice. It had a manic tint to it Oliver had not heard before. "The alarm indicated it came from the foggy section, *not* the open water!"

"Won't it just be easier to see if any of the students are out of bed?" said Desmoulins peering into the fog uneasily. "Could *Xihuacota* have learned to use magic?"

"I seriously doubt it," said Watkin's voice. "If we start quizzing her about it, she'll complain we should be asking the golems too – look, there go some of them right now."

Watkin had pointed right at their ice raft as it neared the shore. The golems continued to paddle, oblivious that the faculty could be a threat to Oliver, Emma, and Lance. Oliver wanted to shout at them to turn to make shore somewhere – anywhere – else, but he couldn't risk the noise.

## * Chapter 18: Under the Willow Tree *

Howling with frustration, Blackwood shot a fireball at their ice raft.

But water shot up from the lagoons, intercepting it and creating a rolling wave of steam and mist in the air.

"Now listen here, Broderick," snarled Watkin in a tone they hadn't heard before. "Don't take it out on the golems, they're just making shore for the evening!"

Oliver praised the heavens for the mist created by the sudden heat because it allowed them to leap off the ice raft onto the muddy shore, the golems right behind them. Pulling hard, Oliver dragged Emma and Lance to drier land where footprints would be less likely to show.

"I think you're right, Dionysus," growled Blackwood, storming up the hill. "If we can catch Oliver out of bed, then we've as good as confirmed he's the one who performed the magic!"

"That boy lives in your head rent-free, Broderick," said Watkin. "Aren't you going to apologize to the golems?"

The golems took the opportunity to chase after Desmoulins and Blackwood, completely ignoring Watkin. They growled and threw balls of ice, furious at the dean for his fireball.

He turned to glare at Watkin, his forearms bulging as he flexed his fingers. But then his gaze shifted, and he rose his right arm. *"Defenderis,"* he yelled, blocking chunks of ice thrown at him by the golems. Oliver wondered if Blackwood wore a sleeve like Emma, hidden under his frock coat. As red sparks flew, Blackwood turned to leave. "No, I don't think I will, Cato. They're rocks, not humans. I know it was Oliver, and I'm going to catch him!"

# NOVA 01

A sudden rushing noise sounded behind where Oliver, Emma, and Lance were hiding, causing everyone to stop, even the golems. Fearing *Xihuacota*'s return, Oliver squeezed Emma's hand hard.

Nothing was there. But when he looked down, he saw that their muddy footprints had been wiped clean as if by an enormous, invisible iron. Confused, he stooped to investigate, but Emma began dragging him up the hill. "C'mon!" she whispered into his ear. "We have to get back to Founders before Blackwood does!"

"W-what was that?" stuttered Dionysus. "Is she here?"

A wretched scream echoed across the water from the far side of the lagoons.

"Ah, that'll be her," said Cato, placing his hands behind his back and approaching Blackwood. "Do what you must, Broderick, but I take my leave of this nonsense. Nobody's ever wrought magic from deep within the fog. It must have been a mistake. Maybe the golems found a staff imbued with a shooting star and used it by accident."

The golems nodded their heads in disorderly fashion.

Blackwood scowled and responded but Oliver, Emma, and Lance were too far up the hill to hear.

"Quickly," hissed Emma, continuing to guide them back to Founders. Oliver lagged slightly, wanting to hear what Blackwood was saying.

"Oli!" implored Lance. "He's going to check for us first!"

"Fine, fine!" said Oliver, starting up a trot. Their boots crunched noisily in the packed snow.

# * Chapter 18: Under the Willow Tree *

"If anyone asks, we were playing cards in my room all night," whispered Emma when the hill began to flatten out. "Nobody else in my hall stayed over for Christmas Break!"

They only slowed when reaching the moat surrounding Founders Temple. The wooden bridge proved slippery, but a moment later, they resumed their sprint to Oliver and Lance's ground-level window.

Thanking the heavens for their secret entrance, Oliver pushed it open and crawled through. Emma hopped in next, followed by Lance.

"We made it!" said Lance, huffing and puffing on his desk chair.

Emma shook her head. "Not yet, we haven't. Here," —she removed her puffy coat and gloves, handing them to Oliver— "hide these, I can't be seen with them. Both of you, go straight to the showers. I'll be doing the same in my hall!"

"Right," said Oliver, chucking Emma's coat and gloves into his closet.

She opened the door to leave without another word, taking two steps at a time down the short staircase and then slamming the door to their hallway.

Oliver turned to Lance and nodded his head. "*Frighteningly* good at lying, isn't she?"

Lance laughed. "We all are now, aren't we? C'mon, let's get to the showers before Blackwood kills us."

## Chapter 19: The Teacher's Lounge

*Unsurprising that Europe had no secrets left. I even checked Machiavelli's tomb. If anything worth snatching had been there, it's long-gone. Tio did tell me checking the tomb would be a waste of time, but I could say the same about this entire trip.*

*17th of February, the second year of the 10th Age*

"You said we couldn't ask anybody about the scroll!" said Emma indignantly.

"Not too loud!" hissed Lance.

He and Emma were huddled around Oliver in the observatory deck above the Simulation Room. A great cheer echoed around them as Stevie led the Hutch dungeon team through a practice simulation below. The Dungeon-Simulation tournament was only a week away.

"We can't!" said Oliver, his brows furrowed in frustration. "But we can ask around about Tenoch's temples and the Forgotten Wood. We already covered this!"

A lizard skull crumbled against the viewing glass garnering another roar from the crowd.

"Fine," said Emma, completely ignoring the crash, "but how are we supposed to bring either of those things up in normal conversation?"

"I don't know," said Oliver, impatiently, "we can just say we read about it in the Research Lab. They already know we've been in there according to Stevie, remember? Aren't you supposed to be our liar in chief, anyway?"

# \* Chapter 19: The Teacher's Lounge \*

"Can we talk about anything else," shot Lance, nervously. "People keep staring at us!"

"You're just imagining it," said Emma dismissively.

"Sup', Wise King," said a voice Oliver had grown to hate. He looked over Lance's shoulder and saw Beto sauntering over, his curls bouncing up and down with every step. He'd regained a swagger to his gait after scoring several important goals when the Coatlball season resumed. Founders continued to have the second-best record, only behind Champayan. Anticipation was rising ahead of the Dungeon-Simulation tournament as a good performance by Founders could take them ahead in the Magical Five standings.

"Oh, I might kill him," Emma muttered, openly scowling. "If he brings up dueling one more time …"

Oliver had to agree with Emma. Beto had been asked to represent Founders as a two-seed Duelist, stinging Oliver's pride in the process. Oliver knew he didn't deserve the spot since he'd missed most of the inter-dorm scrimmages Professor Zapien used to determine Founders' two tournament representatives, but if he were being honest, he thought he was guaranteed a call up since he was a Trinova. His overconfidence betrayed him, however, and Beto had taken his opportunity well, winning his first match and securing a spot in the playoffs in March and April.

"Don't you have dueling practice to worry about?" shot Lance, nastily. "Why do you care about dungeon practice?"

Cristina and James, who had walked up with Beto, frowned.

# NOVA 01

"It's good research for my dueling actually," said Beto. He tossed a lazy look below as Elton crushed a poisonous toad. "A shame you couldn't have been selected as our other representative, *Oli*. It would have been fun to embarrass you in front of the whole school during the Final."

Oliver rolled his eyes. "Normally, Beto, I'd love an opportunity to wipe that stupid smirk off your face, but we're busy here, so would you mind bothering somebody else?"

"Everything alright back here?" interrupted Professor Watkin. He supervised Hutch's practices as the Dorm Head.

Cristina spoke quickest. "Oliver just threatened to punch Beto in the face!" Beto nodded his head gravely, feigning embarrassment to be associated with Oliver's rude behavior.

Unable to stop himself, Oliver spoke up. "Technically, sir, I threatened to wipe the stupid smirk off his face, not punch him."

Emma and Lance snickered while Beto and Cristina scowled. James just looked confused.

"Well, that's not very polite, is it?" said Watkin, looking from one trio to the other. "Oh, to be young and so worked up. Oliver, consider this a warning. At Tenochprima Academy, smirks must remain on faces, no matter how insufferable they may appear. Understood?"

"But, sir," interrupted Beto, "he just threatened to attack me. Shouldn't detention be in order?"

Watkin contemplated Beto for a moment, forcing him to look away. "Your subtlety needs refining, Mr. Warren. The Academy punishes goading

# * Chapter 19: The Teacher's Lounge *

just as sternly as petty threats of violence. Consider this a warning for you, as well."

Glowering, Beto, Cristina, and James retreated.

"Thank you, sir," said Oliver.

"You might not be so lucky next time," replied Watkin. He watched Beto settle into the crowd. "With them as your teammates in this weekend's tournament, you might consider a friendlier approach."

Oliver grimaced inwardly, knowing Watkin was right. Going into the weekend, he'd developed little to no chemistry with his Dungeon-Simulation teammates. To be fair, he was fighting an uphill battle seeing as three of his four teammates were his worst enemies other than maybe *The Damned* if he ever escaped.

Watkin surveyed him, seemingly absorbed in his own thoughts. "Ask your RA, Abe, if you can switch to his team. It will give your dorm the best chance of placing in the top 3 if one of your dorm teams isn't self-imploding."

Oliver nodded his head. "I didn't think I could switch teams, sir."

"Never hurts to ask."

"Sir," said Emma interrupting. Oliver looked at her nervously. "Have you ever heard of something called Tenoch's Temples?"

Lance managed to choke on his spit. Oliver closed his eyes in frustration.

"Tenoch's Temples?" asked Watkin. When Oliver opened his eyes again, he thought he saw the briefest of smiles nestled on the corner of Watkin's mouth.

# NOVA 01

"Are you three saying you'd like to discuss some *additional subject matter* you've uncovered during your *studies?*"

"Um," said Emma looking at Oliver for support. "I *think* so?"

"Well," butted in Lance, "we just wondered if you'd heard of it. We like to umm—,"

"Research," continued Oliver, "additional subject matter in our free time."

"Indeed," said Watkin. He didn't speak for almost a minute, staring absently at the simulation unfolding below. The crowd had congregated several feet away to get a better look at Stevie who was giving her team a pep-talk before entering the boss room.

"*What is he mulling over?*" Oliver thought.

Just as Emma opened her mouth to speak again, Watkin held up a hand.

"The Tenoch Temples are the cornerstones of a seventeenth century myth tied to this very school … it's a myth very few people have studied." Watkin paused, peering at them with a raised eyebrow. "Fortunately for you three, I am one of the few. The myth states that after fleeing the Spanish during the Fall of Tenochtitlan, our co-founder, Cuahtemoc, oversaw the creation of more than just one temple north of the Río Norte. You see, outside of Tenochprima, we've only ever found temples in the southern half of North America and Central America. The myth purports that more temples were constructed in an attempt to preserve indigenous cultures while also providing safe havens for users of magic. Whether that vision ever came to fruition remains to be seen, but it was a mixture of each of

## * Chapter 19: The Teacher's Lounge *

the Founder's goals." He paused for a moment, taking a sideways glance at Lance who blushed in response.

"But the Temples, if they ever existed, have been lost to the sands of time. The only fact associated with them is their connection to a letter written by Madeline Desmoulins."

"Desmoulins," muttered Oliver, thinking back to when Dionysus had offered to help them find the Iguana's scroll. Archie had warned him Dionysus had been involved with *The Damned's* movement later that same day. But Watkin ... Watkin had not. Archie's words echoed dimly in his head. *"I don't know who you can trust, but I do trust you to make the correct decision. Do not do so hastily."*

"Professor?" said Oliver, feeling a rushing thrill in his hands and neck.

"Yes, Oliver?"

"Did Madeline leave behind any advice on how to find the Temples?"

Watkin raised his other eyebrow. "Certainly not. And I must stress, none of her *descendants* would know either."

Oliver thought hard before answering, feeling like he was beginning to understand Watkin for the first time.

"Certainly not," he echoed.

The same flickering smile appeared on the corner of Watkin's mouth.

"But ..." continued Oliver, "there was a letter? What did it say?"

"Yes. It was addressed to Cuahtemoc, and it said something very intriguing. Madeline wrote, 'The Forest Temple – painted shut, it cannot be found.'"

# NOVA 01

Oliver felt his stomach twist in excitement. *Begin with the Forgotten Wood, for there, your Gift has stood, its entrance lies within our grounds, good luck – it cannot be found.* Could the Forgotten Wood be home of the Forest Temple? One of Tenoch's forgotten Temples created by Cuahtemoc himself?

"Dionysus still has the letter today," said Watkin, snapping Oliver's attention back to the conversation. "But I've given you every word of it."

Oliver chose his words carefully before responding. "Do we know what she meant?"

"You tell me," said Watkin, finally looking at him directly. His hands were on the pommel of his staff.

Oliver's nerves and gaze faltered at Watkin's stare. *Does he know about the scroll? About the Gift?*

"What does 'painted shut' mean?" asked Lance.

Watkin sighed. "I've wrestled with that same question for years, Lance, but the trail goes cold there. Your guess is as good as mine."

Another cheer reverberated across the room as the Hutch team completed the practice simulation.

"As I mentioned not too long ago," added Watkin for only their ears to hear, "you are now being monitored rather closely. Should your research continue, be careful with whom you discuss it."

Without another word he stepped away, his staff clunking.

"Just how much does this guy know?" muttered Emma as Watkin congratulated Stevie and the Hutch team for their time.

# * Chapter 19: The Teacher's Lounge *

Lance continued peering at Watkin. "Didn't Archie tell you not to trust anyone? How do we know he isn't someone we're supposed to steer clear of?"

Oliver didn't reply immediately, instead he followed Lance's gaze. After Watkin finished congratulating the Hutch team, he began shepherding the students out of the building.

"'Painted shut,'" Oliver repeated, thinking hard about what Watkin had said. "Are there any paintings on campus?"

"I don't think so," said Emma, "just tapestries, sundials, and weird pots and pans hanging around in crevices. Why? Do you think painted shut is connected to the Temples— ouch! Lance watch where—,"

"There *are* paintings on campus!" said Lance putting a hand to his head. He'd stopped in place directly in front of Emma as they exited the front door. "Remember my detention?!"

"Of course not," said Emma, pushing him aside. "Were we there?"

"No! I told you! Remember, oh my gosh, it was there the whole time!"

"What was there?!" said Oliver, feeling his earlier goosebumps spread from his arms to his neck.

"Tenoch's temples!" said Lance, a goofy smile across his face. "It was just staring right at me the whole time ..."

Oliver grabbed Lance's arm. "Words, man! Use your words! What are you talking about?"

"Yeah, what are you talking about?" said a fourth voice.

It was Beto again. He, Cristina, and James had followed them outside.

# NOVA 01

Oliver threw up his hands. "Beto! What did we say about your smirk! We've got better things to do than listen to you!"

Whatever Beto had expected Oliver to say, it wasn't that. For the first time, he didn't even pretend to smile; instead, he openly snarled. "Guys, I think it's time we give these three a lesson on manners."

Lance put a hand on the head of his hammer, ready to pull it from his belt, but Oliver grabbed his arm for a second time, stopping him. "Remember what Abe and Brantley said? He's just goading us – trying to get us expelled."

But Oliver was wrong.

With one look around the courtyard, Beto confirmed the rest of the viewers had dispersed back to their dorms. Then, with a hand on his sheathed scimitar, he stomped the ground, popping up a mound of Earth. He followed up the move with a forceful punch of his fist, firing the rock directly at Oliver's back.

"*Defenderis*!" shouted Emma, and just in time. Red sparks flew as Beto's missile collided with her shield, showering Oliver and Lance with dust.

"Beto!" roared Oliver. "We'll all be kicked off the team!"

Beto snarled and raised two more spheres. "Too scared to fight? Not so Brave without Watkin here, are you?" He fired the missiles – this time at Emma.

With a shout, Lance pulled out his hammer and swung at one of the spheres, redirecting it towards Cristina who sidestepped it. The other, however, connected with Emma's stomach, forcing her to double over, completely winded.

# * Chapter 19: The Teacher's Lounge *

Outraged, Oliver felt for the energy in the Earth before raising his ringed fist into the air. An enormous wall of hardened dirt quickly followed. Without thinking, he opened his fist, commanding the Earth to envelop Beto, Cristina, and James. To his amazement, the rock and clay wall folded over and around them just as he'd wanted it to, forming a brown and red igloo with no entrance.

Ignoring the yells from inside the dome he'd created, he knelt down next to Emma.

"You alright?"

Emma held her eyes shut, and she shook her head.

"We should take her to the infirmary," said Lance, grinning despite Emma's condition. "That was brilliant, Oli. Listen to them squirm under there."

"What should I do with them?" Thudding noises sounded, indicating Beto was trying to break down the walls.

"Who cares?" said Lance putting away his warhammer. "If they try and blame us, we can say they started the fight."

"They did start the fight," gasped Emma, beginning to sit up. "We've got nothing to lie about." Refusing their help, she got to her feet. "I'll be fine, just got winded is all. Nice work, Oli."

"Nice work yourself," said Lance, wiping dust off his coat. "Quick thinking with the shielding spell. Can't believe they actually attacked us."

"Absolute moron," said Emma. "Would have gotten us all kicked off the Coatlball team if we got caught."

"Forget about it!" said Oliver, giving the Earth igloo a look before pulling them behind a stand-alone classroom. "Lance! What were you saying about a painting?"

"Right! I'll take you straight to it."

"Straight to it?"

"Tenoch's Temples remember?!" hissed Lance.

"If you knew where the Forgotten Wood was, why did you let us ask Watkin?!"

"Of course I didn't know! We just started talking about paintings and it made me realize I've seen one before – and I told you about it, months ago!"

"No, you didn't!" said Emma, wincing as she tried standing tall.

"Yes, I did!" said Lance. "Remember, during my detention? There was a painting of three temples in the teacher's lounge!"

"Lance, we're looking for a painting of a forest!" said Emma, rolling her eyes. "That might be Tenoch's Temples, but the scroll said Oliver's gift was in the Forgotten Wood."

But Oliver raised his eyebrows as he realized what Lance was thinking. "What if the Forgotten Wood is home of one of Tenoch's Temples? If Madeline painted a Forest Temple shut where it cannot be found, and there's a painting of Tenoch's Temples on campus, maybe the painting can tell us more about how to find the entrance to a Forest Temple or something!"

"Exactly!" said Lance. "But, Oliver, you better do some light refracting first. I don't think we'll be able to barge right into the teacher's lounge."

# * Chapter 19: The Teacher's Lounge *

It was as if a light switched on in a dark corner of Oliver's brain. "You really think it'd be that easy?"

A scraping noise sounded from the other side of their hiding place, followed by crumbling rock.

"I think that's them escaping," said Emma.

Oliver nodded understandingly. "*Sorbelux!* How do I look?"

Emma squinted. "Hmm, it's easier to see you in broad daylight – slightly blurry around the edges."

"That's just 'cus you know where to look," Lance countered.

At the sound of Beto's voice – "where'd those sinovas go?! I'm going to stab 'em this time!" – Oliver grabbed their hands and began guiding them down the hill towards Founders. To their left the sun was setting over the Swampy Woods, casting shadows over water and land.

"Hang on," said Lance, slowing them down. Though Oliver couldn't see him, he didn't like the tone of concern Lance's voice had carried.

"What is it?"

"I've just realized," Lance continued. "Watkin's the reason why I had that detention to begin with."

"What are you talking about?" asked Oliver, slowing down with him. "Brantley gave you detention after you pulled out your hammer last time Beto threatened us."

"No! Blackwood was leading us to the kitchens when Watkin showed up and said he should take us to the teacher's hallways and lounge instead…"

Emma began to slow down too. "So, let me get this straight. So far, Watkin has told us we can ask him about anything we want, nearly choked to death when Oliver saw the glowing willow in the lagoons, and put you in detention in front of the painting we're looking for? Seems a little too good to be true, doesn't it?"

Oliver frowned. "Are you saying we should ask him some more questions?"

"I'm saying, he knows more than we've given him credit for."

"Do you think he knows where the Forgotten Wood might be right now?"

"At this rate, I don't think so – he probably would have just told us."

"I don't think we should trust him," Lance blurted out as if he'd been holding onto a bomb. "Archie warned us not to!"

Uninvited anger and frustration boiled up inside Oliver. "Archie told me he trusted me to make my own decisions and I think I trust Watkin!" He tugged both their hands hard. "If Watkin was working with *The Damned* in secret, he'd be more like Blackwood – trying to chuck me into detention all the time instead of giving me hints!"

Lance kept his mouth closed, but Oliver could feel he had more to say just by the touch of his invisible hand. He didn't push him, however, because they were approaching Founders Temple.

Although the magically enhanced snow had taken a back seat since the beginning of the new semester, most students opted to spend evening hours inside where it was warmer. Unless, of course, you were out searching for your worst enemies. Hiding behind the osorius statue, Beto, Cristina, and James crouched.

## \* Chapter 19: The Teacher's Lounge \*

"They'll have to come back inside eventually," said Beto, openly frowning. "And when they do, we'll see who's smirking after we're done with them."

Resisting the strong urge to laugh, Oliver tugged Emma and Lance past the statues unseen before entering the Founders Temple foyer. "Imagine how long they'll be waiting out there," whispered Lance.

Oliver's own satisfaction soon faded, however, upon entering the Dining Hall. Almost every table was occupied with students eating dinner, sipping hot cocoa, or licking ice cream cones. The staircase to the faculty apartments lay on the opposite side of the foyer, behind the stone and quartz table where the Guides ate. Archie sat there now, sharing an enormous slab of meat with Rasmus and Merri.

Lance sighed on his left as they waited on the outer edge of the room in front of them. "How are we supposed to get all the way to the other side without running into someone by accident?"

"Let's just stick to the edges," said Oliver. He didn't feel nearly as confident as he sounded.

Sidling along the outer edges of the cavernous room, they made slow progress to the staircase, managing to only garner one set of curious eyes – Headmaster Lalandra's – when Emma stubbed her toe against one of the mahogany tables in the rear of the room.

"Sorry!" she whispered. "Hard to walk when I can't see my feet!"

When they finally reached the Guides table, Archie straightened up from the meat he was devouring and peered in their general direction. The tendrils on his upper mandible quivered as he sniffed the air.

# NOVA 01

*"Oliver?"* he asked telepathically.

"Uhh," Oliver managed.

*"Never mind, I do not want to know."*

"Can the others sense me too?"

*"Only I can sense you. But if your usual trio is intact, Rasmus and Merri will sense Emma and Lance."*

As Archie spoke, Oliver felt both Emma and Lance's grips tighten.

"Well, if you wouldn't mind swearing them to secrecy, I don't think we need the world to know I've rediscovered light refraction."

*"Indeed,"* said Archie turning back to his food. *"I'd be careful around Guides and beasts in general. Your species is the only sentient one so dependent on sight. I smelled you before I saw your outline or felt your consciousness."*

"Noted," grumbled Oliver, pulling Emma and Lance up the staircase. Unlike the steps down to Founders Temple, the white marble steps leading up to the faculty apartments were wide, forming one long turn. When they reached the landing above, Lance tugged them left, past smooth stone floors and walls. Every few yards, large gaps in the stone walls revealed short overhangs overlooking large swaths of the campus grounds. The sun poked its final few beams through the gaps, distorting around their bodies instead of forming shadows.

After a few more windows, Lance stopped them before a double set of mahogany doors.

"In there," he said, breathlessly. "It's the teacher's lounge."

"I can't exactly open it seeing as I'm holding each of your hands," said Oliver as politely as he could in a curt tone.

# * Chapter 19: The Teacher's Lounge *

"Oh, right ..." said Lance. To Oliver's horror, however, the door cracked open just as Lance had begun to turn the handle. Out popped a gnarled hand and sleeve.

Fearing the worst, Oliver pulled Emma and Lance back against the opposite wall hard, tripping as he did. For one terrifying moment, Emma became visible as her hand slipped out of Oliver's. Fortunately for them, whoever was coming through the door had paused in their step.

"I don't care if you didn't find anything in his room," said Blackwood's deep voice from the other side of the door. "He's searching for all the same things, and I know he found something out in those damned lagoons. He might even already be looking for the painting—,"

Lunging, Oliver reached out and grabbed Emma's ankle, bringing her back under the spell just as Blackwood emerged into the hallway. When he did, he paused, looking from side to side with his eyes squinting suspiciously. Behind him, Desmoulins followed, a haughty expression on his normally relaxed face.

"And why aren't you the one doing the poking around? It's not *your* orders I'm following, Broderick!"

"Silence!"

Desmoulins' nostrils flared. "Who do you think you are—,"

"You fool! There's somebody here! Shut up!"

Blackwood sniffed the air, reminding Oliver of a chupacabra. He squeezed Emma's ankle hard at the thought of the memory.

After a few tense moments, the Dean straightened his back and stormed off to the stairs, Desmoulins on his heels.

"Don't be stupid, Dionysus. We only follow his orders, not mine. But it'd simply be too obvious if I charged into the boy's room. Besides, Cato is always sniffing around. He suspects something. If he hadn't delayed us at the lagoons, I'm sure we would have caught the mutt! I swear, we ought to consider Wisers when Tío escapes – Lord knows we could do with fewer of them running around!"

The rest of the conversation faded to whispers as Blackwood and Desmoulins turned to go down the stairs.

Seizing the opportunity, Oliver shifted his grip from Emma's ankle to her arm. As she let out a soft yelp, he pulled her and Lance through the mahogany doors and into the teacher's lounge. Several breaths later, when they were confirmed alone, did he let go of their hands and stop the spell.

"Did you hear that?" whispered Lance, sounding dumbstruck. He collapsed into a wingback chair in front of an enormous fireplace. "Were they talking about what I think they were talking about?"

"Yes," said Oliver, feeling slightly sick.

Emma paced the room absentmindedly. "This is bad. But boy were you right not to trust Desmoulins! To think some of our teachers are waiting for *The Damned* to escape so they can follow his orders!"

"What do you mean, waiting?" scoffed Lance. "The way they were talking, we've got about five minutes before they bust him out from wherever he's imprisoned."

Oliver shuddered. "I don't think he's just in a prison. The way Archie talked about it, it sounded like a lot worse than a simple prison."

# * Chapter 19: The Teacher's Lounge *

Emma threw up her hands and shook her head at the ceiling. "How are we supposed to figure all this out without knowing the facts?!"

"No clue," said Oliver, taking stock of the lounge for the first time. "I never thought that if *The Damned* did escape he'd have an easy time of it. Now that we've heard Blackwood talking, we gotta find whatever Gift the Founders left for me in the Forgotten Wood, and fast. Where's that painting, Lance?"

Lance jumped out of the chair where he'd been sitting and guided them to a corner of the room Oliver hadn't yet surveyed. Past the fireplace, and to the right of an enormous tapestry detailing the fall of Tenochtitlan, a small fresco hung, depicting three haggard temples.

"They're identical to the one we found in the lagoons!" said Oliver, excitedly. He peered closely at the painting trying to glean as much as he could and commit it to memory.

Emma pointed at the outlines of the temples. "Each of the outlines is a different color. Green, red, and blue. Is that supposed to mean something?"

Oliver felt his heartbeat quickly in his chest. "Those are the same colors as the Founders Flame! And I'm willing to bet the words around the frame are another hint!"

"What does it say?!" asked Lance. He peered uneasily at the door behind them. "I didn't even notice words last time. Be ready to *sorbelux* at any moment."

Impatiently, Oliver read out the words for them to hear. "Emma, move your head, I can't see with your shadow in the way. Ok, it says, '*Forest of green, crater of blue, moat of red, we leave these paintings for You.*'"

"But it's only one painting," said Emma, frowning. "What does it mean we leave these paintings for you?"

"It means!" said Oliver, grabbing Emma's shoulders, "there *are* other paintings!"

She huffed some hair off her face. "With more clues? I don't know about you two, but I'm sick to death of clues. We need answers!"

"Wrap it up!" hissed Lance, dashing towards them. "Someone's on the other side of the door!"

"*Sorbelux!*" whispered Oliver, grabbing both their hands.

The door opened.

It was Professors Chavarría and McCall, their math teacher.

Oliver cursed their bad luck.

But then the door swung open again and Lalandra entered.

"Mind if I join you two?" she said looking right through Oliver at Chavarría and McCall. "Want to hear what everyone's thinking about final exams."

"Sure thing, Elodie," said Chavarría barely looking up. "We just came in to warm our feet and get away from the extramen. Incessant with their questions."

"Even at dinner time!" seethed McCall.

"One moment," said Lalandra, still holding the door open, "I've dropped something."

Seizing the opportunity, Oliver pulled Emma and Lance forward. With a loud bang, Lance's foot rammed into one of the double doors, knocking them all into the ground.

## * Chapter 19: The Teacher's Lounge *

By some miracle, Oliver managed to hold onto both sets of hands as they fell. Wincing, he opened one eye, expecting Lalandra's face to be right up against his. But Lalandra barely seemed to register the noise.

"You alright there, Elodie?" said McCall from inside. "There's a door there, you know?"

Chavarría chuckled.

"Always running into things, I am," mused Lalandra. Oliver stared at her, dumbfounded. His left hand was going numb from the crushing force of Emma's panicked grip. Did Lalandra really think she'd banged her own foot into the door while holding it open?

Once again, the Headmaster surprised him. This time, as she shut the door, she winked directly at him, causing his heart to skip a beat entirely.

He was still invisible.

## Chapter 20: A Yeti's Decor

*The pyramids and tombs in Egypt didn't have anything we're looking for — though a mummy did almost corner me in Amenemhat II's tomb. I got excited in Petra because the detection tool went off — but it was just a useless cup.*
*I'm desperate to write about my secret, but I can't risk it.*

*15<sup>th</sup> of March, the second year of the 10<sup>th</sup> Age*

"Absolutely not," said Abe, shaking his head.

Next to him Oliver scowled. "What do you mean absolutely not? Three of my teammates hate me!"

He, Emma, and Lance were in the Dining Hall eating lunch just before the Dungeon-Simulation tournament, and Oliver had followed Watkin's advice to try and switch teams.

"That's just as much your fault as it is Beto's! Our A-Team has been cruising and I'm not risking a potential first place finish so our B-Team can get along better."

"But we could get two top five finishes instead of just one!" said Oliver, trying a different angle. "That'd position us better to win the Big Five tournament!"

Brantley jostled up next to them at the table. "Win the tournament? Counting our chickens too early, are we, Oliver? Founders hasn't won since Watkin was an extramen."

# * Chapter 20: A Yeti's Decor *

"Listen," said Abe, ignoring Brantley, "if you had asked earlier, I'd have considered it. But an hour before the tournament kicks off? *Pshh*! I can't allow it."

"Fine," grumbled Oliver, pushing back his chair. "I'll just watch my back and make sure we don't finish last." He stormed off to the circular staircase to change, Emma and Lance hot on his heels.

"You're making a mistake," said Emma, pointing a finger at Abe as she retreated to catch up with Oliver. "Those three are going to intentionally sabotage the team – they're already thinking about being in Champayan next year and don't care about winning for Founders!"

Abe waved a dismissive hand back at them.

"What are you going to do?" asked Lance, reaching Oliver first.

"The only thing I can do," he said. "Just show up and do the best I can. Even if that means getting pushed into a bucket of lava or something."

"Here," said Lance, grabbing his arm. "Take my hammer. You may find yourself in there wishing you had a weapon instead of a ring."

An hour later, Oliver found himself and the rest of the Founders B Team jostling for space in the Dungeon-Simulation lobby.

"Scared, García?" shot Beto, his scimitar drawn.

Oliver shook his head at him. "You realize I literally can't get scared, right?" This wasn't entirely true, especially after his near capture by *Xihuacota* over the break, but Beto didn't need to know that.

Beto scowled.

"YES, CHILDREN!" boomed Tolteca, announcing the start of the simulation. "ANOTHER YEAR, ANOTHER DUNGEON

# NOVA 01

SIMULATION TOURNAMENT! EACH DORM HAS TWO TEAMS AND ALL TEN TEAMS WILL FACE AN IDENTICAL CHALLENGE AT THE SAME TIME. TOP EIGHT FINISHES EARN FROM 100 TO 800 POINTS! BOTTOM TWO FINISHES WILL LOSE THEIR DORM 100 TO 200 POINTS!"

Looking up, Oliver could see parts of the observation deck. He thought he could just make out Emma's red hair through the crowd but there was too much activity to be sure.

With a push to his back from Katie the RA, Oliver followed Beto, Cristina, and James to a door with Founders B above it. All around them the other teams assembled behind their own respective doors.

"Good luck, Founders!" shouted Abe encouragingly from the Founders A line.

Beto turned to give Oliver a glare.

*Boom!*

In a mad scramble, the teams barged through their respective doors and immediately found themselves slipping on a sheet of ice.

By the time Oliver and Katie had entered, James was already nursing a sore backside after falling and slipping all the way from one end of the room to the other. Beto and Cristina, meanwhile, kept their balance by holding onto each other's shoulders. Oliver and Katie followed suit, just barely maintaining penguin shuffles on the surface.

"How are supposed to move to the next room if we can't even walk?" growled Beto.

# * Chapter 20: A Yeti's Decor *

A good question, Oliver thought. Looking around, only ice and torches occupied the otherwise empty stone room. Large pewter tiles formed the floor, walls, and ceiling. Over the floor, however, the thick sheet of ice was causing them trouble.

"Katie?" asked Oliver. "We haven't been taught to perform fire elementals yet. There's stone below us – can you melt the ice?"

"Better yet," said Katie. "I'll just turn the ice to water. *Derrateth!*"

The ice beneath their feet melted instantaneously, leaving them in ankle deep water.

Beto, who was wearing knee high boots, snickered at Oliver, who'd opted for sneakers which were now completely soaked with cold water. Ignoring him, Oliver filed *derrateth* into his head for future use.

Splashing in the water, Katie proceeded to the next room on their right. Oliver made to follow but then changed his mind. At the door frame, he stopped, pretending to adjust Lance's hammer on its buckle as Beto, Cristina, and James passed him. *Want to keep you three where I can see you ...*

In the next room, they found Katie darting away from several golems in a foot of snow. Brandishing Lance's hammer, Oliver stepped forward and swung at the one closest to her, smashing it against the far wall. It collapsed, dazed. *Just a simulation*, Oliver reminded himself as he felt a twinge of sympathy for the golem.

To deal with the other two, Katie grabbed a torch from the wall and waved it menacingly.

"Are you three planning on helping?" yelled Katie as the other golems retreated to a corner of the room.

# NOVA 01

Beto, Cristina, and James managed to shrug but otherwise didn't respond.

With his feet freezing, Oliver pushed ahead to the next room where he stepped onto a stone landing. From there, he inspected his new surroundings.

In front, a pool of deep water sloshed. Although he couldn't tell what caused the disturbance, the Wisdom in the nape of his neck warned him he may yet find out. Above the water, a platform floated, taking a circular path around the room, potentially providing passage to the stone landing on the far side of the room.

"Okay," said Oliver, "looks like we have to get to the other side by jumping onto the—,"

Hearing a scuff of feet behind him, Oliver stepped quickly to his left. As he moved, a desperate arm tried to grab hold of him. But it was too slow.

Yanking his arm away, he saw Cristina topple off the platform. She hit the water with a soaking splash. From the maelstrom, her hands emerged, thrashing in an attempt to pull herself above the surface. Ominously, the churning water reversed direction. Barely a moment later, a half-scream escaped Cristina's lips as a blue and white tentacle wrapped around her and pulled her into the depths.

*Boom!*

Livid, Oliver turned to face Beto. Using the length of Lance's hammer, he pushed him back onto the snow in the preceding room. "Next time you want to sabotage this team, do it yourself!"

# * Chapter 20: A Yeti's Decor *

"She just tripped!" shouted Katie, grabbing Oliver on the shoulder and pulling him back to the center of the stone landing. "Do you really think she'd try and push you in?"

"Not her!" yelled Oliver. "Him!" He pointed down at Beto with the hammer, its heavy weight forgotten by the added strength he felt in his limbs.

"Oliver!" Katie shouted, slapping the hammer away. "Pipe down or I'm going to disqualify you!"

Despite his boiling blood pleading for him to crash the hammer down onto Beto, Oliver turned and readied himself in front of the floating platform. With two leaps, he jumped onto the platform and then the second stone landing.

When he stopped, he was surprised to hear Tolteca's voice again.

"FOUNDERS B UNDER REVIEW FOR SERIOUS FOUL PLAY!"

"See!" shouted Oliver, "they're reviewing the push …"

But Oliver's stomach twisted as a floating mirror magicked into existence and replayed *him* pushing Beto over with Lance's hammer, not Beto pushing Cristina into Oliver. Then, in slow motion he watched Cristina trip as she stepped onto the landing, her trailing foot catching on something unseen in the previous room. Then, she tumbled in Oliver's direction before falling into the water.

From across the sloshing pit of water, Beto smirked as he wiped snow from his coat.

"CAPTAIN'S CHOICE!" rang Tolteca.

# NOVA 01

"OLIVER!" shouted Katie. "WE'RE ALL ON THE SAME TEAM – IF YOU SO MUCH AS FROWN AT BETO OR JAMES, YOU'RE OFF – GOT IT?"

Oliver nodded, keeping his face as calm as he could. Inside, however, it took everything he had not to scream right back. The replays didn't show what caused Cristina to trip in the previous room, where Beto had been, and Oliver *knew* Beto was to blame. He'd likely stuck a foot out so she would tumble straight into him and then fall into the water.

When the rest had joined him on the landing, Oliver did his best to maintain a stoic expression. Beto, whose smirk was still intact, patted him on the shoulder when he sauntered off the platform.

"Easy there, Wise One."

"Alright you three," growled Katie, "keep your heads on straight and we might get through this. Beto, you lead front with me. Oliver and James, y'all form the rear."

Oliver obliged, happy to have Beto in front of him and not beside him. James tried his best to intimidate Oliver with a growl as they formed up, but it caught in his throat and came out as a cough instead. Ignoring him, Oliver kept his head in motion, analyzing for threats from every direction.

In this formation they proceeded through the next several rooms. Katie kept them at a slower pace than Oliver would have normally liked but given the possibility of being tripped at any moment by Beto or James, he didn't complain. Better to finish the dungeon slowly than get eliminated for trying to rush through too quickly with enemies nearby.

# * Chapter 20: A Yeti's Decor *

One room they encountered featured enormous blocks of ice and a locked door. James, to Oliver's great surprise, figured out how to unlock the door before anyone else could. The solution was to push the ice blocks around until they reflected the pattern on the ceiling above them.

Shortly thereafter, animated skeletons attacked them, brandishing swords capable of freezing any limbs that they touched. Oliver just managed to slap a sword away with the head of Lance's hammer when Katie dispatched them all with a glowing white sword she summoned into existence.

Just as they thought they were about to enter the dungeon's boss room, they darted into a foyer with a crackling fire, an enormous chair, and a fully set dining table. A ten-foot yeti sat in the chair by the fire, warming its toes. Rather than attack them, the yeti stood up, bumping its head on the ceiling in the process, and greeted them with a deep bow at the waist.

"It's dangerous to go in unprepared," it said to their stunned faces, "take some soup." Somewhat suspiciously, they each drank from bottles the yeti dipped into a pot that bubbled over the fire. As Oliver drank his portion, he looked above the fireplace and nearly choked.

Above the mantle, a painting hung. It depicted a temple, half-covered by a blizzard within a freezing landscape.

Ignoring the tickling effect of the stew spreading warmth throughout his body, Oliver addressed their strange host. "Thank you, Mr. Yeti. Nice painting you got there – is that your winter home?"

# NOVA 01

The Yeti looked almost as surprised as Beto by the questioning. It peered from side to side to confirm Oliver had spoken to it and not one of his teammates.

"Thank you, small one. The painting shows where I came from."

"And where—,"

"Oliver!" interrupted Katie, "we don't have time for this! Boss room – now!"

The yeti almost looked relieved at the opportunity to stop speaking and return to its place by the fire.

Begrudgingly, Oliver turned away from the yeti, but not before taking one final look at the painting hanging above the fireplace. The Temple stood out from the snowy backdrop; it was surrounded by the same blue outline he'd seen on the edges of the second temple in the fresco from the faculty lounge. Oliver couldn't help but wonder if he was making a mistake not asking the Yeti more questions before moving on.

His thoughts quickly subsided, however, upon entering the boss room.

Like the other rooms they'd encountered so far, ice and stone clacked against their shoes upon entry. But this room was much larger than all the rest, and it possessed a gradual incline in its stone floor. They entered at the highest point of the incline, and in front of them, several yards away, a still body of dark water occupied the bottom half of the room.

No sooner had Oliver begun to dread the water when it began to churn. White froth bubbled from it in waves as the surface rose, eventually splashing out as a horrible, muffled roar sounded.

"Stay in formation!" shouted Katie.

# * Chapter 20: A Yeti's Decor *

*How is a formation going to help?*

A slimy, green head emerged from the water, challenging Oliver's Bravery. The roar turned from muffled to deafening, reminding Oliver of a video of an elephant being chased by a pack of lions. From the slimy head's left and right, four purple-blue tentacles shot forward, seeking to drag each of them into the icy water while four others fired chunks of ice at them.

With a scream, James broke formation, retreating to the back of the room where the tentacles couldn't reach him.

Oliver, meanwhile, tried raising a wall of stone beneath them and the squid in the water, but its strong tentacles broke through the stone as if it were no thicker than a sheet of paper. Beto's scimitar proved useful against the arms that got too close, leaving several gashes wherever it swung. He even managed to sever one limb entirely when it made a lunge towards Beto's legs.

A roar sounded from the squid monster as its severed tentacle thrashed on the stone. In retaliation, three tentacles shot directly for James, who continued to cower.

Like a squealing pig, James pressed himself as far as he could into the furthest recesses of the corner where he hid; but the squid monster had moved forward, and the reach of its tentacles could no longer be escaped. With a desperate poke, James cut open one of the tentacles with the freezing sword he'd picked up from the skeletons. Just as Oliver was ready to write James off, the entire tentacle froze as the blade struck it. With a great thud and splash, the tentacle fell onto stone and water.

# NOVA 01

But James had only accounted for *one* tentacle.

The other two pulled him to the water so quickly, he didn't even have time to scream.

"Katie!" shouted Oliver, thinking fast. "Can you freeze the water? James' sword barely scratched that tentacle and it completely killed the arm!"

"I – I don't think I can," she said, dodging a block of ice thrown by the watcher. "*Conjelareth!*"

*C'mon* thought Oliver as the water began to freeze under Katie's spell. It started at the shallow end and trickled deeper at a slow pace.

But only the surface of the water froze under Katie's spell, and it didn't take the squid monster long to break free.

Time slowed down as Oliver's upper neck vibrated.

*You should do it.*

*But Watkin warned me not too.*

As Oliver deliberated, the watcher seemed to grow wise to their plan. With a roar like a bull, it sent its seven remaining tentacles directly at once. Poor Katie didn't stand a chance. She fell to the ground hard as three tentacles wrapped around her legs and drug her into the depths. A swish and clang, however, told Oliver that Beto's scimitar had sliced through air and flesh again.

But Beto kept swinging blindly, coming dangerously close to Oliver, forcing him to back away.

He stumbled.

"What are you doing?!" he roared angrily, looking to where Beto had been.

# * Chapter 20: A Yeti's Decor *

But Beto was gone. A second later, Oliver saw him, or what was left of him, disappearing under the water now, too. Dread shot through his veins as he felt a tentacle wrap itself around his ankle. Reaching out for the hammer, he clasped his fingers around a handle, but instead of the hammer, he found James' spear in his hand. With a lurch, the watcher pulled him into the water at great speed. As he felt the icy liquid envelope his legs, he took the sword in both hands and channeled the heat from the torches to fuel a spell on his lips.

"*Conjelareth*!" he shouted, slamming the sword down into the water with both hands.

With a sound like crackling glass, the entire body of water froze, leaving Oliver's bottom half completely encased in ice. Only his top half was free. Rotating, he looked towards the squid monster.

It was frozen solid.

*Poof!*

Relief rushed over him as the monster vanished in a puff of smoke. A moment later, he'd been teleported to the observatory deck upstairs.

A wave of noise slammed into him as he popped into existence next to his hallmates. Abe ruffled his hair shouting, "well done! Why didn't I think of freezing the water?!" while Katie clapped him on the back and yelled, "was that your first time freezing something? Amazing!"

But Oliver only had eyes for Emma and Lance who broke through the crowd to embrace him.

"You did it!" shouted Lance.

"How'd we place?"

"Fifth!" said Emma, grinning.

"Fifth?!" he shouted incredulously. "How? We were so slow!"

"You were," agreed Lance, laughing, "but the other five teams didn't get past the boss! That octopus thing looked terrifying from up here – can't imagine facing it down there!"

In the celebrations that followed, Se'Vaughn and Trey led a boisterous crowd back to the Dining Hall to celebrate. They chanted as they went, bellowing, "Foun-ders Tem-ple! Foun-ders Tem-ple!"

Close behind, Oliver, Emma, and Lance chatted animatedly over the results.

"According to Abe," said Lance, rubbing his hands together excitedly, "we're now in first place in the Magical Five Tournament!"

Emma couldn't stop grinning and pushing Oliver in the back excitedly. "We actually might win this thing! But no time to relax. We've got the Dueling tournament next and then the Coatlball playoffs."

Lance shrugged. "No chance Beto puts up a fight in the Dueling tournament. After his stunt on Oliver in the Dungeon-Sim, we know he's got his eye on Champayan next year."

"He still has his pride," Emma countered. "In the Dungeon-Sim, he could sabotage us – easy enough, right? But if he loses a duel … well, that makes only him look bad."

# * Chapter 20: A Yeti's Decor *

As Oliver listened, he felt a shudder of anxiety surface; a sensation that had become all too commonplace since finding the Iguana's Scroll and learning that *The Damned* could bust out of his imprisonment at any moment. He thought back on the shadow he'd seen at the airport all those months ago. At the time he'd dismissed the threat as a figment of his imagination, but could it have been something more sinister? Was it an omen of things to come? Or worse yet, could it have been *The Damned* already watching him, out in the open, waiting for an opportunity to strike him down? But that didn't make any sense – *The Damned* was imprisoned. Everyone knew that.

*The Iguana's Scroll says he'll escape.*

His anxiety doubled, rolling like a wheel in his stomach. He tried pressing it down, but the wheel resisted as his mind kept racing back to the scroll or the Forgotten Wood ... or the shadow ... or the painting ... the painting!

Oliver skid to a halt, grabbing onto Emma's forearm. "I just remembered! Did either of you see the painting in the yeti's room?"

"Painting?" asked Lance. "What painting?"

Emma closed her eyes, reimagining the scene. "We didn't see any painting, Oli, just a chair with a yeti and then y'all barged in from behind."

"You're joking!" said Oliver incredulously. "Y'all must have been above it, looking down the opposite way I came in."

Their heads nodded.

"Well, there *was* a painting. I asked the yeti about it – but it wasn't of a Wood or a Forest Temple – no, it looked more like a snowy field – but there was definitely a temple on it!"

Emma's eyes popped. "Do you think that means we should be looking for a snowy forest instead of a green one?"

"I don't know," said Oliver. "But aren't the faculty the ones designing the simulations?"

"Yeah?"

"Because, if we can find out which teacher designed it, we can ask them why they chose that specific painting!"

Emma's smile dashed off her face. "I've got a nasty feeling I already know who designed it."

"You're just assuming the worst!" said Lance, chuckling. "I, for one, like to think positively!"

Oliver paced around them, keeping his ring-hand on his chin. "Slim odds, they'll tell any of us who's behind it, though." Looking back up, he resumed their walk back to the Dining Hall at a quickened pace. "Maybe we can ask Watkin."

Lance caught up to him and tugged his arm to slow him down. When Oliver faced him, a frown was on his face.

"Oh, we'd go to war for you. But are you sure we can trust him? You heard Blackwood and Desmoulins in the lounge – what if he's just like them? Waiting for *The Damned* to escape? We don't know enough about him yet."

# * Chapter 20: A Yeti's Decor *

Oliver bristled. "What happened to thinking positively? We don't have to mention the painting. Just let *me* do the talking."

Lance's frown thickened, but he nodded his head.

Entering the Dining Hall, Oliver scanned desperately for Watkin but couldn't see him. He pushed his bangs up in case they'd blocked his sight but still couldn't see the History Professor anywhere.

"There he is!" hissed Emma, pointing.

Next to the staircase leading to the faculty lounge Watkin appeared to be holding a conversation with Archie.

"*Archie!*" said Oliver telepathically. "*Whatever you do, don't let Watkin go upstairs – we've got a question for him.*"

"*Goodness gracious, Oliver. It is incredibly rude to interrupt someone's conversation telepathically.*"

"*You're right – very sorry – we'll be right over to interrupt in person.*"

"*Hmm.*"

Applause broke out when Oliver passed the table where Se'Vaughn and Trey were seated. The attention caught him by surprise and forced him to slow down. Some of the older students celebrated with the seated extramen, just as sincere with their applause as their younger counterparts; it looked as if a great deal of people were excited by the possibility of Founders winning the Magical Five tournament, or at least the possibility of Champayan *losing* it.

Before Oliver could stop entirely to grin and wave awkwardly at the onlookers, Emma grabbed a fistful of his shirt, forcing him in Watkin's direction.

"Well done!" said Watkin once they were near enough to hear him. He grinned in a boyish way Oliver hadn't yet seen, wiping away the age around his eyes and cheeks. "Founders stands a good chance of winning the trophy this year after today's finishes!"

"Thanks!" said Oliver. "I—,"

"Owe your teammates Beto and Cristina an apology," interrupted Watkin.

"*Yes, I daresay I agree,*" mused Archie. "*Professor Watkin's just told me about your push against Beto in the arena.*"

Oliver couldn't believe what he was hearing. He had not expected the conversation to steer in this direction.

"He pushed Cristina into *me* to try and knock me off that platform! The replay failed to show what Beto was up to in the previous room!"

"You are prejudiced against him," said Watkin. "Learn now while you're young to abandon your pride and do what's right."

Oliver wanted to yell, to tell Watkin and Archie they were both idiots, to drag Beto over from wherever he sat and force a confession out of him, but an annoying voice in the back of his head calmed him down. *Tell them what they want to hear. You need to find out about the painting.*

"Fine!" said Oliver, ignoring the urge to yell. "I'll talk to Beto ... and Cristina. *But I won't apologize to them.*" He'd kept the last bit to himself.

"Good," said Watkin. "Now how can I help you?"

Lance took the lead, garnering raised eyebrows from both Emma and Oliver. "You know how we love to research, sir? Well, we really liked the

# * Chapter 20: A Yeti's Decor *

look of the Yeti's room in that simulation. Do you know who designed that room?"

*"What on Earth?"* said Archie, lifting a mustache-like tendril confusedly.

Watkin surveyed them for a moment, his expression neutral. "Anything in particular catch your attention? I'll be honest I didn't notice anything eye-grabbing from where I stood behind Emma and Lance."

"Umm," said Oliver, "well we wondered who among the faculty had experience being up in front of a Yeti like that. Wanted to ask them more about it."

"Hmm," said Watkin, his left eyebrow raising. "Well, if it's Yeti knowledge you're looking for, I'd be remiss not to point you in the direction of Professor Desmoulins. But if it's anything else that caught your eye, Professor Zapien designed that particular room."

Relief coursed through Oliver at hearing Zapien's name. She'd be easy to get answers out of.

But it took them until the following Monday to track her down, and only then because they had her class. When asked about the Dungeon-Simulation, she laughed, causing her curling locks of hair to bounce up and down around her warm face.

"You liked my Yeti room? I always have a blast designing the rooms before the boss. Gives the players an opportunity to gather themselves. This year's boss was so tricky, I thought giving y'all the stew might help."

Emma flipped her hair as Zapien spoke. They'd sidled next to her as the rest of her Channeling 101 class attempted to use energy within stone deposits to lift their partner into the air.

# NOVA 01

"That's so neat!" said Emma, her eyes misty, "but you know what I *really* loved? The décor, you know?! So cozy, right?"

Oliver looked at Emma with disgust. Even though he knew she was trying to goad a reply out of Zapien, the misty-eyed schoolgirl approach just felt wrong; especially when it came from Emma.

"Did you really?" said Zapien, slightly suspicious. Maybe Emma was overdoing her persona. "Well, my husband had a lot of influence on that one. He met a Yeti during his travels long ago and suggested the simple fireplace, chair, and painting." Oliver felt his heartbeat quicken. "Well, to be honest, the painting was a last-minute addition."

"Oh?" asked Oliver, slightly raising a hand so Emma and Lance wouldn't interrupt.

"Mhmm," Zapien continued. "Headmaster Lalandra suggested adding some more décor after reviewing the dungeon. And then we had dinner at her apartment and there it was – an enormous fresco – it looked straight out of the Renaissance – she suggested we add a smaller version fit for the dungeon."

Goosebumps exploded across Oliver's back, neck, and arms. He took a breath before replying. "Was Headmaster Lalandra's fresco the exact same?"

"The painting? Oh, most certainly *not*. Hers depicts a sunnier landscape. A beautiful green forest I should say. And instead of the cold, icy temple, there's a mossy, green one."

Lance gaped.

## * Chapter 20: A Yeti's Decor *

"Thank you, Professor," Oliver managed. He grabbed Lance by the shoulder. "We better get back to today's exercise, right?"

Zapien nodded, ushering them to an open space in the classroom.

As they practiced, they didn't say a word other than *"levantaris"* as they lifted inanimate objects like Lance's hammer. They didn't need to. They finally knew where the painting was, and all that was left to do was break into the Headmaster's apartment to see it.

# NOVA 01

## Chapter 21: Family, Honor, and Reputation

*The boat from Johannesburg took forever but the wait was worth it. Machu Picchu is stunning. I'm starting to slow down a bit, though. Haven't let go of the light refraction staff since China and have almost forgotten what talking to other people is like.*
*Tío owes me big time for this.*

*23rd of April, the second year of the 10th Age*

Breaking into Lalandra's apartment was easier said than done. For starters, Oliver needed to know which apartment belonged to the Headmaster, and he didn't like the idea of breaking into the wrong one by accident.

"We should just ask Zapien where Lalandra lives," groaned Lance. "We've been posted up here for days!"

In an attempt to spot Lalandra entering her apartment, they'd taken it upon themselves to perform all their studying in the Dining Hall. For anyone that asked why they didn't study in the B4 observation room like they normally would, Emma would smile and say they needed the proximity to Ms. Joan's hot cocoa for their late-night studying sessions.

Oliver felt a prickle of impatience at the suggestion. "We've already told you! Asking Zapien would be too obvious. Trust me, she'll show up eventually."

But so far, they'd found that Lalandra only ever went down the stairs from the faculty apartments, never up them.

# * Chapter 21: Family, Honor, and Reputation *

"Maybe she has another way inside?" suggested Emma.

Oliver almost replied but refrained as he could hear someone approaching their table from behind.

It was Stevie, and Elton wasn't far behind.

"Now, what are y'all really up to?" huffed Stevie. "I don't want to hear any of this hot chocolate nonsense – I see you looking up at the faculty staircase every few seconds. Y'all are about as subtle as … a flamboyance of flamingos? A murder of crows?"

"It's none of your business what we're up to!" said Lance, narrowing his eyes.

"None of our business?" said Elton gleefully. He grabbed a chair and sat down next to Oliver, picking up the paper he was pretending to work on. "I see you've made a lot of progress on your essay on," —he squinted his eyes dramatically at the gibberish Oliver had written— "yeti paintings. Oliver what the heck? Even for a dummy paper this is garbage."

"Is that what this is about?" said Stevie, grabbing another seat. She looked into the space above Emma's head dreamily. "I saw the Yeti's painting during the Dungeon-Simulation. So did Elton, but he's too dumb to register anything that isn't food."

"Amen, sister," agreed Elton, saluting lazily.

"Well, what's the painting then? Official Trinova business only?" Oliver stiffened at their jokes. How could he have been so stupid to write down what he was searching for? For a Wise Trinova, that was pretty stupid.

# NOVA 01

Emma scoffed. "You said it yourself, Elton, that's just gibberish. We're posted up trying to catch Blackwood—,"

Stevie laughed. "No use, sweet, innocent child. Poor Lance-a-lot went stiff as a board when we started talking about the painting."

"We can help you!" said Elton. "Give us a shot!"

Oliver wanted to slap Lance on the back of the head, but it was no use now.

"Fine," he said sternly. "But you have to swear not to tell anybody about the painting. If the wrong people find out … well, let's just say everything the adults won't tell us, everything about *The Damned*, it'll all come back."

Stevie's grin fell.

Elton tried laughing. "Don't say stuff like that, man. That's not a joke."

"Does it look like we're joking?" Oliver retorted. He wore a grim expression.

"Point taken," said Stevie. "Alright, alright, alright, cross my heart and hope to die, you have our word."

Lance poked Elton in the stomach. "Yours, too?"

"Yikes! Yeah, mine, too!"

"Alright," said Oliver, leaning in. "We need to find a way into Lalandra's apartment."

"Groovy," said Stevie. "Why?"

"Does it matter?"

"Not at all." She leaned back into her chair, grinning goofily. "Alright, we'll help you. Won't we, Elton?"

"Never doubted it."

*431*

# * Chapter 21: Family, Honor, and Reputation *

A chair scraped and Joel sat down. "What's going on here?"

"Cross your heart and I might tell you," Elton grunted.

Joel shrugged. "It's crossed, my guy."

Stevie shushed them both. "Her apartment is the top one, obviously."

"Obviously," Joel echoed. "What are we talking about?"

"How do you know?" Emma interrupted, ignoring Joel.

Stevie leaned forward again, waggling her eyebrows. "Cause, I've been in it, haven't I?"

"What?!" Oliver hissed.

"Yeah, if it's paintings you're looking for, she's got a room that's full of 'em. Not sure why you didn't consult me sooner."

Oliver wanted to flip a table over in frustration. Stevie had known all along about where to find paintings.

"Look, Oliver," said Stevie, leaning back in. "I know you're the Prophet's Advent and everything … and that you've got a big secret you're keeping from the rest of us … but at some point, you're going to have to start trusting people. Not everyone in the world is evil."

With a scrape of chairs, Stevie, Elton, and Joel left. "Y'all better come soon," said Elton. "Seats fill up pretty quick."

"Oh!" said Emma. "I'd completely forgotten about the Dueling final!"

Oliver hadn't, but he'd been trying to ignore Beto's successes since the tripping incident in the simulation.

With a sigh, he sunk into his chair gloomily. "Stevie's right. Look at how much time I've wasted us by not asking around sooner."

# NOVA 01

"Hang on, though," said Lance, shaking Oliver's shoulder. "We've been right not to trust people. Archie understands the situation better than any of us could. He's ancient, and we should trust that he'd be right about the Founders — if they only thought the Trinova should know about *The Damned's* return, it's because they knew only you could be trusted with that knowledge. We've been over this!"

"He's right," said Emma begrudgingly. "We can ask people for help, but we don't need to tell them *everything* we know. It's a fine line we'll have to balance here on out."

Oliver buried his head into his arms. *Speed is of the essence, to defeat an evil presence.* At least when he lived with Santiago his problems were limited to going hungry or being bored.

Shutting his anxiety to the side again, he sat straight in his chair.

"Yeah, y'all are right … as usual."

Lance beamed at him.

"Of course, we are," said Emma. "Now, let's go see about that painting."

"Wait? Now?" said Lance. "Don't we need a plan?"

"I think … I've already got one … What we've gotta do is…"

A few moments later, Oliver and Lance walked outside Founders to join the crowd of students milling towards the Dueling Strip.

## * Chapter 21: Family, Honor, and Reputation *

"Are you sure I shouldn't be going instead?" asked Oliver. "Might be better to have someone using *sorbelux* if they're searching the *Headmaster's* apartment."

Lance sighed with annoyance. "Look, nobody's gonna notice Emma's absence, but someone like Blackwood may kick up a storm if he sees you're not at the duel."

Oliver nodded but still looked back at the Founders temple nervously. "If you say so."

"And besides," added Lance cheerfully, "it'll be good to see Beto lose a duel for once."

The stands on either side of the Dueling Strip were fuller than they'd yet seen. And for good reason. The Tournament had been well under way for the weeks since the Dungeon-Simulation, and in that time, Beto had proven to be quite the capable duelist. Oliver had been right. Beto's pride and honor seemingly outweighed his desire to sabotage Founders.

After qualifying for the Tournament as the eighth seeded entry, Beto had soundly defeated the second and third seeds to make it all the way to the final against his cousin John Tupper, the number one seed.

From what Oliver had heard from Abe and Brantley, John competed at another level entirely. Nobody had been able to stay on the strip for more than thirty seconds against him, and nobody was betting on that changing today.

And yet, the crowds were boisterous, and it was a well-known secret as to why. Regardless of Beto's performance, regardless of whether John obliterated the young extraman, Founders would still lead the Magical Five standings going into the Coatlball playoffs. Even Oliver had to admit Beto's commitment to the tournament was commendable, but that didn't stop him from harboring animosity. Beto had been slacking off in Coatlball training and continued to express negative interest in the Magical Five tournament standings. It drove Oliver crazy. If he didn't care about the Magical Five tournament, why was he here today, competing in the Dueling Tournament final? What was his motivation?

Unable to guess an answer Oliver sunk into the stands with Lance close by. Many of the older students brought drums to the strip like they had during the Coatlball matches. They played a beat as old as the campus itself, more brooding and sincere than the quick anthems heard at the Coatlball strip.

Seated closer to the drums than he would have liked, Oliver had a hard time hearing anything Lance was saying. Resigned to his thoughts, he set about looking around. On one side of the strip, Beto warmed up with an expression like stone painted across his face. He sprinted in place for a moment and then jumped a few times as high as he could. Professor Zapien tried speaking encouraging words to him, but he kept shrugging her away.

On the other side of the strip, Oliver's eyes met Blackwood's. An evil, thin smile split the Dean's face before he looked away; clearly, he was glad to see Oliver at the event. Next to Blackwood, John Tupper sat lazily on a chair facing the strip. Tall, athletic, and emotionless, John looked to be made of a different fabric than the rest of the student body. He kept his attention on the other side of the strip, directly on Beto.

## * Chapter 21: Family, Honor, and Reputation *

Oliver didn't like the look of John. The boy seemed a little too casual, a little too unencumbered by the stakes at hand. Beneath his long, dark-brown hair, he observed the world with deep-socketed eyes that took in more than they returned. Even Beto, who always wore a smug expression, looked grim ahead of a final. But John ... he looked just plain bored.

Either way, Oliver reminded himself, it didn't matter much. Right now, for all he knew, Emma could already be in Lalandra's apartment, writing down everything she could about the forest fresco. By the end of the night, she might have even gathered enough information to lead them to the entrance of the Forgotten Wood.

"LADIES AND GENTLEMEN," boomed Tolteca, floating from one set of bleachers to the next. "WELCOME TO THE DUELING FINAL. THE RULES ARE SIMPLE – THE COMBATANTS WILL USE ANY MAGIC AT THEIR DISPOSAL TO KNOCK THEIR OPPONENT OFF THE STRIP. LAST COMPETITOR STANDING IS THE WINNER!"

The hum in the crowd stopped, leaving only the sound of tinkling torches. The flames licked at Beto, John, and even Tolteca, reflecting off him in a pinkish glow.

After a nod from the sundial, Beto and John stepped onto either side of the white marble strip. Every scuff of their boots echoed around the bleachers as they moved to the middle and clasped hands. Beto tried smiling but looked more like Tolteca than himself. John, however, looked at his cousin in a way that made Oliver fear for Beto's safety.

## NOVA 01

Unable to help himself, Oliver leaned forward in his seat as Beto and John returned to their opposite ends of the strip. Something about John was so off-putting that Oliver found himself doing the unimaginable – he was rooting for Beto, his worst enemy.

*Boom!*

The duel began.

As he had done during his previous duels, Beto began the fight with a furious barrage of Earth elementals. Brandishing his scimitar, he fired sphere after sphere at his older cousin, creating a storm of projectiles capable of ripping through almost any barrier. Oliver could *feel* the Power Beto imbued into every missile. The world warped around his scimitar strikes as they connected with Earth, transferring Nova's Power as instructed.

But none of Beto's shots landed. To everyone's surprise, John, who was famous for quick duels, simply side stepped them. Right and left he swayed, looking as if he were warming up for a dance, not competing in a Dueling Final. A flash of light caught Oliver's eyes as the boy moved. It came from John's index finger. *He's Powerful enough to just use a ring.*

"I'm disappointed in you, cousin," said John, his voice carrying across the quiet arena, imbued by his own Power. His words hung in the air, staying on one's ears longer than welcomed. "You think reaching this final will gain my respect? You've put your own honor before your family. Family *always* comes first."

# * Chapter 21: Family, Honor, and Reputation *

Beto lowered his sword, taking a moment to catch his breath and peer at his cousin. "I – I have fought well," he stuttered. "I've made it to a final as an extraman, representing the family all the way!"

Oliver wanted to scream at Beto to tell him to put up his defenses, but it was too late.

John shifted his weight, flexing his arms and legs as he bent them. With an audible breath, he shot fire from his ring-hand at an alarming speed.

*"Defenderis!"* shouted Beto, holding his sword with both hands. His shield charm *exploded* as the stream of fire met it, showering the onlookers with sparks. Desperate, Beto rose a wall of Earth to defend himself further, but John turned the Earth into mud with a lazy flick of his wrist, and as the wall collapsed, he yelled, *"estalla."* For a moment, Oliver couldn't see if the spell had accomplished anything, let alone affected Beto. But then, almost as if in slow motion, the air in front of Beto concentrated into one location and then expanded in a devastating explosion, firing the younger boy up and out of the ring.

As Beto flew, Oliver let out a breath he didn't realize he was holding. *It's over.*

Only it wasn't.

Just as Beto began to cross outside the marble strip, John twirled his wrist, creating an artificial whip in the air and lashed it around Beto's foot. With a yank, he slammed his cousin down onto the marble in front of him.

For a brief moment, the arena lay quiet as the crowd waited. By the rules, the match wasn't over yet; nobody had been knocked off the strip.

# NOVA 01

Stepping forward nonchalantly, John approached Beto. His whisper carried across the bleachers like wildfire. "Family *always* comes first!"

He flicked his wrist again and slammed Beto onto the side of the ring he'd just vacated. Then, with a savage cry, John rose his ring hand towards the setting sun and then down towards his motionless cousin, ushering as much heat as he could muster. With a rotation of his arm, he released the energy onto Beto like a beam of star fire.

Unable to cast a shield, Beto had enough sense to use his remaining strength to roll to his side. But the fire was too quick, and it struck him directly on his thigh.

Beto screamed as his clothes and skin melted away. The noise made Oliver's stomach turn, sounding more animal than human; he'd never heard anything, or anyone make a noise like that.

Boos and projectiles descended upon John, but he waved them away with lazy puffs of air. Before anything else could be said or done, he kicked into the ground, cruelly popping up a section of rock beneath Beto to send him flying from the strip. Only the Champayan students cheered as John bowed to each section of the crowd with a sadistic grin.

Where Beto landed, Professor Watkin arrived, his lips moving noiselessly to place Beto's motionless form onto a magical stretcher. Headmaster Lalandra, meanwhile, had taken to the ring and grabbed John by the ear.

What she yelled as she dragged him off the strip, Oliver didn't hear past Beto's guttural screams. All around, students held hands over their mouths as they watched Beto continue to yell and Watkin tend to his twitching leg.

## ∗ Chapter 21: Family, Honor, and Reputation ∗

*"Champayan wins the duel,"* said Tolteca solemnly. *"Please follow your dorm-heads and RAs to the Dining Hall."*

"Founders with me!" shouted Zapien, bringing the extramen viewers out of their shocked disbelief.

"C'mon," said Lance, pushing Oliver up.

As they walked out of the arena, a round of applause went out from the extramen because Beto had sat up from his stretcher, no longer screaming. Watkin pushed him back down though and continued muttering spells.

"Looks like he'll be alright," Lance tried saying jovially to James and Cristina.

They glared back.

Moments later, Oliver and Lance sat down, silent, in the Dining Hall. Only when Emma joined them with a wide grin on her face did Oliver remember he might have some good news waiting for him.

"I found it!" she said, as they sidled up next to her for dinner.

"The painting?"

"*Better.* The Forgotten Wood."

"What do you mean you found the Forgotten Wood?" hissed Lance.

"The painting *is* the entrance!" whispered Emma gleefully. "I'll show you!"

*"Its entrance lies within our grounds,"* muttered Oliver, repeating the prophecy.

"Exactly!" said Emma.

"Did you enter it?"

## NOVA 01

Emma nodded. "I stuck my head through and saw the forest – looked a little spooky but otherwise fine. I wouldn't want a vacation house there or anything." She paused and looked around the Dining Hall. "Why does everybody look like they're coming back from a funeral?"

Oliver and Lance exchanged a look.

"We almost did."

Emma frowned. "What are you talking about?"

"That John kid," said Lance. "He's messed up in the head."

"Beto's cousin?"

Oliver took a moment to describe what John Tupper had done to Beto at the Dueling Strip. Her frown turned to a scowl as he spoke.

"Is he going to be alright?"

"Watkin was looking over him when we left, so he'll probably be fine," said Lance. "But I've never even heard of the kind of magic John used. It looked like he fired the sun at Beto or something. I'm sure there'll be a nasty scar by the time they're done fixing him up."

"That boy is messed up," said Oliver, frowning. "Did you hear what he said? Family comes first? How could you do that to your own cousin?"

"Brantley and Abe tried warning us about him," said Lance, his eyes wide with shock. "He makes Beto look like a fairy princess."

Silence followed as they ate their dinner. The rest of the student body did the same, marking the most depressing dinner Oliver had ever experienced.

On the one hand, he felt sorry for Beto – John had been cruel, and they'd want to beat him thoroughly if they met him in the Coatlball playoffs. On

## Chapter 21: Family, Honor, and Reputation

the other hand, it was difficult to care about Beto or the playoffs when they could be searching for the Gift in the Forgotten Wood. Now that he thought about it, the Gift was more important than anything else if the Iguana's Scroll was even remotely accurate.

"I think we should focus on—,"

"The playoffs," said Emma.

"The painting," said Oliver.

"Final exams," said Lance.

Oliver scoffed at them both. "How can you two be worried about school right now? *Speed is of the essence, to defeat an evil presence, that has lusted for release, since the dawn of divine peace.* I'm not waiting around for *The Damned* to bust down the Dining Hall door and kill us all!"

"Keep your voice down!" said Emma. Oliver had attracted a few weird looks from Valerie, Se' Vaughn, and Trey.

"Listen," said Lance. "We have no idea what's waiting for us in that temple in the Forgotten Wood. We need a plan – a good one – before we go waltzing around. We've got a month left of Coatlball and academics. Let's learn everything we can and make a plan of attack first."

Oliver hated the idea of waiting, but Lance was right. If they went in now and came across anything like John Tupper's star fire spell, they'd be eaten alive. Slowly, he looked at Lance and nodded his head.

"You're right. We'll learn as much as we can for the rest of the year and then go for it after exams and the Coatlball tournament. Deal?"

Emma smile broke out, looking mischievous. "Can't wait to see what Augustus, Madeline, and Cuahtemoc left you. I bet it's good."

# NOVA 01

## Chapter 22: The Forgotten Wood

*Tío said the Aztec sites wouldn't be worth a visit because Cuahtemoc stripped their vaults clean before he left. And even if he didn't, the Spanish certainly did.*
*I had to check anyway. It's crazy to me that an entire civilization followed the Mayans and then disappeared just as quickly. It breaks my heart to see all this history and culture restricted to just museums — imagine what it would have been like to pick your crops from your own floating garden in Tenochtitlan!*
*I used to think the problem was unique to North America. But I've seen the rest of the world now. Humanity's corruption is seamless, without border. It stains our entire history like blood on a tapestry. We're going to stop it.*

*7$^{th}$ of May, the second year of the 10$^{th}$ Age*

Since the incident at the Dueling Strip, many of the extramen began viewing Beto as a rallying point for the Magical Five tournament. Founders' odds of returning the Emerald Trophy to the extraman hall were now better than they had been for the first time in decades, and all that remained was for the Coatlball team to beat Champayan in the Coatlball final.

Initially, Oliver, Emma, and Lance agreed with the rest of the extramen. After all, Beto had stood up to his cousin, giving Founders a real shot at glory.

Within five minutes of Beto emerging from the infirmary, however, all sympathy and respect they had for him faded away entirely.

# * Chapter 22: The Forgotten Wood *

Despite his now using a walking stick to support his heavily bandaged leg, Beto's gait had somehow become even *more* annoying. With his curly hair bouncing, he often took it upon himself to wave at every nook and cranny of the Dining Hall that stood and clapped for him. Nine times out of ten, he'd end his rounds across the room with a firm simper directed at Oliver, reminding him that Founders loved the boy who'd nearly delivered the Emerald Trophy, not the Prophet's Advent.

"If he comes over here to gloat," growled Emma, "I'll take his cane and beat him with it."

She, Oliver, and Lance were back in the Founders eastern viewing dome, applying finishing touches to their final research papers for Watkin on the origin of the Cradler's Rocks. The task ended up being incredibly difficult given the scarcity of pre-first-age primary resources, but they feared it far less than the grade Blackwood might give them for their abysmal essays on the three major types of defensive spells: elemental, casted, and conjured.

With one eye on Beto, Cristina, and James as they took their seats in the opposite observation dome, Oliver put down his notebook. Emma didn't bother pretending; she scowled openly at them with her notebook and essay lying forgotten on the coffee table.

"Are y'all done with your essays yet?" asked Oliver.

"Nah," said Lance. "But I'll finish it tomorrow – I'm sick of looking through ancient sketches of wizards and rocks."

Emma nodded her head.

"Good," said Oliver. "Let's go over the plan then, one more time."

Emma sighed. "We may as well just go now. We're not learning any new magic at this point, are we? Just waiting for our exam results."

Oliver ignored her. "So, after the Coatlball final tomorrow against Champayan ... no matter the result, we'll hang back to 'celebrate' and then we'll go on a walk with our good friend *sorbelux*. We'll get into Lalandra's apartment while everyone else is at the feast, take a quick peak at the Wood, see what kinda danger there might be, and come *right back*." He emphasized the words while looking at Emma. "Then, we'll wait for our final exam grades and go back later in the week to find the Gift in the Temple. Got it?"

"Works for me," said Lance.

"You're the boss," said Emma. "Then what?"

"That'll depend on what the Gift is—,"

Applause from the main common room distracted him.

"You're joking!" said Lance.

Beto came strutting towards them despite his cane. He waved at those clapping for him in the common room before entering their dome.

"What are you three up to?" he said coldly. "Planning for the game?"

"Finishing our Watkin paper," growled Oliver. "What do you want?"

Beto didn't respond immediately. Instead, he shook his head at Oliver and began to limp towards the couches where they were sitting. Emma and Lance stood up, their arms stiff.

"Calm down, you three. No need to be so feisty." He narrowed his eyes, taking a second on each of their faces. "Can't an injured player wish his team good luck before a big game? I mean, it is a big game after all. Though,

## * Chapter 22: The Forgotten Wood *

I suppose I've done most of the heavy lifting for you already. All you have to do is win *one* game. It'd be a real shame if you lose … imagine losing the Magical Five tournament after I gave you a lead going into the final game? The embarrassment …" He paused to smirk at Oliver directly. "Well, it'd be impossible to recover. You'd be known as a loser. Not that you aren't already."

Lance, who'd gone slightly white, looked like he'd love nothing more than to swing his hammer at Beto. Instead, he took Emma's lead and frowned at them with his arms crossed.

"You're still too hurt to play, then?" said Oliver, pointing at Beto's cast and cane.

Beto's smile dropped for a moment at the mention of his leg, but only for a moment. "Yeah … I still can't put any weight on it while the solar radiation seeps out. It was quite fortunate Dean Blackwood was there to bandage me up, otherwise that buffoon Watkin might have amputated the leg instead."

A red mist threatened to cover Oliver's eyes, but he resisted. *He's just goading you.*

"Get outta here," said Oliver, growling. "If you're here for trouble, I'll gladly embarrass you again. How long did you wait by those statues in March to get revenge? All night?"

Emma and Lance laughed.

"Don't worry, García," said Beto, "I'll leave you weirdos alone. I'm just here to pass on a warning. From what John tells me, he'll be coming straight for you tomorrow. Last kid he man-marked ended up missing for a month, didn't she?"

Emma scoffed. "How can you talk about your cousin like that when he nearly destroyed your leg? Family comes first? Yeah, right – that guy's a maniac."

A flicker of an emotion Oliver couldn't place flashed across Beto's eyes, but it quickly turned into a curling lip.

"As a sinova, I wouldn't expect you to understand the expectations of a great and honorable family like mine. Just know, you've been warned."

Still glaring, he limped away. Applause greeted him again in the main common room, making Oliver's blood boil.

"I don't like the idea of John Tupper coming after you tomorrow," said Lance, his eyes wide.

Oliver scoffed. "I'd like to see him try."

With their nerves itching, they went upstairs to sleep, garnering some applause along the way.

It was a miracle Oliver managed to sleep at all with the game, grades, and threat of *The Damned* looming over him.

Once again, he found himself thinking, and in this case, dreaming, about the shadow from the airport. In a flash, he stood in the same clearing where he'd first seen the threat. This time, however, the shadow stalked towards him. In a whirl of clouds and smoke, the scene shifted, placing them in what

## * Chapter 22: The Forgotten Wood *

Oliver imagined the Forest Temple to be. He envisioned a similar setting to the golden willow temple in the lagoon, but with trap doors and puzzles like the simulations he played at school. No matter what room or challenge he faced, the shadow always followed, just behind, and never quite in sight.

"Why are you following me?" he asked, kicking at a loose rock in a moss-eaten room.

He didn't know why he bothered asking the shadow questions. It never responded to him.

But this time, it did.

The churning wheel of anxiety in his stomach turned to absolute *dread*.

"I should ask you the same thing," the shadow breathed. Its voice was exhausted, raspy like *Xihuacota's,* but then deep like Blackwood's. It made Oliver want to scream.

But he couldn't, his lungs were weighed down as if something were sitting on them. He tried peering left and right, up and down, but the shadow had disappeared entirely.

Then a new noise struck his ears; one that made his skin crawl. It differed from the first voice in the same way a feathered serpent's differed from a human's, only far more monstrous. From a great distance he heard it, echoing through the tunnels, a collection of screeching, clicking, and sniffing, imbued by a hateful, crushing desire to infect his soul.

"It followed me," said the tired voice again, still out of sight. "But I've hidden from it every day. And now ... we are *so* close ... so very close."

# NOVA 01

"Close to what?" Oliver screamed. He covered his head with his fingers and hands, anything to protect him from the specter that haunted the shadow.

The clicking, screeching, and sniffing drew closer, immobilizing him.

"My *release*."

---

The next morning Oliver ascended the marble stairs into the Dining Hall with Lance. His eyes were red and puffy from a nightmare he couldn't quite remember. Every time he thought he came close, the memory slipped through his grasp.

Applause broke out when they sat down. Lance went pale in the face at the attention.

To their surprise, it wasn't just the Founders students doing the clapping; most of Hutch – Stevie, Elton, and Joel loudest among them – sang or cheered along with the extramen. The frock coats had returned, as well. Seemingly every student that wasn't a Champayan wore one with Founders' colors. Those that didn't, queued up in lines to be dressed in feathers and body paint to look like either Archie, Rasmus, Merri, or Espie.

"I'm going to be sick," said Lance when they sat down next to Emma and Se'Vaughn. "If that John kid is coming for us—,"

"We'll just have to beat him," said Emma, shrugging. "Every great team has to beat their bogey team."

## * Chapter 22: The Forgotten Wood *

Se'Vaughn nodded his head. "Nothing to worry about Lance, we've got a Trinova on our team, they don't. And Ronnie, too, for what it's worth."

But Oliver wasn't feeling all that well ahead of the game either. For the first time in his life, a dream that he couldn't remember began to trickle back into his conscious. Had that nightmare been just that, a nightmare? Or had it been a vision? Who was the Shadow? *The Damned?* What on Earth had the clicking creature been? Maybe Emma was right, maybe they'd have to find the Gift sooner than later.

"Oh no," said Se'Vaughn. "Oli, you feeling sick, too?"

"No chance," said Emma. "He just thinks a lot. It's all the Wisdom, you see."

Oliver nodded his head at them and tried eating the platter of eggs and hash browns he'd ordered. Ms. Joan had left him a "good luck" message written in ketchup over the potatoes.

A few short minutes later, Ronnie led them past the thicket to the Coatlball trench for light warm up drills.

"Now remember, Champayan will never stop hounding us for the ball. You've gotta be quick and decisive with your passing! Even if you mess one up, forget about it and play the next pass just as aggressive and fast!"

Getting in the air managed to take Oliver's mind off his nightmare. Lance, however, still looked like he might vomit. His condition seemed to worsen as the crowd filled the bleachers. From the front, Tancol's drums beat again, but this time in support of Founders.

With ten minutes until kick off, Ronnie let them know he and Abe would start in defense, Lance and Oliver in midfield, and Emma and Se'Vaughn on offense. Pouting, Cristina took the bench where Oliver expected to see Beto cheering them on.

"Hang on," he asked Abe as they formed a line to shake hands with the Champayan players. "Where's Beto?"

Abe shook his head and pointed at the eastern bleacher.

Jumping up and down with the Champayan crowd, Beto cheered as loud as the rest of them, his ties to his dorm and teammates entirely forgotten.

Emma snarled. "What a slimy piece of—,"

"Can't say I'm surprised," interrupted Lance, finally showing some color.

"Focus on the game!" shouted Ronnie, queuing them up in a line to shake hands with Champayan.

Composed of juniors and seniors, the Champayan team was much bigger than Founders'. They each made sure to crush Oliver's hand one at a time, shifting his bones around painfully. Still, Oliver made sure he met John Tupper's eyes when they came face to face for the first time.

Where John quickly went through the motions with the other handshakes, he lingered on Oliver's for a moment longer than necessary.

"This is the Trinova?" he said, his lip curling. "Your reputation exceeds you."

"Aren't you tough?" said Emma, scoffing from the front of the line. "You met him during the regular season already. And besides, you're talking smack to an *extraman*. Get a grip, little man."

## * Chapter 22: The Forgotten Wood *

Ronnie and Abe laughed, but poor Lance squealed as John shook his hand last, crushing it entirely. Tupper didn't even bother *looking* at Emma, let alone responding to her.

"He's probably gonna come after you as well, Emma," said Ronnie. "Abe, work on protecting the team more than anything."

"Yes, *sir*."

As they mounted their Guides and took their starting positions, the familiar voices of Elton and Joel reached their ears.

"Exciting final this year!" boomed Elton. "More than just bragging rights on the line, the winner of the match takes the Emerald Trophy!"

"GET READY TO RUMBLLEEEE," shouted Joel. "You're absolutely right, Tolteca. In an underdog season to remember, Founders has made the final. They will try their hardest to bring an end to Champayan's decade-long run and return the Emerald Trophy to Founders Temple for the first time since our very own, Professor Watkin, guided his team to a first-place finish."

Boos and hisses emanated from the Champayan bleacher.

"In an interesting twist," continued Elton, "the Founders boy who has put his extraman dorm in the position to win, has already tied his allegiances to Champayan ahead of next year. In fact, you can see him jumping up and down on his supposedly maimed leg in the eastern bleacher!"

"Bless him," said Joel. "So blissfully unaware of how stupid he looks."

At Joel's words, tomatoes, banana peels, and conjured ravens pelted the commentator's box.

# NOVA 01

"Oh no," said Elton, blasting away the projectiles with a pulse of Power. "Anyway, Headmaster Lalandra takes the field to kick off the game."

Instead of her usually whimsical expression, Dr. Lalandra frowned at both sets of players this time around.

"I remind you," she said to Ronnie and then Tupper, where her eyes lingered, "flagrant fouls will result in a swift ejection."

"Yes, ma'am," said Ronnie.

Tupper grunted.

Satisfied, Dr. Lalandra tossed the ball high into the air, starting the final.

In the bedlam that followed, fireballs sizzled, *defenderis* shields sparked, and chunks of Earth hurtled from one direction to another. For a moment, it looked as if Se'Vaughn might snatch the ball from the air first, but Charlie Holding, a barrel-chested Champayan midfielder, forced him off course by summoning a flock of ravens. With a yelp, Se'Vaughn ducked beneath the onslaught of black feathers, allowing the ball drop below where Tupper caught it.

With a roar, Tupper's osorius charged forward, pushing aside Abe and Reggie on their way. Between the strength of his steed, and the power behind his spells, Tupper seemed almost impossible to slow down. He didn't just defend himself when he held the ball, he attacked everyone else as well. Jets of fire, conjured sling projectiles, and summoned swords of light hunted those around him, enabling his steady progress down the field. Desperate, Oliver felt for the ring in his finger and rose an enormous wave of Earth covering the width of the trench. The crowd gasped. Unsatisfied,

## * Chapter 22: The Forgotten Wood *

however, Oliver descended to where he knew Tupper would have to play a pass upward.

But Tupper didn't pass the ball. He didn't need to.

"*Estalla!*" he yelled.

Just as Oliver remembered from the duel against Beto, an ominous howling noise sounded as the air in front of the wall along the width of the trench aggregated to a spot directly in front of Tupper's charging osorius. With a sound like fireworks, the air exploded, shooting chunks of wall in every direction.

Archie dodged the debris and Oliver swore, realizing it would take something really clever to stop Tupper. He looked to the stone leading up to the Founders goal. What could he do? *Stop him.*

Unsure of whether his plan would work, Oliver opened his fist and concentrated on removing the stone flooring of the trench in the defensive third of the trench. With a sound like a chain gun, stone bricks dispersed haphazardly, leaving nothing but solid Earth. Tupper's osorius slowed as it neared the modified course. Then, while Tupper looked around confused, Oliver raised his palm again, turning the Earth into a thick mud.

Whispers rushed across the crowd. But Oliver didn't care. He couldn't let Tupper win. The boy was *evil*.

With hardly any time to react, Tupper's osorius sank into the mud, its feet thrashing wildly in the muck. Begrudgingly, Tupper tossed the ball upwards for Holding to catch.

## NOVA 01

In a series of blur-like passes, the ball ended up in the hands of Min Ahn, Tupper's co-attacker. With a feint to his left, he juked Ronnie entirely before firing a shot straight into the net.

"GGGOOOOOOAAAAAAAALLLLLL," boomed Joel, over the intercom as the Champayan crowd erupted. "That should be six points — no, it's only three thank goodness — yep, replay just confirmed Ahn shot from twenty-nine yards, not thirty."

"Yes," agreed Elton, "you can see his captain yelling at him now. Could have been six points with better positioning."

Looking down, Oliver saw Elton was right. Tupper had escaped the mud and was now giving his fellow attacker an earful as he pushed wide to block Abe from progressing the ball.

With few options available to him, Abe tossed up to Oliver who caught the pigskin with his fingertips. Seeing Holding and Jim Karnegie, the other Champayan midfielder, descending upon him, he shuttled the ball immediately towards Emma, yelling, *"defenderis!"*

A shower of sparks rose and fell as the two players battered against his shield with summoned swords of light. They kept swinging at him long after Emma had darted away and launched a pass to Se'Vaughn, who caught the ball thirty yards out from goal.

"*Archie!*" Oliver yelled. The Champayan midfielders kept swinging their swords. "*Get us out of here or we'll be in pieces!*"

With an exhale of hot steam, Archie circled downwards, attempting to sneak between both assailants.

*Whoosh!*

* Chapter 22: The Forgotten Wood *

One of the swords went through the air, narrowly passing over Oliver's head as they broke free.

Ignoring the blade, Oliver urged Archie forward, making a late move towards the goal where Emma and Se'Vaughn poked and prodded for an opening. Seeing Oliver out of the corner of his eye, Se'Vaughn dropped a pass downwards for Oliver to catch as he zoomed up towards the goal. But he could only hit the backboard and not the net.

"GGGOOOOOAAAAAALLLLLL," boomed Joel again. "García makes the score three to one! We've got a game on our hands, folks!"

Berating himself for missing an easy three points, Oliver pressed Archie back to the middle of the trench to get back into position.

But he was too late.

In one pass Champayan skipped over Oliver, Se'Vaughn, and Emma, and held the ball in the middle of the trench. Too far behind, Oliver watched, crestfallen, as the play progressed from Holding to Ahn down the right flank. They laughed when they lobbed a pass over Lance who stood no chance without Oliver in his position.

Just as Oliver thought to raise a last-effort wall of Earth, a rumbling noise sounded, distracting him, and out of nowhere, a forty-foot pillar of rock struck Merri, sending Lance flying. Far below, Tupper grinned with satisfaction as Lance fell and fell until he magically decelerated to land softly on the ground. Desperate, Ronnie darted forward to block Holding and Ahn, but they easily shuttled it below to Tupper who made no mistake, scoring three points. He quickly raced back to midfield before Founders could reorganize, closing his fist along the way to fix the stone floor Oliver had destroyed.

Lance got back onto Merri as quickly as he could while Abe and Ronnie passed the ball back and forth to buy some time. Karnegie, however, had other plans. Popping up between Abe and Ronnie, he intercepted a weak pass from Abe, and after some gloating, he passed to Ahn who connected with the backboard.

"Ggggoooooaaaalll," yelled Joel, beginning to sound subdued. "Seven to one! Champayan is threatening to break away here!"

Se'Vaughn, who'd so far been isolated at the front of Founders' attack, dropped deep to receive a pass in midfield. Ronnie threw it to him, but when the ball arrived, Se'Vaughn was yanked right off of Xhak and pulled towards the Earth; Tupper had summoned a whip and latched it onto his ankle.

The pass sailed just past Xhak and into the arms of Karnegie who immediately shot for another point against the backboard.

"Eight to one," shouted Elton through the intercom. Joel had buried his head in his arms. "Annnddd surely the Founders captain must call a time out soon …"

But Ronnie shook his head. "Quick passes!" he yelled at the team. "Keep your heads up!"

This time Lance dropped deep to receive a pass and was able to hot potato with Oliver up to the midfield, dodging a parliament of owls and a jet of fire along the way. Then, Ronnie made a move forward from deep, catching a pass from Lance to occupy the right wing. Seeing the hole in

## Chapter 22: The Forgotten Wood

their own defense, Oliver dropped back to fill it, keeping an eye on Tupper who was barreling back towards the Champayan goal.

Se'Vaughn caught the ball next and made a diagonal, return dash, preparing for a shot.

"*Estalla!*" rang Tupper's voice. Oliver watched him open both fists as he yelled.

Again, the air compressed and expanded in a rush of wind, sending Xhak spiraling out of control.

Somehow, Se'Vaughn managed to get the ball to Emma with a desperate pass. She fired at the goal immediately.

The net rippled.

"GGGOOOOOAAAAALLLLLL," yelled Joel, coming back to life. "Emma Griffith scores for Founders! Eight to four."

With fewer than five minutes remaining in the half, Brantley subbed in for Abe, Katie for Ronnie, and Cristina for Se'Vaughn. The fresh set of wings helped defensively, but anytime they tried attacking, Champayan boxed them out completely with either smart movements or advanced magic. Tupper's *estalla* spell in particular was giving them a hard time. Any time they made it past the halfway line, Tupper would force a turnover by blowing up the air in front of them.

By the time the whistle blew for half-time, Champayan led twelve to four.

Red in the face, Ronnie insisted they keep going for shots from close range.

"Unless you have all the time in the world to line up a shot, don't even think about it! You're never going to make it!"

"Ronnie," said Lance, tentatively, "is there anything we can do about Tupper's explosions? Why can't we do the same thing?" Abe piped in before Ronnie could answer. "It's an incredibly difficult piece of magic. Tupper is the first person in a few years that Belk was able to teach how to do it. It's taught in one of her elective courses – she calls it air compression."

"What's the theory behind it?" Oliver asked casually.

Abe gave him a wary look. "Well, with *estalla* you're supposed to suck in air quickly, and then expand it from a small space even quicker. The counter spell, *abrilla,* would be to expand the concentrated space as the air attempts to concentrate. But don't try it, Oli – Trinova or not, it can kill you if you do it wrong."

Oliver thought back to Tupper's hand motions, mirroring them as Abe spoke. "Can any of you at least do the *abrilla* counter-spell?"

Brantley shook his head. "We'll just have to dodge it. Any time you feel the air moving around you, *move*, because an explosion *will* be coming."

"If we pass quick enough," said Ronnie, "it shouldn't be an issue."

Oliver and Emma exchanged a look, both agreeing the spell was absolutely an issue. How were they supposed to pass or throw the ball with the air exploding around them every few seconds?

The whistle sounded.

"Alright team!" shouted Ronnie. "High percentage shots!"

After five more minutes, they would have settled for any shots.

## * Chapter 22: The Forgotten Wood *

Since the game resumed, Tupper's explosions increased, making it nearly impossible to progress.

After a particularly nasty one, Cristina turned over the ball, allowing Champayan back into Founders' half, just twenty yards from goal. Feeling frustrated, Oliver thought back to Abe's explanation on the advanced magic.

He'd been able to freeze water when that was supposed to be too advanced. Why not compress air, too?

With a deep breath, he closed his eyes and opened his fists. From his ring finger, he felt the wriggling strands of chaos in the world. He'd begun getting used to the feeling. From the mass of activity, he picked out a twitching line that somehow felt *connected* to the air in front of Tupper. Then, he filled it with Power.

*"Estalla,"* he whispered.

Howling wind *billowed* towards a needle-point's worth of space in front of Tupper. Banners and signs were caught into the hurricane-like gale, whipping and fluttering through the air. With a stunned expression, Tupper pulled on the reigns of his osorius, desperate to get away.

Finally, the wind stopped, and for a half-second that seemed the end of it.

But then, the air in front of Tupper *exploded* like cannon fire, shimmering with Power. The shockwave from the blast was so powerful it sent Tupper flying off his Guide. He landed, hard, on stone nearly thirty yards away. Where the explosion had occurred, a ten-foot crater had been created, blasting away the playing surface entirely.

Silent and dumfounded, the crowd and players turned to stare at Oliver with terrified expressions. Then, a voice broke through the quiet.

"ATTA BOY, OLI!!!" yelled Trey, igniting the crowd like gunpowder. The cheering that followed was deafening.

"FOUN-DERS, FOUN-DERS!!"

Terrified by Oliver's onslaught of magic, the Champayan players grew timid with their passing. They glanced at their captain, John Tupper, for support, but he looked just as disturbed as the rest of them. Every time he tried air compression again, Oliver yelled *"abrilla!"*, completely shutting him down.

With the Champayan passes growing less and less confident, Lance began intercepting quite a few of them.

"A *fourth* interception by Wyatt!" yelled Joel over the intercom. "That's your little brother, that is! Best defensive performance we've seen in a final in years!"

But Elton had temporarily jumped out of the commentator's booth to join the cheering crowd. He foamed at the mouth, screaming obscenities as he picked up random extramen and shook them.

"GOOOOAAAAAAAALLLLLLLL," shouted Joel. "BRANTLEY MONTGOMERY MAKES IT TWELVE TO TEN! THAT SHOT SAILED INTO THE NET!"

Brantley fist-pumped as he retreated back to defense. He'd subbed in for Abe again and scored a six pointer from forty yards out.

"Hit 'em with another one, Oli!" he yelled.

# * Chapter 22: The Forgotten Wood *

Oliver nodded. Seeing Karnegie passing the ball to Ahn, he opened and closed his fists.

"*Estalla!*"

The banners that were left in the crowd fluttered as the air around the stadium sucked towards Ahn. Eyes wide with fright, he tried passing the ball back while yelping an incoherent string of syllables. The pass ended up missing Karnegie entirely, sailing directly into Emma's arms instead.

Then, just as the entire arena winced for the oncoming explosion, the concentrated air dispersed.

Frowning, Oliver looked down and saw Tupper holding an opened fist high into the air. He grinned with satisfaction.

"Uh-oh!" said Joel. "Looks like we've got a game of chess on our hands between Tupper and García! Two minutes left!"

"HIGH PERCENTAGE SHOTS!" screamed Ronnie, his voice going hoarse, as Emma thought about a shot from more than twenty yards out.

Frowning, she tucked the ball close and darted to her left, passing to Oliver. But he quickly shuttled the pigskin to Se'Vaughn, opting to keep an eye on Tupper instead of contributing to the offense; just in time, too, because the older boy had begun attacking whoever held the ball with the same strands of star fire with which he'd scarred Beto.

"*Estalla!*" Oliver yelled. "*Estalla! Estalla!*"

Even though Tupper dispersed each attempt, it forced him to focus on Oliver's magic instead of the game, allowing Emma, Se'Vaughn, and Lance to progress down the trench.

# NOVA 01

"Only thirty seconds remaining!" announced Elton. He'd returned to the commentator's box as Joel had ceased commentating and covered his face with his hands. Through the gaps in his fingers, he watched along with everybody else, hoping and pleading.

Every Champayan player barring Tupper had fallen back to defend, harrying any Founders player that held onto the ball for more than a second. Se'Vaughn and Emma led the attack by darting around the defenders, quickly passing off to one another, hoping to eventually connect with a penetrating move made by Abe, Brantley, or Lance.

"Twenty seconds!"

The wind rushed towards Se'Vaughn, making Oliver's stomach lurch. *"Abrilla!"* he yelled, dissipating Tupper's spell just in time.

*"Oliver,"* growled Archie, *"remember your fundamentals. You and the boy below won't get anything done using verbal spells. Try an elemental."*

Catching Archie's meaning, Oliver raised his ring hand, feeling the Earth beneath Tupper.

It rose, more like gravel than solid Earth, forcing Tupper's osorius to stumble for more secure footing.

"Ten seconds!"

*"Estalla!"* Oliver shouted.

Once more the wind howled as it congregated in front of the Champayan goal; its defenders eyed each other nervously.

Below, Tupper had regained his composure. "No!" he shouted. *"Abrilla!"*

But he was a fraction too late.

## ∗ Chapter 22: The Forgotten Wood ∗

The air in front of the goal pushed away the defenders with the force of a hurricane.

Only Charlie Holding was left in position when the wind stopped howling. Seeing the opportunity, Emma darted forward to receive a pass from Se'Vaughn. Holding raised his hands desperately, scrambling backwards to try and block her shot.

"Use magic you troglodyte!" screeched Tupper. "*Estalla! Estalla! Estalla!*"

But Oliver stopped each attempt.

Against Charlie's outstretched arms Emma faked a shot, once, twice, until, finally, she let loose.

The net rippled.

"I DON'T BELIEVE IT!" screeched Joel over Lalandra's whistle. "SHE'S GONE AND DONE IT! FOUNDERS SEALS THE MATCH, SEASON, AND TOURNAMENT! THE EMERALD TROPHY IS GOING BACK TO THE EXTRAMAN HALL!"

Utter jubilation followed.

Reeling with passion, Oliver urged Archie to chase Emma down, who'd wheeled off to the extraman bleacher to celebrate with tears streaming from her eyes. She raised her arms at the crowd, orchestrating roar after roar. When Oliver and Archie arrived, they yelled themselves hoarse screaming congratulations as they hugged her. From Rasmus' back, she hugged Oliver back, trembling with emotion. A second later, the rest of the team arrived, forming a dogpile on top of them as everyone tried to catch hold of the girl who'd snapped Champayan's streak.

## NOVA 01

In the bleachers, older students grinned stupidly with their hands behind their heads, wishing they could have been the team to knock Champayan off their block instead.

The extramen, meanwhile, led by Trey, Ogden, and Valerie, stormed the trench to jump up and down with the team.

Only after the faculty entered the trench to return the non-participants to the bleachers, did Oliver, Emma, and Lance emerge from the dogpile, still embracing. By the time they recomposed themselves, the Champayan team and crowd had stormed off. Champayan's players could be seen, skulking through the thicket on their way back to their temple. Only Blackwood remained behind, a murderous expression on his face.

In front of the cheering crowd, a stage rose from the ground, and on it, the Emerald Green trophy glinted in the setting sun. Ronnie got to it first, raising it high for the crowd to see with ecstasy etched across his exhausted face.

The rest of the celebrations, Oliver always had a hard time remembering. What stuck out were memories of Ronnie and Emma being hoisted up and crowd-surfed, and Elton single-handedly throwing Lance up and down after Lalandra announced he'd won MVP for his four interceptions.

A quarter of an hour later, however, Oliver heard a conversation he wasn't likely to ever forget.

As planned, he, Emma, and Lance stayed behind in the locker rooms, waiting for their adrenaline to die down, so they could slip away into the Forgotten Wood unnoticed. Unfortunately, however, it proved to be much

## Chapter 22: The Forgotten Wood

harder to steer clear of the celebrating mob in practice than it had been in theory.

Between Emma having won the game, Lance winning the MVP trophy, and Oliver keeping Tupper at bay, the hugging and congratulating seemed never-ending. It was only after a teary embrace from Zapien when they managed to finally find themselves alone in the locker rooms.

"Ok," whispered Oliver. "Ready?"

Emma and Lance nodded.

*"Sorbelux!"*

He pulled them outside.

But before they'd made five steps, the icy voice of Dean Blackwood froze them in place.

"You're sure you didn't see them head to the Dining Hall for the celebratory feast?" He was standing just outside the bleachers, in the perfect position to see anyone exiting. Oliver thanked the heavens he'd cast the spell before they exited.

Desmoulins looked nervous. "I'm telling you, Broderick, they're still in there."

Blackwood spat. "You idiot. I'll just check."

A moment later, he'd banged open the door to the locker-room foyer and stuck his head through the door. "We're closing the room for the night!" he roared in his deep voice "Last chance to leave for the feast!"

Oliver, Emma, and Lance held their breath.

"I can't believe it," said Blackwood, seething. "HE'S ALREADY GONE UP TO THE TEMPLE!"

## NOVA 01

"What difference does it make?" said Desmoulins. "We can just keep an eye on him during the feast."

"We saw the Griffith girl already enter Lalandra's apartment – they know where the painting is!"

Emma's hand twitched in Oliver's.

"Sure, but there's no way they'll actually find it! We've had fourteen years to locate what Tío was looking for and we're no closer to finding it than we are to rediscovering light refraction!" Blackwood looked like he might punch Desmoulins. "If that *wretched* boy gets to it before we do – you know what? I don't care how dangerous it is, we are going into that painting *tonight*."

"Tonight?!" repeated Desmoulins. He looked towards Founders Temple and shuddered.

"Yes, tonight, you miserable coward. I've been looking at the stars, and the patterns are changing. Nova is almost fully upon us. Soon enough we'll have more than just its moons Powering us. And when we do, Tío can make his escape."

Desmoulins went white. "Escape? How?"

Blackwood's thin lips split into a grin. "Yes, Dionysus, *escape*. How? I wouldn't presume to know. I for one, however, do not intend on telling him we didn't break him out sooner because we were scared of enemies he defeated when he was a teenager. Tonight, we go to the damned Forest Temple and, at long last, we'll find the artifact. Then we go straight to the Sage's Sanctum to bust him out ourselves. I doubt the Trinova could hope to impact his plans. The end always arrives."

# * Chapter 22: The Forgotten Wood *

"The end always arrives," repeated Desmoulins. Though he was white with fright, he spoke in a monotone voice as the words crossed his lips. Then, so quickly that Oliver almost didn't catch it, Desmoulins and Blackwood exchanged angled nods of the head with their right hands over their hearts.

The rest of what they had to say, Oliver couldn't hear as they'd entered the thicket and passed out of earshot.

Lance let go of Oliver's hand, looking just as pale as Desmoulins had. "How are those two allowed to be teachers?!" he stammered.

Emma popped into sight too, having also let go of Oliver's hand. "This is bad – Oli, I know you just wanted to check things out tonight, but we have to go all the way—,"

Oliver ran his hands through his hair but nodded all the same. "If those two get to the Gift first … it sounds like they can use it to bring *The Damned* back. And there's something else I haven't told you."

Emma and Lance exchanged a look.

"I dreamt about him."

"You what?!" said Lance.

"Blackwood's right. I think he's escaping soon. We've got to find that Gift before they do. And we have to hope it will help us stop him from escaping."

Lance gulped. "Yikes. You think he's about to escape and even if he isn't, those two are going to try and bust him out."

Oliver grimaced before leading them onward. They dashed as quickly as they could, making their way through the thicket, then past Hutch, where

## NOVA 01

fireworks were going off to celebrate Founders' win and Champayan's demise. At the moat, six osori batted at unattended Tancol drums, sniffing at the air when Oliver, Emma, and Lance breezed by them.

To Oliver's frustration, it took them ages to get past the Dining Hall; every nook and cranny was occupied by noisy students celebrating the win. They managed to just navigate through it by sticking close to the wall that hid Ms. Joan's kitchen. As they sidled, Oliver felt a surge of disgust at the sight of Blackwood and Desmoulins conversing in hushed tones near the faculty table. *"Search all you want,"* thought Oliver, *"you're not gonna find me tonight."* He resisted the urge to grab Lance's hammer and smack their heads.

When they finally reached the faculty stairway, Oliver excitedly pulled Emma and Lance onward. But just as he was about to take the first step, Emma tugged his hand hard, slamming him and Lance against the wall.

"*Ouch,*" whispered Lance. "What was that for?"

But a second later, it was obvious what the pull was for. Descending the stairs in front of them was Headmaster Lalandra.

She whistled a merry tune as she went, slow for some steps and then quick for others. When she reached the bottom, she stopped and looked directly at them.

"Make sure you lock the door behind you," she said.

A quick look up and down the staircase confirmed she couldn't have been speaking to anybody but them. Oliver thought about saying *"thank you!"* but by the time he'd mustered up the resolve, she'd moved on. With raised hands she entered the Dining Hall, and clapped, sending a Founders banner flying across the room to enormous cheers and applause.

## \* Chapter 22: The Forgotten Wood \*

"Do – do you think we should be trusting her too?" asked Emma. Oliver laughed nervously. "Not sure if we have a choice!"

## Chapter 23: Boy, Shadow, and Ghost

*I'm taking a break with Tío's parents in Connecticut before checking the last remaining sites in North America. They've been super understanding. Told me to rest for a while before exploring the woods in Oregon. Thank goodness, too. I'm not sure how many steps I have left in me.*

*13th of May, the second year of the 10th Age*

With the threat of *The Damned* fresh on Oliver's mind, it didn't take him long to breeze past the ten flights of stairs leading to Lalandra's apartment. His shoes squeaked noisily against the marble steps as he went, but it hardly mattered anymore. Even if anyone could hear his footsteps over the bedlam ensuing from the celebrations in the Dining Hall below, the moment for sneaking around had gone.

When he, Emma, and Lance reached the top landing, a large, brown door stopped their progress. On his right, Emma released herself from his hand and popped into existence.

"Only one apartment on the top floor?" Lance whispered, still holding onto Oliver's grip and invisibility.

"Shh!" hissed Emma. She tried turning the long door handle. It opened, seemingly on its own volition.

"Emma?" Oliver asked as they stepped into Lalandra's foyer. He released *sorbelux*, bringing both himself and Lance back into the light.

"What?"

## * Chapter 23: Boy, Shadow, and Ghost *

"Was the door unlocked last time, too?"

"Umm, yeah I think it was."

Lance finally let go of Oliver's hand, leaving behind some sweat.

Oliver held his tongue. After having had to cross the lagoons to find the Iguana's Scroll, finding an unlocked door felt a little too easy. Before he could stew on the dilemma any further, Emma grabbed his hand again, dragging him further into the apartment.

Had the nature of their visit been less stressful, Oliver might have insisted on inspecting the various rooms in further detail – a seven-foot porcelain chicken, for instance, clucked at him with its head cocked when Emma dragged him past the kitchen – but for all he knew, Blackwood and Desmoulins had a shortcut to the Forgotten Wood. Lalandra's eccentricities would have to be explored during a later visit.

"There it is!" hissed Emma, pulling Oliver into the dining room. She pointed at a painting of green and brown situated above a cupboard.

Oliver followed Emma's finger towards the painting with a frown on his face. Just as he opened his mouth to express his doubts, his eyes locked onto a pattern among the darker hues of the artwork. Nestled behind dozens of green and brown trees, stood a Temple, overgrown and forlorn.

"I think this is it!" he said, breaking the silence.

"Hmm," said Lance, looking thoroughly unconvinced. "I thought it'd be bigger – one we could step into."

Emma rolled her eyes and swung her fist at the fresco. Instead of ripping through canvas, the better part of her forearm disappeared, oscillating the surface as if she'd disturbed a trough of water.

# NOVA 01

"See!" she said, stirring her arm through the painting. "Let's get going before Blackwood or Desmoulins show up!"

Oliver went first, stepping through the painting by awkwardly climbing over Lalandra's cupboard on his arms and legs.

When he pressed through the disguised passageway, it felt a lot like when he first crossed into the Other Side. After a brief resistance from the paint and canvas, he broke through, stumbling onto a bed of leaves, needles, and twigs.

He rolled into a standing position, checking for enemies.

Nothing moved.

He stood in an old forest, surrounded by thick trees. When a late-afternoon breeze ruffled his hair, the branches creaked and sighed, breaking the silent deadlock around him. Unlike the South-Carolina coast he'd left behind, here the sun hadn't set yet, and the air was crisp and clean in his nose. Behind him stood a half-finished brick wall. It looked serenely out of place in the middle of the forest. On it, someone had nailed a painting of Lalandra's dining room.

Suddenly, a noise like ripping paper broke through the forest. Throwing caution to the wind, Oliver tapped into the energy stored in the Earth beneath him and rose a wall to defend himself.

A second later, Lance entered the clearing and rolled straight into Oliver's wall.

Wincing, Oliver helped Lance up and mouthed an apology.

Lance cursed at him fluently under his breath as he rose, rubbing a red bump on his forehead in the process.

## * Chapter 23: Boy, Shadow, and Ghost *

When the ripping noise sounded for a second time, Oliver lowered his wall, allowing Emma to roll into her own standing position.

She rolled further than he had, stopping in front of a pathway Oliver hadn't noticed before. It led straight to a monolith.

Like a sentinel lost in time, the Forest Temple loomed over them, covered in overgrown trees, vines, and brush, making it difficult to see in the setting sun. The sheer size of it was enough for Lance to stop rubbing the welt on his head and look up, his mouth agape.

Oliver reached into his pocket and took out the Iguana's Scroll. *Begin with the Forgotten Wood, for there, your Gift has stood, its entrance lies within our grounds. Good luck – it cannot be found.*

He read over the text several times. "Okay, you two," he said, "no telling, what's in there. But I'm willing to bet it's going to be more like one of our Dungeon-Simulations than the golden willow."

Lance raised his eyebrows. "But what happens if we fall into a trap or something?"

Emma patted him on the shoulder, consolingly. "You'll be dead, bud." Only then did she notice the reddening bump on Lance's forehead. She gave it a confused look.

Oliver shook his head, stepping towards the temple. "We'll be fine if we're careful."

He led them slowly, at first, through a thicket of bramble, and then over a deer path that led directly to the temple. After several minutes down the winding pathway, they arrived at a dark entryway underneath the temple's front façade. A stone-laden landing preceded the façade, covered with green strands of ivy. The bits of masonry and stonework that were still visible crumbled at the corners.

More ominously, scorch-marks formed a perimeter around the entire entryway itself.

"We're definitely still on the same Side of the Key," Oliver mused, looking at the scorch-marks.

"How can you tell?" said Lance.

Emma used her sleeve to magically raise one of the larger pieces of rubble. "That's how."

"Right."

"This entryway used to be blocked up," said Oliver, ignoring them. "It's been blasted apart – look you can see the scorch-marks."

Emma stepped closer to inspect the damage. "Hmm. Blackwood and Desmoulins said they'd tried to get in before. Maybe they blew apart whatever seal used to be here?"

"By the looks of it," said Lance, "someone used air compression to destroy it. Can either of them pull off the spell?"

"I bet most adults can," said Oliver, running a hand over some of the scorch-marks; they left a black residue on his fingers that he had to rub away. "But it may have been *The Damned* who broke the seal. These scorch-marks make me think the magic involved a more explosive spell. *Estalla* just moves the air in and out quickly. Either way, let's move slowly in there."

Feeling a growing sense of trepidation, Oliver stepped forward, leading them inside.

## * Chapter 23: Boy, Shadow, and Ghost *

They found themselves in a foyer not too dissimilar from the one in Founders Temple. A double-sided landing loomed above them, accessible by the same set of semi-circular stairs seen in Founders Hall. But where the Founders front room buzzed with light and activity, here, only a single torch flickered from the upper level. On the wall in between the double stairs, a black-soot outline of a sundial stood out. Only when they were at the top of the stairs did they see an immobile sundial, flat on the tiles below. Its ruby and emerald grimace had been frozen in time and now lay covered in an inch of dust.

Doing his best to ignore the bad omen, and the dryness of his throat, Oliver led them on.

The next room opened to thirty-foot ceilings and haphazardly spread-out torches. Before Oliver was comfortable stepping inside, Emma went ahead anyway.

"No, wait!" he tried shouting. But it was too late.

A bell rang as soon as Emma crossed inside, making Oliver's neck tingle in apprehension.

When the toll dissipated, grunting and scuffing noises began to echo from across the room. Breathing in, Oliver took a moment to exchange nods with Emma, and then Lance, doing his best to convey confidence. Among the three of them, he did genuinely believe they could fight *anything*.

But then their foe stepped into the light, shattering his confidence entirely.

An eight-foot knight stood before them, covered, from head-to-toe in seamless, black armor. In one hand it carried a claymore sword large enough to cleave an oak tree from its roots. In the other, it held onto a green shield emblazoned with the same symbol Oliver had seen in the temple beneath the golden willow.

It was *his* symbol – the symbol of the Trinova.

The figure swung its blade a few times before slowing it to a pointed halt. Torch light shone from the base of the blade to its tip, inviting a challenge.

Oliver almost laughed at the impossibility of the task. No wonder Blackwood and Desmoulins hadn't dared enter here. How were they supposed to get past this?

The knight roared, forcing them to cover their ears. The noise sounded like it belonged to a monster, not a human, and it reverberated in the air around them long after they'd heard a jaw slam shut.

The beast approached after the air settled, shaking the ground with every step.

*"You must defeat me,"* it finally said with a deep, snarling voice, reminding Oliver of Reggie. As it stepped forward, it clanged its claymore and shield together, bringing a whimper out of Lance. *"She,"* the monster continued telepathically, *"waits for only the Advent. Can you claim the title?"*

*"Who's she?"* Oliver thought.

But then the beast charged.

"Oliver!" shouted Emma. "What's the plan?!"

Time slowed as Oliver surveyed the situation. He narrowed his eyes, glancing at the knight and its bulky armor, sword, and shield. Then, he

# * Chapter 23: Boy, Shadow, and Ghost *

locked onto Lance and Emma's smaller frames. He'd need Emma's Bravery for this to work.

"Alright," he shouted. "Lance, fire rock blasts at the knight! Make 'em Powerful!"

Lance saluted and began firing a barrage of Earth towards the oncoming monster with a series of yells. Every time he launched a chunk of rock with his warhammer, the air *warped* from the Power he imbued within his strikes.

Satisfied, Oliver turned to Emma. "We'll need you to press forward every now and then to keep the knight occupied." Nodding, Emma immediately moved to rush the giant, but Oliver grabbed her arm to stop her. "Make sure," he added with raised eyebrows, "you back up when he swings."

Emma met his eyes with fire and anger as he held her. "I can take care of myself, Oli."

Oliver nodded but didn't feel any regret. She needed to hear Wisdom to balance out the Bravery in her. This wasn't just a simulation like back at school.

Understanding dawned in her eyes as they held contact, and then her frown turned into a smirk. "Obvious advice doesn't count as Wisdom, Oli. I'm not going to give that thing an opportunity to lop off my head. Don't worry."

Oliver's grip faltered as he blushed. She released herself easily just as Lance yelled back at them.

"ARE YOU TWO FINISHED PICKNICKING YET?"

## NOVA 01

Though Lance's rocks of Earth connected with the knight's shield, slowing its pace, it still progressed towards them. Nodding at Oliver, Emma turned and dove into the fray. Oliver forced himself to look at the knight as Emma rolled beneath its swinging blade.

Now, it was his turn.

"*Estalla!*"

The air compressed in front of the giant, streaming to a needle's point near its chest. With a glance at Oliver, the giant tossed its shield to the side and buried its claymore into the ground with two hands. Not a second later, the air expanded, pushing Emma and Lance backwards while also tearing away bits of armor off the grounded giant. With a clanking noise, its helmet came loose and flew off, revealing the terrifying head of not a man, but a *wolf*.

As the howling wind subsided, the wolf-giant snarled, brandishing two rows of sharp teeth. It pulled the claymore from the Earth and severed the ties to its gauntlets and greaves. As the heavy pieces of armor fell, the giant barreled towards Lance at a much greater speed than before, almost as fast as a charging osorius. Seeing the panicked look on Lance's face, Oliver raised a wall of Earth under the beast, sending it skyward. It backflipped off the Earth, changing course to charge Emma.

"*Estalla!*" Oliver yelled again, unable to keep the desperate tone out of his voice.

With no way to bury its claymore, the giant took the full force of the spell and hurtled towards the far wall, arms flailing helplessly.

*Crunch.*

# * Chapter 23: Boy, Shadow, and Ghost *

Oliver's heart thundered in his chest as they stood still, waiting for the dust to settle.

"Is it dead?" Lance shouted. He eyed the fallen wolf with his hammer raised in front of him.

*"No,"* interrupted the deep voice of the wolf-giant. Slowly it rose to its feet. *"But I concede to the Advent."*

Lance gasped as the giant's wounds began to knit over, healing themselves. Around them, the shorn-off pieces of armor sped towards the knight, returning to their original places.

"Have you conceded to anyone before?" asked Oliver, ignoring the magic unfolding around them.

The giant snarled. *"Yes."*

"Who was it?"

*"Can you not guess? Be gone with you."*

Oliver wanted to stay and ask the wolf more questions, but the threat of Blackwood bursting in at any moment urged him forward. Reluctantly, he kicked his feet into action, leading Emma and Lance through a door that had begun to scrape open behind the giant.

When they entered a smaller, but similarly unadorned, room, his heart finally slowed. He exchanged a look of relief with Emma as he wiped his sweaty bangs off his brow. The challenge had been tougher than he'd anticipated but they'd survived.

Movement in front of him returned his attention to the new room.

It was Lance.

## NOVA 01

He'd moved towards a torch on the wall to their left. Everything to their right ... was enveloped by complete darkness. Fearing a pack of chupacabras, Oliver stiffened.

When Lance reached the torch, blinding flames from an unknown source erupted from the right-side of the room, cascading like thick drops of magma.

*"Iuxtairis!"* Oliver shouted. Despite his Gift of Bravery, he backed away towards Lance at what he saw.

Clicking its pincers in front of them, was none other than an escorpius. Flames licked its eight-foot-long and four-foot-tall body from gaps in its carapace, lighting a glossy liquid stuck to its skin. The liquid ignited, blasting them with a wave of heat that threatened to remove their eyebrows.

*Skrreeeee!*

Emma rolled from the stairs towards Oliver and Lance, narrowly avoiding a pincer that clicked above her head.

Lance brandished his hammer in the direction of a small alcove behind the monster's right flank. "It's blocking a staircase!"

Oliver had seen the staircase but was too worried about Emma to concern himself with much else. Behind her, the escorpius had planted its two pincers in the dirt and begun to arch its stinger. He could see more liquid coursing through its slightly transparent carapace.

Panicking, he attempted to raise a pillar of Earth beneath the scorpion to unsettle it, or hopefully crush it into the ceiling where it might explode into a million pieces. But the Earth didn't budge for some reason.

"Emma!" he shouted. "Get outta there!"

\* Chapter 23: Boy, Shadow, and Ghost \*

With one final roll she clattered into him.

"Oli," shouted Lance, "it's about to breathe fire on us!"

The liquid behind the carapace had reached the creature's torso.

Desperate, Oliver tried raising Earth again, but this time as cover for themselves.

He thanked the heavens as it worked, trapping the escorpius in the other half of the room just as flames erupted from its terrifying maw.

Lance cheered as a thick liquid met the other side of the wall. "Now what?"

Oliver thought hard.

He couldn't remember much about the escorpi other than the fact that some had been sighted earlier in the year in the Swampy Woods to the east of the lagoons.

"All I can think of is a defensive shield!" said Emma. Her eyes were furrowed in concentration. "This is why I never made the Dungeon-Simulation team!"

"That's it!" said Oliver, thinking back on the Dungeon-Simulation tournament. "I defeated that squid monster with ice – maybe we can freeze this escorpius, too!"

Emma and Lance exchanged a look.

"For all your Wisdom, Oli, sometimes you're pretty stupid," said Lance, echoing Emma's earlier sentiments. "There's no water in here – what are you going to freeze?"

"Gimme your hammer," Oliver directed at Lance. "Don't worry. I'll give it back."

# NOVA 01

Hesitantly, Lance offered him the hammer by the handle. Oliver gripped it and ran his fingers over the course of the steel. Could he imbue a freezing spell into a weapon? Even if clumsy, it could just save their lives.

"*Conjelareth*," he muttered.

Emma gasped as crystals popped into existence across the hammer. "How did you do that?!"

A blue aura now emanated from the steel.

"Dunno," he said, handing the hammer back to Lance. "I doubt Miyada would approve but we're gonna need you to hit that thing with everything you've got while we distract it."

They could hear the escorpius battering against the rock wall as Lance took the hammer and nodded.

*Skrreeeee!*

To the left, Oliver collapsed a large section of the wall and a wave of heat followed.

Eyes smarting, Oliver charged towards the opening, followed by Emma.

The escorpius stepped through the gap on six legs, clicking its pincers overhead. With little pause, it lunged a pincer at Oliver.

"Now, Lance!" Oliver yelled.

Roaring, Lance broke through the wall on the right before swinging in an uppercut motion through the creature's belly.

*Skrreeee!*

The escorpius writhed with pain at the hit but did not freeze.

Oliver's stomach sank.

"Plan B!" shouted Emma. "Make for the stairs!"

## * Chapter 23: Boy, Shadow, and Ghost *

Dodging around the flailing stinger, Oliver and Emma dived into the alcove and sprinted up the steps of a long circular staircase, Lance not far behind.

Once the escorpius was no longer visible, they paused, leaning against the walls to catch their breath.

"No rest for the weary, huh?" said Lance gesturing up the stairs from his slumped position against the wall.

Oliver desperately wanted to stop and gather his thoughts, even if only for a moment, but Wisdom urged him on.

*Speed is of the essence.*

A new room waited for them at the top. Oliver went first, slowly, ignoring the *skreees* of the escorpius below, until he found himself on soft grass that left a sweet smell in the air.

He was tempted to take a deep breath of the sugary smell, but a noise like crossing blades sounded on his right and left. Instinctively, he rolled forward and just in time, too, because behind him, two scythes met with a clang, before resetting in their starting position on either side of the room.

"Hold up!" shouted Oliver at the stairs. Emma had stuck her foot into the room. "When you come through, do it quickly because there's a trap!"

Emma nodded and entered, rolling as Oliver had. He caught her so that she wouldn't go past him and set off another potential trap.

"Thanks," she said, quickly removing herself from his arms.

Lance came in next, clattering to a halt next to them on the floor. "Don't mind me," he muttered.

Settled, they took stock of their surroundings.

## NOVA 01

They were in another small room, albeit much more illuminated than the last. Apart from the scythe trap at the doorway behind them, the only other objects in sight were the torches lining the walls and a giant bronze scale. In front of the scale, an elevated platform loomed above, inaccessible. It was covered in moss, and at its far end, an open doorway beckoned.

"Huh," said Lance. He pushed up with his free fist, but no Earth rose. "Earth elementals don't work in here for some reason."

Puzzled, Oliver tried raising the stone flooring too. But it didn't budge.

"Maybe it's not Earth," suggested Emma.

Oliver shrugged and pulled himself onto one side of the scale. It descended with his weight, raising the other.

"Uh-oh," said Lance. He looked at the other side of the scale rise up all the way to the platform above. "I think only one of us is going to be able to go on. Two of us on one side and one on the other."

"Hmm," said Emma. "How would *The Damned* have gotten in here before if only one could proceed?"

"It's possible he didn't make it this far in," said Lance. "That escorpius wasn't exactly dead down there."

"Maybe," said Oliver. "But if I'd come in by myself, how would I proceed?"

Emma scowled. "Well, what if we raise some Earth from the level below and bring it up with us? We can use it as a counterweight."

Oliver laughed. "There's a raging escorpius down there."

They scratched their heads, puzzled.

## * Chapter 23: Boy, Shadow, and Ghost *

Lance pointed at Oliver. "It's really simple guys. Only Oli is gonna be able to keep going."

Oliver paced around the room, looking from the scale to the scythes and then the dust. They didn't have many options in front of them. Maybe Lance was right. At any moment Blackwood or Desmoulins might barge through and stop them and they shouldn't be sitting around …

"Hang on!" said Oliver. A sudden thought had crossed his mind. "What if we use Blackwood and Desmoulins as counterweights?"

At first, Emma and Lance only returned confused glares. But then, at the same time, they grinned mischievously.

Lance rolled his hammer around his hands like a lacrosse stick. "Oh, that's good. A little bit of *sorbelux* and I can dink their heads in for a good night's sleep. I've been dreaming about doing it all year to Blackwood, anyway."

Satisfied, they sat down and waited.

It wasn't long before they heard scuffles from further below.

"That'll be them fighting the wolf-giant," said Emma.

Blackwood's voice echoed up to their hiding place, confirming Emma's suspicion.

"How the blazes did they get past the escorpius?!" his voice growled.

"EWW!" screeched Desmoulins. "Are those escorpius guts on you?!"

"Don't be a fool, Dionysus, they'll already be at the artifact!"

Lance gave Oliver a shove. "It's go-time, cap'."

"*Sorbelux,*" whispered Oliver. They grabbed hands and edged towards one of the scythes.

# NOVA 01

A moment later, Blackwood entered the room, narrowly avoiding the scythes.

"There are the scales," he said, snarling at Desmoulins who stumbled in after him. "But how did they know to freeze them in place?"

"He *is* the Trinova, after all," suggested Desmoulins.

*Clunk!*

Desmoulins crumpled to the ground.

Blackwood jumped. "What the—,"

*Thunk!*

Blackwood collapsed and Lance appeared, laughing.

Emma couldn't resist a kick to Blackwood's ribs. "That's for poisoning Oli with the chupacabra!"

"Idiots," agreed Oliver. "Okay, let's drag them on."

Grunting, they piled Desmoulins and Blackwood onto one side of the scale and quickly jumped onto the opposing scale to reach the platform above.

"Good thinking," said Emma, offering Oliver a fist bump.

He took it and looked up through the opening in front of them. A long, uniform staircase waited for them, stretching upwards almost indefinitely. Without delay, he began the ascent, dreading what might lie ahead.

"Listen," he said to Emma and Lance as they passed torches of red and yellow that flanked the stairs. "I don't think we'll find an artifact just waiting for us up here. The Founders would have left something to protect it."

Lance scoffed. "What? The wolf and escorpius weren't enough?"

## \* Chapter 23: Boy, Shadow, and Ghost \*

"The wolf seemed embarrassed about what beat me here when I asked him. I'm worried there may be more than just the Founders' protection waiting for us."

"What are you saying?" said Emma, a concerned expression on her face. "That *The Damned* is waiting for us up there? That this has been his prison?"

It was a thought that had crossed Oliver's mind. What if the Forest Temple *had* been *The Damned's* prison all this time?

"I'm saying," continued Oliver, "that we shouldn't rule anything out. Let's be careful."

"Yikes," said Lance, raising his hammer. "Why not just leave him in there, then?"

"Because," said Oliver, "whatever that artifact is, I think it will make him even stronger. That's why he risked getting it in the first place. And in my dream, he said he was close to *his release*."

Oliver couldn't stop himself from shuddering as he relived the nightmare in his head. That voice ... it had sounded so tired. And the clicking that followed? What could that have been?

Lance gulped, bringing Oliver back to the present. Inwardly, he berated himself for showing fear in front of his friends. They needed to see him being confident and Brave, not nervous.

He donned a smile and pushed on, but it was with a much grimmer mood that they continued their ascent. Glancing back, Oliver saw Lance looked downright scared in the torchlight. *Why shouldn't he be? A second ago he thought he was on an adventure. Now he knows he might be on a suicide mission.*

# NOVA 01

Emma, meanwhile, looked resolute more than anything else. Her lips had been drawn into a thin line beneath her freckled nose.

With slow and steady steps, they eventually reached the top, where a set of mahogany doors waited for them. They were twice as tall as Oliver and their iron, ring handles were as wide as his head.

"Ok, guys," he said, putting a hand on one of the handles. "Only I have to go in there. Don't feel like—,"

"Good grief," protested Lance, "if we didn't want to keep going, we'd have waited down by the freaking scale. Let's get this over with!"

"We went into the lagoons with you," agreed Emma, "we're not about to abandon you now." With a snort she pulled the handle for him.

Air sucked beneath the door as it opened, whooshing past them with a bone-chilling swish. Ignoring common sense, they entered.

Another seemingly empty room waited for them – this one, as small as Oliver and Lance's dorm room. When Oliver stepped further inside and made sure nothing waited in the shadows around them, he allowed himself to focus on the only object inside the room.

In front and center, moonlight filtered inside through a gap in the ceiling, illuminating a standing podium. Slowly, they approached it, Lance holding his hammer high, Emma flexing her sleeved arm, and Oliver clenching his ring hand.

Nothing stirred as their footsteps echoed across the room.

Once close enough, Oliver saw a pillow at the top of the podium's surface. On it, lay a simple necklace made of a gold chain and a solitary blue stone. Moonlight glinted off the gold but not the stone.

## * Chapter 23: Boy, Shadow, and Ghost *

"That must be the Gift," whispered Emma.

Lance shook his head. "I don't understand. How is a necklace supposed to help you stop *The Damned* from returning?"

Oliver shared Lance's skepticism but reached out a hand to take the necklace all the same.

As soon as the gold chain touched his skin, a whirling noise of gusting winds sounded behind him. As he turned to face the intrusion, he put the necklace on, barely registering a rush of energy he felt in the process.

The wind came from a mass of red and black smoke aggregating near the double doors they'd just entered. As it continued to twist and twirl, dread invited itself into Oliver's stomach. There it gnawed at him in the same circling motions made by the smoke.

*This can't be happening.*

A shadow had begun to form within the dark cyclone. A shadow he'd come to know.

With one final twist, the smoke ceased rotating, and a figure stumbled out from nowhere onto one knee. Its ribs rose and fell with haggard breaths underneath the folds of a tattered, forest-green overcoat.

Oliver stared at the figure as its breath rattled, too scared to think lest it could read thoughts. After several tense moments, the figure rose, revealing a gaunt face with amber eyes and long, grey hair.

The amber eyes surveyed them, tired, cold, and terrifying, until they locked onto the necklace around Oliver's neck.

# NOVA 01

"Boy!" shouted the figure, forcing goosebumps to erupt on Oliver's arms. He recognized that voice as the same exhausted, deep one he'd heard in his dream. Now, it haunted him in person.

The man in front of him was the man everyone feared. He was *The Damned*.

"You have done well to retrieve the necklace. But where is Broderick? I would very much like to address his delay."

Oliver thought hard. *The Damned* didn't seem to have any idea who he was. That *might* give him a chance to survive. But he had to act quickly.

"Broderick is waiting downstairs," he lied, "making sure the coast is clear for our exit."

*The Damned* took in a deep breath, rotating his neck around before speaking. "Indeed? Cato still prowling about, is he? And what is your name, boy?"

Oliver thought of the evilest person he knew and lied. "John Tupper."

*The Damned* twitched, flicking his eyes up and down. "I think not."

*"Defenderis!"* Oliver shouted, barely in time.

His shield *exploded* against an unknown spell that he knew would come, showering the room with sparks of red and yellow.

"Fool!" growled *The Damned* as the magic cut off. "Are you attempting to become the next Trinova?" He paced towards the podium and leaned on it. "Nobody can withstand my Power. But I am tired … very tired. And yet, I have endured my purgatory and emerged stronger for it."

Oliver held *The Damned's* eyes despite the strong urge he felt to run back down the stairs.

# * Chapter 23: Boy, Shadow, and Ghost *

"How did you escape?"

The Damned narrowed his eyes. "You are *bold*, boy. I suppose that's expected for your ambitions. I'll answer your questions – it matters not." He paused to cough, holding onto the podium for support. Did Oliver imagine red and black smoke continuing to congregate around the man? "You will know me as *The Damned*, though that's not who I really am, or was. I used to be much, *much* more. But it would appear that my true self has been rewritten.

"I escaped because you drew me here to the necklace."

Lance and Emma exchanged looks from either side of Oliver. "Yes," he continued with a handsome, but manic grin. "When I was not much older than you three are now, I came here and placed a spell on that stone." He coughed, looking irritated. "I could not touch it despite all my efforts, but I placed a spell to bring me here if and whenever someone else could. I never expected anyone but Broderick to do so, but I thank you all the same."

He doubled over to cough again, keeping a hand on the podium. There was no mistaking it, he grew more and more solid by the moment.

"Tell me, Trinova," he said, changing to a tone that didn't sit right on Oliver's ears. "Would you do anything in your Power to safeguard our future against the threats of the next Age of Darkness? When Nova abandons us yet again during its long orbit, would you do what was necessary to better the world as our forefathers commanded?"

Oliver looked at *The Damned* more closely now. He appeared tired, and sick – the coughing alone proved that. But in his eyes, Oliver could see a fire he'd not seen in any other living thing. It twisted and raged, making Oliver shudder at what the man might consider to be necessary to better the world. *What did you do all those years ago that erased your name from memory?*

Finally, Oliver spoke. "I would protect our future against evil."

*The Damned* began to laugh. Slow at first, then long and hard, only made more insane by various bouts of coughing. "And what do you consider the opposite of evil? Will *you* serve as an arbiter for good? As a man of principal? Fools looks to morality. True politics require we remain agnostic of self-inflicted burdens. No, *boy*. The end always arrives. Are you ready to die? I've humored your questions thus far. Anyone else? You, girl? Anything stupid to ask?"

Emma glared back defiantly.

"Ah," he said, leering right back at her. "Gift of Bravery I see. Such a waste."

"You're stalling!" Emma shouted. "You're too weak to fight us, aren't you?"

More coughing. "I think you'll find I'm more than capable enough to do anything."

This time, Oliver attacked first.

*"Estalla!"*

*The Damned* waved his arm impatiently. *"Abrilla!"*

"Elodie will have to teach you more than that to stop me!" He closed his fist, ushering a vibrating wave of dark energy at them. It moved slowly, ebbing forward two feet and then back one every second.

*"Defenderis!"* they shouted.

## * Chapter 23: Boy, Shadow, and Ghost *

The vibrating spell seeped through their defensive shields as if they were walls of paper, forcing them to back away.

"Oli!" shouted Lance, desperation in his voice. "What do we do?!"

The vibrations seeped closer, threatening to consume them.

Oliver didn't know what to do. He was just a teenager. Not a seasoned warrior ready to fight *The Damned*.

But then a chill erupted on the back of his neck and Archie's voice sounded in his head, unbidden. *Remember your fundamentals!*

Thinking fast, Oliver rose both hands and opened his right fist, raising a wall of Earth and hurtling it towards *The Damned*.

With a lazy flick of his wrist, *The Damned* turned the wall into powder, but Oliver continued the channel, sending the now dissolved wall directly towards the man's face.

The dust hit him like a stream of dry water, forcing an eruption of coughing and hacking. Unable to see or focus, *The Damned* began to shoot spell after unknown spell wildly into the air.

The vibrating waves had stopped, but the new magic came at them in dangerous spurts, narrowly missing their heads on more than one occasion. For a moment, Oliver hesitated.

"*Defenderis!*" Emma yelled. "Oli! He's using a ring, just like you!"

Oliver locked his eyes on *The Damned's* right hand, where a blue ring glowed with each new burst of magic. Feeling a surge of energy vibrating around his neck, Oliver dashed forward, dodging collapsing floors, beams of energy, and psychic waves until he was back-to-back with *The Damned*.

# NOVA 01

Without further hesitation, he grabbed the rampaging man's hand with his own, holding it still. Then, he pulled off the ring.

The room went quiet as the magic ceased to manifest. Oliver took the opportunity to step away and slip on the ring he'd stolen.

"AARGH," shouted *The Damned*. From his robes, he began pulling out a stained dirk.

*Whoosh!*

An enormous boulder hit him squarely in the chest, knocking him off his feet. With a thud, the back of his head hit the floor, bringing his attacks to a halt. To his right, the dirk clattered onto the floor.

Breathing deeply, Oliver looked over his shoulder, expecting to see Emma smirking.

But it was Lance who stood with his fist pointed out, looking as pale as his bedsheets.

"Nice shot," said Emma, just as impressed as Oliver.

"Don't mention it," said Lance bleakly.

Oliver looked back at the still form of *The Damned*.

"You knocked him out cold, but I can still feel his breath. We should go get Lalandra or Watkin before—,"

Suddenly, the room went cold, tightening their skin unnaturally.

Oliver tensed when a puff of dissipating red and black smoke replaced *The Damned's* figure, leaving them alone.

"There is no need for reinforcements," said a faint voice that could have once been warm.

## * Chapter 23: Boy, Shadow, and Ghost *

Oliver turned, raising his fists in anticipation for another battle. But he dropped his hands just as quickly, eyes wide and his mouth open.

A woman dressed in furs *levitated* next to the podium. Barely visible at first, she became more and more solid with every word that crossed her lips.

"Who are you?" asked Oliver.

Lance whimpered behind Emma, his heroic moment entirely forgotten.

"I *was* Madeline des' Moulins," said the figure. "But you already knew that, didn't you, Oliver?"

Madeline's breath rattled at times, making Oliver's hair stand on end. She passed through the podium and approached him.

Oliver's arms tingled. "This is your necklace, isn't it?" he said, touching the blue stone that now hung around his neck. Unless he was mistaken, he was conversing with a ghost.

"It was," said Madeline, "but it is my Gift to you."

She floated closer to inspect Emma and Lance.

"Augustus, Cuahtemoc, and I" —she looked over her shoulder as if her co-founders were nearby— "we founded this school to prepare the magical community for the upcoming Age of Proximity and the following Age of Darkness. We saw no need for the world to descend into chaos for another eight hundred years. We were so confident of our aspirations ... but then Augustus' visions began to haunt us. Wisest of us all, he saw the rise of *The Damned* ... and then you, Oliver."

"Me?"

# NOVA 01

"Yes, you. The False Prophet followed by the Advent. We left you this necklace to defeat your predecessor. It is the only way."

"What do you mean?" asked Emma. "Oliver's the Trinova, isn't he?" She took a quick look at where *The Damned* had been. The smoke had dissipated.

"Yes, Oliver is by nature," said Madeline, following Emma's gaze. "But *The Damned* almost possessed enough Power to match any Trinova."

"How?" asked Oliver. "That's impossible!"

"There are ways," said the ghost. "Forgotten ways." She floated back over towards him, a pained expression on her sallow face. "I have few precious moments left for you, Oliver, but know this. We don't know how or why, but over the millennia, whispers of ancient artifacts have afflicted the magical community, tearing it apart every time Nova leaves us. The artifacts, though impossibly scarce, enable magic during ages of darkness and grant users with a Gift or enhance an already existing one. My necklace is one of these artifacts. It possesses the Gift of Bravery."

Madeline's shape flickered in the moonlight.

Oliver looked from the necklace to Emma and Lance, who gaped at him. "Did Augustus and Cuahtemoc have artifacts, too?"

"Yes," said Madeline, sounding tired. "You will need all three to defeat *The Damned*. His might will be equal to that of a Trinova's when he escapes his purgatory."

"We just knocked him out cold," Emma piped in. "What do you mean we'll need all three to defeat him?"

## * Chapter 23: Boy, Shadow, and Ghost *

"You faced but a shadow of his power and evil," said Madeline, frowning. "In his youth, *The Damned* came here, looking to find an artifact to grant him a second Gift. Augustus foresaw his arrival, however, and placed a spell on the necklace allowing only someone who possessed the Gift to touch it. *The Damned* did not take the setback well. He murdered the sundial that guarded this place and placed his own magic on *my* necklace. A clever spell I'd not seen in life. It allowed him to transport here the moment anyone *did* touch the necklace. Thankfully, you defeated him before he fully transported. For now, he remains in his prison, running and hiding. I thank you for that."

"Where is he trapped?" Oliver asked. "What is he running from?" He thought back to his dream … to the clicking and scratching.

Madeline's form turned more translucent.

"I am out of time," she said, looking directly at Oliver. "The greatest evil known to man haunts him. But you *must* understand his purgatory is only temporary. *The Damned* will rise to Power again, and when he does, trust your Wisdom. You must demand good for all, not just the greater."

With one last flicker, she vanished, allowing warmth back into the room.

Several moments passed before either Oliver, Emma, or Lance spoke. After a long pause, however, Emma broke the silence, approaching Oliver. "Well, chief, we've got good news and bad news." She held out a finger with one hand and grabbed it with the other. "Good news – we stopped *The Damned* from escaping." A second finger followed. "Bad news – Madeleine's ghost seemed to think he could still find a way out."

## NOVA 01

"And we have this necklace now," added Oliver, placing a hand on the blue jewel hanging from his neck.

"What about the ring?" said Lance.

Oliver's heart skipped a beat. The blue ring! How could he have forgotten?

But it was nowhere to be found. Oliver tried looking around to see if it had fallen to the floor but couldn't see it anywhere. Lance and Emma watched him move clumps of weeds around and inspect the corners of the rooms.

"It must have disappeared when the shadow did too," said Emma. "Why does it matter?"

But Lance's eyes had gone wide. "Oliver! You don't think the ring was an artifact, too, do you?"

Oliver nodded fervently. "It was blue like the necklace, wasn't it?"

Emma frowned, looking around too. "Well, it isn't here anymore, so there's no use crying about it."

"Don't you get it?" said Oliver more shrilly than he would have liked. A knot was beginning to form in his stomach, mirroring the dread he'd felt when *The Damned* first appeared. "If *The Damned* has one of those artifacts too ... well, what if the Founders' Gifts won't be enough?"

A new voice interrupted them. "That's not how fate works, Oliver."

It was Professor Watkin, standing at the double door entrance, Jaiba on his shoulder.

Oliver formed a fist with his ring hand, raising a wall of Earth threateningly.

# * Chapter 23: Boy, Shadow, and Ghost *

"How did you get in here?" he yelled at Watkin. Next to him, Emma and Lance rose their arms ready for another fight.

Watkin rose his hands calmly and grinned. "Same way as you – using those useless excuses for human beings you left behind on the scale."

"Were you hoping to free *The Damned?*" Oliver asked, his tone still fierce.

"What do you think?" said Watkin, folding his arms. At his shoulder Jaiba squawked at them jovially.

Emma fired a warning rock past Watkin's shoulder.

Watkin didn't even flinch as the Earth crumbled against the wall. "Answer the question!" she shouted.

Watkin folded his hands behind his back and let out a sigh. "Not now, nor have I ever, wished to free *The Damned*. I did, however, try and take that necklace around the same time he did. Now that you've discovered it for yourself, I can speak to you openly about it."

Oliver, Emma, and Lance exchanged confused looks.

"Don't trouble yourself, Oliver. Search your heart, you know you can trust me. I'd wager you've already decided it's the Wisest course. Am I wrong?"

Assurance spread warmly through Oliver, blanketing him in a sense of comfort he'd not felt all year. Truth be told, he *did* want to trust Watkin, to have an adult ally on This Side of the Key for once. But he needed Watkin to prove himself first before he did.

"You've been giving me hints all year – why not just flat out tell us how to get the necklace if you were on our side?"

Watkin pursed his lips together contemplatively. "Because I believe the safeguards placed in this room allow only the Trinova to remove the necklace. As such, I couldn't aid you earlier. If I had, you would have been assisted by someone who had already been prevented from obtaining the necklace in the past. I could not take that risk given the stakes at play."

Lance lowered his hammer and scratched his head, confused. "But Madeline's just told us anyone who already had Bravery could take the necklace. She never said anything about it being obtainable only by Oliver."

Watkin closed his eyes and held them shut as he took in a breath. "I see." A flicker of an emotion passed over his jaw line and Oliver had it narrowed down to either anger or frustration. "I suppose that worked just as well to stop *The Damned* from getting the necklace to begin with. If that's the case, I apologize for having not been more direct with you three earlier."

"What did you do with Blackwood and Desmoulins in the room below?" said Emma, still fierce. "Who do you serve?"

Watkin laughed. "Whom do I serve? Humankind. But I suppose that means I *serve* Oliver if his goal is to rid the world of humankind's greatest threat. Is that your goal, Oliver?"

Oliver didn't hesitate. "Is my goal to defeat *The Damned*? Yes, it absolutely is."

"Excellent," said Watkin unclasping his hands and rubbing them together. "Shall we get started?"

THE END

NOVA 01

*The Iguana's Scroll*

THE TRINOVA SAGA CONTINUES IN

THE SERPENT'S TONGUE
---
NOVA 02

## Bloopers

Inside his chest, Oliver felt his heart pound. He thought he knew what lay in front of him. A letter from Tenochprima Academy.

He stooped down to pick up the parchment and glimpsed cerulean ink.

*"Wait!"* Archie implored. He had resumed smiling like a mischievous cat. *"Before you read the Instruction Manual,"* —Archie paused to frown— *"oh, no. My dear boy, I'm afraid there's been a mistake. Your application has been denied. I must take my leave."*

La Chancla smacked Oliver on the back of the head.

"Sorry!" Oliver strained. "I swear I didn't try to freeze anything!"

"Shhhh," said Emma, waving a hand impatiently at him. She tapped the glass where the catfish blinked at them, still frozen in time by Oliver's spell. "Lance, get me filleting knife."

They didn't stop perusing through the map's scribbled hints until they'd joined Stevie, Elton, and Joel outside Hutch for the snowball fight. Grinning at the opportunity to push away the anxiety he felt, Oliver ducked and weaved to join the fray with Emma right behind him. They barreled into Elton to dodge a well-placed missile from Joel, collapsing into a heap behind a thick wall of snow. When they landed, Elton looked down at them past askew, blonde hair, his eyes red with Power. He gestured rudely towards Lance, who'd just slid into safety within a rickety fort hiding Joel and Stevie.

"So that's how it's gonna be, little bro?" Elton shouted as Lance took cover. "You were supposed to destroy the Sis, not join her! Bring balance to the teams, not leave them in dark—,"

"Steady, flyboy," Emma interrupted. She whipped out a blaster, and her hair had somehow turned into two buns on the sides of her head. "Let's not get dinged for copyright infringement."

"We're definitely still on the Other Side of the Key," said Oliver, looking at the scorch-marks on the walls.

"How can you tell?" said Lance. "I don't feel no different."

Emma rose her magical sleeve in disgust, gesturing towards an open chest full of Aztec gold. "The curse is still upon us!"

From the chest, a skeleton-iguana popped into existence, screeching and scattering gold coins in every direction.

Oliver grinned at Lance, flashing a set of rotting teeth. "We named the iguana, Mack."

# ABOUT THE AUTHOR

C. T. Emerson lives in North Carolina with his wife and two fluffy cats. He's the author of the *NOVA* series and enjoys eating ice cream. If you must know, his favorite flavor is salted peanut butter with chocolate flecks.

After growing up in México from 1994 through 2010, he graduated from Davidson College in 2016, earning degrees in political science, Spanish literature, and procrastination.

He believes writing is much more fun than anything else and is happy to update you on all his dealings on CTEmerson.com. Flock there – consumable goodies await. Either that, or a more up to date about the author section.

Made in the USA
Columbia, SC
06 September 2022